ON THE
CHESAPEAKE

ROBERT F. LACKEY

Heron Oaks, Murrells Inlet, SC

Copyright © 2016 Robert F. Lackey

All rights reserved.

ISBN:0692688676

ISBN-13:9780692688670

Other books by Robert F. Lackey:

Pulaski's Canal ISBN: 0692625267

(Kindle ASIN:B01BPEIYM0)

As Pug Greenwood:

Bim and Them ISBN: 0692569561

(Kindle ASIN: B017MW4K5Y)

Tooey's Crossroads ISBN: 0692566198

(Kindle ASIN: B017OL09JE)

DEDICATION

To Betty Lackey Hoke Darden Fisher,
who has the most appealing soft spoken southern accent
that ever kissed ears.
If the sweet scent of honeysuckle blooms had a sound,
it would be the lilting southern lullaby of
Aunt Betty's voice.

-    *Robert F. Lackey*

ACKNOWLEDGEMENTS

No book can make its way to print without the hard work of many people.

I wish to acknowledge the valuable assistance of stalwart beta readers

and thank them for their contributions.

Notably

Judee Cooper of Edgewood, Maryland

Kathy Cullum of Havre de Grace, Maryland

Lori English of Las Cruces, New Mexico

Jeanne Hawtin of Havre de Grace, Maryland

Trista Smith of St. Leonard, Maryland

Nancy Testerman of Havre de Grace, Maryland,

who aided significantly in finalizing this manuscript.

Also,

I once again offer my appreciation to the wonderful efforts of

The Susquehanna Museum at the Lock House,

for saving priceless information and artifacts about an amazing period in the development of our country, the State of Maryland, Harford County, and that exquisite gem at the head of the Chesapeake Bay:

Havre de Grace

- Robert F. Lackey

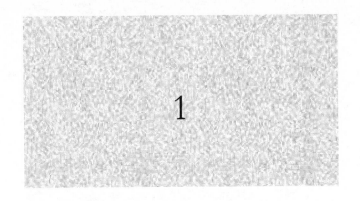

Havre de Grace, Maryland. 8:17 o'clock, the morning of September 16th, 1842.

"That sounded like a gunshot!"

Nancy called out to anyone listening, wiping her hands of spilled beer and trading worried looks with the proprietor as he came out of the kitchen. She moved to the front door, then gently pulled it open just enough for a one-eyed peek. Barely disturbing the brass bell dangling from the curled spring just above the door, she looked across the street toward the Tidewater Bank and Trust Company. No one came out of the building. She hesitated at the narrow opening of the door, listening intently for another sound. She was sure she had heard gunfire. These new wooden buildings on Oyster Street were thrown up of the cheapest pine planks to catch the brisk canal and harbor business.

A body could hear yelling two and three doors down when the wind was low.

"...biscuits!" someone yelled. She turned back toward the tables and almost bumped into her boss as he leaned over her and stuck his head all the way outside the door.

"Mrs. Palmer, get that grouchy mate his hot biscuits. He's getting on my nerves, and I only heard him speak the once."

"You be careful, Carl," she whispered as they pirouetted together to change places at the door, their bodies only briefly touching, both pretending it was of no consequence, neither looking back at the other. Carl grabbed the doorbell to muffle its ring and stepped softly onto the boardwalk in front of the tavern. Nancy rushed to the kitchen and scooped up four hot biscuits off the pan fresh out of the oven and covered them with a thick warming towel. She plated the four biscuits and quick stepped back to the table of the grumbling sailor.

"'Bout goddamned time! Shitty service for a place charging fifteen goddamned cents just for a breakfast!"

Nancy gave the leather skinned sailor her best smile and told him she'd be happy to get him more biscuits as soon as those were gone, if he still had room.

"It's the best deal in town," she added.

"Goddamned robbery," he grunted, reaching for the next biscuit with one hand and scooping a large helping of fresh butter with the fishing knife he wielded in the other; the table knife and fork set out by the waitress untouched.

"Enjoy your meal, mate." She tried a final time to entice the belligerent seaman into a better mood while he ate, but to no avail.

"Captain. Goddamn it! Captain! Captain Randall Hoagg of the schooner *Raven*." His

2

booming shipboard voice echoed within the little tavern. Biscuit crumbs escaped between the gaps of missing and broken teeth as he spoke. A young couple at a nearby table turned to look at the noisy patron, catching Hoagg's attention.

"Eat your goddamned grub."

The couple quickly returned their attention to each other. Nancy gave the Captain a shallow curtsy and flew to the safety of the kitchen, wishing she had stepped outside with Carl instead.

Carl stood on the boards of the sidewalk. Bright yellow sunlight painted the building fronts across the street. The autumn breeze gently kissed his cheek with cool lips. Inside the big sunlit windows of the bank, a clerk moved back and forth at his counter. The owners of the dry goods store and hardware store stood on either side of Carl.

"Thought it sounded like a gunshot, Carl."

"Maybe not."

Something hard pressed against the small of Carl's back. The sea Captain used his beer mug to push the proprietor out of his way, for his own look at the Bank. He held a biscuit stuffed with cured ham and continued to bite at it as he stepped in front of the three men. Carl leaned to the left to see around this man just as the bank door opened. He had heard of bold bank robberies although he had never witnessed one himself, and was suddenly glad that the rude man, who drank beer with his ham and eggs, had stepped in front of him. All he saw though, was very normal. The bank clerk accompanying a woman.

His name is...Brown; has his lunch here

3

occasionally. I have seen her before. Pulaski. Her name is Pulaski.

The clerk handed the woman a small sack, glanced in the Tavern's direction, then tipped his hat to her and walked away. It was all very normal.

The gunshot couldn't have come from the bank. Maybe it wasn't even a gunshot.

The woman's dress was faded, but snug about her body, showing a pleasing form still worthy of far more than a mere glance. Her hair golden in the sunshine, uncombed and teased by the faint breeze drifting cool off the bay, whispering among the strands. Her boots banged on the wooden planks, looking more like a man's, but at odds with her graceful walk.

"Who is that woman," the hardware owner asked, watching her stoop to pick up a cloth from the road and shake the dust off. Without looking about she stepped further into the road and walked slowly toward the end of Oyster Street .

"Fine looking wench," the Captain said.

"...Mrs. Pulaski," Carl finally answered.

The sea Captain whirled in front of Carl to face him.

"Would that be Ben Pulaski's wife?"

Carl stepped back a half step.

"Why, yes. She is. Do you know Ben?"

A smile slowly spread across Hoagg's unshaven face, Carl's question hanging unanswered. Hoagg turned his eyes back at the woman as she made her way toward the end of the street.

Speaking only to himself, "So, that's the fair Sonja. I heard o' her 'til I was sick of it. Figured Pulaski was just as full of shit about that as he was everything else. Goddamned if that sonofabitch don't really got himself a looker under the covers."

He turned to share his observation and a wide grin with the men behind him, but they had quickly returned to their businesses while he was admiring another man's wife. Hoagg sniffed at their departure, and then reached a curled finger deep into his jaw to loosen a piece of ham trapped amongst the crags of his back teeth. He examined it briefly before flicking it into the street, and then tilted the mug to his lips to drain the last of the beer. Looking at the pole mounted clock in front of the Hardware next door, he saw that it was only a little past eight thirty. He still had plenty of time to go back to the table and finish eating his fifteen cents worth.

"Goddamned robbery," he mumbled to himself and then smiled again. "Almost bad as me," then he chuckled once and stepped back into the tavern. He eyed Carl standing by the kitchen door talking to Nancy and raised his empty mug toward them.

"Beer! And get it from the cellar this time. This shit up here is warm!"

Carl nodded to Hoagg, while Nancy went to the Captain's table to retrieve the mug. There was no cellar in the Tavern. It was a single-story pine plank building. Carl smiled to himself as he pulled a fresh mug from the shelf in the back room and drew a beer from the only beer cask he had pegged open so early in the day. It was Friday, and he would open two or three more casks before the day would be over long after sundown.

But for now the grouchy son of a bitch will get his beer from this cask or none at all.

Nancy breezed in, knowing full well what Carl was doing, traded the empty mug for the fresh one and quick stepped to Hoagg's table.

"Here ya' go, Captain. Fresh from the cellar."

Hoagg snatched the mug and took a gulp, glancing at the waitress over the rim.

"It'll do, but on second thought I think I'm done. Not that it's been worth fifteen cents."

He dropped the coins on the table in front of the woman, scooped the rest of his ham into another biscuit and then left. Outside, he stepped off the plank walkway onto the dust and crushed oyster shells, pacing the woman he had seen moments before. He watched her met by a man. Hoagg leaned forward, gazing intently at the man. Then he watched them walk away together, with the mule walking untethered behind them like an obedient dog. She broke away from the man and ran back toward Hoagg, her breasts dancing and the space between her thighs molded by the dress fabric as she ran against the breeze.

Come to me, little darlin.

She scooped up a small parcel lying in the road, then returned to the man and the mule. Lingering at the corner of Oyster Street and Canal, he watched the woman and her man walk up the slope to the little bench at the tree. Watched the autumn leaves blow across the hillside. Felt the cool breeze brush against his cheek. Drew out his knife and wiped ham grease off the blade onto his stained trousers, then stood there cleaning tar from under

6

his fingernails. He watched the couple intently when they made their way back down and onto one of the canal barges, pulled by its mules past the warehouses and beyond his view. The man shook his head slightly, picked another piece of ham gristle from his teeth and spit it onto the ground.

Benjamin Goddamned Pulaski.

He absently traced his fingertips along the ridge running down the front of his belly under his shirt. There was a horrific wide red scar meandering from his breast bone nearly to his groin, like a long twisted lightning bolt, puckered in several places from hard battles with infection that took an agonizing year in Hell to heal. He turned and walked back to Oyster Street with a wide grin on his face, remembering the man who gave him that scar, gave him the agony. Pulling his watch out of his pocket, he checked the time again. He had a nine o'clock meeting with the owner of the bank on that street. He made his way back up Oyster Street and walked in through the door at two minutes before his appointment.

"We're closed," Herbert Binterfield whined from behind his desk, holding a mirror shard in front of him and wiping the ink from his face with his oil soaked handkerchief. "Had to let my clerk go," he added, "No one here to give you receipts this morning. Come back this afternoon."

"Didn't come here to see no goddamned clerk." Hoagg spoke into the shadows at the rear of the bank.

"We're closed, I said."

"I've got an appointment," Hoagg insisted, "with a guy named Binters, Binter-something."

"Do you mean Binterfield," the other asked, straightening his shoulders slightly.

"Yeah, that's it. We're supposed to talk about...loading cargo from here onto my ship..."

"And?" Binterfield continued to wipe at the ink, and finally making some progress.

"And taking it to Charleston, ... for auction."

"Oh yes, yes! Excellent! This may improve my day after all. Come through the gate, come back here to my desk. Please don't mind the, uh, disarray."

Hoagg pushed at the gate watching it swing unchecked into the back of the counter. "Seems to be sprung," he said more to himself than the figure at the back of the bank. As his eyes corrected to the shadows of the back office area, he could see the strewn papers, spilled ink pot and a puddle of some other liquid on the floor beside the massive desk. Binterfield started to rise, but then quickly sat back down, pointing an upturned hand at the recently righted chair in front of his desk. Hoagg noticed the great stain at the man's crotch before he sat back down and then looked around the office more carefully. Glass mirror shards covered much of the rear floor, and some were even on the man's desk. The rear door frame was shattered about shoulder high, with jagged white pine splinters showing from the mahogany stain. The smell of gunpowder was heavy in the air.

Hoagg nodded to himself. "Thought I heard gunfire over this way."

"That crazy Pulaski woman," Binterfield whined, smoothing his chestnut colored mustache with the side of his finger, and rolling the tip of his tongue along the edge of the small chip in his tooth.

Hoagg looked wistfully at the splintered door frame, smiling at the thought of the small blonde form he had seen from across the street, the shape of her body as she ran toward him, and visualizing her causing the damage around him.

"I believe I'm falling in love, Binterbean."

"BinterFIELD"

"Yeah...so what do ya have for me, BinterFIELD?"

"Our mutual acquaintance, tells me you have participated in the legal slave trade in the deep south?"

"Yeah..."

"And that you could be interested in fresh sources of more...labor?"

"More slaves? Yes."

"We are awash in untethered blacks, I tell you. The cotton and rice plantations farther south are absolutely begging for additional slaves to work new fields."

"Yes, at least the part about deep south demand."

Binterfield described the black village of shanties growing near the cattails along the southern shore of town at Concord Cove.

"Each one not much bigger than a privy, but full of blacks. I am sure many of them are escaped slaves. There are one or two that work for friends of mine, that I would not want taken - I will give you

9

their names and whatever description I can put together."

"And the rest, Mr. Binterfield?"

"The rest you can take whenever you... get the opportunity. I can be of great value in identifying loose blacks, and, uh, others you might, well, take away. And mind you, we will keep track of the numbers. I expect fifteen percent from each sale. You would not know of many of them without me."

"I expect there'll be plenty to go around after the sale. There be hundreds of free bucks and runaways all over Maryland and Delaware, fair and easy game from the Bay. I'm looking to make a handful of loads from up here, so I ain't gonna toss it all into the shitter, just to cheat you outta your finder's fee. I got fees in other places too, but I still make more than any captain that used to bring them over from Africa. You'll get your money, Binterfield, long as I get my niggers up here."

Binterfield watched him closely. "Captain, I am informed good slaves are selling in Charleston for five hundred to a thousand dollars apiece..."

"And comely black wenches for as much as three..."

"How many, er, slaves could fit on your ship, Captain?"

"Couple hundred, easy," he chuckled, "well, easy for me, kinda tight on them," then he chuckled again.

Binterfield flicked the tip of his tongue along the chipped edge of his front tooth, and rubbed his chest where the Pulaski woman had pressed her knees. She had him pinned on top of his desk – and stuck her gun in his mouth.

"Oh, Captain, I can find you far more than enough...cargo, to fill your ship, and more than once."

Fifteen percent of two hundred thousand dollars! Thirty THOUSAND dollars EACH load! More than I make in three years! This would more than replace the piddling sum I lost to the Pulaski woman this morning.

"There's another buck you should look after, Captain"

"Yeah?"

"He may be more difficult to handle, but will probably bring the best price of your load. His name is Simon Bond, and you'll have to go up canal a couple miles north to catch him."

"Simon Bond, do you say?"

Binterfield almost giggled as he spoke.

"I am told that he stays at the farm of that Pulaski woman."

"Bond? Did you say Simon Bond? Big man?"

"Yes."

"Staying at the Pulaski place?"

"Yes, yes. I said all that."

Hoagg's eyes sparkled like a young child with a Christmas gift.

---<>---

An hour later, Randall Hoagg stood at the edge of the wharf in front of another new warehouse added to the line of wooden buildings shouldering their place along the waterfront of Havre de Grace from the Canal Basin down toward the lighthouse. Chesapeake Bay Schooners, scows, and shallow bottomed Jacks were nudging one another in the morning sun to take on their next cargo or off load goods brought in during the night from Norfolk, Baltimore, or Philadelphia. The safety of the Concord Point Lighthouse, and a near full moon the night before, made their final run up the bay an easy sail. Their captains took every opportunity to get their cargoes quickly to this market and were eager for their return loads. A man in a leather apron carrying a wooden box of tools walked nearby. Hoagg grabbed the edge of his sleeve as he walked close.

"Hey! Where's the closest Blacksmith?"

The man stopped and smiled. "Well sir, we got two. One set up at the Canal barn, Charles Briscoe, does mostly nails, bolts and horseshoes for the Canal Company. Th'other is down at Concord Cove. Don't recall his name. New man. Does most anything, chains and tools and such. His shop is on th'other side of Tuttle's. The Boatwright."

Hoagg nodded and looked away without saying anything. The man stood another moment then hurried on his way toward the tallest ship along the wharf. Hoagg absently felt the weight of the coin purse in his pocket, then took his own course up the gentle slope to Market Street and made his way south down to the point. Just past the lane to the lighthouse, a thinned stand of trees gave some shadow to the morning sun and a narrow lane made its way west from there, while a well trod footpath continued south into the trees. Once in the trees he could see the little shanties set randomly at the edge of the water, rags for curtains as well as for some doors. There was hard-packed dirt pathways among the shanties, and a modest clearing with stump stools arrayed around a large fire pit.

Ought to find some 'cargo' here.

He went back to the narrow lane and followed it to its end. There was a fair sized workshop with ankle deep piles of wood shavings at various spots around its perimeter. A rowboat laid bottom up across sawhorses in the final stages of building. Beyond that, the lane narrowed to a well trotted footpath among saplings, the smell of burning charcoal and the steady ringing of a heavy hammer on anvil. He stepped from the footpath into the clearing near the blacksmith shop and spoke to the Smithie who looked up as he neared.

"Got some work for you."

Edward Lesko dropped the hinge he was bending into the water trough to harden, laid his tongs against the anvil stump and stepped away from the forge wiping his hands.

"What can I do for you?"

"Can you make slave manacles?"

"Excellent ones. What kind and how many?"

"You made them before?"

"I worked for years at a shop in Virginia. Made hundreds of them. Then moved up here to start my own shop."

"You do straight bar wrist manacles and chain strung ankles?"

"Single or double ankles?"

"Singles. Five to a chain. Three feet apart."

"I can do that, though three feet apart might giv'em too much room to misbehave. How many of each do you need?"

"They got to be able to go up and down ship's steps. I got a few on board my ship, but need much more. Need enough for at least a hundred slaves. Do'em in sets of twenty with each set having their own key, so one key can't open them all."

"Sounds like a man who knows his business. I can have it done in a month, maybe three weeks."

"Th'hell you will. One week. One week or I go to the other blacksmith."

"Briscoe don't do chains or manacles. Ten days."

After a short haggle on price, the two men shook hands and Hoagg headed back up the footpath into town.

Ten Goddamned days! I just need to start with what I got. And catch some that won't be missed by business or the law. That's something ol'prissy Binterbean can actually help me with...

Hoagg headed for the Sheriff's Office. The small office was wedged between two storefronts on a side street off Union. Inside, it held a simple office in front with a small desk and narrow pot belly stove, an iron strip door behind it opened to a single empty cell. The desk and stove were old, moved in from somewhere before, but the rough cut planks of the walls and floor were new. A broad shouldered man sat behind the desk examining a large seaman's knife with a whalebone handle as Hoagg walked in.

"You the Sheriff?" Hoagg looked keenly at the knife. His hand floated up and gently touched the thick scar beneath his shirt.

The man put down the knife and folded his hands together on the desk. "Deputy Sheriff Lyle Mattingly. Some folks call me Constable, but I don't like it. I'm the Sheriff's Deputy for Havre de Grace. Sheriff stays up in Bel Air, at the County Seat. What do you want?"

"I represent several slave owners in Virginia and the Carolinas..."

"So?"

Hoagg exhaled slowly and gritted his teeth. "So, I wanted you to know who I am, so you are informed that I am performing legal services for my employers, in your town."

"So, who are you?"

"Captain Randall Hoagg of the Schooner Raven."

"So, how many you looking for?"

"Couple dozen."

The deputy sighed, made a pencil note in a ledger book on his desk and put down the pencil. Then he picked the knife back up and leaned back in his chair, giving the knife his full attention. "I'm informed."

"You got any leaflets of local runaways or black felons?"

He looked back up at Hoagg. "Why?"

Hoagg took in a slow breath and spoke softly.

"So, if I come across any of them, I can bring

them to you... and you can collect the reward."

"Oh," the deputy smiled broadly. "Well, sure!"

He snapped opened his desk drawer and pulled out several leaflets. Some were old and coffee-stained, but several were recent papers, all of which he handed to the Captain.

"Here, Cap'n. See what you can find. I'll even split the reward with you!"

Hoagg shifted through the leaflets, looking at printed drawings of black men made from woodcuttings, that all looked alike – probably printed by the same printer using the same woodcarving. Different names, different vague descriptions, varying rewards, different owners. He stopped while looking at one of the older leaflets, printed a year earlier in 1841. Same drawing for the name Simon Bond, wanted for murder in St. Mary's County, two hundred dollars reward. Hoagg smiled.

Why in shit would I turn in Simon Bond for half of the reward, when I could get five times that for him in Charleston? Plus, maybe introduce myself to that sweet Pulaski woman as part of the same deal - maybe even share time with her while her husband lays gutted on the floor, dying next to us - and watching.

"You see one you know, Cap'n? You're smiling."

The smile disappeared. "Just noticing all the drawings look exactly alike."

"Well, what d'you expect? All darkies do look alike, Cap'n."

"You care to sell that knife, Deputy. I'll give you a good price for it."

Mattingly looked carefully at the knife, and slowly shook his head. "...Nah. Had to take it from a citizen. Have to give it back next time I see him."

Hoagg left the office slamming the door behind him. He walked back down to Market Street and entered the first saloon he came to, ordering a large whiskey at the bar. As he stood there draining the glass, two men arose from their table to join him.

"Buy you a drink, Cap'n?"

He glanced over his shoulder and barely nodded to the men off his ship.

"Surprised you two are sober and have any money left to buy yourselves another drink, let alone someone else."

"Me an' Freddie had a bit of luck last night."

"Yeah," Freddie said, "Me and Dicky met an old friend who owed us money, and was just pissing to pay up."

Both crewmen chuckled at the shared joke and ordered whiskey for the three of them. When the bartender served them, Dicky paid with a smooth five dollar bill. Hoagg saw the bill and grabbed Dicky's wrist in a death grip. Then he quickly released his grip and let the bartender take the bill. He remained silent until the bartender set three whiskeys, four dollar bills and coins on the bar in front of Dicky.

"Where'd you get that kind of money?" Then he lowered his voice, "Am I going to have to deal with the law over it?"

Freddie answered in a whisper, "Nothin to worry about, Cap'n. Just a drunk ol'farmer who didn't know what was going on."

"And nobody saw nothing," Dicky added. "It was in an alley with just the three of us."

Hoagg looked into each man's eyes and sighed.

"Alright, but if this comes back on me I will slit your throats – or worse. Now buy me lunch."

2

Five miles north of the twenty-acre Havre de Grace canal basin, which accepted the water and barges coming down from Wrightsville, Pennsylvania, the Susquehanna and Tidewater Canal drained past the growing settlement of Lapidum. At the southern end of Lapidum, on the last level ground before the steep rise into the hillside, sat the Pulaski farm. The house was perched on the western bank of the canal, framed between two massive oak trees. The morning sun floated above the crest of the eastern hillside, shining across the Susquehanna River from Cecil County. The first bright rays of the sun slipped between the curtains of the Pulaski front room, bathing it in yellow light. Sunlight accented the rippled sides of the single room that marked the walls of the original log cabin.

Ben Pulaski, owner of the canal barge *Ugly Boat*, sat in the kitchen on the back side of a double fireplace, across the table from his wife, Sonja. The fresh bandage around his head was pristine except for the small dot of darkening blood showing through high above his left ear. Both stared at the stack of money in the middle of the table that was far greater than any they had ever owned. Next to the money were two signed documents. One deferred final payment on a bank loan four years for his barge, which had been due paid-in-full only yesterday. The other paper approved a bank withdrawal for six hundred dollars.

"But Sonja, I closed that account two years ago..."

"Mr. Brown, his clerk, had kept it open, waiting for the opportunity to get it to us. It was every penny Binterfield had ever cheated out of us. It was all ours. It was all still in his damned bank, still in his books. Mr. Brown put it in the correct account – ours."

"I can't believe Binterfield won't come after us for this..."

"Brown swore he would stand up in court as witness to Binterfield approving the withdrawal as well as deferring the loan payment. Brown said I could trust him. He said that you would."

Ben nodded to her and reached out to touch her hand. "Yes. I think I can trust Brown, but I am worried that this is far from over."

"Ben, it was over the moment I killed him..."

"But you didn't kill him, Sonja. The powder was wet and didn't go off..."

"Doesn't matter. I pulled the trigger. In my heart and mind and soul I killed him – before you could. It was only his spittle in the powder that kept him from being dead, and that keeps you from being hung. Brown and these documents will keep him from changing his mind."

"I still should have killed him myself. Meant to when I followed you into town yesterday. He will come after us. He will cause us pain, somehow. I know it."

Ben stood to ease the stiffness in his back and the pull of the long scar running along his side . "Something will yet come of this. Something evil."

She stood next to him, the morning light highlighting the golden strands of her hair, and smiled into his eyes. "We came of this, Ben. We came back to life, a new life. I feel hope, Ben. First I have felt that since I lost Alisha, since we lost Alisha. Now let him be."

She pulled on his dark beard drawing his face near to hers, pressed back the lines on his forehead and kissed him there. He tilted back and then to the side, reaching to her shoulder to steady himself. The little spot on his bandage had grown slightly larger.

"You need to lay down," she said and helped him to the bedroom. Then she dashed to the kitchen, scooped up the money and the documents and returned them to the wooden lockbox in the chest of drawers against the opposite wall. She sat on the wooden chair next to the bed and took his hand.

---<>---

The afternoon air was heavy with the dust and aroma of dying leaves. Already the oak and maple leaves were turning to the early pallet of fall colors and taking to the air on cool breezes. The warmth of the noontime sun was a failed promise, and its arc slightly lower than yesterday.

Ben still lay on the bed talking with Sonja, as they tried to make sense of what each had experienced.

"What happened on the Canal, Ben?"

"First, tell me about Mickey. Why did he leave, where did he go?"

She pictured Mickey on his hands and knees in their front yard, vomiting whiskey in the night rain, unable to walk to his room in the barn that he shared with Simon, crying out to his dead wife.

"He said he promised his wife he would do something with his life; something better."

"Where did he go?"

"I didn't see him leave. He just said he had to go. Said someone told him he had healing hands."

"Yes. He sewed up my head..."

"What? That drunkard? And you let him?"

Ben raised his hand slightly to wipe away the comment from the air. "Him and Miss Mauzey did. She's the one told him he had healing hands. He told me that later..."

"Miss Mauzey? Who? - Ben, tell me what happened?"

"Miss Mauzey was a runaway slave. Anthony had escaping slaves in a hidden compartment in his barge..."

"Anthony! I should have known. Whenever he is around you, disaster strikes us!"

Ben raised his head from the pillow and frowned at her. "You want to hear what happened or not?"

Anthony Renowitz had known Ben long before

Sonja entered his life. His grandfather had been a successful slave trader until the African slave trade was made illegal. Rather than chase the remaining legal slave trade among the states, he spent his last few years in cotton and coffee. His death bestowed a large fortune upon his family in Philadelphia, who ironically became staunch abolitionists. An excitable son of that abolitionist generation, Anthony had a propensity for taking poorly made plans of good will to extremes.

"When I found out about the slaves, Anthony convinced me to help get them across the Line into Pennsylvania..."

"Of course-" Sonja stopped her own comment as Ben raised a single finger to her.

"I agreed to distract the slave catchers hanging around Lock One, so Anthony could take the *Wilhelmina* on through, into Pennsylvania. I guess I distracted them too much. One of them pointed a gun in my face. I thought he was going to shoot me..."

Sonja caught her breath. Ben continued.

"...so I hit him with the tiller handle. I hit and he shot at the same time. Everybody thought we were both dead. Anthony got through. Mickey and Simon took me on to Wrightsville, after Miss Mauzey and Mickey sewed up my head. The bullet only grazed my skull bone."

Ben shrugged his shoulders. "Turned out, most of the slaves weren't even in Anthony's barge at the time. They couldn't trust us enough to take the chance. Went on their own way through the woods. One of those was captured and killed. Only Miss Mauzey and Toby went on to Wrightsville with us.

When we got there that doctor said I was doing fine and tried to hire Miss Mauzey."

Sonja nodded. "Wallace Harper was coming back from Wrightsville. Had been there visiting that other doctor. He told me about a canaller being shot when he stopped at father's farm in York Furnace. The doctor in Wrightsville said the canaller was with a big black man and an Irishman. That's when we figured out it must have been you, and then I came home."

"So tell me what happened with your father? Things had not gone well there while I was at sea. Is everything alright between you two now"

Sonja gave up a broad smile. "Oh yes. I got rid of our problem."

"Tell me..."

"Not now. You go to sleep."

They squeezed each other's hand and he drifted off to sleep for a while. She laid down beside him and covered them both against the early autumn chill with an old quilt she still had from their first house.

As the sun began to set over the western ridgeline behind the house, Ben rose and took his pipe and tobacco pouch from the mantle over the fireplace in the front room, then stepped out onto the porch to settle into his favorite chair and view. Down the gentle slope of their front yard, framed by the two massive oak trees, beyond his barge tethered to its mate, and beyond the canal wall on the other side, the Susquehanna River slipped by with only the slightest ripples on its way to the Chesapeake Bay. The river gave a near mirror image of the blue-gray cloudless sky above. On the eastern bank the lengthening afternoon shadows of the trees behind his house and farm rose up from the river, clawing their way up to darken the hillside in Cecil County.

Behind Ben, his sons Aaron and Isaac chattered in their shared bedroom. They lay in bed waiting for sleep to come, earlier than they wished, but necessary for their awakening at four o'clock the next morning. Other voices in easy conversation, muffled by the wood wall containing them in the tack room of the barn, drifted across the front lawn to the porch. One was the baritone of Simon Bond. The other was Toby, still full of curiosity and questions, believing adults had the answers, finding comfort in Simon's company. Down canal, far beyond his view, he knew Anthony was on the *Wilhelmina* in the Havre de Grace Canal Basin five miles south. Dozens of other barges waited their turn to advance from mules along the towpath to steam tugs to Philadelphia, Annapolis or Baltimore, and finally relieved of their cargo.

Anthony, my friend. You almost got me killed this time. And now I have lost Mickey from my crew. Sometimes your schemes cost me far too much.

Ben fingered the empty scabbard lying on the table next to his chair. Regretted losing it to the Deputy. Felt uneasy without it comforting his side, where it had always been before, had allowed him to save his life then. He rose and walked down to the barn and into the tool room, picked up the older iron knife set there to help butcher the pig later in the Fall. Rust had begun to spot the blade. He picked up the sharpening stone and carried it with the knife back to the porch. Watching the sky settle to gray, he gently rubbed the edge of the knife blade back and forth across the stone, like the steady pendulum swing of a mantle clock. The rhythm of the strokes were soothing, the feel of the blade reassuring, the cutting edge rubbed thinner and thinner, as sharp as a barber's razor. The rhythm of it all helped soothe the ache in his head, and helped his mind remember a few more details of the blackness in his memory of the night before, before waking up in the alley near the tavern with his money belt gone.

Two men helped me walk. Maybe? Was that here, or in China? Last night, maybe? Some other time?

Satisfied with the hone of the blade, he slipped the knife into his scabbard, slipped his belt through the loop and stepped off the porch. The first stars began to shine overhead as he walked down the pathway past the barn, through the saplings and across the little wooden bridge that connected his property to Lapidum. He walked past the general store to lockhouse number nine, across the swing bridge there and onto the towpath, where no mule ever travelled at night. On his right the canal water drifted empty and lazy to the south, and on this left, with only the towpath separating them, the Susquehanna flowed south as well, but faster and with the quiet power of a mile wide river determined to shove itself into the Chesapeake Bay.

Mickey had named the power of the river an evil presence. The Bitch, he had called her. Ben came to accept that. The Bitch had taken Mickey's family. The Bitch had also taken Ben's daughter and their home on Pearl Street, the first winter he was gone.

Alisha.

He never met the infant. It was two more winters and a spring before he at last found his way home. Sonja had been told he was dead, and her heart had frozen harder than the ice gorge that had killed their daughter and crushed their home. Sonja's heart was almost completely thawed now, almost, but there were times...

---<>---

When Robert Hannah stepped out of the company warehouse to make his way home, the sun had been down for hours and most of Havre de Grace was deep asleep. The chorus of boisterous snores coming from the barges in the canal basin told him there were still many barge captains prisoners in their own barges waiting for a tow down the Bay. The swing bridge near the main lockhouse was across for the night, and he took a leisurely stroll along the outer towpath. Happy to be in the fresh air coming off the Susquehanna Flats, away from his clip board and dust in the warehouse. He felt proud of his day, wasn't quite ready for it to end. The Warehouse Supervisor had been promoted to company Shipping Master this morning, and before noon he had named Robert his replacement. He was anxious to be home and tell his wife of his promotion and the extra five dollars pay a month they would be getting. Rent had just gone up again and little Robert Jr. needed new shoes. This would more than take care of that. He would tell her at breakfast, but for now he wanted to enjoy his moment a little longer before he went home.

The sky was a dark sapphire field sprinkled with stars. A few small clouds drifted across the face of a three quarter moon bright in the southeastern sky. He stood at the edge of the towpath with his hands in his pockets. The basin behind him and the Susquehanna River slipping by in front of him, he listened to it whisper to the rocks as it passed. Along the rippled surface he could see the moon's reflection, and he breathed deeply of fresh air rolling up the bay. He felt a sharp pain in the back of his head. A lightning bolt shot down across his vision, splintered in all directions and then disappeared, taking all light with it. In the darkness there was another sharp pain to his forehead as he fell face down on to the rocks, and then all feeling was gone. He was deep into the darkness, falling without any feeling, only the sense of falling, and he fell until the senses stopped and he had travelled far from consciousness.

The man who had hit him from behind looked around to ensure no one else was close enough to see his work. He kneeled down to roll the body over and ripped open its shirt and loosened its belt, yanking the waist of its trousers down below its bellybutton. Gripping the handle of his long bladed knife with both hands, he leaned his shoulders high over the lower abdomen and drove the razor sharp blade deep, the tip finding its way in to the bone at the back of the pelvis. Pulling the knife part of the way back out and pushing it toward the head at the same time, he sawed his way up to the belly button where he changed direction slightly toward the right of the body. Then he stopped and withdrew the knife. He looked around again, and then examined his cut, tilting his head to the right and then to the left; as a painter might review his last few brush strokes. He reinserted the knife into the pool of blood and writhing intestines with minor direction changes and continued up the abdomen, cutting a meandering slit running all the way to the lower end of the man's breast bone. With his hand almost buried in the oozing blood of the massive wound, he brought the blade up toward its head and made a final side-to-side sweep of the blade tip across the inside of the belly and lower chest, slicing open stomach, lungs and the still beating heart.

He looked around again, then sat there in the moonlight looking at his handiwork, tilting his head one way then another. He reached out with a bloody hand to rearrange one of the jagged edges of the ghastly wound, picking at the edge of the flesh and pulling it until it laid in the manner he wished to see it. He stared at it in silence a long moment, then looked up at the sky, took in a shivering breath and blew it out. He pushed the body over to roll it off the towpath into the river, and followed it down to the wet rocks. Leaning over, he pushed the body farther out into the current with its face up and the gaping wound filling with water. Watched it float away, drifting south and deeper in the water as the river took its gift. Knowing it would soon sink, and not rise later to complicate his life. Knowing the gutted abdomen and sliced lungs would not fill with the putrid gases of dead bodies, which caused the drowned to come back up to the surface like the dead coming back to life. He smiled to himself, kneeling down to wash his hands and forearms in the cool river water, knowing the plume of fresh blood was there even without seeing it again in the darkness, humming softly to himself.

---<>---

On the front porch, Ben wiped his hands with the wet rag from the barn. The well oiled blade of his knife rested snugly in its borrowed scabbard for the night. In the fading moonlight, a heron glided silently into the shallows on the canal in front of the Pulaski farm. Immediately on the hunt, it waded deliberately with his head cocked back, slowly tracking a sluggish fish not paying enough attention. The heron's head shot down into the water taking the fish and quickly holding it up in the air so it would slide down his throat. Ben watched as the Heron walked stiff legged into the little cattails growing in the shallows and settled into a pose for a night's wary half-sleep. Relaxed and content for the moment, Ben closed the front door as he entered the cabin and joined his wife for the night.

At four in the morning, Ben walked down to the canal, over the little dock built by his son Isaac, and onto the deck of the *Ugly Boat*. Her cargo holds were full of coal, as were the holds of *The Turtle* tied in front of her. *The Turtle* was a Pennsylvania built canal barge with a single small cabin in the center sandwiched between two large cargo holds, and could carry much more than his first barge, the *Ugly Boat*. She was intended as a barge, but damaged during building and finished as a scow, able to fit within the narrow and shallow canal, but beveled at the bow to let it sail, once into the Bay and her mast raised. The ability to sail his own cargo kept him free from the long waits and exorbitant fees charged by the steam tugs, but cost him cargo space in her odd hull.

Aaron came from the barn leading two harnessed mules, the single tree used for towing mules in line was still lashed to the back of Nadja to keep it from banging against her ankles until they were on the towpath and hitched to the tow rope. The lead mule, Sarah, was well rested from her dash into Havre de Grace the day before and eager for a short pull back to the Canal Basin.

Isaac worked with Simon to bring the *Ugly Boat's* heavy wooden mast, boom, and gaff from the barn. The mast to hold up the sail, the boom to spread the sail at the bottom and give better direction to the wind's push, and the gaff at the top of the sail to hold it out taught from the mast and better catch the Bay's light winds there. Next they brought out the side boards, the amazing Dutch innovation that allowed a flat bottom boat without a keel to push back against the windward nudge to her side and transfer her motion forward; the forces that bestowed upon all sailboats the ability to travel at angles from the wind.

Once all was ready on the two barges, Simon, Isaac and Ben used poles to push them to the other side of the canal where Aaron and the two mules waited on the towpath. Isaac tossed the bow tow rope from *The Turtle* to Aaron, who tied it to the single-tree that would take the combined power of both Nadja and the older Sarah within the single file harness. The early dawn light was visible only at the edge of the sky and the canal was still in darkness. Ben hummed as he sat at the stern tiller of the *Ugly Boat,* then whistled for Aaron to lead the mules down the tow path. There was a feeble jerk as the mules reached the lead of the rope and the barges began to ease forward. Nadja stumbled back a half step when her harness took the drag of the barges, but the more experienced Sarah was ready for it, leaning into the momentary resistance and drawing them all forward. She settled almost immediately into an easy pace helped by the gentle southerly current within the canal. They would be through the basin within the hour and through the outlet lock into the bay a half hour after that.

---<>---

At sunrise, Captain Hoagg loitered near the Raven's double wheel, his ship still tied to the Havre de Grace wharf. Fresh coffee steamed from his mug. He absently fingered a small canvas bag and hummed to himself as he watched the activity on deck. The crew of the Raven unloaded the last of their cargo of cotton. The buyer eagerly pushed his slaves to grab the bales and shove them into his wagons for their short trip to waiting looms along the southern Post Road. The weaver was excited at the low price this sea captain had taken for such a lovely cargo of Georgia cotton, and had wasted no time getting it picked up and out of Havre de Grace.

He was such a FOOL!, the weaver thought as he bumped along Market Street in his lead wagon.

Captain Hoagg hefted the bag of gold in his hand; payment for the cotton, and smiled in the early light. His face was lost in the shadows of the sun rising behind him, bright yellow across the Susquehanna Flats in Perryville.

The fat little fool thinks he has cheated me, when I paid no more for that cotton than I have for this ship. Nothing! A simple slice across the throat of a drunken captain, and it was all mine. Easy work and fresh food for the crabs and fish in Charleston Harbor.

He turned to the First Mate approaching him.

"Get me that carpenter, Wilson! We need shelves built for our next cargo. And remind th'bastard to put the chain holes through the sitting boards, not the damned support posts. If my deck sags anywhere, I'll come back and cut his throat – and his wife's."

Once the carpenter and his apprentice came on board to begin work on the shelves, Hoagg turned the ship over to Wilson and walked down the gangplank to the wharf and back to the Tidewater Bank and Trust.

The bell jingled softly as he opened the boarded front door. Inside, a man was on his knees, repairing the little office gate, another man was on a ladder, painting the door frame behind Binterfield's desk and still another was mounting a new oil lamp on the nearby wall. Morning sunlight sprayed from the front windows that faced the street. Golden light painted the area around the desk. The air was rich with the scent of turpentine and freshly sawed oak. Hammers and saws added their cadence to the activities in the bank. A young man was busy moving ledgers from the wall near the clerk's counters and taking selected volumes into the large walk-in safe at the rear.

Binterfield was sitting behind the desk wagging his finger at another man probably ten years his senior with a ridiculous looking bandaged nose and bruised eyes, folding his spine and nodding his head to the banker like a servant. Binterfield noticed Hoagg and gave a beaming smile, beckoning him with a finger to join him, then turned and with a flip of his hand dismissed the older man at his desk.

"Get out, Briscoe! Come back later and maybe I

can find use for you again. Go see your brother at the mule barn."

Captain Hoagg had his hands in his pockets and did not remove them as he stood in front of Binterfield's ornately carved mahogany desk.

"You got my list?"

Binterfield clapped his hands to get their attention and then dismissed all the workers. Once the last man had closed the front door behind him, Binterfield motioned the Captain to the leather padded chair beside his desk. He withdrew a carved glass decanter and two small matching glasses from a bottom drawer, briefly examining the decanter.

At least this made it through Sonja Pulaski's visit.

He poured an ounce of whiskey into each glass and handed one to Hoagg.

"A drink, Captain. If you indulge so early in the morning."

"I indulge more than you could possibly imagine."

"I am in good spirit this day," he said toasting the captain, then downed his drink.

Hoagg smelled then sipped his drink. "You got my list?"

Binterfield opened the center drawer, newly relined in fresh cedar, and with a flourish withdrew a crisp white sheet of paper containing three columns of names, laying it in front of the captain.

Hoagg swallowed the remainder of his meager drink and leaned forward to examine the list, but without touching it. "What are these letters after

34

the end of the names?"

"*S* is for known slave, *R* is for runaway (or possible), and *X* is for, well... expendable. Do with those as you wish."

"A lot of the *X's* have a *w* after them. What's that for?"

"Well, captain, those are white people I'd like to see gone as well."

"Want me to clean your dirty little house while I'm collecting slaves?"

Binterfield smiled an almost perfect smile with almost perfect teeth – except a little chip missing from the corner of one front tooth, but the smile did not reach up to his pale blue eyes.

"Well... if you would be so kind."

"ONLY, if doing it suits me."

"Oh, of course. Of course..."

"And, each *X* I attend to, costs you your commission on one of the *S's* or *R's*."

"Oh, well, er, I see, um, yes, I guess that is only fair – unless, of course, you manage to find one of those a buyer, somewhere?"

Binterfield pulled back the slip of paper and reviewed it, then dipped his pen into the inkwell and lined out several names and slid the paper back to Hoagg.

"Maybe I was being a little exuberant in those instances."

He tapped his finger next to one of the remaining *Xw* entries, that for Nathaniel Brown, his recently resigned lead clerk.

"But, Captain, if you could make this one a priority, I will gladly sacrifice <u>two</u> commissions from the other categories."

Hoagg pulled up the paper, blew on the fresh ink lines to dry them and began folding the paper.

"One more thing, Binterfield. I need someone to point out these people to me. You gonna do that?"

"Oh no, I can't be seen doing that. I'll send you Mr. Briscoe, Samuel Briscoe. He and his brother, the canal company's blacksmith, know everyone in town."

Hoagg nodded. "Send him to my ship this morning. Morning, mind you. I'm moving my ship off the wharf before noon. This goddamned town of yours charges me every day for being tied up, and will charge me another day if I'm still there after noon. It's almost October. I need all this finished quickly, so I can be on my way to Charleston long before the heavy ice shows up down in the mouth of the Chesapeake. Send me your man!"

---<>---

Coming into the upper Canal Basin along the long thin ribbon of tow path, Ben steered the *Ugly Boat* from the canal proper to the riverside containment wall enclosing the basin. The two barges following their mules appeared almost mirage-like in the early morning images on the water showing unwrinkled sky above in rare mirror calm surfaces. Only the outward single bow wave marred the surface with a thin line that drifted out behind them a hundred yards. Nearing the center of the lower basin along its outer edge, another barge emerged from the pack of barges near the main lockhouse, making its way north, empty of cargo and high in the water. As the two travelers pass one another using the same towpath, the mules pass each other first. Aaron slowed to drop his line into the water and allowed the upcoming mule to walk over his line while the northward bound barge could glide over it. As barge number 26, company owned and captained by Dan Bartlett, neared the tethered *Turtle* and *Ugly Boat,* he called out.

"Ben on board?"

Aaron left Sarah and Nadja to nibble on sparse grass growing along the towpath and walked back to the *Ugly Boat* to hear whatever news Dan brought. Ben waved from the tiller. "Good morning Dan. What things do you hear from in town?"

Dan whistled for Thomas to halt his mule, and barge men from both boats grabbed at each other with boat hooks. Dan looked down, speaking as quietly as he could. "Sound travels too far in a calm, Ben, but you should know. Deputy Mattingly is asking about Simon Bond. Said he's wanted for murder in Southern Maryland."

Ben said nothing.

"There's a reward for his capture and return to St. Mary's County. Fifty Dollars. That's a lot of money, Ben. Could loosen some tongues."

Simon moved to the side of the barge near Dan. "He say anything else, Dan?"

"No, just that, Simon. Asked if anyone knew of you. Asked me and I said never heard tell of you, but I can't say what others might have told him. You do something down there?"

"Only what needed doing."

Dan looked back at Ben. "You know about it?"

Ben nodded yes.

Dan whistled for Thomas, his company rented slave, to move on. "You two be careful." His eyes moved on Isaac. "All of you. This could fall onto all of your heads. Simon, you ought to ride with me. Ain't no time to be going on into Havre de Grace. I'll drop you off in Lapidum."

Simon and Ben looked at each other, then Simon hopped onto number 26 before it slid beyond the *Ugly Boat*. Ben nodded to Dan, "Much obliged, Dan."

Ben looked around the deck of the *Ugly Boat* and up at the towpath, speaking to Aaron and Isaac.

"Well boys, it's just you and me this trip. Think I need any more help than that?"

Both young men grinned and shook their heads No. Ben kept his eyes on them a moment longer to take in the details of each son. Isaac tilted his head and frowned.

"What? Something wrong?"

Ben smiled.

"Nothing's wrong with either one of you. I am proud of you both."

The smiles that crawled across their faces came quickly and strong, lasting for long minutes, and returning again and again as they had moments to pause. Their shoulders moved with confidence of purpose and their backs were straighter when they stood.

I don't tell them that nearly enough. That's got to change.

As the double barge eased next to the Outlet lock in front of the main lockhouse, Aaron unhitched the mules and trotted them over to the company barn. Ben looked across to the Lockhouse, missing Will Boyd and wondering how his wife was doing back in Delaware, where Sonja mailed the checks for Will's portion of the profits on the barges. Will had been his partner and kept the unfinished *Ugly Boat* until Ben found his way back from China.

Will drowned in the Basin. Thrown by his horse and broke his neck. Closed casket- the crabs. So wasteful of a good man.

Now Stephen McGraw sat in the Canal Superintendant's office, and his family lived in the other rooms of the house.

Ben stepped forward to help Isaac raise the mast into its hinged mount in the forward deck. They attached the boom to the mast, the main sail kept tied to the boom. The gaff pole was tied to the upper edge of the sail for quick raising once they were clear of the outlet lock. Aaron returned from the barn and helped attach the hemp rope rigging, and then the three of them poled *The Turtle* and *Ugly Boat* through the outlet lock. They had become more efficient at the evolution from mule-pulled barges with the *Ugly Boat* in the rear, shifting to sail power with *The Turtle* taken to the stern of the *Ugly Boat*. It took no more time now than hitching the mules along the towpath.

The wind on the Bay veered southerly, forcing workboats from Chesapeake City coming north with catches for Havre de Grace to tack back and forth across it, laboring their way slowly up the Bay. The air smelled of freshwater fish and the forest back along the canal. The breeze played with his shirt collar and laid a chilly kiss on his cheek. Ben smiled again. Once the sails were set, a southerly wind would push them half way to Annapolis before those poor workboats could beat against the wind to make their way up to Havre de Grace.

Aaron and Isaac worked together to drop the side boards down into the water on both sides of the hull and lock into place. Without instruction, the three Pulaski's each completed their tasks to bring up the sails and hold them taught for the push of the wind that would take them forward. Next came the gentle bump when the tow rope yanked *The Turtle* into line behind them. Aaron pulled the main sail tighter and brought the boom over against the coming wind.

The *Ugly Boat* came alive and leaned gently away from the wind taking her crew and her loads forward as Ben pushed out the tiller just enough to steer them south toward Annapolis. He was rewarded with the timid gurgle of the surface water as the blunt bow shouldered it aside. Looking back at the cobalt blue of the river where it slipped into the Chesapeake and ahead to the translucent green of the upper bay, they crossed the Susquehanna Flats and passed the Concord Point Lighthouse near the southern tip of Havre de Grace. His holds were full of Pennsylvania coal, and the growing number of steamboats going in and out of Annapolis were hungry for it. Prices had never been so good for his business. The word around the canal basin said coal prices had doubled since his last load. Free, unlike most other canal barges forced to wait for steam tugs to pull them to their destination for heavy fees, the *Ugly Boat* and *The Turtle* needed only the wind.

Pulaski Shipping? Pulaski and Sons Shipping?
Yes, that is it. Pulaski and Sons!

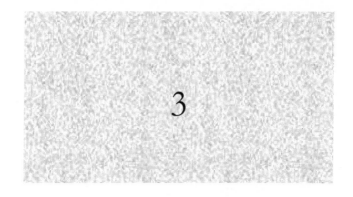

3

Simon stepped off Barge 26 while Dan signed the clipboard and chatted with his brother John. It was a short walk south from the canal's Lock Number 9 down the twenty yards of Stafford Road. There the road turned west while Simon continued on to the little bridge crossing over Deer Creek and the wagon path back down to the Pulaski farm. They had passed the farm coming into the lock. From the canal, the view up the slope with the house framed between the ancient oaks was a handsome scene in all seasons. He came first to the barn and tack room that served as his bunkroom. He and Ben had worked on it for weeks to make it habitable for mules, cows and farm hands. Mickey was gone now, so little four-year-old Toby would sleep there until Simon could manage other arrangements for him.

Toby had still not been told that his Uncle Jedediah never made it to freedom across the Maryland-Pennsylvania Line. Jedediah had been Toby's only family. Cornered by slavers while still in Maryland, he fought too courageously to keep from returning to slavery. The slave catchers lost thought of their bounty and gave in to their rage. After walking a thousand miles to get there, he was hung in the woods just yards south of the Line. It was near where Ben was shot. Near too, where Simon and Mickey buried that little runaway girl and her dead baby. But that was on the other side of the Line and they had been placed into freedom soil.

Simon pushed open the plank door to the bunkroom. "Toby? Toby? Where are you, youngster?" He looked in the stalls and up in the hay loft, hoping Toby had not managed to get into mischief again. The boy had a penchant for not doing what he was told.

Simon left the barn, giving the woodpile a quick glance as he passed, then headed for the house. The Pulaski frontage rose up gently from the canal to the barn among the huge oaks and then up to the front porch of the house. The wagon track ran along a level stretch slightly above the barn, but below the house, and served as the plateau across the front. Originally a fair sized two room log cabin, vertical plank rooms had been added on either side of the main cabin. The front porch had been enlarged to run the full width of the house, giving generous welcomed shade in the hot months and shelter from rain and snow. The wood of the old logs and the vertical planks had aged to similar gray in the years it stood before Ben and Sonja began renting it the year before.

After Ben and I came back from the dead. After the flood. After they lost Alisha.

Simon turned before he got to the house and went up into the back field, to the hog and chicken pens and finally the outhouse. No Toby. He stood there with his hands on his hips looking across the back field at the steep wooded hillside that ran up to a granite crest high behind the property. He sighed, shaking his head.

Now, Toby. Don't you dare be up in those woods.

"Simon!"

He spun around to the sound of her voice. Sonja Pulaski stood on the steps at the back door from the kitchen. Golden curls spiraling naturally down the side of her face.

"Simon, I saw you looking out at the field. Are you looking for Toby?"

"Yes, Ma'am. Do you know where he got off to?"

"He's in here having breakfast. Why don't you come in."

Simon smiled and looked up at the sun.

Morning's half over and he's just now eating breakfast!

She poured him a cup of coffee and set it on the table in front of him as he sat next to Toby. Simon ruffled the boy's bushy hair.

"You up here botherin Miz Sonja, young'un?"

Toby shook his head no, his mouth full to overflowing. He kept his attention focused on his plate full of biscuits and sausage gravy. His legs dangled over the front of his chair, swinging in time with his chewing.

"You gonna spoil him, Miz Sonja."

"I know boys, Simon. Just like my own. If they're not eating, they're hungry. Now you tell me what is bothering you."

"Ma'am?"

"Don't you Ma'am me, Simon Bond. You've lived with us almost two years now, and I know a lot of your ways."

He looked at her over the rim of his coffee cup, his eyes half closed and eyebrows high on his forehead, sipping loudly from his cup. She pointed a finger at his face.

"You were better educated down there in St. Mary's county than either me or Ben, where we came from. Ben pointed it out to me first, but I have seen it for myself. When you start talking like a field hand, something is not right."

Simon lowered his cup from an empty smile, "If we could wait until later, please." He rolled his eyes down toward Toby, so she could see, and she nodded yes.

Simon patted Toby's shoulder. "Come on, Boy. We got some chores to do in the barn." As Simon rose from the table he said, "Thank you, Miz Sonja." He squeezed Toby's shoulder as he slipped off his chair, clearing his throat loudly to ensure the boy got the message. Toby spun around to face Sonja saying, "Thank you, Miz Sonja."

Sonja followed them out onto the porch carrying a large bowl of freshly dug potatoes, taking a seat in one of the porch chairs and setting the bowl in her lap, as Simon and Toby went to the barn. The breeze pushed back the limbs of the saplings on the towpath, giving her quick glimpses across the river of beech trees with early patches of yellow.

Inside the bunkroom Simon sat Toby on his

bed.

"Wha'd I do?" Toby asked. "Was I not s'posed to go in the house?"

"No. That's not a problem. The Pulaski's don't own slaves. They treat people like people, brown or white."

"Well, but you look like I done something."

"No, Boy. I just got some bad news to tell you." Simon took in a deep breath. "Slavers caught your Uncle Jedediah before he could cross into Pennsylvania."

"They take him back?"

"No, Boy. They hung him."

Toby's lip trembled. "Hung him dead?"

On the front porch of the house, as Sonja peeled the potatoes meant for supper, she heard Toby cry out long and wailing. She bowed her head. Tears slipped down her cheeks and into the bowl.

Long minutes later Simon stepped out of the barn and slumped onto the chopping block near the wood pile. He sat loose with his elbows on his knees and his hands hanging limp between his legs. He dropped his chin, shook his head and surrendered a ragged breath.

Sonja placed her hand on his back in silence as she walked by. "Simon, I am meeting Margaret and riding one of the Barges into town." She walked down the wagon road toward the little bridge.

He watched her walk away. Out over the river, the gulls dipped out of the sky to pick up menhaden from the river for their lunch, the coot and loons landed among the quiet eddies near the large rocks squatting in the river.

Sonja and Mrs. Bartlett, standing on one of the company barges, slipped into view on the canal in front of the Pulaski place as it made its way south toward Havre de Grace. Sonja raised her hand and waved to Simon, but he did not wave back.

What would Mrs. Bartlett say about that? Say to people in Havre de Grace? Say to the Sheriff's Deputy? Uppity Nigger at the Pulaski Place?

Toby pulled on his pant legs.

"What I s'posed to do? Where I s'posed to go now?"

Simon pulled his hat off and scratched his head.

"You got anybody already made it into Pennsylvania?"

Toby shook his head no. "Momma got sold down Mississippi. That's when Uncle Jedediah told me we was goin walk to freedom. Ain't got nobody else I know of."

Simon looked down at the little boy who had seen enough to make a grown man cry. Toby's eyes still swollen and watered.

"Well, you got me. So, first thing you've got to do is start calling me Uncle Simon. I'll be your family and you stay with me for now. Someday soon we'll go get your Aunt Lettie, then we'll all go to Pennsylvania, maybe New York or even Canada."

"I got a Aunt Lettie?"

"You will have when I go back down into St. Mary's County to get her."

---<>---

Hoagg snapped his pocket watch closed, and called Wilson to his side.

"Get this ship off the docks and settled in at the island. I'll have to join you later. If you run her aground, I'll..."

"Not to worry, sir, I'll have her neat and pretty, backed into the channel like you said."

Hoagg grunted and walked down the boarding plank onto the dock.

I told the goddamned banker to have his man here well before noon. Damned near that now.

He walked slowly into the little town. People swirled around him, eager to stay out of his path. Intending to deliver his choicest oaths to the banker on Oyster Street, he instead ambled farther into town, looking at the shops, seeking out a tavern for a morning beer and whiskey. At the next corner he read the street sign, *Market.*

---<>---

Walking away from the Lockhouse, Sonja steered Margaret past the entrance to Oyster Street and made their way along Adams Street. Passing the home of Dr. Wallace and LuAnn Harper, she saw Eudora, the Harpers house servant, sweeping the broad front porch. Sonja waved to her and received Eudora's wave and a bright smile in return. Then they turned down the side lane to the new General Goods Store on Market Street.

The new store was almost full glass across its front, with a small inset in the middle for the door, tucked back off the boardwalk. A shiny new brass bell jangled cheerily as the women entered. The store smelled of fresh wood, lamp oil and lilacs. There were already four or five other ladies moving up and down the several long aisles. Sonja and Margaret gleamed at each other like happy children. They had never seen a store this large, or with such a range of choices. Several feet of shelves and racks on the right hand wall were devoted entirely to factory made clothes for men and women. Their eyes went first to the lavender dresses hanging like troops at the line.

"Margaret, how can they think to sell several dresses already made like this? Surely they will need re-sewing to fit one lady or another."

"Why, maybe not, Sonja. These little tags have different sizes written on them - and, oh my goodness, it matters not to folks like us!"

"Why is that?"

Margaret whispered, "These prices. My gosh. These dresses must be from England or France. The price is a full dollar and thirty-five cents. We can make them for less than half that." She added, "John would be furious with me if I ever spent that much money on a dress."

The women released the garments and quickly pulled their hands away. There were two clerks in the store, both waiting on other ladies. This allowed Margaret and Sonja the liberty to just walk up and down the aisles, looking and whispering at all the merchandise the store offered. As they rounded the far end of the second aisle, Sonja found a carved wooden stand with glass windows holding an array of sheath knives laid on red velvet. One drew her attention immediately. It had an intricately etched whale bone handle and a long blade of mirror-like steel with an edge so sharp it caught the light from the lamps above like a pinpoint star. It was so similar to the one Ben had before it was taken by the Sheriff's Deputy, and she knew Ben was now using an old iron blade. She thought for an instant, perhaps she could buy it for his Christmas gift. Leaning close to read the price tag, she gasped and straightened up, walking away.

Margaret saw her movement, grasped her arm gently and whispered, "How much?"

Sonja shook her head and whispered back. "THREE dollars and seventy-five cents."

They both looked wide-eyed at each other and quickly headed for the front door to find the business where they had always shopped. Halfway back up the aisle, Sonja stopped abruptly. Frozen. Rounding the front end of the aisle and turning to come toward her was a little blonde headed girl about five years old. Her face was in modest shadow, morning sunlight from the front windows shining a halo through the fine strands of unruly golden hair curling around her head. The little girl moved slowly down the aisle picking up and touching almost everything she came by, feeling the fabric or items and smelling the cloth of some. Sonja could not move. As the little girl neared, Sonja stepped aside to let her pass. The girl looked up and smiled into Sonja's face, her blue-grey hazel eyes and rosy cheeks illuminated by the sunlight.

"Thank you," she said in a soft musical voice.

Small tears slipped along the edges of Sonja's eyes.

"Mos!" The hoarse whisper flew down the aisle as the speaker rounded the corner to come after the girl. The woman did not look at anyone except the girl. She took the girl's hand gently into her own leather hand.

"I told you, sweetheart, to stay close to me."

"Yes, Momma."

The woman led the girl back up the aisle and out the front door. Sonja followed closely behind them, nearly bumping into the burly seaman entering the store. The man stepped back, holding the door and lifting his cap.

"Ma'am," Hoagg said, staring into her eyes, lingering with an open mouthed grin, breathing whiskey vapors over her face as she stepped out. Then inhaled her scent deeply as she passed.

Margaret saw the expression on his unshaven face, met his own cold stare with one of her own, and firmly escorted Sonja forward. Hoagg stood there, letting the door to the shop close. Sonja leaned out to keep her eyes on the little girl as she walked slowly down Market Street, staring after the two forms until they rounded a corner and were gone from sight. Standing in front of the Deputy Sheriff's Office, tears filled Sonja's eyes and streamed down her cheeks, and she could no longer see anything but light and shadows.

Margaret stepped beside her and offered her a handkerchief. "What is it, dear? What did you see?"

Sonja wiped the tears from her eyes and drew in a ragged breath. "Alisha would have been five years old now. That little girl was almost the perfect image of Alisha that I see in my dreams."

Margaret put her arms around Sonja's and let her weep on her shoulder, noticing the sailor still standing on the boardwalk.

"Mrs. Pulaski? Mrs. Pulaski?"

Margaret turned her head toward the voice. "What is it, Constable?"

Mattingly lowered his eyelids and exhaled.

"Deputy Sheriff , Mrs. Bartlett, as you well know."

Sonja wiped her eyes again and turned to face the Deputy.

"Yes, Deputy?"

"I have had it in my mind to get this knife back to your husband and seeing you here allows me to pass it to you to give to him. The Sheriff saw no reason to keep it and had no authority to do away with it."

Sonja accepted the knife.

"Thank you, Deputy. I will give to him."

"Good. And kindly remind him that I don't want to have to take it away ever again. That business between him and Binterfield has to be done. Tell him that."

Sonja smiled at the Deputy. The steel of the highly polished blade in her hands reflected in her own blue eyes, untouched by the smile.

"I can assure you that he will never allow events to come to that again."

Hoagg smiled.

Sonja said nothing more as they walked back down the street, but instead of turning at the corner of the new store, she continued on St. John Street to the new Post Office. Hoagg stayed several paces behind them, lingering along the nearby trees as the women went in. Sonja found a letter to herself from Alice Boyd and another from her father in York Furnace. She also found a letter posted to Ben. Slipping the letters into her handbag, she took Margaret by the arm and headed toward her fears, boldly marching onto Oyster Street. Her back rigid and the steel frozen in her eyes, as they neared it she turned her head and looked directly into the bank windows as she passed. Her heart was galloping in her chest, walking without breathing, waiting for him to burst out onto the boardwalk. She saw Binterfield in there, looking at her. Pressing her lips together, she forced a broad smile across her face and gave him a little coquettish wave. The blood was pounding in her head. Margaret's chatting was lost in a muffled drone broken by the thunder claps of her own heartbeats.

"...Pulaski!..."

Margaret gently pulled on Sonja's arm. Chills spread along Sonja's spine.

Oh God. He's coming after me. Why did I come this way??

"Mrs. Pulaski?"

"Sonja," Margaret said. "Isn't that Miss Estess from the school?"

Sonja stopped and turned toward the other voice. The galloping in her chest slowing to a muscular trot.

"Miss Estess, so nice to see you." Her heartbeats losing their thunder. The pulsing of her neck against her snug collar fading. "Hopefully my boys are not too much of a challenge for you?" Her heartbeat and the stiffness of her back drifted toward calm.

Curious to see the rest of the interchange, Hoagg spied Briscoe coming out of the tavern on the opposite side of the street, scurrying along the walkway, and stepped off to intercept him.

"No. No, not at all, Mrs. Pulaski. They have done well. In fact, both have performed admirably. You obviously taught them well while they stayed at home..."

"Yes?"

"I apologize for stopping you on the street like this..."

"No. Not at all. What is it?"

"Well, Aaron has advanced as far as our school program goes...And Isaac, your Isaac is ready for much more than our school can provide..."

"What do you mean, Miss Estess?"

"Isaac has read everything in the school, supremely, even a book I brought in that I studied in college. His comprehension is quite good..."

"Yes?"

"He should be enrolled in a college. They are both of advanced age for school; older than my other pupils. I was going to put all this in a letter, but when I saw you from the milliner shop, I thought it the opportune moment to talk to you."

"You wish to graduate them?"

"Yes, Mrs. Pulaski. And it would be my pleasure to write a recommendation for Isaac to attend a college or university. He is so academically bright."

"Well...I am... almost speechless...thank you...Miss Estess."

---<>---

Hoagg spat tobacco juice into the water within his own shadow and swung easily around the upper post of the ladder. He made his way down to water level and his waiting skiff for the ride to the Raven, safely anchored south of the town away from needless eyes.

Briscoe sat down in the center of the boat, still trying to convince Captain Hoagg he needn't go along.

"Sir, I provided you the amended list from Mr. Binterfield, and I will gladly meet you at a time of your choosing to assist you later..."

Hoagg did not even look at him when he spoke.

"Bullshit! I told that banker I wanted you at the ship before noon, 'cause I had to move her out. It was damned near that when I sent her on. Then I had to wander around this wharf, looking for your sorry ass! One o'clock! You finally show up at one o'clock. If I had waited on you, it would have cost me another fifty dollars, still tied up at that damned dock. You got fifty dollars to give me?"

"N-No sir, but..."

"But nothing. Your ass stays on my ship and moves on my orders, until we do what we need to do."

"Sir, I can't stay on your ship all day, I need to..."

"You will stay, if I have to chain you to the deck."

"But, sir…"

"Briscoe, if you speak again before I tell you to, I will gut you like a fish and throw your useless carcass into the Bay!"

The two mates in the boat knew not to speak to this captain unless in response to a direct question, so in silence they pushed the boat away from the wharf and tilted out the gaff off the short mast presenting the boat's single sail to the wind. The captain took the tiller as he always did and let the two others set the tension on the gaff line as to catch more of the breeze. A small white churn of water grew at the bow and the wake spread out behind the skiff as the wind took her on the stern quarter, pushing her south. Ducks quacked in protest as the boat slipped though a mass of mallards, coots and seagulls milling near the warehouses, slurping the littered surface with their bills searching for morsels. The hand at the bow looked up from the numerous flocks of ducks near the town to an incoming log canoe, its hull almost dangerously low in the water. Its deck was piled high with oysters. He turned his attention to his closest shipmate.

"A man could just live off what he could catch up here, ya know that? Wouldn't have ta pay fer nothing ta eat." The other hand nodded his head and opened his mouth to speak, but the sound of the captain's voice filled the ears of both men.

"Mind the goddamned boat, or I'll put you out right here so you can go after yer free food."

---<>---

Kent Island came fully on Ben's east. He reluctantly surrendered his enjoyable downwind run to the south and called his sons to help tack the *Ugly Boat* to the west for their turn up the Severn River toward Annapolis. Isaac and Aaron had been asked to do only very little over the last four hours, once they had set out the mainsail and forward jib sail 'wing and wing' like a huge canvas butterfly. The main sail, held out by its boom at the bottom and gaff pole at the top was almost all the way to its side. The triangular jib sail, normally aligned in front of the main sail, stood out the opposite side with a spare gaff pole at its lower edge. Now they scrambled to reconfigure the sails so they could slice across the wind, putting the sideboards to work again. Annapolis harbor was only thirty minutes away, even working across a dying wind partially blocked by the Sandy Point peninsula now slipping past. The surface of the Bay behind the peninsula was a gentle roll, with waves less than a foot and yards apart.

Anchored south of the peninsula, but not far out enough to interfere with ship traffic was a side wheel steamboat. The *Ugly Boat* was close enough to make out individuals walking her decks and waving flags. While Ben and the boys watched the men waving the flags, the steamboat let out a long shriek from its steam whistle. At almost the same moment, a light skiff set sail from the side of the steamboat and made its way directly toward the Pulaskis. A man was in the bow of the skiff waving another flag. The flags from the steamboat and skiff seemed to be different colors, meaning nothing to Ben. Some flags just looking like old coal rags tied on sticks.

"Ahoy" bellowed the man in the bow of the skiff, as it neared the *Ugly Boat*.

Ben stood up and pulled his father's old flintlock pistol from the storage box near the tiller. He held it up so the oncoming man could see it, then yelled out to him. "What do you want?"

"Easy, friend. Easy." The man spoke across the shortening distance, holding up his hands. He turned to face the man at the tiller. "Drop the sail, Ned. This man don't know us and we came in kinda quick. Shear away."

The speed of the skiff dropped off and the bow swung parallel with the *Ugly Boat*, coasting to a gentle roll about thirty feet from the barge.

"Mister, you carryin Pennsylvania coal to market in Annapolis?"

"Maybe." Ben rested his foot on the storage box and laid the pistol across his knee, still pointing it at the skiff. "I asked you what you wanted."

The man in the bow kept his hands up, and as soon as the man at the tiller lowered the sail and could see Ben's pistol, he snapped his hands up in the air as well. The bow man chuckled nervously, "Well...I want to stay alive and my Cap'n wants to buy your coal, if that's what you're haulin."

"Why doesn't he go on in to Annapolis and buy it from the colliers?"

"Cause there's a run on coal between all the steamships and the railroad..."

"Doesn't sound like a problem for us, Mister." Isaac and Aaron came to stand beside their father. Aaron was holding a grappling pole.

"...the colliers will pay you three times what you usually get for it..."

"Still don't see a problem for us."

"Well, then they're chargin SIX TIMES the usual price to us."

"Maybe you should take that up with the colliers."

"That didn't do no good. Cap'n says he'll pay you FOUR times the usual rate, if you let us off-load you out here. That is, if you got coal."

Ben turned to his sons, but each could only shrug their shoulders.

"So, you got coal?"

Ben opened the storage box and placed the pistol down onto the canvas wrap, but did not cover it, then turned back to the skiff. "Yeah. I got Coal. How much you want?"

"How much you got?"

"Twenty eight tons within the two boats here. How much you want."

Then men in the skiff lowered their hands. "All of it, sir. We want to buy it all."

Minutes later, the *Ugly Boat* eased up against the high wooden hull behind one of the side wheels. On the outer housing towering above the deck of the *Ugly Boat* and *The Turtle*, Ben read the three-foot high ornately painted letters arching with the curvature of the housing.

"Po...Ca..."

Isaac, knowing his father never fully learned to read and write, stepped close to his ear and began to whisper. Ben grabbed his son by his arm.

"No. I can do this. I've been practicing. Now, hush."

Ben turned his eyes back up to the giant letters.

"Po...Sa, no, Ca, Ca...Hon...T-Tis, no,..Ta...Tas. Po-Ca-Hon-Tas. Pocahontas." He nodded in satisfaction to himself and turned back to his sons, pointing at the lettering over his shoulder with his thumb. "Pocahontas. Says Pocahontas up there. That's the ship's name." Isaac and Aaron solemnly acknowledged the information provided by their father.

The steamship captain came down to meet Ben and shook his hand.

"Captain Pulaski, I would appreciate it if you would look for us as you come back down to Annapolis with more coal. Looks like we may do this a while until the sanity comes back to the coal market. In the meantime, I'd rather pay more to you than yield to the robbery of the damned colliers."

"Captain Weems, we will be coming by here about every three to four days."

"Good. You tell any other barge captain up in Havre de Grace who can make their own way down here that I will buy all the coal they can bring. Just fly a burlap bag up your mast if there's coal for sale." He handed Ben a very thick packet of money, and shook hands again.

Fifteen minutes later, the *Ugly Boat* and *The Turtle* were riding high in the water and scooting away from the Pocahontas. Surprise swept across the boy's faces when Ben instructed them to set sails for a continued trip on to Annapolis.

"Pa, what are we going to do there now that the holds are already empty?"

"We are going to buy as much cotton as we can fit in the holds. And any space left after that, we're going to fill with anything that will sell in Havre de Grace, Lapidum, York Furnace or Wrightsville. And I'm going to get your grandfather's old flintlocks re-worked for firing caps. And then after that, we're heading to Wrightsville to take on another twenty eight tons of coal and come back here looking for the Pocahontas!"

4

South of Havre de Grace, on Spesutie Island, the Spesutie Narrows was itself almost a small, fully enclosed bay, except for the tight entrance between two steep tree lined shores. Little more than a hundred yards at its widest by three hundred long, it was mostly less than three feet deep above the death grip of a muddy clay bottom. But, it did offer a deep entrance in a single deep trough near its western shore, where even at low tide, the water was well below the Raven's keel. The tree-covered isthmus at the northern end of the narrows made it a perfect place to hide a sloop. Even the massive pines at the center of Spesutie Island helped hide her masts from the bay. Hoagg had ordered large pine boughs tied to the upper masts in an effort to mimic the surrounding forest, although only single boughs hung at the tip of each mast. Still, to the unwary eye, that could be enough. Swampland to the west kept people and traffic away on that side. The skiff slowly rounded the shoreline within the narrows and came into view of the Raven.

Hoagg smiled at the downward curve of the beak and menacing orange painted eyes of the figurehead on the bow. There was not enough deep water to turn her around, so she had to be dragged in by her stern, but the wind coming though the scrub and pine trees on the northern isthmus would allow her to fly out if trouble came her way. The skiff slipped alongside of the Raven and under the run out muzzles of the three six-pounder cannon she carried on each side. Six-pounder cannon had fired more than once during voyages to Africa, and would match anything the Chesapeake Bay had to offer.

He ignored the smell drifting out from the holds, almost no longer noticed it at all. Even though it was illegal since 1808, the five years since she was built had been spent hauling terrified slaves from Africa to southern ports. The slaves were crammed screaming and trying to breathe in their own retch and feces, in a space the size of a white man's coffin. It had left a smell in the once fresh oak that would never come out.

A familiar voice growled among the men on deck above the skiff as the man in the bow hooked onto the chains bolted into the Raven's sides.

"Cap'n's comin on board. Git yer shit outta the way and stand by the entry. First man speaks before the Cap'n does I'll break his jaw for him."

Hoagg smiled briefly to himself and climbed easily up the side ladder to the main deck. He enjoyed the nearly flush deck, more like that of an old pirate ship and always ready for action. The captain's cabin peeked above deck no more than a few feet near the stern. Open companionway steps down into the interior near the bow and just before his cabin gave great ship access without spoiling its simple lines. The ship had rare side-by-side double wheels sitting behind the main mast, making it close enough to his cabin for his own convenience, but far enough away so he didn't have to hear the crew talking. The double wheels let the wheelman see beyond the bow regardless the set of the sails or the lean of the ship. And finally, the Raven had a monster cargo hatch that ran from just behind the forward mast all the way back to the main mast. He loved this part of being ship's captain. God help any man that tried to take it from him. He spat tobacco juice back into the water below him and wiped his mouth with the palm of his hand. Hoagg's first mate made an attempt at a salute while the Raven's Bo's'n blew his whistle as sharply as any Navy Bo's'n had ever done for any captain.

Bo's'n Findley is drunk as usual and too damned knife happy, even for me, but he can blow that whistle like a sonofabitch.

Hoagg returned the salute by touching the brim of his cap and then dug into his pocket for a small piece of silver for Findley.

First Mate Wilson approached the captain as the Bo's'n stepped away. Wilson had been with him even before they signed on together to the *Philadelphia Star*. Hoagg thought him almost useless as a First Mate, but he would always do exactly as Hoagg had instructed, and he was quick to report anyone that spoke ill of the Captain. Hoagg always wanted to know what was going on behind his back.

"Couple darkies came to fish on the bank of the narrows this morning, saw the ship and came to get a closer look."

"You kill'em?"

"Just one, Cap'n. It was a Buck and a boy. Let'em get close to the ship in that thicket over there, then signaled our pickets to bring them in at gunpoint. Kilt the young'un – he was more trouble than he was worth, but the buck was prime property so I got him chained below with the rest."

"You didn't shoot'im did you?"

"Naw, no noise, like you ordered, Cap'n. Slit his throat and tossed him in the shallows near shore."

Hoagg looked into the shallow water where the Mate pointed and saw dozens of blue crabs crawling over each other near the shore.

"Body's mostly gone now, Cap'n." The mate looked intently into the shallows. "Almost puts a man off crabs, ya know?"

"Did you have to cut the buck?"

"No sir, Cap'n. Not a scratch on that'un, just a bump on the head from a belaying pin. Got real riled when we had to kill the boy. Must have sired him or something. But he ain't damaged merchandise, Cap'n. He'll fetch full price in Charleston."

"Good man," Hoagg said, smiling into the mate's face, and then allowed the silence to linger until it had gained the man's attention. "Guess who lives a few miles north of that little port town I was just in?"

Wilson could only shake his head slowly in ignorance.

Hoagg announced, "Ben Pulaski" speaking each syllable slowly and deliberately.

The silence grew while the man retrieved a singular hate he had stored since his last voyage to China, put back within a space others occupied with

65

souls or spiritualism, held there molding in hope of some future reckoning.

"Pulaski..." the man said as a smile slowly began to trace its way across his leathered face. "God damn," he said to his captain. The smile stayed broad on his face as he looked north into the trees on the isthmus that stood between him and Havre de Grace.

"God damn...Pulaski," he almost chuckled toward the trees.

---<>---

After supper in an Annapolis tavern near the dock, Ben, Isaac and Aaron settled onto the deck of the *Ugly Boat*. The coolness of early autumn air was still comfortable and they lingered on the deck talking.

"Boys, we took in more money on this one trip than all I brought back with me after three years at sea. And I thought I was a rich man then. With all this, we can pay Simon for past wages, send a share to Mrs. Boyd, put some back for Mickey and even put some back to pay off Binterfield. Even with all that we can fill our holds with cotton and other cargo and earn back almost all of that again."

"What about us," Aaron asked.

Ben looked at Aaron in the fading light. "Well, you boys are doing men's work. No reason you shouldn't earn full wages. At least when you're not in school."

Isaac cleared his throat and leaned toward Ben. "About school, Pa. It's time for us to come out of that."

"You boys were out a long time while I was

gone, and you've only been back the past year."

"Pa, we've done all we're supposed to do," said Aaron. "Miss Estess says we're ready to graduate."

Isaac nodded.

"That's right, Pa. I read that whole new McGuffy Reader in two days and she tested me on it. She even brought a heavy book she used in her college and a new story just published by a writer up in Baltimore – Edgar Allen Poe. I was able to read them both and answer all her questions."

"Is that so?"

"Yes, it is. Pa, some fellas my age are already married with sons of their own. I CAN'T go back to the school."

"Son, I'm not so sure we can get you to college. They're really expensive. Maybe..."

"There is one that won't cost anything, Pa. Miss Estess says the Army College up in New York teaches Engineers, and the United States government pays for it."

"Isaac, I guess we can talk about it more when we get home."

"I can't go back either, Pa!" added Aaron. "We're too old to be in school. I'm sixteen!"

"Aaron, if you graduate too, what do you want to do next? You have any ideas?"

"Sure do: anything except school!"

They chuckled together and began getting the boats ready for the night, then settled into their bunks in the small cabin of the *Ugly Boat*.

---<>---

Hours after midnight, the launch from the Raven rowed against the wind with four unconscious forms bound and gagged lying in the middle of the boat. Six crewmen grunted as they strained at the oars to push the boat into a northerly wind that had shift completely around since sunset. The wind was cold and wet knuckles only added to the sailor's discomfort.

"Damn the wind to hell! Against us rowing north, and damned if it ain't turned around to be against us rowing south."

"And it be a cold wind," another complained. "Coming off early ice somewhere."

"Shut up," Hoagg snapped.

After another hour, the launch finally crept around the bow of the Raven. The ship's crew swung out a boom from above and lowered a cargo net into the launch.

"Roll them bodies into the net, and get'em hoisted on deck. We need to make sure they're alive. I swear to god, I heard a head bone crack when you hit that one coming out of the last shanty, Johnson. If I lost a sale, you'll take his place in the chains."

Hoagg climbed up the side of the ship while the launch crew worked to get the limp bodies on board. As the full cargo net was swung inboard and lowered to the deck, Josh Holden checked the forms for life and injuries. He poured water on their heads and slapped their faces.

"Alright, Holden. You're the one served as a surgeons mate once. They gonna live?"

"They look all right to me, Cap'n. This big one's

got a gash in his head I oughta sew up some, but it don't look deadly." He snickered as he stood up. "Course he may not be as bright as he should be when he heals."

Hoagg pointed a finger at Johnson.

"Any lost profit on him comes out of your share. You understand me?"

Johnson exhaled deeply and nodded yes to his captain.

"Captain," Briscoe called. "I pointed these boys out to you. Now can your crew take me back?"

The launch crew moaned at the thought of another long pull against the wind. Hoagg ignored them, but turned toward Briscoe.

"Briscoe, your ass stays on board until I'm through with you. Johnson! You're on sentry watch the rest of the night. Holden! You check on that big buck through the night. Keep him alive if you can. If you can't come get me. I'll need you to sew up Johnson after I'm through with him. Briscoe! You help Holden."

Johnson swallowed hard and moved away from the captain. Hoagg turned toward the other crewmen around him.

"The rest of you, get these things in chains and get'em down in the hold, then get some sleep as you can. Tomorrow night is going to be busy."

Hoagg turned and stepped down into the captain's cabin and slammed the door behind him.

---<>---

As soon as the first warehouse opened in Annapolis the following morning, Ben took his sons looking for unconsigned cotton bales. He soony had all that he could take into the hulls of the *Ugly Boat* and *The Turtle*. After assessing the size and number of cargo spaces left, the three went to an iron foundry and bought five unassembled iron stoves. Ben left Isaac and Aaron to assist loading the stoves and went to a pottery shop he had visited before. He bought all the crated complete sets of dinnerware in the shop. Ben had worked with the proprietor on consignment the year before, and had faithfully delivered the agreed price after he had sold them. This visit he could proudly pay on receipt, but even as he received payment for the dinnerware, the proprietor happily offered several crates of glass oil lamps and tins of whale oil for Ben to take on consignment. Ben paid cash for the lamps and oil as well, and the bubbling man joined the workers pushing the cart to dock, chattering all the way down the street to ensure Ben would come see him again on his next trip.

Ben stopped next at a gunsmith, leaving the storeowner and his workers to see to the delivery of the cargo to his sons. As soon as the crates were loaded in and on the barges, the shop owner gave his workers a rare day off and then closed his shop. Their children in school for the day, the shopkeeper arrived in his home before lunch with a bouquet of flowers for his wife, a bottle of wine for them both, and lust in his heart.

Ben left his pistols with the gunsmith and joined his sons at the dock with an armload of ham biscuits and a jug of apple cider from a nearby cart vendor. By noon, the *Ugly Boat* and *The Turtle* moved ponderously out of the Annapolis harbor, looking for a stiff wind to take them back to Havre de Grace. Although the large bales of cotton were lighter than equal volumes of coal, the iron stoves and additional cargo brought the two barges as low in the water as they were hauling coal. The lower set actually improved their sailing qualities, by keeping the bulk of the hull in the water and improving the resistance of the side boards. The warm winds from the south continued to battle with the northerly winds trying to bring cold air to the Chesapeake Bay. The wind had veered completely around and was blowing mild toward the north, Isaac and Aaron once again set the main and jib sails 'wing and wing' to run before the wind.

This is the luckiest of all trips. Even the wind works for us.

As they passed Spesutie Island, Aaron spotted the masts of the Raven, even though the view included the tall pines on the west side of the island and the masts had pine boughs tied at the peak. His keen eyes easily picked out the straight limbless masts below the pine boughs. He pointed at the island and called out to Ben.

"Pa, there's a two-masted ship sitting in Spesutie Narrows."

Ben shaded his eyes against the brightness of the afternoon western sun above the island.

"Yeah. You're right. Looks like a fair size one. A sea goer. Must have brought something big to the island. Or, maybe taking on cattle, but there's a better wharf for it on the northern side of the island. Looks odd to me."

The island slipped by and Ben's thoughts returned to his anticipated revelry of telling Sonja about the successes of their trip. Shortly after three o'clock they were able to take down the sails and mast, return *The Turtle* ahead of the *Ugly Boat*, and pole the barges through the outlet lock and into the Canal Basin. The autumn sun was still well above the hills behind the Pulaski farm, after the barges had been tied to the Pulaski dock, and the mules munching hay in the barn, when Ben, Isaac and Aaron burst into the house.

"We're hungry," they yelled, as boots were thrown into bedrooms and three boisterous men invaded the kitchen area. Ben swept Sonja up into a floating hug and twirled her around in a circle. Sonja pinched Ben's nose and pushed his hands down so she could stand, but held onto his hands.

"Looks like you boys had a good trip."

"Not good, Ma. Great!"

Ben nodded his head in agreement.

"It was a VERY good trip, Sonja. The price of coal has soared! There is some kind of big competition going for coal among the steamships and the railroads. One steamboat actually stood out at the mouth to the Severn River buying coal before we could dock! It off loaded our coal and paid us cash right there! We paid four dollars a ton for it and the steamboat captain paid us twenty-eight dollars a ton. We made well over six hundred dollars profit!!"

"And Pa said I could be finished with school!"

"And I can go to a university!"

"Now wait, boys, what I said..."

"I spoke with Miss Estess, Ben..."

"What? Wait. What? What did she say? Isaac said she told him..."

"One at a time, Ben. One at a time," she said.

"What's for supper, Ma?"

"Aaron. Sit. Isaac. Sit. Benjamin. Sit! Everyone just take in a deep breath."

"...Supper?"

"Beef stew. Now shush."

"Beef Stew!!"

"Shush, I said!" And she stomped her foot.

"Ben, Miss Estess says the boys have learned what they were supposed to and have outgrown school."

"Sonja, she said pretty much the same thing to them as they tell me. I'm not so sure about college or university."

"Ben, she told me she would be happy to write a recommendation."

"I want to be an Engineer, Ma," Isaac said. "And the country pays for men to go to the Army College in New York."

"Yes, son, I know about West Point," Ben said. "They take fifty or so young men each year from the whole country. It is very hard to be accepted."

Sonja placed her hand on Ben's. "Ben, maybe you could write a letter to General Jackson."

The boys' eyes popped wide.

"Andrew Jackson??"

"President Jackson?"

"Yes, he knows your Pa."

The boys spoke in unison, "Knows Pa?"

"Knew me, more like. I was with him at New Orleans, but I was just a drummer boy and that was a very long time ago."

"You were at the Battle of New Orleans?"

Sonja placed her hand on Ben's arm. "He told you more than that, Ben Pulaski. You said he told you to let him know if there was ever anything he could do for you."

"Yes, right before he turned me over to my Pa to get the worst beating I ever had."

"Ben. You telling me he never made that promise?"

"No. He made it."

Isaac and Aaron still sat staring at each other with their mouths open.

"Pa knows Andrew Jackson," Isaac said to Aaron.

"You need to write him a letter Ben. Write it for Isaac. I'll help..."

"No. I'll write it myself."

"Pa, you were at the Battle of New Orleans??"

"Enough! I don't do anything like that anymore," Ben said.

"Your father was a Lieutenant in the United States Army when I met him, Boys."

"What??"

"I said, enough of this. I will write the letter when we get back from Wrightsville."

"But, Pa..."

"Enough!"

They sat in silence through most of supper.

"Ben? Ben? I think they deserve a little more information than that," Sonja said.

After finishing his stew, Ben exhaled a deep breath. "All right, sons, I will tell you more during our trip to Wrightsville."

Sonja patted him on his arm. He smiled at her then at his sons.

"You boys were a great help to me in Annapolis. You are ready to become men. Maybe almost already there. Maybe as much as any man ever is until he faces his worst tribulation."

Ben was unaware that he had just spoken a prophecy.

"We need to be up before first light, so we can be toward the front of the coal line across from Wrightsville. We need to get in bed."

"In just a few minutes," Sonja added. She pulled an old rippled and water stained bible from a nearby shelf and spread it open on the table. Before Ben's long absence, before the ice flood of '39, before the loss of Alisha and their first home, it had been Sonja's routine to read to them from the Bible on Sunday afternoons. This wasn't Sunday, but it was time.

- - <> - -

Early October produced the first morning with frost on the ground. The grass alongside of the Raven was dusted in white. Hoagg sipped his coffee and scowled at the land.

"Goddamned frost."

"Sir?" asked a nearby sailor.

"Frost. I hate it." Hoagg regretted sharing the comment. "Mind yer goddamned business. Get me Wilson."

As soon as Wilson stepped in front of Hoagg, the captain gave him orders.

"Send that whining old woman, Briscoe, back to town and start getting this ship ready to sail. I want to get down to Charleston, sell the cargo, then be on my way to Jamaica before winter comes."

Wilson grinned and scurried off to implement the orders.

Hoagg called after him. "Send Briscoe to me before you put him off."

"Aye, Aye, Cap'n," he yelled over his shoulder.

Hoagg stepped down into his cabin to review his ledger.

The word spread through the ship's hands like fireworks. Charleston meant money in their pockets. And Jamaica meant a wonderful warm drunken winter spending it.

The numbers in the ledger were not great. Barely half full in the hold. All his new chains and manacles lay unused in a storage room below deck. But even these slaves would bring Hoagg more money than he had ever seen.

Briscoe rapped on the open doorframe. His face was smudged and his expression sour. Loose straw was sprinkled in his hair, since he was forced to sleep in the goat locker during his weeks aboard.

"Ah Briscoe, have I made my point about being on time for me?"

"Yes, sir, Certainly, sir. I am here to serve as long as you need me, sir."

"Quit kissin my ass. I'm sending you back to Binterbean. Tell your master I'm only half full, but I'm heading south before the ice comes. Frost is a sure sign of a coming winter, and I'll not be frozen in with unsold cargo. Tell him I'll bring his share of the sale when I return in the spring. You got that?"

"Yes, sir."

"Then get your ass out of my cabin and off my ship. Wilson has a boat waiting for you. And Briscoe,"

"Yes, sir?"

"When I get back, I want another full list ready to go, so I can fill my hold next time, you hear me?"

"Yes, sir."

"Then tell Binterbutt. Now get the hell off my ship."

Hoagg scanned down his list of 'acquisitions'.

There are still twenty others being held in Chesapeake City, but those have nothing to do with Binterfield. New cotton fields and rice fields open every day in the deep south. Charleston will bid on any black body we put up on the blocks.

Hoagg smiled to himself and sipped his coffee as the ship transformed to move before the wind.

5

The rain was cold, and smelled of ice. October was slipping into November. The canallers on other barges began to talk of 'the freeze', the winter time when the canal becomes ice and barge traffic halts until spring. Barges passed one another, crossing not only tow lines, but coal smoke rising from the cabin iron stoves, smudges like black swords crossed in the air above and quickly blown away in the rain. Another torrential downpour fell from low lying gray clouds and swept along the Susquehanna valley toward Lapidum. The eastern side of the river was hidden in the rain and mist. The waste weirs built into the canal walls to drain overflow waters into the river were gushing torrents. A rare current dashed southward within the canal, spinning leaves and twigs within rows of tiny eddies, a line of pinwheels in the muddy water. The mud atop the towpath next to the canal was dangerously slick, eager for the chance to break a mule ankle or send a careless handler sliding into the canal or the river. The river smashed itself against the boulders, shooting geysers twenty feet into the air, its surface galloping in anger and violence, clawing along the outer side of the towpath like a caged animal.

Safe from the river some called "the Bitch", for her malevolence, Ben kept his sons and his barges out of the fray. He kept them home until the storm marched south and he was satisfied in his decision that cost him a day of business. He had fought such a storm the previous year, and it almost cost Aaron his life. He sat on the porch wrapped in a wool coat while the waterfall from his roof slapped the ground below. He scratched his letters with a charcoal pencil on the backs of outdated leaflets Sonja had picked up at the Post Office. He wrote the sixth line of the same words, beginning 'Your Excellency', then stopped again to examine his work.

"Shit! Looks like a pig scratching in the dirt."

Sonja stepped onto the porch. She placed her hands on her hips under her shawl and leaned over Ben's shoulder to see his paper.

"Well, it's a mighty smart pig, who happens to know a president of the United States of America."

"Knew," Ben answered with a frown.

She bent down next to his head and kissed him on his cheek above his beard. He leaned into her kiss and smiled.

"It looks truly correct, Ben. I don't believe a person who once shot a man for insulting his wife would put much value to handwritings with many swirls. I think he would want each letter to stand up for itself and not pretend to be stitchery."

She ran her fingers through his curly auburn hair and stepped back into the house, closing the door.

"Then I guess it's time to write the letter," he called out as the door closed behind her.

Two frustrating days later Sonja read through the final copy of the letter, while Ben sat nearby watching the river, still fat with storm water, pretending he paid no attention to Sonja.

October 29th, 1842

General Andrew Jackson, President of the United States of America,

'Your Excellency,

I humbly identify myself as a citizen who once had the honor of serving under you at the Great Battle of New Orleans. I was a mere drummer boy at the time, absent from my father, the morning we stood against the British at our line. I served under you again during the wars with the Seminole Indians in the States of Georgia and Florida. There I received a battlefield commission as a Lieutenant in the United States Army Regulars, for actions taken in that campaign, during which I was wounded, and then discharged from the Army in the State of North Carolina for convalescence.

I am a matured man now, self sufficient in every way, surrounded by my family, and still proud of my service. I ask nothing from your hand, except for consideration of a recommendation for my oldest son, Isaac Burl Pulaski, to attend the Military University founded at West Point, in New York State. He has been singled out by his teacher as advanced in his studies for his age and grade, and is suitable for enrollment into a University for further education. It is my son's desire to become an engineer, and my belief in him that he is fully capable of that pursuit. Were he to be allowed entrance to that university, to become an engineer and be considered for a commission as an officer in the United States Army, it would be an eternal source of pride and joy for me and our family.

Your humble servant,

Lt. Benjamin Pulaski'

Sonja laid the letter on the small table near her chair on the front porch.

"The words are perfect, Ben."

She stepped to the edge of the porch, pulling her shawl tightly around her, and looked out between the Oaks that framed their front slope. Most of the leaves were gone from the trees and the saplings along the towpath, laying in piles on the ground. Her eyes centered beyond the canal and on to the hillside across the river, unfocused, not really seeing that, but seeing somewhere else and another time.

"I did not imagine your letter would touch on the time we met."

He stood next to her and placed his hand on her waist.

"It was an eventful year, Sonja. Being severely wounded by an Indian spear, and then being captured by you. Both events equally dangerous," he said smiling.

She jabbed him in his side with her elbow. "And both equally capable of being life threatening."

He pulled her to him and held her tightly, then kissed her. "At least today you are unarmed."

"Good God a'mighty," Isaac said, holding the

letter in his hand. "You fought in the Indian Wars?"

"Put that down and watch your language, Isaac Pulaski," Sonja barked.

Aaron followed Isaac onto the porch and peered over his shoulder at the letter his mother yanked from his brother's hands. "Pa fought Indians?"

"Never you mind," Ben answered, but Sonja pinched his arm.

"Now is as good a time as ever, Benjamin. They are old enough to know it, and they should hear it from you."

Ben looked around, seeking another avenue, some chore to pursue, but Sonja stepped in front of him. "Benjamin, there is nothing else to be done, and you have promised them more than once. It's time you told them."

Ben plopped down in his chair and motioned to Aaron, "Fetch my pipe."

Sonja wrinkled her nose. Her dislike of the tobacco smell was well known. She moved her own chair up wind and motioned for her sons to bring out other chairs onto the porch.

Ben puffed on the pipe and flicked loose tobacco out of his short beard.

"Your grandfather Lenz, my father, was captain of a wonderful Baltimore clipper named the Osprey. Growing up, I spent far more time on the Osprey than anywhere else. I would have lived there if he let me. It was far more enjoyable than...well, I spent too much time there and not enough on my schooling, which is why you have had to watch me struggle writing that letter. It's also why I am so proud of you two for doing so well in school..."

Aaron's excitement was uncontainable. "Indian's, Pa! Tell me about the Indians."

"All right. All right. But, first things first..."

---<>---

In the summer of Ben's 12th year, the United States had declared war with Britain. By late autumn, after initial land and sea skirmishes with the British, rumors of British ships in the Chesapeake Bay flew around Baltimore like fire in dry wood. Occasional reports of attacks on commercial shipping near the mouth of the Bay at Hampton Roads seemed to confirm the fear. A courier arrived at the Pulaski's Baltimore home with a letter from Lenz' old captain. It was one of many sent out to seamen and their descendents who had served during the war of Independence. The American Navy was too small, the letter said, so anyone with a hull they could call their own, was asked to take action to protect the country. Lenz decided Baltimore was safe, protected by Fort McHenry finished only ten years before, and it was unlikely the British would try here. When he sailed his ship down the Patapsco River late in 1812, he was satisfied that his errant son was safely stowed at home with his stepmother.

Washington City was placed on mud flats and not well protected from the water. The Potomac River offered easy sailing within short miles of there. Lenz had seen that on shipping trips to the city. Knew it would be easy prey.

As the Osprey rounded past the white rocks marking the mouth of the Patapsco, and steered south for the Potomac, young Ben Pulaski showed himself on deck. Lenz was furious, but there was no time to take his son back. Two days later, as the Osprey rounded again, passing Point Lookout and steering north up the Potomac, some British ships had indeed entered the bay. A royal navy vessel gave chase after the Osprey, firing its cannon at her, but the distance was too great. The Osprey, a fast running small Baltimore-built ship, quickly out ran the British and was able to carry the warning up the river to Washington City.

Washington was in pandemonium, but the Navy had established an office on a river dock, south of the city. Lenz already had a few tons of canvas for shipment to Philadelphia when he set sail for Washington. The Navy office was extremely grateful to acquire some of the canvas as they worked furiously to convert fishing boats into Navy vessels. In the frenzy of moving supplies back and forth across the Potomac, a supply ship loaded with gunpowder had run aground on boulders near the center of the river. Rowboats had scurried back and forth since early morning unloading the precious powder, but too much of it still lay in the damp broken bottom of the supply ship. In a whirlwind of administrative actions, Lenz was quickly given a commission as a Lieutenant in the United States Navy, the Osprey was registered as a commandeered Navy vessel, Lt. Pulaski assigned as captain of the Navy vessel Osprey, his crewmen impressed into the Navy, and Lt. Pulaski ordered to off load as much of the gunpowder as his ship would hold, then stand by for written orders. In less than two hours Lenz had gone from civilian volunteer to Navy Lieutenant, bringing his ship alongside the grounded supply ship and hoisting bags of gunpowder onto his decks.

"I will hang the first man I see with pipe or seegar," he yelled across the deck, "assuming I can stretch your neck up the yardarm before we blow to kingdom come!!"

His men were good at their job, sober and serious, and none needed to be told to be careful around gunpowder.

"Keep the dry bags stacked on our deck until we can see what we have that's still good! Bo's'on, take all the canvas we have left and line the hold to give it a dry bottom to stack it on!"

"What can I do, Pa?"

"Benjamin, if I had time, I'd take a hickory stick to your ass. But lucky for you, I don't. Stand behind me and stay out of the way!" Then he gripped his son's shoulder. "Pay attention to what I do - And learn from it!" Ben did as he was told and within minutes, his father was sending him darting in one direction or the other carrying messages to his men. They all knew Ben. Considered him a member of their ship family. Had known him for years.

Late in the afternoon a rowboat approached the Osprey, an officer in the stern frantically waving his arms.

"Come aboard," Lenz yelled.

"No time, Pulaski," the officer yelled through a speaking trumpet. "The British are coming up the river. Riders describe ships of the line, a hundred tons or more. They'll have to stay in the main channel and won't be able to get up this far. They gotta have troops. Probably land them to the south. We have to move north. You can't do any more.

Leave now! Try to get by them in the darkness. Norfolk has probably fallen! Break out to sea if you can! Try for Charleston! God speed Lieutenant!!"

Then the row boat spun around and followed the officer's point, heading for another ship still working in the river. Lenz ordered all the dry powder sent down from the decks, which filled the hold to about two thirds. In the fading light, no glims, candles or lamps dared to be lit. The schooner stayed to the outside of the southward river flow, the shallow side of the river. They raised a square sail over the bowsprit to capture what little breeze was there, and men in the bow tossed lead weights ahead of the slow moving ship to gauge the depth of the water. Ben suggested a long pole be tied next to the bow sprit, sticking down in the water with its tip a few feet below the level of the keel. When it tugged forward it would signal the ship was near running on the bottom.

"Brilliant," Lenz had said, patting his son firmly on his back. Crewman spent the rest of the night taking turns laying along the bowsprit with their hand loosely holding the top of the pole, whispering "bottom!" when it tugged forward. The word was quietly passed to the wheel man at the stern.

At full dark they drifted around the major bend in the Potomac River, just south of Aquia Creek on the Virginia side of the river. A line of several ships were anchored bow to stern in the deep channel that ran near the Maryland side, but none of the ships were the big three-deckers Lenz expected. Most were ships not much bigger than his. All the lamps were lit on the other ships, men were milling about, some were sitting and eating, some were actually playing musical pipes.

"They are not attacking," Lenz said to himself, and wished he could send a message to the Navy office, but it was far too late, and he was too far away to even consider it.

Two days later the Osprey was running before the wind in Hampton Roads on a course that would take him out into the Atlantic. He had seen no close sails and was reassessing his orders to go to sea. Even as he entertained the thought of turning north, a large British Man-of-War moved ominously out from the mouth of the James River with all sails set. Two miles off from him smoke clouds erupted from the bow of the Man-of-War, and a few seconds later a huge splash erupted from the ocean not far from his ship.

"They are shooting at us," he yelled to his crew, "and they could hit us from there! Loose all sail!!"

They mean to sink us!

"All hands on deck!! Loose all sail!"

It took hours to finally pull away from the British ship, with the wind pushing hard against the Osprey's sails, and the deck tiled steeply away from the wind as the masts leaned to their limit.

Only the single British ship had begun patrolling the mouth of the Chesapeake Bay. It would be another year before the British Navy came to control the Chesapeake. The young Navy Officer on the Potomac Dock had panicked and sent ships needlessly scurrying away on useless missions. Lenz Pulaski's act of patriotism would cost him months of commerce. The Osprey sailed into Charleston Harbor in early November, the ice collected on the rigging during her Atlantic run beginning to melt. There was no reception from the Navy, except an administrative nightmare of what to do with seventy two tons of Navy gunpowder without either written authorization or bill of sale. Lenz spent long frustrating days waiting in government offices for decisions that would never come. The Navy office accepted his report of Navy registration of the Osprey, but not his commission, but due to Lenz' ownership papers they could not remove him as ship's captain, so they ordered the Osprey to remain in port until formal documentation arrived from Washington City. Winter settled the entire matter, and trapped the Osprey until April, 1813. It also allowed Ben the opportunity to visit Navy ships and learn duties the seamen were happy to have the youngster perform for them.

In December, a message arrived from Washington refuting any actions taken by the errant junior naval officer during the October 1812 panic on the Potomac. Lenz was formally notified of his civilian status, and the Osprey reverted to a commercial vessel. However, the issue of the gunpowder remained unresolved, and therefore the Osprey was impounded at Charleston and the Pulaski's evicted from their ship. Lenz was able to transfer some funds from his Baltimore bank to a Charleston bank and found lodging for him and his son in a rented room near the harbor.

In January, when Ben turned 13, Lenz reluctantly gave his permission allowing Ben to serve as a paid apprentice to the ship's carpenter on the Revenue Cutter Gallatin, which was wintering in Charleston. The winter weather was bleak and cold, but not nearly as much so as winter in

Baltimore. Waiting is harder, when that is the main function.

At last, in March, the Gallatin began patrolling the South Carolina coast as far north as Georgetown and as far south as Port Royal near Beaufort. Ben loved the moments at sea. When he came back with exciting stories of encounters by the Gallatin evading British ships attempting to blockade southern ports, Lenz demanded that Ben stay on shore in the harbor. The newspapers were filled with accounts of British ships all along the eastern coast, and squadrons entering the Chesapeake Bay. Lenz fell into despair at being away from the Bay and trapped in Charleston. His second wife continued to refuse answering his letters. Letters from business associates mentioned seeing her at social activities and plays. The month advanced slowly and Lenz' depression worsened. His moods were pulled down further by an overactive Ben, repeatedly returned to the lodging by constables.

During the morning of April 1, 1813, Lenz sat Ben down in the room for a stern lecture on courteous behavior, when the building was rocked by a reverberating explosion that pounded across the harbor. Out in the street with dozens of other concerned citizens, Lenz and Ben watched a black pillar of smoke climb into the sky above the dock where the Gallatin was moored. In the early afternoon a Naval seaman approached Lenz in the parlor and requested he come to the Naval office . Once there, he was informed by the senior officer that the Gallatin had exploded, most likely due to a spark from a nearby ship. Lenz felt a lump rise in his throat, but he forced himself to ask the question, "Was it the Osprey?"

"No, Pulaski, your ship is fine, and it is full of gunpowder. Washington finally decided what to do about that in a letter received just yesterday, and as much as I would like to impound that cargo for Charleston, you have been ordered to New Orleans. The Navy is forming a new squadron there, and desperately needs that powder. The Chesapeake is essentially a lost cause. British ships are pouring into the Bay and creating havoc with shipping. Short of a fleet of man-of-wars, we have nothing to stop them. We've done well on the great lakes and need to keep the bastards out of the Mississippi."

He handed Lenz a folded paper. "This is registration of the Osprey as a United States Navy Vessel." Then another, "This recognizes the gunpowder as property of the Navy." Then another, "This commissions you as a Lieutenant in the United States Navy." And another, "This assigns you as captain of the Osprey." And another, "And this orders you to join the New Orleans Squadron under Commodore Daniel Patterson 'with all due dispatch'. That's Navy parlance for 'move like your ass is on fire.' Dismissed, Lieutenant." Lenz saluted and turned to leave the office.

"And Lieutenant," the captain added, "the next time you feel the urge to give your ship to the Navy, get it in writing!"

Within two weeks the Osprey was ready for sea and filled with enough food and supplies for three months. The Navy had added four small cannon on each side of the main deck with cutouts for each gun, and a nine-inch long gun at the bow. The Navy also added 10 gunners, a gunner's mate, and 10 more sail handlers to the crew of the Osprey.

"This ain't no pleasure cruiser no more,

jinnelmen," the gunner's mate had said to the Osprey men. "This here's a fightin' ship now."

The April weather turned tropical as the Osprey sailed south along the Atlantic Coast, quickly passing the coast of Georgia and sailing the long coast of Spanish Florida. Several days later the Osprey turned west and entered the Gulf of Mexico, just south of dots on the horizon the Gunner's Mate identified as the Florida Keys. The air was saltier and more humid. Light breezes barely pushed the Osprey westerly and felt like a hot breath on one's neck in a stuffy room. Energy quickly left the body during work, and sleep was slow to come in the heat. Sweat slowly trickled down inside shirts and trousers. The skin stayed wet, the lips stayed dry, and fresh water became precious.

Lenz finally reported to Commodore Patterson in early May. The Osprey was sent on into New Orleans, with orders to resupply other fighting ships when the need arose. Once again, Lenz Pulaski and his rambunctious son, Ben, were left at the shore to wait. Life in New Orleans became the hottest summer either had ever endured. Lenz and Ben both tried every avenue to become engaged in an activity other than the torture of simply waiting. Ben spent more and more time among the growing army camp learning the drums. He tried several times to find a way to pick up a musket, but was considered too young for such an activity, even though everyone seemed to know the army there was too small. As the only thirteen year old among the drummers, he quickly became the senior drummer, and fell into the regimented banging with vigor.

Lenz and Ben originally shared a common tent

in the army camp. Lenz would daily report to the Navy Office for assignments and Ben would find useful activities where he could contribute. As the spring slipped into summer, the two saw less of each other, spending longer times in other areas. Lenz was temporarily assigned as the second lieutenant on board one of the larger armed schooners within the squadron, the *USS Alligator*. He was confident Ben would be safe among the army staff, and act accordingly. Since the patrol route of his ship brought him back into New Orleans every few days, he could search out his son at those times. He was, after all, almost a man.

Among the regular army already posted in New Orleans, Ben met a young Lieutenant from Maryland only five years his senior, and soon developed a casual acquaintance. Ben, while rambunctious and frequently over-energetic to the point of mischief, was far more serious in matters of the military. Lieutenant Osgood Bond, on the other hand was still prone to daydream and consider the impractical. Ben and Osgood often drifted together in the afternoons when duties were complete. The second cousin within a well-landed family in St. Mary's County, Osgood's commission was acquired for him by the Sotterlees, in the unsuccessful hopes it would encourage him to mature. Many of his duties, especially those requiring writing reports, were actually completed by his attendant slave, Simon.

Ben enjoyed the friendly uncomplicated time spent with Osgood, but he was drawn to more serious conversations with Simon during the time around the campfire after Osgood had gone early to bed. Simon was well educated and could read and write. Ben had shunned his schooling after his mother's death in his seventh year. He ran away from school almost daily, to go sailing with his father, who allowed his own grief to overshadow his parental duties. When his father had remarried after Ben's tenth birthday, Ben had run away from his second mother with a father too accustomed to his presence on deck. Simon told Ben of ancient stories originally written in Greek and Latin, but only in the quiet of the night and never in front of other white people.

Ben left a note on his father's bed when he moved into the Army camp as drummer for the second regiment. Osgood had arranged the orders for signature by the regimental commander. Simon had written the note for Ben's father. Summer drifted into autumn, with each Pulaski performing his duties, and rarely seeing each other. Ben learned to perform all drum tattoos for all orders, and helped the other drummers in the other regiment learn them as well. Osgood had a musket issued to Ben and allowed him to participate in drills and marches. Simon introduced Ben to men known as Socrates, Hippocrates, Ulysses and the soldiers of Sparta.

Autumn slipped into winter and brought Ben's 14th birthday. Ben was the size of the average soldier and his own clothes were wearing thin. His ceremonial tunic for drummers, given him the previous year, had to be left open, since the buttons no longer reached their button holes, so Osgood had Regular Army uniforms made for Ben. Lenz had remained on board the Alligator as acting Second Lieutenant, and sought out Ben whenever he could. With permission from the ship's captain, he managed to have Ben aboard for a few patrols to teach him the Navy side of the war and spend time together. Lenz' silent wife Beatrice had finally begun writing Lenz short letters, giving him names of British officers to request, should he be captured. Beatrice had always maintained correspondence with that side of her family, even though it was certainly out of favor during those years. The news regarding Chesapeake shipping was devastating. Lenz told Ben he firmly believed that had he kept the Osprey in the Bay, he would have lost her several times over and be far deeper in debt than just his lost business.

In the New Orleans patrol area, engagements with the British had been few, and the use of powder had been minimal. Still, the Osprey sat at the New Orleans docks, waiting for the pleasure of the United States Navy. The powder had remained in the hold for so long, the Commodore ordered the Osprey put to sail and taken to the far edge of the harbor. There she was met by two of the squadron's gunboats. The bags of gunpowder were lifted out and passed from one ship to another until all the bags had been rotated out into the fresh air, having the topmost bags now packed in the bottom, and the bottom most bags now stacked on top.

---<>---

"What about the Indians, Pa? What about the Indians?" Aaron complained.

"Maybe," Sonja suggested to Ben, "You can tell them where you were when the British attacked."

"Just wanted to fill in all the gaps," Ben answered.

---<>---

In August of that year, the British marched on

Washington City and burned the Capitol building and the White House. The following month they tried to take Baltimore, but could not get in.

In Louisiana, early in November, the British fleet in the Gulf of Mexico sailed toward New Orleans. General Jackson arrived and began organizing the army and the citizens into a single army. There wasn't nearly enough powder, flints and balls for the army. Ben joined the men building picket lines in the marsh just outside the city. Commodore Patterson took the squadron to meet the British just off shore in Lake Borgne, at the mouth of the Mississippi River. On December 14th the British attacked the New Orleans Squadron. The British pounced on the ships immediately. U.S. losses were great.

The gun boats were smashed by the British cannon. The Osprey stood out near the edge of the fighting, ready to deliver powder. One gunboat lost its rudder and was blown into the Osprey, pushing her across the rocks and split her hull. Before she could sink, Lenz put on all sail and ran her into the beach just below the city. That gave a little more time for Jackson to prepare the city defenses.

The British landed thousands of troops south of the city. On December 23rd General Jackson led a charge against the British soldiers setting up camp and disrupted their plans for attack.

On Christmas day, Ben Pulaski barged into Andrew Jackson's tent.

"My father has gunpowder on the beach for you, General."

" Is that right, young man? How many pounds does he have and how much money does he expect for it."

"My father says he has over 40-tons of dry powder, and the Navy doesn't need it anymore."

"Well, by God, bring that man in here!"

"Can't, sir. He's down at the beach unloading your powder. Said you should come quick before the British get it."

By New Years Day all the powder was stationed along the picket line south of the city, surrounded by sandbags and dirt barriers. That day, Benjamin Pulaski turned fifteen.

On January 8th, the British Army marched toward New Orleans. British and United States Army drummers beat the angry rhythms of the march and the call to arms. As the British neared in the mist, General Jackson ordered the drummer boys down off the pickets and behind the lines. Ben sent his drum back with one of the other boys, and snatched up his musket, standing next to Jackson.

"You get back, Boy," Jackson ordered.

"No sir, General. I'm fifteen now, and I'm standing right here."

The General laughed and slapped Ben on the back.

"By God, young'un, if I had a hundred like you we'd just step out there and whip the Brits where they stand."

Ben stood on his tiptoes looking out over the picket, leaning forward as if he only waited for the General's command.

Jackson placed his hand gently on Ben's shoulder.

"What's your name?"

"Benjamin Pulaski, sir."

"You just hold your spot, young man. I'll tell you all when to shoot," he said calmly.

By the late morning, Ben's shoulder throbbed from the pain of firing the musket, taking the punch of the rifle butt hammering against him, reloading with the ramrod, firing and reloading, firing and reloading. His hearing was nothing but shrill ringing, the voices of those around him mumbles like trying to speak under water. His eyes burned from the acrid gunpowder smoke that had swept over him in continuous waves. Tears ran down his blackened cheeks, as his eyes tried to wash themselves clean. He raised his ramrod again, moving through the pain, following the motion to reload yet again. A firm hand gripped his forearm, and would not let him complete the motion. A face showing in the smoke, close to his own, saying something, but he could not understand. The face smiled and a hand ruffled the auburn hair on his capless head.

"We've done them, young man," Jackson said. "They're heading back to England, God Damn them all!"

Ben's knees buckled and he plopped down into the mud, but still held his musket upright. Another man sat down next to Ben and put an arm around him. The man held a saber in his other hand and he wiped the sweat from his brow with the back of his hand. Ben looked up to see his father's face, looking as tired as he felt. They smiled at each other, catching their breath together.

"But, what about the Indians, Pa??"

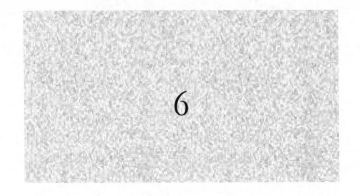

6

Ben and Sonja led their sons to the table for dinner. Ben ruffled Aaron's hair, noticing how high he had to reach to do that now.

"Son, I will tell you more after supper, but I need to say things about the Indians first. Things that will likely surprise you."

Sonja patted Ben's arm. "Not too much gory detail, please, Ben."

Aaron almost swallowed his stew whole with the least amount of chewing, and was sitting in the front room waiting several minutes before the others.

"I know all too much of what you need to tell them, Ben. I will stay in here cleaning up." Then she smiled and added, "I will come in there for the good part."

Ben glanced back at her over his shoulder and winked. He poked the fire in the stone fireplace and dropped another split log on the pulsating coals.

"You need to understand, Aaron. Indians are just as smart as us, and in some cases, a lot smarter. Indians have different languages and different tribes. Their tribes have names like Creek, Cherokee, Iroquois, Seminole, and many many more. Their tribes are like nations, with their own boundaries and their own treaties with other tribes, all of it in this country long before Europeans came here. Of course, I didn't know all that when I joined the army. Like you, I thought of them as less than people, more like rodents and wild animals that inhabited the forests; game for hunting that sometimes bit you."

The excitement slipped down from Aaron's eyes. Isaac leaned forward, dwelling on each word his father spoke. Ben settled into a chair near the fire. His tone was solemn.

"Isaac," Ben said, "You may become an Army Officer yourself, someday. You need to understand what I am telling you. Things are not peaceful between the white man and the Indian. The time for that was kicked away long ago. The wars between us and the Indians may still not be over. You need to understand them and respect them, but you also need accept that you may have to fight them; to kill them so they cannot kill you."

Isaac sat staring silently into Ben's eyes.

"There is so much hatred between the Indian and us, Isaac. The solution seems to be either wipe them off the earth where they fight, or push them into parts of the country we will not want to go."

Isaac let out a deep breath. "Tell us about them, Pa."

"Yes, Pa," Aaron added, "Tell us about what happened when you were in the Army."

"The Indians I fought were the Seminole. We,

the Army, were in the Indian's world, thinking like we were back in ours. Living in the swamps was so different from here. A lot of soldiers died in those swamps, and so did a lot of Seminole. They fought for their country just like we did at New Orleans, only this time we were the British. We took a couple as prisoner once, and I had to guard them. Some spoke English; were even Christian. They saw Florida as their country. They even had Creek Indians and runaway slaves living with them, who thought it was safer with the Indians than with white people. They fought with them against us, too. The British had given them all muskets to fight us before the Battle of New Orleans."

Ben leaned back in his chair, looking up at the rafters but seeing memories as he spoke. "My father had to watch as the poor Osprey, his own ship, was taken apart for the boards in her sides," he began.

---<>---

Lenz dreaded his return to Baltimore. He had left home much against his wife's wishes, on what turned out to be rumors. He had been trapped far away when the British bombarded Baltimore and nearby Fort McHenry, and had now lost his ship. He would have to find his way back to the Chesapeake Bay, to discover if any of his life there was still intact. A sentry came to his tent with orders to report to General Jackson. When he entered Jackson's headquarters, he was surprised to see his son standing in the room.

"What's he done now, sir?"

"It's what he's about to do, Lieutenant. Thought you might want to watch."

A sergeant held a Bible in front of Ben and

recited the Army Oath of enlistment. After each phrase, the sergeant paused and Ben repeated the line. Lenz was not surprised at Ben's action. Ben had told him he was going to do it. Still, he was surprised at being invited to Jackson's headquarters to watch it. Even surprised that Jackson was having it in front of himself.

"So help me, God," the sergeant said.

"So help me, God," Ben repeated.

The sergeant looked back at General Jackson, awaiting his next order.

"Alright, Sergeant. Get his ass out of here and start teaching him how to be a soldier."

Jackson motioned for Lenz to approach his desk.

"Lieutenant, I am informed that the ship you lost, was your personal property. Is that right?"

"Yes, sir."

"And that you sailed it out of the Chesapeake Bay to help your country fight the British."

"Yes, sir."

"Well, I see where young Private Pulaski gets his back bone."

Jackson handed Lenz a thick envelope, carrying the seal of the United States.

"This country doesn't have a God damned penny, Pulaski. Between everything the British destroyed, and everything that fool Madison pissed away; as a country, we're paupers. But, it won't stay that way too long. In several years, when the pain of the blood-letting fades, and the balls of the leaders in Washington City come back to them, there will be a major effort to recognize people like you, and maybe even me..."

Not knowing what else to say when Jackson paused, Lenz said, "Yes, sir."

"That document is one of the last official acts of the United States Commander of the Southern Territories, before I follow my orders into the swamps of Florida, where Congress hopes I get killed."

"Yes, sir, I mean, No, sir."

Jackson chuckled and lit a cigar. Still standing, he leaned across his desk and offered his hand to Lenz. As they shook hands, Jackson continued.

"That document authorizes you to be compensated by the United States Treasury for the loss of your personally owned ship, at whatever fair market value exists, when they get around to doing it. The size and tonnage and number of decks was furnished to me by the Navy Squadron and signed by Commodore Patterson."

"T-Thank you, sir."

"Well, we might both be dead before they get around to it, but it's all I can do for now. Dismissed, Captain."

"It's... Lieutenant, Sir."

"Nope," he said, flipping his hand at the envelope in Lenz' hand. "That's in there, too. Dismissed." He waved Lenz away in a cloud of blue smoke.

Captain Lenz Pulaski was next assigned by Commodore Patterson to take command of one of the small Jefferson Frigates and deliver its passengers and cargo to Washington City. Some of the cargo included British battle flags and officer's swords taken during the fighting, sent as souvenirs to Dolly Madison. When Lenz appeared surprised at the recipient, the Commodore related, "General Jackson is known for saying that between the two Madisons, Dolly was the only one with balls."

Lenz and Ben had dinner together that evening at a tavern in New Orleans. Lenz shared the news about the compensation, his promotion and his destination. Ben told his father that he would soon be marching into Georgia under General Jackson. The rest of the meal was nearly in silence. When they finished they embraced, and since both were in uniform, they stepped back and saluted each other, then went their different ways. It was the last time father and son would see each other for several years.

Ben spent the next two years in southern Georgia, with occasional marches into northern Spanish Florida. He marched and drilled far more than he stood into battle. His unit was frequently held back from the worst fighting, held in reserve and rarely used. Skirmishes with the Seminole Indians in late 1816 found him as a corporal in the front line, shoulder to shoulder with other soldiers. The Seminole were fierce and adaptable warriors. Usual military advances in the swamps were frequently out-maneuvered by the Seminole. When attacked by the Indians from many directions, larger Army formations dissolved into platoons and squads standing back to back on small rises above the swamp water.

Ben's Lieutenant was Osgood Bond, a poor

leader of the Second Platoon who frequently looked to Ben for suggestions, even before consulting with his own sergeant. Ben's advice generally made Osgood look like he knew his job. With Osgood's permission, Ben would take Simon on scouting moves ahead or beside the platoon, spoiling many Indian ambushes. Simon was an excellent tracker and a dependable partner scouting the swamps with Ben. Ben had developed a keen intuition of likely Seminole movements and in several instances helped guide his fellow soldiers to safer places for self-defense.

Against Ben's advice, and that of the platoon sergeant, Osgood ordered his platoon onto a long dry strip of grassy land surrounded by thick forest, so he could dry his feet. The Indians attacked as soon as Osgood had his boots off. Osgood and the sergeant were killed almost immediately. Ben rallied the soldiers and led them off the island and back into the swamp where they formed a circle around a large Cypress tree in waist deep water. He then sent Simon up into the tree limbs as a lookout for coming Indians. The soldiers' gunpowder was wet. The new muskets issued them by the Army were almost useless. A mist enveloped the swamp and was followed by darkness.

Ben ordered the men to fix bayonets and put their backs against the tree, touching each other's shoulders. Each man would know the other was there and nothing could get between them or behind them. When Simon alerted them to an Indian attack, Ben ordered "Strike" and all the men lunged outward as one with their bayonets. They gave the bayonet all their strength, whether they could see anyone or not. The spring-like circle of bayonets killed several Indians during the night, and the men reformed with their backs against the Cypress.

The attacks dwindled, and finally stopped altogether. Simon slipped down the tree and informed Ben he had seen an Indian fire ring on the dry strip where Osgood had been killed. Quietly, Ben led his men back toward the grassy strip, but held them in the water. He reformed them by silently pulling each man into line abreast, in preparation to charge. When the first faint light of gray dawn brightened in the eastern tree line, he led his men in a silent advance of bayonets. Many of the Indians were still sleeping on the ground. Without gunfire, several Indians were killed before a Seminole cry rang out. The soldiers made a steady killing advance. Like a reaper machine, the line of soldiers marched through the dying warriors, saying nothing. There was only the grunts and groans of fighting and dying men. The soldiers left no one alive behind them. There were fewer and fewer Seminole in front of them. As the soldiers neared the end of the grassy strip, only an old man and a girl still stood before them. The old man appeared to be almost blind. The girl held his arm with one hand, and a knife in her other.

"He is a medicine man," Ben said. His were the first words spoken since they left the circle around the tree. "He is their priest, not a warrior." Ben ordered half of his men to face behind them with bayonets out, in case another attack might come. "Let the old man and the girl go."

The old man was indeed a medicine man, and the girl his granddaughter. The incident became known among the Seminole as the night of the cottonmouth, after the deadly snake that strikes silently without warning. The story was shared among the Seminole and was heard by Army scouts who reported to General Jackson. Among the Seminole, a story was passed along about a young army warrior of the cotton mouths who respected the life of a medicine man and his granddaughter.

The week after Christmas 1816, Ben was promoted to sergeant. He managed to sew the new chevrons on his sleeves by the light of his campfire at Fort Scott on New Year's Eve. The following morning he turned seventeen, and was the youngest sergeant under General Jackson's command. The new officer for Second Platoon arrived that same day. Lieutenant Anthony Renowitz, of Philadelphia, assumed command of the Cotton Mouths and informed them that their success on the grassy strip had earned them the right to wear the skin of a cottonmouth snake as a distinctive band around their Shako hats. The greatly feared venomous snake loathed by most Army soldiers, soon became highly sought after for its skin, and the second platoon proudly displayed their snake bands.

Ben and Anthony improved the concept of deadly silence, as they called their approach. Typical Army advances in the swamp were noisy. Men stumbled over roots, splashing in the water, while trying to stay in line. Metal dishes and loose items in their packs clanged together when in a rush. Sabers rattled in their metal-capped scabbards. Item by item, much of the noise was silenced. Palm leaves were inserted into back packs to separate the utensils. Rag strips were tied around saber and bayonet blades to keep them off the metal caps. Powder horns were slung on shorter leather strings to keep them higher out of the water.

The men were led in loose order, allowing each man to move flexibly within the swamp. Finally, the men were taught to walk more carefully with their toes down first when wading through water, following the motion used by the Indians. During an overnight visit by the Regimental Commander and his personal guards, Anthony and Ben were able to move the entire second platoon into attack positions within ten feet of the Colonel's own tent before his guards became aware of them. Overcoming his own embarrassment at being surprised, the Colonel commended the stealth of the second platoon. He ordered Lt. Renowitz and Sgt. Pulaski to teach the "Cottonmouth Method" around the regiment, but other events soon robbed them of the time to obey his order.

Angered over stolen cattle taken by white settlers raiding into Florida, the following week Seminoles began attacking farms in Georgia territory near Fort Scott. When the Cavalry pursued them, the Indians slipped back into Spanish Florida. Company A, which included Anthony's platoon among three others, was sent into Spanish Florida to find the main Seminole settlement. Early in the morning, Captain Henderson met with his platoon officers to give his orders for the movement. The Platoon Sergeants were not invited into the Captain's tent, but remained close by, easily hearing the words of the officers. Anthony tried to convince Henderson to spread his platoons out in loose formations, and let second platoon scout ahead, but the Captain insisted all platoons keep in parade formation, with second platoon in its proper place behind the first.

"We have paid Indian Scouts for that work, Lieutenant Renowitz. Your job is not as a scout.

Your job is to keep your platoon in line where I put you, and to make sure those pirates in second platoon fire and keep firing when I order it. Am I understood, Lieutenant?"

"Yes, sir!"

Two days later, the company crossed into Spanish Florida. They were met by scouts who gave them the route to the main Seminole settlement, a low tree covered island in the middle of a swamp connected by a well guarded narrow dirt path. The Captain led his men into the swamp, around the settlement with the intention of attacking from the south. The Seminole were well aware of the soldiers long before the Army neared the settlement, and were waiting in large numbers. The surprise Seminole attack quickly separated the platoons. Captain Henderson was among the first to die. First Platoon charged the Indians, but were outnumbered and driven back after their Lieutenant and Sergeant were killed. Lt. Renowitz led the second platoon to their aid. He placed Ben in charge of the Cotton Mouths and formed the first platoon around a large cypress.

Ben formed the Cotton Mouths around another cypress nearby. With the big trees behind them, the soldiers could face the Indian charges. With little time to re-load the muskets, the fighting soon fell to silent bayonet lunges. Darkness fell over the swamp while the fighting continued in surges. The ring of soldiers grew smaller as men were killed and wounded. A ring of Indian bodies formed at bayonet distance from the cypress. Throughout the night, the two platoons lunged out at the sound of ripples in the water. The iron rings of bayonets were more than the Indian Warriors wished to test.

As the sky above the trees began to lighten and reflect off the surface of the swamp water, a final lone Seminole dashed in toward the soldiers. Just before the Bayonets found his heart, he managed to drive a stone spear into the chest of Benjamin Pulaski. As Ben sank into the dark water he could hear bugles sounding and musket firing in the distance.

---<>---

"Pa! What happened then? What happened next?" Aaron was wrapped in dread.

Ben looked deep into his eyes, with sadness over his face, and said, "I died."

His sons stared blankly at him. Sonja slapped his shoulder. "Don't you dare do that, Benjamin Pulaski! You tell them what happened!"

Ben let slip a small smile and looked into her eyes, "You just like hearing the next part."

She smiled. "Yes I do, so tell it properly."

Aaron and Isaac spoke in unison. "What?"

"That spear felt like a boulder full of lightning grinding in my chest," Ben said. "I slept a lot. I guess it was sleep. I woke up from time to time in different places, and each time my bedding was soaking wet. When my head finally cleared and I could sit up, I was in a room back at Fort Scott. I could hardly move my left shoulder and I was as weak as an infant. Colonel Clinch led the rest of the Regiment right up the front road to the settlement and drove it into the swamps. Our Cotton Mouths, the first and second platoons, were the only parts of the company to live. Lt. Renowitz was made Captain and put in charge of the company. I was made a Lieutenant, then told I was being sent out of the Army on convalescence."

"What's Convalescence?" Isaac asked Ben.

"It's a time to heal, Son. But they knew I wouldn't. Not enough to fight in the Army for a long time. General Jackson had me made Lieutenant, so I'd get half officer pay during convalescence."

"Now, tell them about my Father, Ben," Sonja said.

"I will. I will," Ben said.

Aaron turned toward his mother. "Was Grandpa Jundt in the Army too?"

"No," she said. "Let your Pa tell it."

Ben shifted in his seat. "It took weeks before I could get around on my own. I fell in with one of the Army suppliers who had a cargo business and a farm up in North Carolina. He told me when he was a boy, he was a powder monkey on a ship under Captain John Paul Jones."

Aaron's eyes went wide, "John Paul Jones??"

"Keep listening," Sonja whispered.

"Since my father had always said he had done the same thing," Ben said, "I asked him if he ever knew a Lenz Pulaski. As it turns out, they were best friends at that time, and both on the *Bon Homme Richard*, when Jones fought the British."

The two boys shared open-mouthed amazement with each other.

"So, that spring when Mr. Jundt made ready to return to North Carolina, he offered to bring me to his farm in one of his wagons. I could stay there a while to get stronger, and then make my way up to Baltimore. He hadn't mentioned he had a beautiful young daughter named Sonja."

Ben slipped his hand around Sonja's.

"Well, I was only thirteen then..." she said.

"And a bit of a spoiled brat..." Ben added, and received a gentle slap on his arm from her, accompanied by a poorly hidden smile.

"I stayed there two years," Ben said. "Partly to get better, partly to help Burl in repayment for his generosity, and partly to watch that girl grow into a woman, so I could be first in line for her hand..."

There was a frantic knock on the door. Ben stood and opened the door to find Margaret Bartlett standing in the dark on their porch, grasping a crumpled piece of paper. She shoved the paper into Ben's hand.

"Ben. Deputy Mattingly nailed this on the poster board in front of the lock house this afternoon. I thought you ought to see it."

"Come in, please, Mrs. Bartlett."

Sonja rose from her chair and stepped next to her. "What is it, Margaret."

Ben held the paper up to the lamp light. "It is a wanted poster for a murderer, a runaway slave named Simon Bond. Two hundred dollars for his capture, dead or alive."

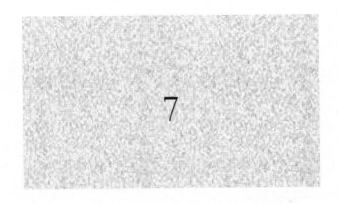

"This drawing could be any black man," Ben said.

"There's two or three Simons around here, Mr. Pulaski," Margaret answered and looked at Sonja. "I don't know how many people in Lapidum and Havre de Grace know your man's full name is Simon Bond." Margaret looked around the front room and back to Ben. "I am so sorry to barge in like this, Mr. Pulaski, but John and I thought you needed to know right away." She wrung her apron in her hands in front of her, her brow furrowed.

Sonja rose from her chair and extended her hand to Margaret. "Thank you dear."

"Yes," Ben added. "Yes. Thank you for bringing this to us, and please give my respects to John."

"Yes...well. I should get back to the house." She skittered down the steps of the porch and quick-stepped down the pathway toward Lapidum in the fading light.

Sonja leaned her head against Ben's shoulder as they watched Margaret round the path. "What will you do?"

"He needs to know," Ben said. He stepped down from the porch and headed to the barn.

In the bunkroom, Simon was playing checkers with Toby under the oil lamp hanging in the center of the room.

Simon chuckled as he spoke to the little boy. "No, Toby, you can't move your checker to another spot after I jumped it."

"Can too..."

"Simon," Ben spoke.

Simon looked up at Ben, his smile fading as he noted the deadpan expression on Ben's face. "Something wrong?"

Ben handed the wanted poster to Simon, who read over it and exhaled deeply. "What else?"

"John Bartlett's wife just brought it to me. Said Mattingly nailed it up on the post board near the lock today.

"He still around?"

"No. I don't think he came up to the lockhouse either, so he must be putting them up all around Havre de Grace and here."

Simon held the poster up to the light again. "Says I'm a runaway slave. This picture doesn't look anything like me."

"You know those pictures never look like anybody. Probably the same engraved picture they use for all black men."

"Probably."

"Simon, what name did Osgood use for you when he freed you?"

"Well, he didn't actually use any name, Ben. It was sort of a gentlemen's understanding."

"A gentlemen's understanding? Do you mean he never wrote it down, Simon?"

"Well, he always intended to, Ben. That's what he said when he got drunk, and as you know, he got drunk a lot."

"He never freed you?"

"Well, he never objected when I brought it up that last time. I said 'Osgood, you always said you would free me', and he didn't object, so I wrote up the papers."

"You...you wrote up the papers?"

"Had to. He had been dead three days then. Just me sitting in that tent alone, waiting for Captain Renowitz to decide what to do with all Osgood's personal effects. I had been signing his name in reports and letters to home for over a year. I did a fine damn job of it too."

Ben stared open-mouthed at Simon, frozen in silence. Finally, his mouth snapped shut. "Anthony knew. All right. What does your freedom paper say is your name?"

"Simon Bond."

Ben spun around and left the barn. Simon began packing his clothes while Toby watched, pestering Simon with questions.

Minutes later Ben returned with several sheets of linen paper, an ink well, and a steel tipped pen. Simon raised his eyebrows and stared into Ben's eyes as Ben set the material on the table.

"Sonja picked these things up in Havre de Grace so I could write that letter for Isaac. You do what you can with it."

At sunrise the following morning, Ben rapped his knuckles against the bunkroom door as he pushed it open. Toby was still asleep in his bunk, covered with a well-worn wool blanket. Simon was at the table, twisting his shoulders and looking down at an official looking document. As Ben walked into the room, Simon snatched up the paper and wadded it into a ball.

Ben stuttered, "What the..."

Simon then dropped the wad of paper onto the floor and stamped it with his boot. Then he picked it up and gingerly opened the document onto the table, pressing it out with his hands. Once it approached its original size, he folded it into quarters. Before Ben could ask a question, Simon motioned to him with a jerk of his head, and led them out of the bunkroom to the mule stables. He rubbed the paper on Sarah's haunch, then raised her tail and rubbed the paper firmly across her anus.

With a broad smile spreading across his face, Simon chuckled. "A white boy once told me 'Niggers smell like a mule's ass.' I wouldn't want to disappoint him." He withdrew an empty leather folder from his back pocket and slipped the paper into it, then returned it to his pocket.

Ben shook his head and smiled at his friend. "What does it say is your name?"

"Silas Burrows."

"Well, *Silas*, how do we explain that we've been calling you Simon the past couple years?"

Simon fell into a thick-tongued plantation drawl. "My previous white boss done had a son named Silas, and he couldn't bring hisself to call me by his son's name. So, he named me Simon and I gots used to it."

Ben stiffened his back and puffed out his chest. "You got freedom papers, boy?"

Simon reached for his back pocket. "Yassah. Yawanna smell'em?"

"Oh hell, no!" Ben chuckled briefly, then dropped his smile. "Are you ready to take it this way?"

Simon nodded. "I think it'll work, Ben. This way we don't have to try to get people to call me something different. They just keep calling me Simon. And if Mattingly wants to investigate me, he gets a face full of mule ass."

"Who's getting a face full of mule ass?" Toby asked.

"You get up," Simon ordered, then dropped onto Toby, tickling him.

---<>---

Deputy Mattingly wiped his hands with an old rag. This shack was uninhabited as well. It was dark there in spite of full daylight outside. There were no windows, only a front doorway with part of an old moldy blanket hanging in it as a door, flipping in the wind. A couple holes in the roof and gaps between mismatched boards allowed arrows of light to dive into the darkness. Two ramshackle bunk beds nailed and tied together leaned against each

117

side wall. Stained pillows and threadbare blankets lay crumpled on the sickly pads. A single cast-off chair held together by rope stood near a short counter holding a few battered pots at the rear. The smell of the nearby marsh hung heavy in the room, the air thick with the scent of rotted vegetation and exposed mudflats, like an old outhouse, forcing him back out into the light and the fresh air slipping across Concord Cove. A black woman stood there in the winter sun waiting on him. Her faded dress unable to hide the curves of a young body that men of any color longed to touch.

"They been got, Dep'ty. I told you. They been got." Her breath formed thin clouds in front her mouth as she spoke.

"Yeah. The shacks are empty all right, Sissie. But how do I know they're not working someplace in town, and will be back here tonight?"

"You come back and see. They been gone five days. I heard a scuffle, and come sunup they gone. Catchers got'em I think."

"Sissie, You telling me there were runaways down here?"

"No sir. Only be freed or tagged stay down here. Maybe one came through that wasn't, but not no more. Freed or tagged is all we do. That's what you said and it's what we do."

"I should have set fire to this mess last year. Run all you out of here."

"No sir. Ain't no reason to do that. No trouble happens here. Or if it do, it don't go past the woods. I swear."

"Maybe. Maybe not, Sissie." Mattingly threw

his rag into the fire pit at the center of the shanties. "You got six shacks down here. I know others built them, but you run them. Six shacks. Ten cents a week. Or I burn them and run you all off." He held out his gloved hand.

She stepped close to him, letting her breasts slide along his forearm, moving slowly toward the palm of his hand. "Maybe, we could work out a better arrangement..."

Mattingly stepped back. "Bull shit. I burned for a month the last time you paid in something beside money. Sixty cents. Now."

She slapped six dimes in his palm and turned her back on him. He dropped the coins into his pocket and rubbed his hand gently across her bottom as he walked away toward the trail leading through the woods.

---<>---

"Ben," Sonja yelled. "Ben!"

Ben dropped the horseshoe tongs and let the mare's hoof slip back down to the ground then stepped through the open barn door. Sonja was standing on the porch with her arms folded, eyeing a man in a suit coat nailing a board on the front wall of their cabin. "What the..."

"Ben," Sojna called out as he approached the porch. "This man..."

The man turned around as Ben hopped up onto the porch with fists balled. The man's nose was badly broken. He held his hammer high between them.

"You may remember, I am Samuel Briscoe, General Manager of Tidewater Real Estate

119

Corporation," he said extending his hand. "We met in Herbert Binterfield's office..."

Ben folded his arm across his chest.

Briscoe continued, "And you had the pleasure of breaking my nose last fall, when you tried to break into the bank."

"Just trying to pay off my account. So..." Ben answered.

"So, now come-uppance is at hand, Mr. Pulaski."

Briscoe stepped back and pointed his hammer at the sign.

PROPERTY OF

TIDEWATER REAL ESTATE CORPORATION

APPLY HAVRE DE GRACE, MD.

"What the Hell is this," Ben demanded. "I rent this farm from old man Walker through his lawyer."

"Not anymore, Mr. Pulaski. My corporation purchased the property from Mr. Walker as of December first, and you are now my tenant. You will pay your rent in advance by the first day of each month." He stepped back slightly, keeping the hammer between them. "Since you have been paying at the end of each month you have been here, you are now a month in arrears, and you have two days to make the payment or vacate."

Ben rested his fists on his hips and spoke through gritted teeth. "Fine, Briscoe. I'll get you your money right now." Ben stepped past him, bumping his shoulder slightly.

"Not necessary, sir." Briscoe edged past Sonja

and quickly slipped down the steps. Turning at the bottom, "I only accept payment to my corporate bank account at the Tidewater Bank and Trust in Havre de Grace." He began walking toward the path down to Lapidum. "You will have to make your payment there." He stopped several yards away and turned. "Oh, and by the way, due to overhead costs on the property, we are forced to double your rent. Good day, sir." He then quick-stepped down the path to the Pulaski crossover.

Sonja stared open-mouthed at the man's back. Ben's face twisted into a grimace and turned deep red. "That son of a..."

Tap. Tap. Tap. The sound of more nailing arose from the canal. An old man in coveralls was laying on the deck of the *Ugly Boat,* leaning over the edge near the bow nailing another sign.

Ben marched stiff legged down the slope.

"What the hell is going on here," he yelled.

The old man raised his uncovered head, silver strands of hair floated in the air like corn silk. "Sorry, Ben. Canal Board demands all barges show ownership on the bow."

Ben stopped and frowned at the sign, still too far from it to make out the letters. "Hope you spelled my name right, Ed. You could have just told me and I would have been glad to do that."

The old man moved awkwardly up onto his knees, then slowly pushed himself up to his feet. "Ain't your name, Ben. Says Tidewater Bank and Trust Company, Herbert Binterfield, President."

"What??"

An hour later Ben stormed through the front

door of the Tidewater Bank and Trust then abruptly stopped with his hand on the swing gate to the office area. Herbert Binterfield and George Milton sat at the large mahogany desk in the rear of the bank. Arrayed behind the desk were four men holding rifles, Mattingly, and three other deputies. In the far corner, wedged onto a small stool sat Sam Briscoe. Mattingly nodded in Ben's direction and another deputy behind Ben stepped to the front door and locked it.

"Ben," George said. "We need to talk. Mr. Binterfield invited me here since I have been your lawyer in the past. May I stay as such?"

Ben looked at the man behind him, saw his rifle with its hammer cocked. Then he eyed the other men in the room, settling his gaze on George. He nodded in agreement.

George rose from his chair and pulled another out next to him. "Come have a seat, Ben. Legal actions have been set in motion that you need to understand. Legal actions that are firm and demand compliance. "

Ben felt the pounding in his head, the rushing drumbeat in his ears, the flames rising up his face. His hand drifted up to the handle of his knife. His eyes focused on the smiling face of Herbert Binterfield. His vision grew black and red webs around the edges. The web drifted inward like curtains being drawn toward the center around Binterfield's face. The knuckles of his knife hand grew white.

"Ben," George said softly. "Ben, come sit down. Come sit down, Ben."

Slowly Ben stepped toward the desk, still

eyeing Binterfield. Binterfield leaned back away from Ben as he approached, his eyes on Ben's knife. Mattingly stepped forward and gently tapped Ben's right forearm. "Don't make me take the knife again, Pulaski," he whispered.

Ben sat down with his back military straight and kept his attention on George.

"Ben, I have reviewed the purchases and written requirements for your rented house and your barge. Neither are your property. The house rent must be paid the first of each month. Since the new owner demands payment in advance for each coming month, you owe two month's rent to be in good standing. This is legal, and becoming very common practice."

Ben nodded in silence, still only looking at George.

"Real estate prices are soaring," George said. "The new rental amount is in keeping with current prices. Mr. Walker gave you exceptionally generous rates that are not consistent with customary rates now. So, unfortunately, the doubling of your rent is commercially justified."

"And the *Ugly Boat*?" Ben added. "The bank note on that was deferred four years. We have signed papers."

Binterfield gave a broad smile and spoke. "Yes, but..."

George raised his palm flat in front of Binterfield's face, and continued to speak to Ben. "It is fair practice for banks to require regular payments to ensure closure at the end of the term. It is within the rights of the Tidewater Bank and

Trust to demand monthly payments to retire the loan on time."

"And if you are late on either, Pulaski, you forfeit either barge or farm," Binterfield said. "I have the right..."

George held his hand up to Binterfield again, and the banker exhaled, nodding to the lawyer.

"The bank has the right," George said, "to demand payment on time, and lateness or missed payment can be declared by the end of the business day on the date due. Even if that is before the final deferred date of the loan. Do you understand that, Ben?"

Ben nodded understanding to George.

Binterfield flipped copies of the loan agreement in front of Ben. Binterfield's signature was already written. Ben glared at Binterfield, then looked down to review the paper, struggling with the wording, but understanding. He paused while reviewing the finance numbers.

I may not read well, but By God, I know my numbers!

Ben tapped the line describing the monthly payment. "This amounts to far more than what I owe on the *Ugly Boat!*"

"Current rates, Pulaski." Binterfield smiled as he spoke. Ben noticed a small chip gone from one of his front teeth that was new since the last time he had seen him.

"It's legal, Ben, and enforceable," George said. "Loan rates have gone up a great deal in the past several years. Unfortunately, since the note was, um, re-negotiated last week, the original rates no longer apply. Those are customary rates now."

Ben signed the two copies of the loan agreement after ensuring both copies included the same information. Then Briscoe leaned forward and dropped the rental agreement on the desk. Ben reviewed and signed both copies. The deputy at the front door unlocked and opened it. Ben accepted his copies of the papers, then paid cash for his two months' rent and his first monthly payment on the barge. After one of the bank clerks handed Ben his receipts, Ben moved toward the front door. He stopped and looked back at Binterfield. Binterfield produced another beaming smile, then looked away. George gently nudged Ben's arm under the elbow and they stepped out onto the boardwalk together.

"That was shitty business, Ben. But, damn it, it was legal."

Ben took in a deep breath and exhaled it slowly, letting the roar in his ears fade until he could once again hear the seagulls in the sky overhead. He nodded at George, and produced a smile that stopped well below his eyes.

"The man is a snake. Thank you, George."

"Be careful, Ben. Binterfield is working every approach he can muster to do you harm. That incident with Sonja will drive him for years."

"She seems confident he can do nothing. She has a witness."

"One that will soon go to court, Ben. Binterfield has filed charges against Mr. Brown."

Ben raised his eyebrows and peered intently into George's eyes. "Mr. Brown has helped me and

Sonja both since I have been back. "

"Mr. Brown is my client as well, Ben. I will do all I can for him."

They shook hands and George began to move away, but Ben kept him in his grip.

"Someday, George, I will kill Binterfield," Ben said in a rasping whisper.

"I did not hear that," George said as he stepped off the boardwalk.

Ben heard a boot heel scrape behind him and turned. The deputy from the front door stood inches away staring at Ben with wide-open eyes.

---<>---

Ed Archer finished his chore on the *Ugly Boat* for the Tidewater Bank and Trust, and a small carpentry job in the cabin of Barge number 43. As the light of the day faded through the trees, he left the canal basin and stopped off at a little tavern on Market Street. He took his time with the single ale he typically bought there one or two times a week, and chatted with some of the regulars at the bar. Most of the others made their life on the canal, as he did. Many he had known since childhood or his early adult years before his Emily died, when he still went to church and sang in the choir. He lingered a while after his ale, smoking the little cigar handed out by a young man celebrating his first born, then bid his friends a good night. Beside the tavern, he entered the narrow lane that took him to his modest basement room and stopped to help a man bent over in the shadows.

Ed lifted the man's elbow, expecting to help him to the lamplight or toward the man's home.

The man spun around, driving a knife blade deep into his abdomen. At first there was only the pressure, like a punch from a young man, and for a second Ed remembered the years he would often find himself in a tussle outside a tavern. Then the pain exploded like lightning and ran up into his chest, down into his groin, and out to his shoulders. The man worked the blade in and out like a wood saw, but Ed was paralyzed and unable to move as the pain burst over him again and again. He felt the heavy breathing of the man on his cheek, smelled the whiskey and tobacco, and just the whiff of an aromatic scent used by gentlemen. The man pulled Ed out of the lane into the narrower space between the back of the tavern and the warehouse behind it. He gently laid Ed on his back, urging him in a hoarse whisper "Sssshhhhh. Quiet old man. Ssshhh," even as he continued to saw the blade in and out, working up to his ribs. The pain was incredible, but gripped in the midst of the spasm he could neither inhale nor cry out.

The man bent over Ed's body, driving the knife point all the way into the spine, scraping the bones with its tip, searching for the main artery.

There.

It was like pulling a plug from a keg of warm water. The blood rose up and washed over his hands, running over at the edges of the huge wound, pulsating down onto the ground. The bone handle lost its white luminescence in the overhead moonlight, and disappeared into the blackness of the bloody pool. Ed's body spasmed, his legs and arms twitched, and his final breath escaped from his lungs.

No need to cut his heart and lungs this time.

He ain't going into the water. Not from here.

The clouds partially covering the moon parted and allowed an arrow of silver light into the little gap between the buildings. The man pulled Ed's shirt and coat aside, so he could see his handiwork. He pushed and pulled at the raw edges, adding an additional artistic slice here and there to finish the work. He lingered, looking at the wound, then inhaled a deep shuddering breath and blew it out, as one might do at the end of a tiresome run. He stood, looking down one last time, then slipped farther along the gap to the far side of the tavern, and then up to the Ordinary where he rinsed his arms in the horse trough. There in the shadow from the street lamp, he washed off the blood, rolled his sleeves down, and adjusted his vest. Setting his hat straight, he ambled back up Market Street toward the center of town, humming a Christmas carol.

---<>---

Ben walked up the slope to the farm, with the moon slipping in and out of the clouds high above him. He loosened his coat sleeves to shed some of the water. Up on the porch, he stopped to sit on his favorite chair and pull his boots off. The house was dark and silent. The whispering among the trees was the only sound around him. He left his wet boots on the porch and eased open the door, then quietly placed the bar in its home on the inside. The ticking of the clock on the mantle above the open fireplace sounded loud in the near silent house. There was a faint squeak of the door hinge as he opened it and tiptoed into the bedroom. He removed his shirt and absently felt the sleeves as he hung it on the back of his dressing chair.

Probably won't be dry by morning. Morning

not too far off.

Sonja stirred under the bed sheets and blankets. "You were gone a good while," she mumbled.

"Just a few things to get done. Water in one of the holds. I couldn't sleep anyway. That damned Binterfield..." he whispered.

"Let it go tonight, Ben. Try to get some sleep." Her eyes were heavy, barely opened.

Ben laid his trousers on the chair and slipped under the covers. He lay on his back, placing his hands under his head, certain he was still too disturbed to sleep.

If she speaks again I will tell her about Brown.

Sonja turned on her side and laid her hand on his chest. He lay there listening to the slow rhythm of her breathing as she sunk back into deeper and deeper sleep, closing his eyes and feeling the warmth of her hand, he followed her down.

There was a bite to the early morning air when Ben arose. Sonja was content to remain under the covers a few more minutes until Ben started a fire in the front room. The crackling and popping of burning split oak was her signal to get up and move to the iron stove in the kitchen. The floor was cold to her feet and she quickly slipped on her shearling moccasins. Ben turned as he reached for the front door, telling her good morning. His breath fogged in front of his face and the little cloud flashed to brilliance as he opened the door, allowing the early sunshine to burst in.

"Winter is coming," he said over his shoulder. She started to answer, but he was gone and she gave all her attention to the iron stove, jabbing the sleeping coals with a poker, searching for an angry ruby that needed only air and kindling to flame again.

At the edges of the canal where the water was sluggish, the frost still remained among the grass and brush. The grass crunched under Ben's boots as he walked toward the barges.

It will freeze in a few weeks. Must time our trips to be back in Lapidum before that happens. There will be no barging once it freezes. Two more trips? Maybe three? Maybe not. No money to be made during the freeze. More rent to pay, and payments on the barge to be made. God damn him!

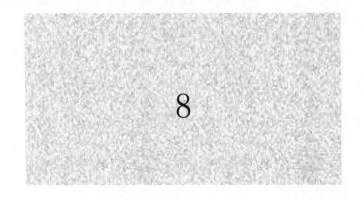

8

On the front slope, the grass was etched in frost, crystal white except for the tracks of his sons, and Simon and Toby, crisscrossing the yard, getting the barges ready to move.

I am behind this morning. They are already at it!

Isaac came up on deck from the cabin as Ben boarded the *Ugly Boat*. "'Bout time," he tossed out through a good natured grin as his father neared."

"You gonna have to dock my time, Boss man." Ben said.

Well-practiced moves had everything following the necessary order. Very little instruction was necessary. The Mast, booms and sideboards were secured on the deck. Sarah and Nadja were in a single trace a hundred feet up the towpath, hoofing at the path and blowing vaporous clouds from their nostrils. Toby was sitting on the back of Sarah, with Simon standing nearby. Isaac was in the bow of *The Turtle* poling the head of the two barges to the center of the canal. Aaron was standing on the deck ready to begin pushing the *Ugly Boat* out as well. Sonja handed up a travel bucket of steaming coffee, and a basket of hot biscuits.

"Two days," she said, but it was a question.

"Two if the Pocahontas is still buying coal. Three if we have to go on in to Annapolis to sell it."

She reached her hand up and he put his down to touch her fingertips. They smiled at each other.

"Push us off, Aaron," Ben said.

Simon stepped off in front of Sarah, not holding her reins, not having to. Sarah leaned into her harness and brought Nadja forward. Within six steps the two mules had the tandem barges moving slightly faster than the meager southbound current, and settled into the pace they would maintain until the canal basin.

Aaron began picking up biscuits from the basket and whistled to Isaac. Isaac whistled as he caught the first biscuit and Simon held up his hands together over his head. Four biscuits sailed in succession to Simons hands. Two he pocketed and two he shared with Toby. Two more stayed with Isaac. Aaron pulled out two for himself. Ben reached into the basket for his first biscuit and bit into it as he snapped his fingers to Aaron and pointed to the little cabin in the center of the barge. Seconds later Aaron came to the stern with a metal cup of steaming coffee. Ben smiled and tilted his head in thanks to his son.

Everybody knows what to do.

An hour later, Ben stepped off the granite wall of the outlet lock in front of the Supervisor's Lockhouse and followed the lock tender up to the office.

"Mr. Pulaski," Stephen McGraw looked up

from his ledger. "You need to pay up all fees before we can let you out into the Bay. New company policy. I see you're in arrears on a couple payments."

Ben frowned at the hated ledger, "I paid up every time I went out. Someone must have missed an entry. It seems to happens a lot, Stephen."

"Sorry Ben, but it says you owe, and it's all I have. Will Boyd sometimes missed things when he was here, but I'm responsible for balancing the books now."

McGraw turned the big book around and pointed to the current total for Pulaski.

"That's more than I ever paid before," Ben complained.

"All rates went up since Mr. Binterfield got on the Canal Board."

Ben exhaled. "God damn that man."

McGraw looked around for his wife, then chuckled. "You ain't the first man to say those words this week, Ben."

"Sooner or later there's going to be murder in this town, Stephen."

"Already been one."

Ben looked up from counting out the fee on the edge of the supervisor's desk. "Murder?"

McGraw picked up the money, counted it quickly, and swept it into the wooden cash box. He spoke as he made payment entries in the ledger and handed Ben a receipt. "Ed Archer. Somebody gut him like a fish. Groin to chest bone. Zig-zag like a lightning bolt they say. Might be another one too."

"How's that?"

"Robert Hannah is missing."

"Robert Hannah? He is a friend of mine. We used to work together building the lock walls."

"Been missing for weeks now."

Ben shoved the receipt into his pocket and walked back out to the *Ugly Boat* carrying a dark scowl on his face. When he stepped back onto the barge Aaron stood looking at him with worry in his eyes. "What is it, son?"

"You, Pa. You look fiercely angry."

Ben forced himself to smile, and shook his head to relieve his son.

I forget that they look to my face to determine the satisfaction of their own lives.

As Aaron turned away to his next duty, Ben stepped quietly to him and grabbed him around his shoulders in a bear hug. He lifted Aaron off his feet and spun him around. When he set him back on his feet, he tussled his hair and chuckled.

"You boys," he said loudly so Isaac would hear as well. "You young men! You are all a father could ask for. I am proud of you and I don't say it enough. Proud," he said.

They smiled at each other.

"More," said Isaac.

"Proud," Ben said.

"More," yelled Aaron.

"Proud," Ben yelled.

Poling the barges through the lock, they waved

at Simon. He had Toby sitting on the back of Sarah, already walking the mules back home. The mule trace was tied to Nadja's back to let their legs swing freely on their way home. Toby ignored the Pulaski's, devoting his attention to the warm penny bag of roasted peanuts Simon bought for him.

The switch of moving *The Turtle* from its tight perch on the *Ugly Boat*'s bow to trailing on a loose line from the stern went smoothly. Occasionally, one of the sons would yell again "More" and Ben would respond with another "Proud!." Isaac shifted to the *Ugly Boat* as *The Turtle* slid by and leant his muscles to raising the mast, dropping the sideboards, and running up the sails. The Mainsail caught the brisk November breeze out of the northwest, and the blunt bow of the *Ugly Boat* was soon churning white water off its edges heading south to Annapolis.

Ben turned over the tiller to Aaron and went below into the cabin to start a fire in the little stove for more coffee. He was still below, preparing to take the fresh coffee on deck for his sons, when Isaac slapped the top of the cabin and yelled.

Ben responded, "Proud!"

Isaac stepped down into the cabin with a big grin on his face. "Pa, I said, 'Pocahontas on the port bow!'. We're coming up on Hackett Point!"

"Already??"

Ben rushed up the steps to the deck and saw the Pocahontas anchored in Whitehall Bay. A man in a blue uniform on the steamship was waving at them to come in his direction. A broad smile spread across Ben's face.

This is going to be a good day after all. With this, I can pay off the Ugly Boat!

---<>---

Herbert Binterfield left a wake of hidden violence within his home on Union Avenue and mounted his carriage for the short ride to his bank. His wife Lydia had confined herself to her room yet again, having the servants bring her all she needed left in the hallway at her door. The bruise on her cheek had just finally faded to the point she could hide it with rouge, but her freshly split lip would take days to recover.

The slave cook worked in a frenzy to prepare another breakfast to replace the one smashed against the wall in the dining room. She knew it too would only grow cold waiting in the upstairs hallway, untouched by the Mistress. She cooked it nonetheless, her daughter crouched in the corner of the Kitchen, sobbing. The master had beaten her with a walking cane for spilling coffee on his shirt.

The clock across the street from the bank clanged its discontent as Binterfield arrived a full thirty minutes later than usual. Briscoe and the cashier were hovering near the front door as Binterfield stepped down from the carriage. Binterfield raised his walking cane to poke the carriage driver in his side, then looked around and lowered his cane. "Get that wheel greased before you come back this afternoon," he ordered.

Binterfield offered Briscoe a cold smile as he entered. "Are they serving the warrant this morning?"

"Yes, sir."

"Go get my mail," he ordered.

Briscoe quickly left the bank and made his way to the center of town. His first stop was to the tavern on Market Street for a leisurely breakfast and a second cup of coffee. The tavern keeper was always quick to serve him and knew his preferences, bobbing his head energetically at Briscoe's smallest request. Briscoe lingered, smoking a cigar, and then left behind more than enough money for his breakfast. He meandered into the new department store, and casually walked the aisles looking at various pieces of merchandise. He halted at a display case showing an ivory handled knife with a long blade of fine steel. "I'll have that knife," he told the shopkeeper.

"Yes, Mr. Briscoe."

Briscoe visited the post office to collect the mail for his real estate company, for Tidewater Bank and Trust, and that for the Binterfield household. It was enough to fill his satchel with a bulge. After leaving the Post Office, he took a few minutes to browse in a book store, but bought nothing. Turning into a shady lane parallel to Union Avenue, he walked past the rear of several prestigious homes and lingered behind the home of Herbert Binterfield. He pulled his watch out of his pocket and stared at it a long moment, then walked up the brick path past the outhouse to the servants entrance, which he opened with his own key. Moments later, he opened the door to Lydia's room.

Barely dressed, with her wig tossed onto her dressing table, Lydia froze in the midst of brushing the rust colored tuft that blanketed her head. She spun around, her eyes wide and red.

"You have mail from St. Mary's County, Mrs. Binterfield."

She threw herself into his arms.

"Oh, Sam," she cried. "I can't stand this much longer."

---<>---

Deputy Sheriff Lyle Mattingly, flanked by two other deputies carrying rifles, walked into the First National Bank on Washington Street. He had his badge pinned to the outside of his coat, so it could be easily seen. He demanded to see the Manager. Moments later, a cashier invited him behind the small barred counter and into the manager's office.

Before the manager could ask any questions, Mattingly announced, "Sir, you have in your employ a clerk named Nathaniel Brown, who is a past employee of the Tidewater Bank and Trust, and for whom this is a warrant for his arrest on the criminal charges of embezzlement."

The manager's eyes enlarged and his mouth dropped open, but he could say nothing.

"Take me to him," Mattingly demanded.

With his mouth still open, the manager awkwardly pointed to the wall on his left. Mattingly stepped to the next door in the hall and opened it. Nathan Brown looked up from his ledger and set down his pencil.

"Nathaniel Brown," Mattingly announced, "you are under arrest for the crime of embezzlement." Even as he spoke, the other two deputies swept around Nathan's desk, pulled him up by his elbows and clamped manacles on his wrists. Nathan babbled a series of questions, requests and emphatic demands, but his comments were ignored by the deputies.

The bank manager stood at his doorway in silent observance as Nathan was led away. He followed them out into the front room as they left and instructed his cashier to return to his window. Then the manager stepped out onto the boardwalk, lowered his head and took in a deep breath. He made his way up the stairs on the side of the building to the office of his tenant and walked in without knocking. "They have taken Nathan to Bel Air," he said.

George Milton released a heavy sigh and slowly shook his head. "I'll get my coat and hat."

---<>---

The next morning, Ben and his sons made their way onto the deck of the *Ugly Boat* to a world of white. During the night the temperature had plummeted. Clouds of vapor surrounded their heads as they spoke. There was an inch of snow on every surface. The water around the barges in Annapolis Harbor was frozen into thin sheets of ice.

"We need to get what we can, boys," Ben said. "This may just be a quick freeze and then it'll thaw, but we can't chance it."

Ben ignored his sons' dashes into areas of unspoiled snow to scoop up snowballs as they made their way to the ironmonger.

"We need to get as many stove parts as we can. They will sell quickly in Havre de Grace and Wrightsville. Nothing like the first freeze to make people pay attention to getting warm. I am going to the wool shop, and will meet you back at the boats."

By noon, the temperature still hovered slightly below freezing and the ice on the water was approaching a half-inch thick. There was only a gentle frigid wind and the sky above Annapolis was turning gray from the columns of black coal smoke rising into the air like onyx tree trunks, feathered in unison near the top. Carts from the iron monger and wooler lined the wharf near the barges, and men moved in lines like ants to move their products down into the holds. Aaron and Isaac took frequent turns eyeing the barges from the deck and from the wharf to ensure they kept level in the water. Most of the iron went into the *Ugly Boat*, while the wool went into *The Turtle* to lessen the drag against its pull. Ben smiled at the sight as he returned with his last parcels. He carried a bag of tulip bulbs for Sonja and Margaret, according to their specific orders. He also had a leather bag holding his father's pistols, fitted with new firing mechanisms in place of the flint locks, and a box of firing caps.

Once the hold covers were wedged in place, the barges were freed from the wharf and the *Ugly Boat* set sails. The wind was lethargic and still out of the northwest, and an hour later they were not yet out into the Bay. Begrudgedly, they pulled out the sweeps, long cumbersome oars, and trudged through the ice sheets beyond Greenbury Point into Annapolis Roads. The wind was stronger there, but still out of the northwest. They would have to sail at angles to the wind, tacking back and forth across it, sailing miles east and west to gain hundreds of yards to the north. It was hard sailing. Watching the oncoming shoreline for hazards as they ran toward shallow water again and again, and working stiff canvas sails and cold stiffened hemp lines at the end of each run. The configuration of the tiller, the sails, the lines and the direction of the barge had to be switched at the end of each run. Changing tack had to be accomplished quickly, otherwise the wind would shove the bow southward, and hours of sailing added just to regain the spot lost at a missed tack.

Sundown came and the wind increased, but at least it veered slightly, giving them a little more push along their runs and a little less resistance when they tacked. Using lights on the shore, they continued to sail well into the night. All three men showed bloody knuckles and split fingernails from working the canvas and hemp. Once tacking was completed at the end of a run, Ben would send his sons down into the cabin to get warm. The waves had grown and slammed against the hulls of the barges. The bucking of the *Ugly Boat* gave too much risk to keep a fire burning in the little iron stove, so the cabin only provided a barrier to the wind, but not the cold. The clouds blew away, leaving a black sky filled with brilliant stars and a bright silver moon. The temperature dropped further and brought a harsher sound to the waves crashing against the hull as more ice formed in the water. The water in the Bay was less salty above Annapolis, and the fresher water froze before salty.

The moon was lower in the western sky when Ben spotted the lighthouse at Turkey Point. It should have been a welcomed sight, getting closer to Havre de Grace. With only a few more miles to go, the wind shifted again from the northwest, stronger and colder, pushing them south. Tacking would no longer work. The longer they stayed on open water the farther away from Havre de Grace they would drift.

"Shit!"

Ben pushed the tiller hard to the left, turning the bow up into the Elk River, and ran before the wind.. They would not make it home tonight. With the wind giving much of its power to the mainsail, the pair of barges made good time up the river and within fifteen minutes sailed into Piney Creek Cove. The shoreline gave them a welcomed barrier from the bitter cold wind. Ben and his sons dropped anchors from both the bow and the stern of the *Ugly Boat*.

"Isaac, I need you to settle on the Turtle, tonight," Ben said.

They hauled in the tow line to *The Turtle* so. Isaac could cross *The Turtle*. They could not anchor the boats too close together, for fear of the wind shoving the barges into one another. Isaac would have to spend the rest of the night on *The Turtle*. He let out another fifty feet of towline and dropped the bow and stern anchors. They waved at one another, then dashed into their cabins to start fires in the iron stoves and drive the chill from their bodies. Each barge had a tin of white bean soup strapped to one leg of the iron stove. It was the tradition on the canal, and the weather always changed.

Aaron started the stove fire while Ben lit the lamp and pulled out a pot for cooking. He took the pot on deck, tied a small line to it and dropped it into the cove. Ice had already formed around the hull, so he had to use a grappling hook to break an opening for the pot. A hundred feet away Isaac was doing the same thing.

"Good night, Pa," he yelled.

"Get warm, son," Ben answered.

He will be safe there, but I wish he was with us.

Alone on *The Turtle*, Isaac slipped back down into the cabin and set the pot of water on top of the iron stove. The fire within the stove was already crackling, and the cabin was growing comfortably warm.

"The captain is aboard, mateys," he bellowed. "Come here, seaman Aaron. Take off the Captain's shoes before I have you flogged!"

He yanked off his shoes and placed them in the gravel filled box under the stove, then he placed his hands on his hips.

"You there, Benjamin. Start my soup right away!"

He opened the tin, poured the contents into the pot, and stirred. He sat down on a nearby chair, resting his feet on the little iron ring that circled the stove, feeling the heat warm his toes. He leaned back in the chair with his hands linked behind his head and surveyed his solitary domain, and smiled.

My own space!

In front of the Pulaski house, Sonja stood on the little dock where the barges usually tied up and looked down at the ice in the canal.

"You stop it," She yelled at the ice. "You hear me? I'll have none of this. Not before they come home!"

It was a long night, waiting for her family to come home.

I hate the night.

---<>---

Before the winter freeze, the *Ugly Boat* made one more trip to Annapolis towing *The Turtle* and Anthony's Wilhelmina, each barge nearly full to bursting with Pennsylvania coal, and every nugget of it bought by the Weems Line at four times the usual prices. The Weems Line managed to finally break the price gouging by Annapolis and Baltimore colliers. The suppliers were left with huge surpluses of unsold coal in the spring that ultimately drove the prices back down.

On the first of December, Ben visited the Tidewater Bank and Trust to pay off his note on the *Ugly Boat*. Binterfield would not receive him personally, but directed his cashier to accept Ben's payment. As the clerk wrote out the receipt for payment and noting the loan was paid in full, he glanced back at Binterfield who refused to even look in Ben's direction. The clerk leaned over the counter toward Ben.

"I understand that you are a friend of Nathan Brown?"

"Yes, so be careful what you say, mister," Ben responded.

"I am, too. His charges were dropped," he whispered. He glanced back toward Binterfield again, then continued, "Insufficient evidence." In a louder voice, he said, "That will be all, sir."

"Not quite, mister. I need to pay my rent. Pretty soon I may be able to pay that off as well."

The clerk made out a receipt and handed it to Ben. He tapped his fingertips on the counter and frowned. "I'm sorry, Mr. Pulaski, but I have orders from Mr. Binterfield. I am to give you this upon receipt of your rental payment."

The clerk slid a piece of paper torn from the county newspaper. It was a list of local real estate for sale. The last parcel at the bottom of the paper was circled.

Lapidum

Lovely small farm on Canal

House and Barn in excellent condition

$100,000.00

Ben stared at the paper. "This is ridiculous! That's two hundred times what it's worth! No one would pay that!"

"I think that is the point, Mr. Pulaski," the clerk whispered.

Ben glared at Binterfield, who sat there beaming at him with a broad smile that wrinkled his eyes and spread over his entire face.

Ben stormed out of the bank and bumped into Samuel Briscoe. Ben began to apologize until he realized who the other man was, and grabbed his coat collar. "Are you insane, Briscoe?"

"No. NO, I am not." He pulled Ben's hands off his coat. "Look, Pulaski, that was not my idea. The bank owns my business. Hell, the bank IS the business. Binterfield set that price, just to keep you from buying it."

Ben stood there, glaring at Briscoe, not hearing him speak, only hearing the roaring in his ears, gritting his teeth, balling his fists, struggling to control himself.

"I want us to be disconnected, Pulaski. I don't want any more of this. Just pay your rent."

Briscoe stepped around Ben and went into the bank. Ben took in several deep breaths and twisted his head slowly to release the tension in his neck. He blew his breath out and then walked away, toward Union Avenue. He stopped on St. John Street to speak with the furrier. He and Simon had been trapping beaver to keep them from damaging the canal waterways, and had several pelts cured in his barn. The furrier would be happy to have them and offered a handsome price, so Ben agreed to deliver them on his next trip into town. He went to the Post Office next and found a letter addressed to him. He read it standing in the post office while others stepped around him.

He took the letter with him and stopped at a tavern on Market Street, where he ordered a coffee and read the letter again, slowly and carefully. The writing was sharp, neatly penned, with no faded tails in the ink at the end of letters, or fat drops at the beginning of them, like his own. The signature was not as clear, the hand holding the pen not as steady as the one that wrote the letter. Still the signature was legible, and one he had seen before. Andrew Jackson. He stuffed the letter into his coat, paid for his coffee, and headed back to Lapidum as quickly as he could walk on the frozen towpath.

Sonja read the letter three times. Her lips smiled, but they trembled. Tears slipped down from her eyes. "I am so happy for Isaac," she said. "But, I am not so ready for this. Summer is not far away, Ben. He will have to leave then."

Ben rubbed her shoulder, letting his thumb glide against her neck and cheek. "It is a short preparatory class during the summer, then the full thing starts in the early Fall."

"Have you told him yet?"

"No, Sonja. I thought we should do that together."

"It is too soon," she said. She lowered her head and wept.

The winter trudged along, simply endured. There were vignettes of milestones, of completed lists, accomplished work, and chores that ran into their thoughts when they were dwelling on the quick passage of time. Spring would mark the beginning of real preparations. It would be too real then. The more they dreaded the Spring and the more they urged it to stay at bay, the more it seemed to rapidly approach. It was the shadow omen of the sundial moving inescapably toward a noon only moments away, they did not want to arrive.

But to Isaac, winter was slathered in molasses. Each day crawled by and seemed to contain a hundred painful hours. The calendar stood mockingly untainted by his desire to rush over the dates toward Spring, as if it would require the entire Spring for him to pack. Time was building a wall around him that would forever prevent Spring's arrival. His mind and his heart shared a common beat, echoing the pounding syllables repeating the same phrase a thousand times a day.

I am going to West Point!

---<>---

The view across the river was easy through the bare limbs. The leaves were long gone, and both the canal and the river were hard frozen. Ben stood on the porch and waved to Forrest McMallery, trotting his cargo rig across the ice from Port Deposit. Forrest had temporarily closed his blacksmith shop and was selling his surplus coal across the river in Port Deposit. He had made horseshoes with iron points that grabbed the ice, and hauled his coal across the river ice in a coal sled. The upper Bay, even close in to Perryville, was frozen as well, but the brackish water farther south let brave watermen bring up their oysters.

Forrest shared the tie-up Isaac had rigged at the river shore. He huffed up the bank and across the plank walkway Isaac had built on the canal ice, leading his mule.

"Morning to ya, Benjamin," yelled Forrest in his customary hearty tone, his breath clouding over his head like white railroad smoke. The sky was palest blue, with only the faintest touch of cotton fiber. It stretched for miles overhead like strands of spider silk plucked from the horizon. Painfully bright beams of sunshine lanced between the bare tree limbs, finding angles and chips in the ice to dazzle the observer with explosions of light. Mac's face was lost in the dark shadow hiding from the sunlight as Ben squinted to look in his direction.

"Good morning, Mac. How are the good people of Port Deposit this morning?"

"Cold as hell and eager for baskets of coal," he chuckled."Are you going south on the ice again today?"

"Yes. The mules had an easy time of it, since you shod them with your ice shoes. I still think you should keep your shop open to make more of those."

"I'm afraid only you and I would be the customers, Ben. Bring me back some oysters, will you?"

"Easily done, Mac. Most of the load will be just that."

Forrest waved over his shoulder as he passed between the porch and the Barn, then turned down the lane toward the short Pulaski bridge over Herring Run into Lapidum. He said good morning to Simon who was emerging from the barn leading Sarah and Nadja, with Toby trotting close behind. Simon and Toby wore thick coats and the new thick wool head covers Sonja had knitted and given them at Christmas. Old blankets draped across the backs of the mules.

"Where are the boys, Ben," Simon asked.

"Just takes two to handle the hauling sled..." Ben started, but then noticed the frown crawling across Toby's face. "That is, er, it just takes us three men to handle the sled. So, I sent the boys up on the ridge to cut firewood while we're gone."

Toby's infectious smile re-appeared, and a swagger blossomed into his walk. Each man took the reins of a mule and led them down the slope and across the canal. Ben, Simon and Toby kept to the plank walkway, while the mules walked on the ice. Once across the canal and over the towpath to the river, they attached the mules to the doubletree trace at the front of the cargo sled. While Sarah was mistress of the singletree trace and controlled it leading Nadja, it was Nadja that took first to the doubletree trace, walking side by side with Sarah. Even after weeks of pulling next to Nadja, she still balked occasionally. This morning she turned and bit Nadja, who went into a kicking frenzy.

"Sarah is the most loyal mule I've ever seen," Ben said, "But she doesn't like a partner worth a damned."

Ben had said this several times before, and Simon always answered the same, but before Simon spoke, Toby placed his mittened fists on his hips and gave his impression of Simon, "Just like some women!"

Ben and Simon laughed loudly, surprised by the act. Simon snatched Toby up into the air and tossed him onto the packing straw in the cargo sled.

As Ben and Simon settled onto their places on the seat board, Ben asked, "Are you sure you are ready to go into Havre de Grace?"

"Mattingly seemed to accept my story, when he approached me early in November. I showed him my papers, and explained that my real name was Silas." He reached into his coat, "You wanna smell my papers, massah?"

Ben just crinkled his nose, shaking his head as he slapped the reins on the mule haunches and the sled moved south. Watermen and cargo sleds formed a chain of transport to move the fresh oysters up from the mouth of the Bush River to Havre de Grace. The Washington to Philadelphia Railroad was hungry for oysters in each direction. With the tracks actually laid on the ice, rail cars were loaded directly from cargo sleds midway across the river. The price of oysters was almost too high for the people around Havre de Grace, except the well-to-do and restaurants – and those with the energy to go get them farther south. Ben's sled simply trotted passed Havre de Grace and went the extra miles south of Spesutie.

North of the Bush River, oyster sleds, pulled up onto the ice near the shore, were selling to anyone at a reasonable price. Ben and Simon filled the sled to capacity, and made the six hour return trip. They stopped in Port Deposit, selling several baskets of oysters to two restaurants and the Union Hotel.

"This is all our profit for today," Ben said, handing half to Simon. "All the rest of the oysters are for us and our friends."

"What about the cost of those fancy ice horseshoes Forrest put on the mules," Simon asked.

Ben tilted his head back at the baskets of oysters still in the cargo sled. "That is all the payment Forrest asked for. He wanted one, so he's getting two. That still leaves a basket for John and Margaret. And..." Ben grinned like a schoolboy, "Since Sonja doesn't like them, all the rest are going into an oyster boil, we'll build in the front yard!"

That evening, the aroma of steaming oysters drifted among the homes of Lapidum. The cold quiet was broken occasionally by singing, and a single gunshot here and there, loud laughing, and children allowed to stay up and stay out much longer than they should. At midnight, as December faded into yesterday, 1843 arose into a black sky filled with brilliant stars and the barest crescent of a new moon. More gunshots were heard around a bonfire blazing in front of the lockhouse at Lapidum. Sonja stood near the fire wrapped in three wool blankets. She leaned close to Ben and kissed him on his cheek, "Happy Birthday, Ben."

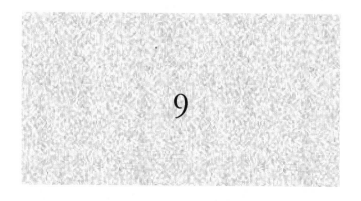

9

Early April brought rain, and the return of the Raven. She slipped back into her private berth on Spesutie Island under a gentle shower, her holds stinking with the misery of a hundred stolen lives, but empty and hungry for a new cargo. The scent made worse by the dampness. The crew settled in for a rare restful afternoon, and prepared for a hard nights work.

When darkness settled in, there was only a quarter moon lingering low in a dark vaporous sky, the weak pretense of moon glow providing precious little light to the six men straining at the oars of the launch. Eight men could have easily taken seats next to the thole pins within the launch and still left room for the Captain to be undisturbed in his thoughts at the tiller, but six could do it. They needed the room in the boat for their cargo. This was the first harvesting night. This was the night for special cargo. Hoagg would have them fly over the water, if he had the power. They rowed past the shantytown near Concord point, leaving old hunting grounds until later in the season.

It was almost as easy as taking baby seals on the arctic icepacks – just wade through the herds with a club, bashing heads until the arm was too tired to swing anymore. But this cargo would bring far better prices than even seal skins.

Hoagg watched the only bright light on the distant shore slip past on his west as they came even with the Concord Point Lighthouse. They continued the long pull north through the last of the upper Bay and into the mouth of the Susquehanna River. The tide was still coming in and there had been no heavy rain lately, so the pull was tolerable to the men. He did not want to risk a long pull with a heavy cargo racing before dawn back to Spesutie Sound. They would go as far north as they planned and work their way back south. Hoagg looked back toward the Lighthouse, not seeing, but knowing the point was there and knowing around that point was the shanty town near the boat builder, where they could take at least two more blacks without waking the others. Hoagg chuckled to himself, enjoying his own game.

A light burned at the stern of the odd railroad steamship nestled into its place on the western shore at the mouth of the river, enduring the long wait for the six o'clock northbound train from Washington City still three hours away. It waited for its chance to be a steamship again for the brief three quarter mile trip carrying the train to the eastern shore of the river, where it would then wait for the southbound train from Philadelphia later in the day. The slowly rising column of steam and smoke from the engine stack blended to gray and drifted up to merge with the haze of settling clouds.

We will soon have fog on the ground.

Hoagg steered the launch closer to the darkened lock house to keep his distance from the steamboat. He did not want the night deckhand to see them pass. The moon glow faded and the crescent moon winked out as the sky filled with weak clouds and more haze. The shore became only a slightly darker dark in a world painted in charcoal hues. Hoagg steered the launch to the east of Garrett's Island, just inside the mouth of the Susquehanna, finally blocking any chance of a steamship's view of the launch.

Swirls in the black water kissed the bottom of the launch, slapped at the rudder, and gurgled past the stern as south flowing river water danced with the incoming brackish tide. The river simply dove under the tide at the mouth of the river and let the tip of the brackish Chesapeake Bay slip over it while it continued its race to join the other cold water flows of the Elk and the Sassafras rivers in the deeper channels. A weak moon meant a weak tide, but it had helped get them this far, and wind had been kind as well. Soon the men pulled beyond the fringes of the bay water and began straining against the full current of the river itself in its own domain. The sky and the river were only slightly lighter shades of coal than the mass of rising shore to the west and the tree studded boulder island to the east. Hoagg thrummed his fingers on the tiller handle, eager to be in action, wanting to scream at his men to pull harder and faster, but knowing they would not, knowing they ought not. He needed their strength to do the night's work, even after the long pull to Lapidum. There was going to be joyous hell on earth at the Pulaski farm.

---<>---

Ben had kicked off his cover and awoke in a chill as the mantle clock struck three times. He lay

154

hoping to return to his sleep, but was still awake when the clock chimed at the half hour. He was eager to be on his way, knowing just the people to contact to sell his cargo quickly. She felt him stir, but he kissed Sonja and convinced her to stay in bed, rather than get up to fix coffee and breakfast.

Within an hour, Simon and Aaron were up. The *Ugly Boat* and *The Turtle* were already configured and loaded, so once the mules were hitched, the trip to Wrightsville and back became only a two-man job. Ben looked at each of his sons standing on the deck of the *Ugly Boat* and decided to send Isaac and Simon back to bed.

"Thanks, Ben. I don't think it would be good for Toby to go through the line again, and I wouldn't want to leave him here alone," Simon said.

Aaron was happy to have his father to himself for a while and Isaac was happy to have the luxury of sleeping until sunrise. Almost instantly, with little more than a grin and a grunt, Isaac returned to the house. As he crossed the swing bridge with Simon at the lock, he tapped on the door for John Bartlett. John had already risen when the mules trotted out over the wooden bridge earlier, and knew it would not be long until it was time to swing the bridge out of the way for Ben's barges.

Minutes later, Ben initialed the clipboard under candle light and whistled for Aaron to walk the mules. Aaron's lamp moved northward on the towpath and the line from the bow of *The Turtle* straightened with tension, then the barge slipped quietly out of the lock into the gentle southward current of the canal. As soon as the stern of the *Ugly Boat* drifted out of the lock, John closed the lock gates behind it. He returned the swing bridge across the canal, and quick-stepped in his slippers back to the lockhouse and his bed. He could still sleep another hour, knowing that no one else would waste good money walking mules on the towpath by lamp light. He shook his head as he stepped back up on the porch.

Lamp oil is just too damned expensive. A man might as well burn money!

The Pulaski farm slept quietly, and quieter still as the mist sank closer to the ground to absorb the little sounds that drifted in the night air near the river. One of the mules in the barn grunted in the dark and shifted in its stall, stamping its left hind foot at a sensed field mouse tittering through the litter hay on its nightly rounds. The last of the embers within the iron stove in the kitchen faded within the mound of wood ash at its center, the coarse black metal sides cooled from the long ago supper and sitting silently in the corner of the kitchen. The clock on the Pulaski mantel in the front room continued to tick away the night, slowly advancing the minute hand, so it could give a faithful accounting of the hours lost during the night, when its owners came to consult it in the morning.

Sonja slid her feet out from her curled position under the quilts and then brought them back again to the warmth near her body, and away from the cold inner surfaces they found without a second body there to give them heated space to stretch. She sighed a faint call across her pillow and formed her hand in front of her sleeping face to hold something not there, but within a jumbled dream pretending to be real. She rolled onto her back to cast away the dream for a more agreeable one, her hand slipping on its own under the covers to where Ben usually slept. She released a heavy breath and her neck muscles relaxed further, letting her face tilt deeper into the pillow as she slid into the full embrace of sleep. Her lingering consciousness of cool feet and troublesome dreams were left on that higher place as it followed her down into the soft black velvet of deep sleep.

---<>---

Hoagg shifted in his seat and said nothing in the darkness.

Pulaski.

Pulaski and his woman.

He recalled the vision of her running toward him in the street. Her breasts and thighs outlined by the thin fabric of her dress.

And that uppity nigger, Simon.

He always said he would sell that bastard if he ever got the chance.

Pulaski.

Hoagg touched his fingertips to the wide scar running down his abdomen and looked farther up the western bank of the river. He had told several men in his past that he would gut them like a fish, had always liked the terrifying picture the threat made. Had even tried it once in an alley when his opponent had wasted all his strength in a knife fight far from over, but was interrupted almost as soon as he started and had to leave the man trying to push his own entrails back inside a hole bigger than his hand. Already tired from his first knife fight, then, he had faced Pulaski.

All that trouble over a little Chinese boy that probably would have starved to death any way.

Hoagg grinned broadly into the night, a low guttural sound escaping briefly from his throat.

Tonight there will be no stopping it. Pulaski held onto his own table, watching what I do to his woman. Simon in chains.

"Cap'n, suh? You say somthin, Cap'n?", said a faceless voice in the darkness.

"Row, God damn you."

Two haloed lights came into view on the eastern shore of the river, now only a hundred yards away. Barely light enough to see a brick building and dozen boat masts.

"Port Deposit" he grunted, and pushed the tiller over, sending them directly toward the western shore, toward Lapidum, toward the Pulaski farm.

There was no shore to step upon on the outside of the canal wall. The launch bumped and shoved along the wall until worked block gave way to piled stones and he finally found a foothold for a step off the boat. Several loud thumps rose into the gathering night mist and echoed off the water. Just beyond the berm the men were mounting, another sound arose not of their own making and all froze in position, not even seeing the hand Hoagg raised to stop them, but stopping of their own instinct. There was a small flash in the darkness of house tucked against the blackness of the hillside, followed by the spreading yellow glow of a freshly lighted lantern. The men sank in their footsteps to bring their silhouettes closer to the edge of the berm. A door swung open clearly outlining a man in a night shirt. The man stepped onto his porch and raised the lantern high above his head, then bent forward to peer into the night mist.

"Who's out there?" the man yelled, but the men hiding at the bank made no movement and no sound. He stepped off the porch and brought the globe of light into the yard, the yellow sphere reaching barely twenty feet into the mist, and moving with him as he walked. The faint light touched the edge of the swing bridge across the canal and the man peered into the lock and up at the holding pond above. A muffled voice came from within the house, not carrying words just the sound of a question.

Probably his wife, Hoagg thought.

The man answered back toward the house. "Don't see anything. Probably just a log in the river." Again, the voice sounded from within the house. Fainter. The message unmistakable even to the men hiding in their stillness on the berm of the canal. Come back to bed.

"I'm coming," the man said.

Hoagg stepped out onto the towpath and silently thanked the man for coming out into the dark with the lantern. He had forgotten about the canal, and would have waded through the canal water. Instead he could cross at the swing bridge. He was too far north, but only by a couple hundred yards. Binterfield had described the arrangement at Lapidum, saying the Pulaski place was the most southern, and the locktender's house the most northern. He could see the lighter band of stone foundation wall to the left of the locktender's house.

Higher up would be the dry goods store and tavern, and other smaller houses stepped into the hillside. The road ran between the houses and the canal, and then up the hill itself to Webster. A lesser wagon trail continued along the canal beyond the turn in the road. That was the trail to Pulaski.

Hoagg shifted the large knife hanging in its sheath from his belt and stepped out onto the towpath toward the swing bridge. He made a first clomp of wooden boot heel onto the oak boards of the bridge, hearing the sound echoed in the stone and water chamber below the wooden walkway, and threw out his arm to halt the others as well.

"Walk on yer toes," he whispered to the others. "Or we'll sound like a herd of shod horses crossing this damned thing." The last man across clomped twice at the end of the boards, almost falling while trying to find the earth for his feet. Hoagg reached out to swat him in the darkness for his clumsiness, but missed the man's head. Again, the seven men stopped as one and listened for a sound coming from the locktender's house, but no light came on. They resumed their walk along the edge of the dirt road between the canal below and the shops above. The road bent sharply to the right and left them to go its own way up the hill. They found the short bridge over the creek and the wagon trail that continued through the stand of trees to the Pulaski Farm.

Within the trees, it was completely dark on both sides of the gang. The men used the gray of the open yard in front of the farmhouse beyond the trees as their guide point, walking slowly, feeling ahead in the darkness. Out of the trees, they crossed the open yard just above the two great oaks nearer the canal, then made their way toward the shape of the house and found the porch and its step. The plank of the step in front of the porch gave slightly under the weight of the first two men to use it, squeaking slightly in protest to the weight. A single clomp arose from the porch boards and the men resumed an ungainly duck-walk they had employed on the bridge. Hoagg was next onto the step, his knife already out of its sheath and hungry to taste someone. He turned slightly, pushing his other hand against the chest of the man behind him and whispered instructions to go with the last man and look into the barn. Slowly five men on the porch felt their way to the door, letting their fingers tell them how it was made and if there were hinges or handle, seeking the quickest – and easiest - way inside. The windows on either side of the door would give them quick entry, but Hoagg did not want to stumble over jagged glass edges in the lightless night. If the door had no bar behind it, he would go through the doorway.

Sonja lay unmoved from the same position she had taken when she surrendered to a deep sleep. She had drifted into the bedroom earlier, half asleep even as she came to bed, secure in the safety of her house. The open bedroom doorway let in the tock of the mantel clock. The dishes waited patiently in the kitchen wash pan. The door bar that was meant to be placed nightly within its braces, leaned against the wall, waiting for someone to remember it.

Hoagg positioned one thick-necked seaman in front of the door, ready to charge his shoulder against it, and the other man in front of the window holding the chair found on the porch. If the door did not give, then the chair would go through the window. They would charge into the house and have Pulaski at knife point before he could struggle out of his sleep. Hoagg rolled the knife handle within his hand, rotating the razor edge full circle on its axis, letting the cutting edge sniff the air. The blood in his arteries rushed up his neck and pounded in his ears. His breathing was shallow. The sounds of the world were muffled in the gathering fog forming in his head. He withdrew within himself, still seeing and ready to command, but looking out from a deeper place, where the blood pounded. He bathed himself in his rising animal anger, ready to let it run loose.

Hoagg looked toward the waiting men inches away from him, only seeing their forms, knew they were coiled like him, springs ready to shoot into action. The pounding in his ears replaced all sound. The thumping in his chest and the sound of his own breathing was lost to him. He could feel something inside wanting to explode at moments like this. He would let it out soon, to become more than himself. He would allow himself to do all that he dreamed about doing in the silent rages that frequented his mind. His penis was in full erection. His mouth filled with juices, and he swallowed in delicious anticipation. He lingered only long enough to enjoy the sensations once again, arriving at the moment when he could totally release himself to his most depraved cravings. He gripped the knife handle, keeping the point directly ahead, the keen edge up and begging to be fed.

His voice trembled only slightly in the excitement, but had to be forced out a second time before it could escape his throat and flow out from the pounding storm raging in his head. "Go!"

The door exploded inward ahead of the seaman's shoulder, the wooden latch shooting across the room, the door slammed back against the wall, and against the unused bar. The man at the window, so primed for his act, began it even though it was no longer necessary. He sent the chair smashing though the panes and thin wood frames of the window. Shattered glass sprayed into the front room. Glass shards and sharp edged geometric beads flew onto the floor and the large woven oval rug in the middle.

Sonja sat up in her bed, not yet knowing why she was sitting and wondered if she had dreamed a sound that was not there. Three men rushed into the room, the window smasher still taking the doorway rather than chancing the raw glass edges of his work. They looked quickly to see the layout of the interior, and were aided to the bedroom by the sound of Sonja yelling.

"What?-"

Fighting off her stupor, she forced her mind to crawl up from her deep pit of sleep.

Men fell onto the bed to grab Ben Pulaski and the woman that was in bed with him. Sonja screamed into the night. The night room air filled with thuds and clomps and heavy breathing and curses of strange men. Furniture was tossed about in the blackness slamming into the walls and each other in the madness. A thick hand emerged from the darkness and grabbed Sonja by the hair and yanked her to the floor. A boot heel stepped on her hand almost breaking her thumb. The men pummeled and grabbed at the covers reaching for their main victim. Half curses and half-spoken questions were shrieked into the air of the room.

Bed covers were torn from the bed. The mattress tossed against the opposite wall as angry hands and fingers grabbed again and again for the body of the man who was not there.

Sonja was grabbed again and quickly discarded aside, then held in place against the lower wall and floor by a boot in her abdomen, to keep her down and out of the way. Heavy breathing filled the room. Unwashed bodies smelling of sweaty wool, tar and tobacco and old fish, heated from the exertion and the excitement, but still unfulfilled by combat. They stood back from the bed in the returning quiet to sort out what had happened and await the next action.

Someone struck a flint in the room and the spark exploded light for an instant and left colored spots shooting through blackness in front of Sonja's eyes. The man holding his boot into her abdomen, shifted to improve his balance, driving his foot slowly and painfully deeper into her and forcing a moan from her as his weight settled from his other foot. The spark erupted twice more from the area near the chest of drawers Ben had brought down from Wrightsville. The flame in the oil lamp caught, first blue then faint dirty orange yellow and then grew to fill the room with bright yellow. Shadows of the men were thrown up to the ceiling, dark giant copies of the men standing around her. Then the shadows retreated down onto the walls as the flame and the light grew. The faces of the intruders gained detail and turned to look down at the half dressed woman pinned to the wall and the floor. Her nightgown was crumpled around her waist and the beauty of her milk white legs gleamed in their eyes.

Ice cold terror swept through Sonja's body. She

shuddered and fought the nausea clawing its way up from the boot in her abdomen, and the dread seeping from her spine into her heart and throat. Hoagg looked down and recognized the fear in this woman's face, and smiled.

10

"Stand her up!" Hoagg commanded and his men grabbed Sonja by her arms, putting their hands under her armpits to raise her up, leveraging her shoulders and forcing her on to her toes.

"Get out of here" she yelled. "My husband will be home any minute with his friends!"

"Good."

She smelled the soured chewing tobacco and rum that were frequent inhabitants of his mouth.

"You won't think it's good when he gets here and teaches you all how to behave."

The men around her chuckled and looked longingly at her form barely contained within the cotton bloomers and shift. Hoagg stepped closer, putting his pock marked nose within inches of hers and looked deeply into her eyes. He brought his knife blade up between their faces.

"Your Ben done taught ol'Randall a lesson. And I been studying on it fer over three years. Now I come to pay it back – with interest."

He moved the tip of the large blade from his face to gently trace its point across her cheek near her left eye. Tiny feathers of steel laid along the razor edge to the blade, put there by the grind stone. Her body trembled, and her breath caught in her throat. He was drawn to her fear, her trembling begging him to go farther, to indulge himself, to satisfy his craving. She shivered and pushed up with her toes to lessen the pain burning in her shoulder joints, but the men only pushed up on her arm pits more to keep the strain. The skin on her arms sent a wave of goose bumps, standing the hairs on her arms, hardened her nipples pushing them against the thin cotton from inside, begging him to act.

---<>---

In the barn, Simon sat up listening to the sounds coming from the house. He went to Toby's bunk, placing his hand over the boy's mouth. When Toby stirred, he whispered into his ear.

"Stay quiet. There's trouble at the house."

Toby had spent months traveling in the woods with his Uncle Jedediah. Knew to stay quiet when he was told. As soon as Simon removed his hand, Toby whispered.

"Slave catchers?"

"Probably worse. Get your shoes on, but you can't have any light right now. I've got to look outside."

Toby obeyed while Simon slipped out of the bunkroom and peeked toward the house from between the edges of the barn door. He had to open the door to see what was happening. Men were standing on the porch. There was a light in the closest bedroom, shadows were dancing across the curtains and he could hear men's voices. He couldn't hear the words, but recognized the tone of desperate men. Silently, he slipped out and made his way to the side of the house. Peeking between the curtain edges, he saw Sonja being held by two men, another man standing in front of her, and a fourth man standing beside him. The man in front of Sonja held a long knife and turned toward the man beside him. Simon saw his face.

Good God Almighty. Randall Hoagg! He was dead!!

Simon heard boots coming off the porch and dashed back to the barn. Gray dawn was in the sky above but a fog was settling on the ground. As soon as he entered the bunkroom he grabbed Toby by the shoulder.

"I need to get you to a safe place."

Light had grown just enough to see each other's face.

"Is it bad, Uncle Simon?"

"You just do what I tell you, and you'll be all right. But you must be absolutely quiet."

Toby nodded yes. They slipped out between the barn doors, and closed them gently behind. Simon stepped to the woodpile and pulled the ax out of the chopping stump. There were men's voices in the front yard. Simon wanted to dash with Toby into the woods, but the dry leaves collecting there and along the wagon trail back to Lapidum would cause too much noise. Instead, he pulled Toby with him, heading toward the back field. As he neared the hog pen, the sow snorted and the nearby chickens began to cluck, so he veered away from them and headed across the open field. At the far edge of the field where the ground rose steeply toward the granite ridge above, he stopped at the base of a strong maple tree.

"Here. You climb up this tree as far as you can get. You stay there until I come back for you, or you know for sure it's safe to come down.

He lifted Toby into the first branch. The little boy whispered. "What if I got to pee?"

"You pee down the back side of the trunk. Don't you let it fall on the leaves, just let it run down the trunk. Now get on up there. I'll be back as soon as I can."

If I can.

Nearing the house again, he saw a man carrying a rifle walk to the barn. The man lit a lantern in the barn. Simon moved back into the field and worked his way around the back of the house and then to the far side. Peeking through the other bedroom window, he saw Isaac getting up from his bed. Simon tapped gently on the window. Isaac stood at his closed door listening to the voices in the rest of the house. Simon tapped on the glass again, hoping it was not too loud.

Two men in the front yard. One went to the barn. Where's the other?

Isaac came to the window and raised it.

"What's happening," he whispered.

"Bad men in the house. You come out here with me so we can figure out what to do."

"No. I need to help Ma!"

---<>---

169

Hoagg sniffed near her neck and the top of her shift, smelled the brass that was mixing with the aroma of the woman that called to him in her fear. Saw the beads of perspiration form on her upper lip and slide down from her forehead to slip into the edge of her eyes, stinging and blurring her vision. She blinked forcefully to keep this man in her vision, to know what was next. Her breathing and his matched in shallow and pace, and he reached up and slowly compressed her right breast in his hand. He stepped back slightly so he could see the breast and his own hand around it, the breast and nipple tight against the fabric almost transparent.

He looked into her eyes, seeing the thing he wanted to be there, seeing her fear and drank it in, swallowed up the brassy air around her becoming a cloud to bathe his face. Slowly he lowered the blade in front of her breast and turned the sharpened edge toward the breast. He watched her twitch and try to pull away knowing it was coming, knowing it would happen no matter how much she screamed, and him wanting her to, needing her to. Slowly and almost delicately he drew the steel feathered razor edge across the outer most layers of skin of her nipple, and listened to the shrill well up inside her throat. He would not let the blade go deep, only enough to find the sense of touch that dwelled just below the surface, where the pain was felt first and most delicious.

Her shrill cry turned into a whimper, a rasping sigh and then a straining groan. The small bead of blood slipped out of the tiny slice in the cotton, stood out shining scarlet in the lamplight, then fell back into the weave of the fabric, spreading out to become a small cherry stain in the cloth. Hoagg looked back into her eyes to drink in the fear once more, to savor it. Her eyes met his, not turning away, not pleading, surrounded by tears but no longer making them, and the blue turned to the shade of the steel in his own knife blade.

She spit into his face. "Go to hell, you sick bastard!"

He fell back away from her wiping the spittle from his eyes and cheek, and drew his left hand back balled into a fist, and even before he could strike she spit again driving his fury almost beyond control. He hit her with a glancing blow, but it still split her lower lip, driving it against her own teeth and filling her mouth with blood. Hoagg brought the knife in front of him, the blade centered below her heart, ready for the killing drive he would use in a successful knife fight. Even as he paused, she turned to her captor on her left and spit a mouthful of blood into his smiling face.

The man loosened his grip on her wrist so he could ball up his own fist, and Hoagg stepped back toward her pushing the blade ahead of him for the kill.

"Bitch!"

But then he stopped himself and held up his hand to the blood spattered face on her left.

"Hold it! Hold it! This ain't the way and this ain't the time. What we do to her we do it in front of her bastard husband."

Hoagg stepped up to her face again and chuckled.

"Spit at me again and I'll break yer jaw, but I won't kill you. You ain't in control here, Bitch. I am. I'll decide when you die, not you."

171

He chuckled again, but the moment was gone. The excitement was swept away by the rising obstinance of the woman.

No pleasure if there's no fear. Not now. Not 'til I have Ben Pulaski tied to watch it. Then I will gut her slowly until I tire of her screams. Tire of hearing Pulaski rage helplessly – No, never tire of that.

"What the Hell is going on here??" John Bartlett stood in the doorway of the bedroom pointing his flintlock musket at the men. The bore of the barrel was large enough to stick a man's finger, and the ball that came out of that barrel would tear a man's arm off, even if it only wounded him. The musket hammer was at full cock and the glassy edges of new flint sparkled in the room light. Neither Hoagg nor any of his men was foolish enough to chance whether the musket would fire properly. It was in perfect condition, and they knew it would be deadly.

"Let her go," John ordered.

Slowly the two men on either side of Sonja relaxed their grip on her and let her sink full onto her feet.

"Oh, John! Thank God you came!"

Before she could say another word the man with the blood spattered face grabbed her again, put his hand over her mouth and his other arm around her waist lifting her off her feet. Sonja's eyes widened and looked into John's face, and she screamed a muffled scream into the huge leather palm covering her mouth, the man behind her speaking into her ear.

"Don't you bite ol'Dicky, woman. Bad things will happen to you if you do."

Hoagg turned full-face to the armed locktender.

Neighbor of this bitch woman. You shoulda stayed in bed Mister.

Hoagg smiled pleasantly at the man even as the man raised the barrel threateningly toward Hoagg's face. The man gave a perplexed look and an arm swept into his view from behind to snatch the barrel up and then yanked the gun from his hand. The other man who had been checking the barn slipped his fighting stick in front of John's throat and pulled back over his shoulders with a hand on either side of his neck. Pulling the stick into his throat harder and harder, it cut off his air almost completely. It threatened to crush the fragile bones in his throat and lifted him almost off his feet. He held him for Hoagg.

Hoagg moved with catlike speed and precision. He buried the blade deep into John's lower abdomen and was already pulling the raw edge back out before John realized that he was being killed. This was what Hoagg wanted. This would feed his knife edge the blood it had been begging to taste. Bartlett tried to scream but the stick against his throat kept him from moving, except to squirm like a caught fish. Hoagg sawed back into his abdomen driving the tip of his knife blade against the back of the man's pelvis. The tip scraped the bone. He pulled the blade upward, sawing the knife up through the meat that held the man's abdomen together.

A shrill gurgle escaped from Bartlett's lips as he

released a scream through his crushed larynx. He and squirmed with his head and pelvis, trying to escape the horrendous pain. The man behind him reasserted his grip on the stick, pulling against the twisting of the locktender. Hoagg continued to work the blade upward toward the chest through cascading blood.

As the locktender looked wide-eyed around the room, struggling to free himself, Hoagg put his face close, sharing his breath, pushing in with his knife, pushing in with his pelvis to give his arm strength, and then pulling up and almost out again, sawing the muscle and tissue. The gash grew and intestines began to slip out of the opening and splash down into the growing puddle of blood at his feet. Again the knife slipped in and out, sawing up through his abdomen, the sound of wet meat fresh cut, sucking and kissing at the knife and hand that held it as both went repeatedly into the bloody cavern.

Semen gushed inside black greasy trousers and no one noticed as Hoagg shuddered and rasped in small short breaths. He bathed in the death throes of the man going insane with agony, hearing his own insides pile up around his own feet and still feeling the fire of the knife blade. Hoagg finally sliced though his liver, opening his main artery. The wound now a chasm big enough to put in a small dog, gave out tremendous spurts of blood cascading onto the floor. The spurts diminished as the still beating heart pumped the last of his blood onto the floor.

Hoagg, near exhausted and satiated, stepped back from the lifeless body, the face turned powder white edged with blue from the lack of air and the horrendous drain of blood. He shivered again and swallowed, catching his breath he stumbled back to sit on the bed. He looked around the room like a man drunk, gasping his breath and half smiling. Thick gore slipped down the blood-soaked front of his shirt and pants. He wiped the sweat from his head with the back of his forearm, leaving a wide smear of Bartlett's blood above his eyes like a scarlet bandana. The dissected body that had been John Bartlett, slipped down into the puddle of his own blood and intestines.

Hoagg looked into each face, belligerent and daring any of them to say a word, and none did. He looked down at his arms again, a school boy giggle floating within the phlegm of his throat.

My dream! I am living my dream.

A gap-toothed grin still spread across his face, he found no camaraderie among the faces in the room. No one could share the thoughts of the sensations he had just experienced; he could not even put it to words himself.

I will do this again. I will do the bitch, and then I will do Pulaski.

Even as he felt that would finally settle it for Pulaski, even then, he knew it would not settle it for himself. He spun around and ran from the room, out into the gray cloud, to the Pulaski's barn.

Blood still ran down his arms dripping off his elbows, off his knuckles, and off the blade. He found the wall to the barn and then the door. A lantern burned in the barn and sprayed him with its light as he stepped in. He giggled to himself and ran to the first stall. The mule shifted nervously in its stall twisting its head trying to see the thing near it, but could not. It could only feel the fire as Hoagg reached the knife far underneath the mule and drew the edge fiercely across, opening the protruding belly wide and dropping its intestines onto the hay as the mule bleated in agony. Hoagg shrieked to himself like a partying child filled with delight and ran to the next stall. Hell visited the Pulaski barn as one after another Hoagg opened the belly of mule and cow and horse. Coming out of the barn, he heard the snorts and clucks coming from the animal pen at the edge of the field. He moved through the growing fog and found them. Sow and piglets and as many chickens as he could swiftly grab. He left them all writhing in their agony, screaming in their own tongue. The blood filled the ground and soaked the hay, forming puddles in the low spots where more blood pooled and congealed.

Hoagg stumbled to the outside pump in front of the house and to wash off some of the blood. He hummed to himself as he rubbed and scraped at the blood that had already crusted around his fingernails and in the folds of his skin. He laughed a small laugh to himself, shaking his head at some silly thought speaking softly to the other of his own conversation, until he was satisfied with his work and had returned to a place occupied by the sane. No more than twenty feet away, the crewman named Freddie lay face down on the grass at the edge of the yard. His head was split open like a ripe watermelon, and Simon crouched behind a bush beyond him clutching the ax, hoping Hoagg would come his way.

Hoagg skipped back up onto the front porch and stopped at the open doorway, gazing into the front room at the form laying on the floor. He kicked at it, thinking perhaps it was the eviscerated body of the nosy locktender, but this body moaned and then cussed when he kicked it. Hoagg reached for his knife handle as he stepped toward this unknown person, but then noticed his hands were tied behind his back and he had been deposited with a seed bag pulled over its head and faced toward the wall.

"What's this?," he yelled at the form, but meaning the question to his men in the house.

The large man carrying the battle stick stepped around the fireplace from the kitchen, munching on a piece of ham.

"Found that one in the other bedroom before...before you went out. He was just coming out."

"Bond?"

Hoagg yelled almost in glee, and then yanked the bag off the prisoner's head. To his disappointment, he looked down at the face of a young man.

"Who is he and who else is around this God damned place?"

Hoagg stepped into Sonja's bedroom, pattering through the puddle of congealing blood formed around the body on the floor. He brought the lamp from the bedroom out into the front room, the wale oil light almost too bright for his eyes.

"Bring her in here."

Sonja was carried in from the bedroom and held near Isaac. Hoagg grabbed the nearest man and shoved him into the bedroom.

"Wilson! Get that God damned thing out of there!"

The man leaned Bartlett's unfired musket against the wall, looked over the body then went outside.

"Need a shovel."

Another man hauled Isaac to his feet so he could see the carnage in the bedroom, his hands still tied behind his back. Sonja gasped as Isaac stood up.

"Have a good look, boy. You're next," the man spoke quietly into Isaac's ear.

Isaac looked down at the pool of blood spread in several feet in all direction, and at the mound of intestines piled beside the body. Only then he noticed that it was Bartlett, his abdomen opened like a gutted squirrel. Bile rose up from his stomach and he turned away, vomiting through the air, and just missing the man holding him. Then he saw his mother held across the room, her arms pinned back by the man behind her, and saw the spot of blood on the front of her shift. Hoagg looked at Isaac and then at Sonja. He pointed his finger at Isaac but looked at Sonja.

"Who th'Hell is he?"

Sonja looked at Isaac without speaking and held his eyes in hers. As Hoagg turned his head back to Isaac, Sonja frowned for just an instant and shook her head so slightly that only Isaac looking directly at her could see the movement.

"Who the hell ARE you?" Hoagg yelled and put his hand on the hilt of his hunting knife.

"Micheal Patrick O'Grady," Isaac answered.

Sonja briefly closed her eyes and thanked God for giving her an intelligent son. Hoagg looked at him longer, cocking his head slightly to one side.

"I heard the pig in town say that nigger Bond stayed out here, and an Irishman named O'Grady. You don't sound at all Irish to me, boy!"

"I'm Irish alright, especially when I try to find work, most people won't hire Irish – even though I've always lived in Harford County. Same problem my daddy had from the time he came here from Ireland 'til he drank himself to death couple years ago."

"Work for Pulaski, do you?"

"Yes, sir."

"Work for his Bitch too, do you?"

Hoagg once again grabbed at Sonja's breast through the thin cotton, making her pull back from the pain of the tight grip. Isaac and Sonja looked only into each other's eyes. Sonja willing Isaac to do nothing to give Hoagg reason to kill him. Isaac willing his mother to believe that he would kill this man grabbing her, as soon as he could.

Wilson came back from the barn with a shovel and began scooping up the loose intestines of the dead man, and tried to toss them out the door, but they had not been severed, so the act only produced a bloody spray as they flew into the air of the doorway and then stretched out from the body to the porch outside.

"Shit, Wilson!!" Hoagg called out. "Carry the damned body out in the yard, then scoop the rest of the shit after it!" Wilson dropped the shovel and picked up one of Bartlett's arms. Its legs and boots were covered with so much shiny blood, any grip was almost impossible. The other man with Sonja's blood spit on his face assisted Wilson to drag the body outside. An horrendous swath of blood covered the floor to the doorway, across the porch, and then down the step out into the yard, like a giant paint brush had been at work. Isaac had never seen so much blood before. Even when a hog was killed, it was over dirt, and he never saw it puddle on a hard surface like this before. The nausea rolled in his stomach again, but he managed to keep himself from vomiting. Hoagg recognized the sickness in the boy's face and snickered.

"You ain't bothered by a little blood, are you boy?"

He huffed at his own joke without waiting for the boy to speak; did not want him to speak. He only wanted the boy to fear him, because fear Randall Hoagg he should.

"When's that bastard Pulaski comin back, boy?"

"Don't rightly know, sir. Could be any minute."

"Good. We're gonna' wait for the son of a bitch and then have a good ol time."

He shared his glance with the men remaining in the room, who returned his grin, but were smart enough to remain silent. Hoagg had been near the edge several times since they had signed on with him, but never this far. They were willing to do almost anything to keep their share of all the money to be made, but it would do no good if they were dead.

Sonja squirmed in Dicky's grip and he rewarded her by releasing one of her arms only long enough to jab her in the back of her head with his fist, and then renewed his severe grip of her elbow. Stars exploded through Sonja's head, dizziness and nausea swept through her. Isaac twisted within the grip of his own captor, receiving the same treatment. Hoagg looked at the two prisoners and only shook his head, again he did not catch the unspoken words sent between mother and son.

"Sit that bitch down," Hoagg ordered, and immediately Sonja was slung onto the chair in front of the fireplace, her foot pivoting among the glass shards from the broken window and slammed into the rocking chair. Fire ran up her leg from her heel as she raised the foot and saw the long glass shard sticking from the side of her foot. She only allowed the smallest whimper as she quickly reached down and snatched the broken glass from her foot. Blood rushed out of the opening in her skin, forming large droplets that ran from her heel, seeping one after another onto the woven rug. She pushed her thumb against the opening to stop the bleeding and tried to lessen the pain. Isaac took a half step toward his mother, but was pulled back off his feet and thrown into the opposite corner. His watcher stood between him and the front door.

One of Hoagg's men returned from the front yard. "Cap'n there's some people gathering back down toward that lockhouse. I heard'em and walked down there to get a closer look. It's foggin in everywhere and almost lost my way back, but they didn't see me. Must be four or five people up and out in the road talking, mostly men. How we gonna get by all them?"

Hoagg moved close to the man, pulling his knife out of its sheath as he moved. His face and the tip of the blade flying before the man in an instant, screaming at the man.

"Holden, you wanna wind up like that man in the yard you just scooped up?!!"

Holden said nothing.

"Cross the canal out in front of this place and make your way along the towpath to where our boat is tied. Bring it down here. We're gonna wait a while longer," Hoagg said

The man still did not move. "Cap'n, the people down there are awake. They might be waitin for that man in the yard to come back."

Hoagg turned the tip of his knife with the same movement of his chin facing the question. The man knew he was risking his life questioning Hoagg, but also knew his life was risked by the people gathering in the road near the lockhouse.

"Cap'n, Sir, we got to get away. If any one of those people see us and we can't kill'em, they seen us and there'll be a hangin' bounty for us all. We kill a couple niggers an that's one thing, but they catch us now we killed that fellah in the yard, and we're gonna have a damned hard time gettin away."

The man held his breath, not knowing what Hoagg would do next. Hearing that her neighbors were gathering at the locktender's house, Sonja screamed out.

" Help! Help! They killed John! Help!"

Dicky turned and drove his fist into the side of her jaw, knocking her unconscious. Hoagg hissed to himself, speaking under his breath, discussing what he would do, speaking to Pulaski, looking out into the fog through the open doorway. Hoagg turned toward Isaac.

"Git him up." Isaac was yanked up by his elbows onto his feet, the hemp rope cutting deeper into his wrists. To the other man on the porch, Hoagg ordered, "Get me a hammer and a big nail from the barn." The man flew into the mist. Hoagg turned to Isaac again.

"You gotta deliver a message to Pulaski. You tell him I got his woman. You tell him come to me, maybe I trade for her. Maybe I trade her for him. If he don't come, I let everyman jack on my ship have her until they are sick of her, then I'll do just to her what I did to that nosey bastard in the yard." Isaac nodded to Hoagg.

"You tell him what I said. You tell him come to my ship in Spesutie Narrows. I can see for a mile from there. More than one boat, more than just him, and I gut her like a fish and haul her kicking body up the yardarms so he can watch her die as I sail away." He rapped Isaac's head with the heel of the knife handle. "You hear me, boy? You understand what I'm telling you?"

Again, Isaac nodded.

"You don't tell those fucking farmers down the road, you wait right here and you tell Pulaski. You hear me?"

"Yes, sir."

"Yes, sir," Hoagg repeated and laughed. "You gonna wait right here til your boss man come back?"

"Yes, sir."

"Yes, sir," Hoagg repeated in a giggle, "Yeah...you gonna wait right here and you ain't gonna tell them people down there a shittin thing til

Pulaski gets back."

The man returned from the barn. Hoagg stepped back, "We gonna leave Pulaski a note tacked to the door so he'll know we been here."

"I'll tell him," Isaac reassured him.

"Oh, I know you will, little man, I know you will." Turning to the remaining deckhand "Hold him up in the door way to that bedroom." The man dragged Isaac across the room, and the other man took a quick look at Sonja, still unconscious in the chair, and stepped over to help hold Isaac.

"Untie his hands," Hoagg ordered, "and hold them up to the doorframe above him." Without delay, the ropes were cut from between Isaac's hands and his hands brought over his head. His hands were numb due to the tight bind of the rope. The seamen held them together against the doorframe. Hoagg placed the point of a four-inch nail in the palm of the outer hand and then slammed it with the hammer, nailing Isaac's hands to the doorframe. Hoagg pounded the nail three more times, driving it deeper and deeper into the wood. Isaac sucked in his breath to brace against the pain, realizing what was being done to him. As he opened his mouth to yell, Hoagg shoved in a bloody rag, almost gagging him.

Hoagg brought his extended finger childlike in front of Isaac. "Sh-h-h-h-h-sh. You gonna stay and you gonna wait for bossman. Just like you promised." Hoagg emitted a girlish giggle as he finished.

"Watch the Bitch!" The voice came from the doorway. Hoagg and the men holding Isaac turned toward the doorway. The sailor, dripping water from his wade across the canal, pointed to the small woman behind them as Sonja flashed around the edge of their vision. Each tracked with their eyes toward the movement, and with each heartbeat the form moved ahead of their sight. The man in the doorway sprinted toward her, but he was too late.

Before the men holding Isaac could turn to grab her, Sonja was lunging onto Dicky, lunging into him. Her feet were completely off the ground and the blood from her hands spraying an arch. A ruby feather lingered behind the movement of her bloody hands flashing down as one, following them down to the man. Sonja plunged the glass shard deep into Dicky's neck. She kept a bloody grip on the razor edge of the blunt end, so she could drive the tapered point deep into his neck. Then she punched the glass blade into the soft tissue, muscle, and the artery just above the collar bone. She screamed in agony and physical exertion, and in animal anger, driving the glass almost its full length into the man's neck.

Even as Dicky swung the back of his hand to knock this crazy bitch down, he knew what she had done. As he reached over with his other hand to grab at the glass amidst the torrent of blood spewing high in front of his chest, he knew she had killed him. His carotid artery was completely severed, spewing the first arch of blood almost to the ceiling. Dicky pulled at the shard again and again, like a drunken man trying to grasp an elusive strand of cloth from his own shirt, but found no grip on the bloody glass.

Sonja spun around and grabbed Bartlett's musket still leaning against the wall. She snatched it up to her waist, slipped her finger inside the trigger guard and swung the barrel toward Hoagg. But he was too close. He slapped the barrel away even as she squeezed the trigger. The gun exploded inside the cabin, shooting the lead ball into Holden's inner thigh. Hoagg struck Sonja hard in the side of her head, driving her to the floor.

Dicky's fingers slipped uselessly off the end of the bloody glass, his palm painted with blood. The sliver of glass twitched with each heart beat, like a metronome, counting the measures of blood.

"Goddam you," Dicky bellowed at the woman on the floor. "Goddam you, Bitch," he yelled again as he sank to his knees. New puddles of his blood marched closer on the floor as his pressure failed and each pulse fell shorter. "Goddam you," he said again, but no louder than a casual conversation.

He turned his face toward Hoagg, pleading with his eyes, knowing his Captain could do nothing. Hoagg looked back without word or response. The man's eyes rolled back toward the woman lying on the floor beside him. Dicky raised a heavy hand, no longer swinging it but only allowing it to drop against the woman's back side with no more force than the pull of gravity.

"Bitch," he whispered, as the others gathered up the woman and their wounded shipmate, moving off the porch.

The lamp was left burning, keeping light in the room, as Isaac struggled to keep his feet under him and keep the pressure of his own weight from pulling his hands against the nail driven though his palms, fighting the growing pain. Dicky watched his mates leave him to sit and bleed to death. A curtain of blackness settled along the upper rim of his vision and slowly began to sink across the light in front of his face.

"Bitch," he thought he said, but no sound escaped from his pale lips, and then it no longer mattered.

As Hoagg led his men down the steps, two of his men appeared from the fog, dragging a limp form between them.

"Now what," Hoagg screamed.

"Got a present for you, Cap'n."

He peered closely at the bound form, and giggled.

"Simon Bond! How wonderful!" He turned his face to the men holding Bond. "Make sure his hands and feet are tied tightly. Then get Freddie and let's be off."

"Freddie's dead, Cap'n. This'n opened his head with an ax."

"Bring the black bastard along. We're going back to the ship."

Hoagg screamed toward the wagon trail, yelling a warning to the neighbors gathered near the lock house. "Keep away from here or we will kill the all? John only got a scratch. Keep away or we will kill John!"

Hoagg smiled and headed across the canal to his waiting boat.

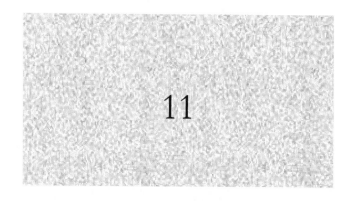

11

The numbness of his hands faded away. Burning pain surged into the void that had blessedly surrounded the iron nail pierced between the bones of his palms. Isaac shifted his feet again. Keeping the shank of the nail in the center of the hole created when Hoagg hammered it into the doorframe. Thick fog stood guard at the open front door where blood seeped under it from the front room. Very little light escaped from the room onto the front porch. Cool damp air drifted into the room, leaving tendrils of grey vapor grasping at it from the doorway as it slipped in.

There was no position without pain, only some with more. He listened to the steady progressions of the tocks from the mantle clock on his left, trying to guess how long he had stood with his hands nailed to the doorframe above him. His stature placed his shoulders blessedly high enough that he could have easily reached far above the doorframe were it not for the nail. Isaac thought of his mother again, his own pain fading slightly for the moment, as he returned to his frantic worry about his mother being taken off by those men.

What are they doing to her? Where did they

take her? Where did they come from? Why did they do this? Why does that crazy man hate my father, so?

Isaac yelled at them when they took his mother away, yelled at the man sitting in the floor in front of him until the man fell over within the spreading pool of his own blood. Isaac was amazed at his mother's action, coming from unconsciousness while the crazed man hammered the nail into his hand. She had leaped from the chair, snarling as she drove the piece of glass into the man holding him. She had not even tried to avoid the blow to her head in order to punch the glass deeper into the man's neck, focused on the kill. He heard them talk through his own pain as the numbness ebbed, and knew she was alive when they took her out into the fog.

Most of the floor in the front room was covered in glistening crimson fluid, the blood of the invader mixed with that of poor Mr. Bartlett. Isaac could feel his own blood trickle down his arms again, his last movement loosening the clots at the center of his hands. The blood ran warm down his forearm, gathering at the first edges of his upper arm muscle, and flowing across his skin there and slipping into the small depression behind his raised collar bone. The small pool had filled. The overflow ran down his chest, staining his shirt with the darker plum of cooling blood.

The lamp continued to burn on the mantel, keeping the room bathed in yellow light, painting the fog as it wandered past and occasionally peeked into the doorway. Isaac wondered again how long he had been there. He peered into the fog, hoping to see someone coming to help.

"Hello?"

He could only see the ends of a few porch floorboards at the center of the doorway, but nothing else. He listened for sounds outside, to hear something other than the tock from the mantel constantly reminding him of the ponderously slow passage of time. He shifted his weight on his feet trying to minimize the pull on his hands, the pain renewed and sent burning spikes from his palm and shooting down his arms. He hissed through clenched teeth, halting his motion to deal with the pain.

Again, he shifted, gently rotating his hands, pivoting around the nail, turning his shoulder to see his hand. The fire erupted in his palms, like holding burning coal. He stopped his movements, gritting his teeth. He forced his mind to plan each necessary joint and muscle movement along his arms and spine and legs so he could look at his owns hands. Isaac clenched his teeth to accept the pain and continued to roll his shoulders. He had to rotate his hands around the spike and arch his back, and then twist his neck to place his eyes directly below his hands. His lower hand slipped down slightly onto the broader coarse shank of the nail. The fire was intense, made worse by his vision of rough iron grinding against raw bone. He whimpered, then growled at himself, growled at the men who had done this and taken his mother.

Hatred grew for the ones who had done this to him. Isaac's anger filtered some of the pain and he continued his turn. Finally, he could see it. The nail had felt as if it were the thickness of a broom handle, but it was less than half the thickness of his middle finger. The square forged-iron tapered shaft had been driven deep into the wood, leaving less than an inch beyond his hand to the nail head. It was a flattened edge extending beyond the width of the shaft, intended to hold wooden boards in place through the years. His legs and arms and shoulders were cramping within the tortuous position he had forced, so he could look at the nail. He could see no way he might remove it.

Isaac yelled at the pain as he rotated back to his standing position, cursing the men who had invaded his home and taken his mother. He returned to the duller pain of waiting, less the monster than he had endured in movement. He had looked closely at the nail. The ache in his shoulders and hips, knees and ankles added to the misery of his fixed position. He could not endure this without limit. He would eventually tire beyond his ability to stand up. Even knowing the horrendous pain to come, he knew he would collapse with only the nail holding his hands in place. The nail would hold its position in the door and he would rip his hands open by his own weight. The nail head would gouge through his hand, split his palm, and tear it apart like shredded venison, leaving him with grotesque useless flippers.

Isaac looked out to the fog again, seeing nothing in the wet yellow-gray smoke. He thought he heard a noise outside, but could not identify the sound or its direction.

"Hello? Is anyone out there? Please help me!"

Maybe it was the sound of my own bones grinding against that damned nail!

No one is coming. No one will help me. Maybe I will have to pull myself down? If it is going to

191

happen anyway....

Just the idea of the pain such a movement could create in his hands added to the fire and the pain.

The pain will be worse, but it will be quick.

"Alright, damn it. Do it Isaac," he said to himslef.

Isaac shifted his weight to even the burden of his weakening legs. He moved to center his head and shoulders directly below the nail. He shuffled his feet back slightly to give himself brace enough to push forward. Clinching his teeth and squinting his eyes against the coming explosion of pain, he began taking fast deep breaths to prepare himself. He bent his knees slightly to provide a spring for his push, feeling the weakness in them and the pronounced, uncontrollable shake that had developed in them. His legs would not hold him much longer and the burning in his shoulders was beginning to rival the pain in his palms. He stiffened the tension in his wrists, but tried to relax the muscles in his palm to lessen the resistance as the nail head would tear through them.

Count to ten. On ten, do it.

He would do it now, or allow his failing legs to rip open his hands into useless bloody paws. He began his count.

"One."

He took several more deep hissing breaths.

"Two...Three...Four..." pausing between each number

He realigned his shoulders.

"Five...Six..."

The blood pounded in his ears.

"Seven..."

---<>---

Gray dawn edged the darkness out of its way, showing Ben and Aaron the last few yards of towpath. Thirty-five miles north of the Pulaski farm, they had kept the mules in harness, and staked down with oats to nibble, so they could move out at first light. Pulling in at the Wrightsville canal basin late the previous day, they had shouldered their way into a prime spot closest to the outlet lock. The lock squatted under the western end of the famous mile-long covered bridge that connected Wrightsville across the upper Susquehanna to Columbia. Aaron yawned as he walked to the mules, then checked their straps and looked back at his father for the sign to move. Ben gave it from his position at the stern, and pushed the tiller all the way to the right. The mules pulled the bow of *The Turtle* through the outlet lock as the stern of the *Ugly Boat* swung wide into the canal basin, and the tandem barges slipped through the open gates into the river.

Aaron led the mules up the wooden ramp to the covered walkway on the side of the bridge. The tow line angled down to the bow of *The Turtle*. Ben pushed the tiller to the left as they entered the water flow and followed the mules across the Susquehanna river. The mountains of coal ahead in Columbia sent lazy steam up into the morning air. Mechanical noises drifted over the water, letting Ben know the coal shovels were ready for the day. They could fill a barge in less than two minutes.

Splitting the load into quarters to prevent sinking the barge, coalers loaded portions stern-and-bow, stern-and-bow, until the barge sat level and low in the water. Minutes later the Pulaski barges followed the mules back across the bridge to Wrightsville, full of coal and moving under the higher tow ropes of the empty barges going over to Columbia. As soon as they touched the earthen towpath Ben and Aaron guided the barges to the down flow lock at the southern end of the basin. As the first of the locks south opened, Aaron whistled a tune and enjoyed the sunshine.

They moved smoothly into the canal. The upper edge of the sun peeked over the treetops on the eastern side of the river. The mules could almost trot along the towpath. Most of the resistance they had pulled against coming north was now nudging the barges along in unison.

We will be in Lapidum this afternoon. Pick up the mast and sails. Be back at the Severn by sunset.

Ben smiled to himself.

Need to take Anthony and the Wilhelmina with us. She still sits in Havre de Grace, full of coal. Forty tons among the three barges. Forty tons for Captain Weems at four times the usual price! Things are finally looking up for us!

Just after passing through the second lock, the barges floated into thick fog. Neither Mule tender nor barge could see the other. While they could see a few feet around themselves, vision beyond them was lost. Ben yelled for Aaron to tap the iron loop on the harness every minute, and he would tap the *Ugly Boat's* bell.

May not make it back to Annapolis this

afternoon, after all. Damn.

---<>---

"Gag that bitch," Hoagg ordered.

The pull down-river with the current had been easy on three of the four men at the oars. Holden's leg throbbed from the bullet Sonja had put through his upper leg. Under a tight bandage, the hole only bled modestly. The bullet had missed both bone and artery. Hoagg kept the launch close enough to the western edge of the river to see the shore rocks, but cloaked within the fog as much as possible. Above their heads, the sky was lighter, still gray, but getting lighter.

Simon and Sonja were back to back in the middle of the boat. Both with bags over their heads, hands tied behind and ankles bound. Simon lay unmoving, barely breathing, while Sonja continued to yell and scream, and kick out with her feet. Wilson pulled the bag from Sonja's head and shoved his wadded scarf into her mouth. Motioning for the scarf of another crewman, Wilson tied it around Sonja's head, holding the scarf in her mouth secure. Sonja gagged, but managed to keep breathing through her nose.

"Check the other one," Hoagg ordered.

Wilson snatched the bag off Simon's head, but the man did not move or make a sound. Blood still trickled forward above his left ear where the belaying pin had struck him.

"He dead?" Hoagg asked.

Wilson shrugged his shoulders and leaned down close to Simon's head. He rolled Simon onto his back, and leaned close to his mouth to listen for breathing. He frowned.

"Stop rowing," Hoagg ordered. "Check him again. I will sell that sonofabitch in Charleston! He can't be dead from that little tap."

The other crewmen held themselves as still as possible, so Wilson could listen for breathing. Wilson's ear moved to less than an inch away from Simon's face. His frown began to fade and a smile grew across his face, looking back at Hoagg.

Then Simon snapped his jaws shut on Wilson's ear like a steel bear trap. Wilson screamed and pulled away from Simon, grabbing at his face and jaw to unlock Simon's clenched teeth. Wilson's movement brought Simon halfway up to a sitting position, allowing Simon to slam Wilson's head into Holden's lap.

"Hit him! Hit him," Hoagg ordered.

Wilson continued to scream as the skin holding his ear began to split. Simon forced his shoulder into Holden's wounded thigh. He pulled Wilson over his other shoulder and onto Holden's lap, then brought his knees under his chest. With Holden, Wilson and Simon all leaning over the edge of the boat, it was near capsizing. Hoagg and the other two crewmen leaned away from the tangled men, grabbing up oars to swing at Simon. Several harsh blows hit Simon's arms and his back, as he continued his roll, pushing up with all the strength in his legs.

Hoagg pulled out his knife and lunged at Simon. The boat tilted wildly onto its side. Hoagg's blade slit across Holden's knee. Holden screamed at the pain and grabbed for the far end of the seat board, trying desperately to stay in the boat. Simon pushed his shoulder into Wilson's chest. Wilson's upper ear began to tear away from the side of his head. Holden pulled himself deeper into the boat, grabbing frantically at the bottom. Simon and Wilson rolled over Holden and beyond the outer edge of the boat. Simon kicked with his feet and pushed himself completely out of the boat, Wilson's ragged ear still clenched tightly between his teeth. Wilson screamed again as they both went into the river.

An oar, already in angry motion, missed Simon and hit Hoagg in the face. Hoagg flashed the crewman a death snarl, then turned toward the water where Simon and Wilson went down. The boat righted and rocked on the surface. Blood ran down from Hoagg's nose and seeped into his mouth. The three men stood with oars cocked above their heads, ready to kill Simon when he surfaced. He did not.

They searched around the boat. There was no sound except the gurgle of the river current pushing them farther south. They had drifted away from shore. All around them was thick gray fog.

"God damn it," Hoagg spat.

The boat hull began to grind into shore rocks.

"Shit. We're on the other side," Holden said.

"Either that or the island near the mouth of this river."

Holden dropped back onto his bench, adjusting the rag covering his bullet wound to include the small bloody slit from Hoagg's knife.

"We going back after them? After Wilson?"

Hoagg looked down at Sonja lying in the center

of the boat.

"We got all we need. Get back to your oars."

The other men retrieved their oars and began rowing again. Hoagg steered the launch back out into the current. Moments later the muffled sounds close on their western side slipped farther away. Beyond that, the hissing heartbeat of the steamer vent on the western shore confirmed to Hoagg that they were at the mouth of the river. The launch slipped past Havre de Grace, across the Susquehanna flats and into the Chesapeake Bay.

---<>---

Isaac realigned his feet, tensed his leg muscles, leaned his body slightly farther forward.

"Eight..."

He focused his attention on a small nodule of blood on the floor in front of him. He let everything else go out of focus. Then he closed his eyes.

"Nine..."

There was a scream.

Was that me?

"TEN!"

There were hands against his chest.

They are back! Damn them to hell! They are back!

He threw himself forward with all his weight, a sound arising from deep in his abdomen roaring out of his throat, growling at these men.

"Easy Isaac, easy lad. We're here! We're here! We're gonna get you down."

It was a voice he knew. It was Delbert Freidman, the owner of the dry goods store. Isaac opened his eyes and bright yellow light filled his brain. Men were coming into the room from the fog, looking at him, looking around the room, blatant shock showing on their faces as they saw the blood that bathed almost the entire room. He could not hear words, only their sounds. He had wrapped himself in a trance-like state, preparing himself to tear the nail through his own hands.

Then there was another pair of large meaty arms wrapping gently around his waist, taking his weight from the ground holding him gently so no weight pulled down on the nail. Another set of hands cradled his arms to hold him still and relieve the pressure on his aching shoulders. The blacksmith's son came toward him carrying tongs and a short block of wood.

What was his name? James? Jeremy? Jeremy, that was it. A year younger than Aaron, but not as tall.

"Hey, Jeremy." Isaac spoke weakly through a dry throat.

Another set of hands took the tongs from Jeremy, leaving him to stand before Isaac, but looking above him, not at him, while Isaac watched Jeremy's face. Isaac could feel the vibration and pressure as the block and tongs were positioned, could read the growing frown on Jeremy's face. It told him when the pain was coming to free him from the nail. More voices. The deep voice of Jeremy's father said something directly behind Isaac's ear. New hands and arms encircled Isaac's chest, replacing the larger arms of Forrest McMallery, who stepped in front of Isaac, gently

199

raising Isaac's hands to the top of the doorway. Forrest looked down between his massive biceps, his meaty face and flame red beard framed between his arms. Deep green eyes met Isaac's gray. Forrest winked, then glanced back up to his work. McMallery grunted slightly and the room air was pierced with the sound as the nail squeaked out of the hard wood.

Hands were lowering Isaac's arms as Mrs. Freidman half-led half-held a sobbing Margaret Bartlett into the room. Mary Freidman, Margaret's sister, looked quickly around the room, uttered "Dear God in Heaven," and steered Mrs. Bartlett back out onto the porch to scream her grief into the fog.

Isaac slumped into the chair pulled out for him at the kitchen table, holding his palms up in his lap, looking at the holes where the nail had driven. McMallery came before him carrying the whisky jug Ben kept in the kitchen.

"Those wounds need to be cleaned out or they'll fester badly."

Isaac looked up as McMallery upended the jug over his palms, flooding the wounds with the alcohol. The whiskey mixed with the blood and liniment rushing into the gashes. Fire again shot along the inner length of Isaac's arms, beginning with hot coals in the palms of his hands. He jumped to his feet, his legs almost giving way under his own weight and clumsily dancing around the room shaking his hands to free them of the added pain.

"Damnation!" he yelled, and continued to fan his fingertips through the air, shaking his hands violently.

Blood droplets flew through the air from his hands as the alcohol thinned the clots and the shaking loosened them from the wound. McMallery reached out with a firm grip on Isaac's wrist and began to wrap his hand in a clean bandage. Snugging the bandage in place and tying the split ends between his thumb and forefinger, McMallery took up Isaac's other wrist to bandage his other hand. The man's thick beefy hands moved almost with a delicacy and precision at odds with their appearance; more at home smashing red-hot iron than tying knots in gauze linen.

"You'll need to change these every day till those holes close up. Ain't big enough to stitch up, but plenty big enough to fester and rot, if you don't keep'em clean."

Jeremy had come to stand next to Isaac, listening to his father's instructions.

"Pa knows about those things, Isaac. You mind him, you'll be all right."

McMallery smiled at his son's confidence and reassurance to the Pulaski boy. His son was only fifteen years old, but already eye level with his father. He had been both mother and father to Jeremy since his wife had passed. Sonja being taken was how his own boy felt about losing his mother, so he recognized and understood the immediate kinship Jeremy felt for Isaac. His mind flew ahead to the possibility of looking for and finding the woman.

If she could be found. If she was still alive.

"I need to find my father," Isaac announced.

Men and women of Lapidum had come and

gone through the front room, taking John's body from the front yard, making a few furtive attempts to wash away the ocean of blood that had splashed within the room. They came and went in two's and three's, helping with the grievous and gruesome tasks, and helping each other find their way through the fog, turning lighter shades of charcoal to ash. Somewhere outside the sun had already risen. When it was light enough to walk the path back to the lockhouse, Mary Freidman escorted her sister home, although it would only be home to her until someone else was hired as lock tender.

A heavy fog shroud had settled over the canal and river and upper Chesapeake Bay, blocking sight except the ground under foot and objects within hand's reach. Sound was muffled, mixing the distant with the near and the two ranges almost indistinguishable to the ear, seeming to come from any and all directions. The smells of the river and the canal and the forest blended into the smoky mist, diluting them with water, mixing them and spreading the concoction over everything, not allowing even the nose to help find the way.

McMallery stood on the porch with Isaac and Jeremy. His hands on his hips.

"Mr. Freidman is riding to Havre de Grace to inform the Deputy Sheriff there. I am sure they will do what can be done."

He put a meaty hand on Isaac's shoulder.

"If you insist on making your way south along the towpath. It will be slow going, Lad. You could miss them in the fog."

"Did anyone find Simon or Toby in the barn?"

"Nothing out there but dead animals, Isaac. Thought Simon would be with your Pa on the barge."

"No, sir. Pa left yesterday with only Aaron. Simon and Toby stayed back."

"Found a body!"

The voice came from the southern side of the farm.

McMallery and Isaac stepped off the porch and around the corner of the house as the voice called out again. In the stand of sapling apple trees, planted for a future orchard, lay a man face down with the back of his skull opened wide. The body was rolled over and a lantern held over its face.

"Must be one of Captain Hoagg's crew."

"Well," McMallery said, "looks like somebody didn't like him being here."

12

Wilson twisted in deadly black liquid that wanted to keep his body. His hands frantically churned the water in front of him. His lungs burned for air, blessed air. The scream he had let out before falling into the water had emptied them. The urge to take in a deep breath to feed his gyrating body was overwhelming. The creature had rolled on top of him when they went in the water and still had his crippled ear in its mouth. There was no light, no air. His face slammed into cold rocks. He couldn't hold his compressed chest another instant. Boots were on his back, shoving him down harder against the rocks. There was no air. There was no stopping his own chest. It expanded in a suicidal gasp for air. Sweet blessed air. He gagged and coughed, desperately forcing the water from his lungs only to fill them again. His flailing hands grabbed at the rocks. Frantic hands clawed for any purchase, grasping for anything to help him get up. He inhaled more water that had no air. His fingernails ripped away, digging for a hand-hold, a way to pull himself up.

AIR! Air! ...air.

Then nothing.

His boots tightly bound together, punching them into the man's back, Simon unclenched his teeth and sprung up from Wilson's body. He arched his head with his hands tied in back. Pushed his nose and mouth above the water. Just his nose and mouth. Nothing more. Drew in the delicious air. He filled his lungs as quietly as he could, hoping it would not be heard from the boat. Let himself sink back down under the surface. His boots tapped against the rocky bottom. He had drifted beyond the body.

Wilson alive? Yelling for help?

Leaping along the bottom of the river like a wounded frog, he let his boots touch the rocks and then kicked away again. His knee hit hard against a boulder. The current rolled him, twirled him around in the blackness. He kicked his boots down again, this time there was nothing there.

Deeper? No shore? Drown?

He kicked again, striking rocks. Found the surface. Savored the fragile air and sunk again. Kicked hard again and again. Paltry sips of air, barely enough. At last, he stood head and shoulders above the water. He flushed his lungs with fresh air. Delicious, miraculous air. Just feet away, the rocky shore of the river waited for him. He kicked again, driving himself toward the shore, but down into the water. Turning on his side to keep his head above water, he crabbed closer to the shore, working his shoulder like a limbless stump. Finally, he sat up with his upper chest and head above the surface. As soon as he felt secure in his perch, he stilled himself to listen for the boat. Nothing.

The rocks around him were slippery with algae.

Using his heels and his shoulders, he wormed his way up the bank to dry rocks. His body abandoned by the buoyancy of water, angry rocks poked hard against it, scraping his skin and hammering new bruises as he inched forward. Eyeing the rocks around him, he targeted one with a sharp ragged edge, and wiggled toward it. He placed his hands on either side of the rock edge behind him and sawed his wrist bindings along its ridge. The hemp rope was tarred for ship use, and soon coated the rock's edge in wet tar. He wiggled to another rock. Then another. His fourth rock finally cut through the rope and freed his hands. He rubbed the raw skin of his wrists and listened again. Nothing.

He grabbed another jagged edged rock and used it to cut the rope around his boots.

Many broken rocks here. How far down?

He stood weakly, only able to see a few yards into the fog, and made his way up the steep bank using his hands and feet. He stooped over on a well-worn dirt path, resting his hands against his knees, taking deep breaths of the cool fog, twisting his body against the stiffness of his muscles.

Towpath. Took me at the farm. Downstream. South from the farm.

He carefully rubbed the back of his head, feeling the tender whelp where he had been hit. Ignoring the pain in his body and its cry to lay down for rest, he stumbled north, back to the Pulaski farm, back to Toby.

Only a few hundred yards up the towpath a figure on horseback came out of the mist, pointing a gun barrel at his face.

"Stop right there, or I swear to God, I'll blow yer damned head off!"

---<>---

Smoke colored mist swirled around him. Ben was the center of a thirty-foot universe. Everything else was beyond that, in the gray roiling fog. The deck of the boat disappeared beyond the forward lip of the cabin in front of him. The edges of the canal slipped into and out of his world. Just enough to keep the barges in the middle of the canal. The bow of the *Ugly Boat*, the entirety of *The Turtle*, and the towline floating out to Aaron and the mules were all memories. Aaron and Ben reached out to each other like blind men tapping canes. Aaron's regular tapping on the single tree chains were answered obediently by Ben tapping his pipe on the barge bell. They had already passed several cautious barges pulled over and staked to the towpath. The two-man crews grumbled and warned him against going farther, even as they dutifully passed his towrope over their heads. He should have stopped hours ago.

"Still good out there, Aaron?"

"Still good, Pa.

Plenty of water in the canal. Scarce traffic makes way for us.

"Someone coming, Pa! Moving fast!"

Ben spun around and flipped open the storage chest that served as his seat. He pulled out the conch shell and quickly blew it three times.

"Damnation," someone yelled in anger.

Sounded like a girl, or young boy.

There was a great splash in the canal and the whinny of a distressed horse.

"What happened, Aaron?"

"She just about ran into me! Run her dang horse right into the canal!"

The sound of canal water cascading back to its home echoed within the mist. Then, sucking 'thocks' heralded feet being pulled from the muddy canal and laboring up the steep side of the towpath.

"Uncle John's dead," she screamed.

"Who is that, Aaron?"

Ben pushed the tiller all the way to the right to plant the bow of *The Turtle* at the base of the towpath.

"Who is that? Who's dead?"

Youthful voices pattered within the fog, words stepping on words, excitement tainted with fear. None of it clear.

"What is it?" Ben yelled.

Their voices were much closer now. The inertia of the barges and the southern current of the canal took Ben to them. The black shape of mules and a form beside them. Then a shape of a horse and another form next to it, slighter than Aaron. The cacophony of words still swirled around the forms. Aaron's face drifted into view, looking toward him, eyes wide. The girl's face was sprinkled with dirt, smeared below reddened eyes.

"Little Miss Margaret?"

"Uncle John's dead, Mr. Pulaski! They murdered him awful! They crucified Isaac and they took Mrs. Pulaski away!"

---<>---

Hoagg held his compass close to the lantern perched next to him and shifted the tiller slightly. The tide had peaked and was waning, not so much as to draw them south, but enough to keep the Bay from fighting them. It had been a long pull from the Pulaski place. Slack tide. The launch could seat eight men at oars, another at the tiller, and still room for baggage in the middle. Six men should have been more than enough to hold one little woman and her man, while he cut them up. Now, only three crewmen pulled at the oars, one of them wounded. Sonja moaned in the bottom of the boat. Hoagg smiled. The sack was removed from her head. She had vomited within it. Holden had pulled it off and tossed it into the water.

Holden stopped rowing again and adjusted the bandage on his leg. Even in the faint light of the lantern, Hoagg could see that the bleeding continued from his wound. He watched the back of the man in front of Holden and frowned.

Freddie? No. He got his head split open. Dicky? No. The Pulaski woman killed him. Who is that? What's his name?

Hoagg checked his compass again, adjusted his tiller and peered into the fog.

Nothing. Nothing but this damned fog. Never seen it so thick. Johnson! It's Johnson up there. Heavy with a club.

Sand hissed under the keel of the launch.

"Sand spit of our island," he said to the little crew.

He pushed the tiller to the right, slipping across the spit and swinging the boat west. Moments later, he turned the launch north and smiled to himself as they glided under the bow of the Raven. Hoagg was a bastard, but a supreme seaman and an excellent navigator.

Nothing but that damned fog. No star, no moon, no shore light, and I brought us ten miles dead on to this here spot.

He smiled again. Johnson was reaching up to grab onto the chains under the bowsprit, when the sentry on deck shouted out.

"Who goes there?"

Hoagg scrambled up the side ladder ordering men to hoist up the prisoner and help Holden. Still very proud of his navigation, Hoagg walked slowly past the sentry, wagging his finger at him like a kindly schoolteacher. He even gave the sentry a small smile. Both Hoagg and the sentry knew that any other time the sentry would have been flogged severely for not discovering the launch sooner. Hoagg hummed to himself as he walked to his cabin, oblivious to his appearance. He was saturated in blood from his hair to his feet. The sentry stood frozen, watching his captain walk away, his throat dry, blood pounding in his ears, surprised at his own survival.

---<>---

The horse knew her way back to Lapidum. The mist still blinded Ben from everything more than a few yards ahead. Aaron and Little Miss Margaret would bring the barges.

Maggie. Aaron called her that.

He resisted the urge to gallop the mare, but she knew her own way. He had to be satisfied with the trot the horse gave him. Minutes later he came to the upper gate of Maryland lock number nine.

"Who's there," a voice bellowed.

"Ben Pulaski!"

"Come slowly, so I can see ya. I've got a rifle and it's cocked, so come easy."

"And he ain't alone," another voice added.

Ben slid from the saddle and walked the horse toward the swing bridge footing, but the opening was empty. The bridge remained securely on the other side of the canal. The stone locks were less than half the width of the canal itself, designed only to accept barges in single file, but still farther than Ben could jump. Ben stood at the outward side of the lock. The two men on the other side stood under a lantern hanging from the clipboard pole. Lars Nilson stood next to the pole holding his musket butt under his arm and the barrel pointed across the lock. His oldest son Eric stood next to him, the handle of his father's old sword gripped tightly in his fist.

"Can you see me, Lars?"

"Yes, I can, Ben. I'm glad you've come, though I wish I had a better greeting."

Eric leaned heavily into the balance bar and slowly pivoted the bridge out across the lock. As soon as it was close enough to step with the horse, Ben crossed.

"Little Miss Margaret came to the boats. Told us some. Tell me more, Lars."

211

"Ben, I probably don't know any more than Maggie. Her mother is in the lockhouse with Mrs. Bartlett now. They're in a terrible state of mind. Best you hurry on up to your house. Forrest is there with your Isaac."

Ben mounted the horse and trotted down to the little bridge over the creek. Two other armed men stood there, one he did not recognize. The other, Tommy McMallery, silently pointed up toward the Pulaski house and Ben did not stop to talk. He halted before his front porch, sliding off the saddle and letting the horse wander away. Lanterns were hanging from the porch posts and the twin oaks in his front yard. Lamplight from the open doorway and smashed window joined the light from the lanterns bathing the porch. Ben stiffened as he mounted the second step. Tommy heard Ben's voice through the fog, and slowly shook his head.

"Jesus God in Heaven!"

---<>---

Delbert Freidman lowered his rifle.

"Ah, Simon. Glad it is you. You are wet. Did you go into the water when those madmen attacked Ben's farm?"

"No. Mr. Freidman. They took me too, but I got out of the boat."

"Is Mrs. Pulaski safe?"

"No, she is still with them, but they aren't hurting her. Is Ben back?"

"I sent my daughter up to fetch him. You go tell him all you know. I must go on to get the Sheriff's deputy. Such horrible men!"

Freidman spurred his horse back into a trot and faded into the mist. Even before he was gone, Simon was striding north toward the Pulaski farm.

---<>---

In front of Ben, the steps, the porch, and the front room floor were painted in blood. Efforts to wash it away had sent it cascading over the edges. It dribbled down the front of the foundation, coated the steps and splattered the front wall of the house. In front of the steps and along the ground in front of the porch, shiny scabs floated like Lilly pads within puddles of red muddy water. The body of a man lay on its back at the far end of the porch. His head arched back off the edge, dripping the last of his thickened blood like tree sap, painting little circles on the surface of his own pool on the ground.

Footsteps ran out from the house.

"Pa! Pa!"

Isaac threw his bandaged hands around his father's shoulders. Ben embraced his son, pushing his hand up against the back of Isaac's head, grabbing his hair, and pressing him tightly against his shoulders. Words were useless. And then the brief quiet moment ran away.

"What happened?"

Isaac sank to the step, sitting in the diluted blood at the edge of the porch and rested his elbows on his knees. He did not look at his father.

"Men broke into the house. They grabbed Ma. Simon was at my window telling me to come out with him, but I couldn't. I went into the front room to help Ma. I didn't get the chance. They hit me in the head and put a bag over my head. Should have gone with Simon –"

Ben sat next down to his son. "What next?"

"I guess one of them knocked me out. Next thing I remember was being stood up and they pulled the bag off my head. He told me his name when he nailed me to that doorframe. Captain Hoagg. I...I wasn't able to help her."

"Hoagg?? Randall Hoagg? He's dead..."

Isaac shook his head 'no'. "Captain Hoagg killed him..."

"CAPTAIN Hoagg did what?"

"Mr. Bartlett was lying on the floor. He was cut open like a gut deer. Captain Hoagg asked who I was..."

"Hoagg is alive??"

"Ma was held between two men. The expression on her face, when they asked me that... She wasn't hurting or afraid for herself – she was afraid for me. Made me think I needed to say something other than my real name."

Isaac looked out into the fog, his eyes wide, seeing it again.

"What happened, next son?"

"Ma was like a bobcat, snarling and jumping around the room before they could catch her again. She punched a piece of window glass into that man out on the porch and she grabbed up Mr. Bartlett's gun. Captain Hoagg knocked the barrel away before Ma could shoot him, but the gun went off into one of the other men. Shot him in the leg..."

"Is your mother alive, son? Was she hurt bad?"

"She was punched hard, I think. Had her hands and feet tied when they left. But they didn't hurt her much more than that. They won't, he said, 'til you get there. Unless you take too long."

"What? They told you where they were taking her?"

"That man hates you fiercely, Pa."

"I should have killed him in China. Thought I had. Tell me exactly what he told you to say."

"He said come to Spesutie Narrows at sunrise. Said, 'Come alone'. If you come with others or come late, he will cut Ma like he did Mr. Bartlett..." Isaac drew in a ragged breath, his hands shaking. "Said, if you're not there before noon, you would find pieces of her floating on the incoming tide."

Men had gathered on the porch while Isaac told Ben what happened, listening to details they did not know. Ben patted his son on his back and stood up.

"I need to get one of my horses..."

McMallery spoke from behind.

"Horses are dead, Ben. That madman gutted everything in the barn. Not a living thing remains in the barn or on your farm. Every horse, mule, pig, goat and chicken has been slaughtered."

"Simon? Toby?"

"Found no sign of Simon, Ben. Don't know a Toby."

"They took Simon, too, Pa," Isaac said. "I heard them talk about him outside. Hoagg wants to sell

215

him in Charleston."

Eric Nilson walked up the slope from the canal, leading the horse Ben had taken from Maggie Freidman, its muzzle wet from nibbling grasses growing in the shallows.

"Eric," Ben said, "Please keep that horse close by. I'll need to borrow it."

"Sure, Mr. Pulaski. 'Sides, Maggie borrowed it from me anyway."

Ben took in a deep breath and went into the house. Ignoring the blood stains, he quickstepped to the mantel where he kept his father's old pistols.

"Left them in the *Ugly Boat*! Damn!"

He snatched up John Bartlett's musket from the floor as he reached up to take his powder horn and shot pouch from the mantel. In the bedroom, he paused briefly before the bloody hand prints on the bed sheet, his teeth clenched. On top of the chest of drawers, he discovered his whalebone-handled knife with a little bow tied around it. He carefully slipped the bow off the knife and laid it gently on the dresser. He withdrew the iron knife from his sheath and replaced it with the steel blade, laying the old knife on the dresser next to the bow.

Hoagg, I will kill you and watch you die. This time I will pull your heart out.

Again on the porch he spoke to Isaac. "Son, you stay here, but not alone. Go with Mr. McMallery here, if no one else stays here. Do you hear me?"

Ben and Forrest traded quick glances and Forrest nodded.

"You know this man, Ben? China, you said?"

"Yes. Sailed on the same ship. Hoagg was the bo's'n then. Thought I had killed him there."

Forrest blinked his eyes. Isaac placed his hand on Ben's arm.

"Pa, I need to go with you. I need to help."

"I know you want to, son, but I will worry less knowing you are safe here. Aaron will be here shortly, or at least by morning. No. I need you to stay here."

"Pa, you ought not to go alone!"

"He isn't going alone," said a familiar voice rounding the corner to the front of the house.

"Simon! Thought you had been taken."

Simon pointed Toby toward Isaac.

"You stay with Isaac until I get back, and this time you stay where I tell you to stay. Don't you be wandering around."

"I hadda poop! You said pee down the tree if I had to, but you didn't say nothin about poopin!"

Ben stood before Simon. "Simon, I need you to stay here at the farm. Watch over Isaac and Toby. Don't let anyone..."

"I'm going with you, Ben. I'm going to help you kill that Bastard."

Ben shook his head as he loaded the powder and shot down the barrel of the musket. "I need to know my sons are all right..."

"You need not to get yourself killed, Benjamin. We both know Hoagg. That lunatic will kill everyone and everything around him, if he gets a chance..."

"You know him, too?" Forrest asked.

Simon looked up on the porch where Forrest stood.

"We sailed together once. Hoagg is an animal."

"I will kill him, Simon," Ben said, as he tamped the wad down with the ram rod. Simon turned and walked over to the barn, returning with the ax and stood before Ben.

Ben blew out a deep breath and nodded his head at Simon. "There's a well sharpened iron knife laying on top of the chest-of-drawers in my bedroom."

As Simon went into the house, McMallery stepped next to Ben.

"I'll watch the boys, Ben. They will be safe with me." Then he handed Ben a pistol. "It's loaded and will use the same powder and balls as that musket. Me and John use the same...well, used to...shit." His eyes centered on Ben's. "Kill that son of a bitch. Do it with your knife if you get the chance."

Simon returned from the house, sliding the knife under his belt as Eric led two saddled horses through the grass. Eric handed the reins to Ben and Simon.

"The swing bridge is over the lock."

As soon as Ben sat in his saddle, he handed the pistol to Simon.

"Get rid of the damned ax."

Simon nestled the ax handle under his arm as he slid the pistol barrel behind his belt opposite of the knife. Then he took the reins in one hand and gripped the ax handle near its head. "Taking this too."

Both horses turned away from the house with boot heels to their bellies, and trotted into the mist. The horses stomped over the swing bridge and were across the canal in seconds, their nostrils already wide and hooves slapping hard on the muddy towpath as they passed the Pulaski farm, charging through the fog to Havre de Grace.

---<>---

In the Captain's cabin of the schooner Raven, Sonja leaned her back against the hard corner of the post in the middle of the room. She was tied against it at the waist with her wrists bound around it, pulling her arms backward. Hoagg sat at a nearby table eating a late evening meal, and watching Sonja.

"You just stand still and behave yourself, woman. Maybe your man will show up before my deadline. Actually – I know he will. He's the honorable kind. They face the cannon and make the charge and they're the first over the wall and at the enemy. Huzzah! Huzzah! And the first to die."

Sonja would not look at him, but studied the room.

"You see something you like, woman? See some pretty trinket, ol' Randall can give you for your charms? Hmmm?"

She sneered at him and then looked away. Her blue-hazel eyes were red-rimmed. The artery in her neck tapped against her lace collar. Her bladder screamed for release.

Hoagg sliced off a thick piece of breast meat from his roast duck, sucking it loudly off the fork

219

and into his mouth, grinning at Sonja. "Yeah, sweetie," he said as he chewed. ."..you and me gonna dance for your man. I'm gonna show him all the things a woman can do to please a man. Most of em you never did for him, I'm sure."

Sonja shifted her feet. "He is going to kill you."

"Ol' Ben had his chance, bitch. This is Randall's turn. I'm gonna cut a map of the Mississippi River from his balls to his ribs."

Hoagg focused his attention on the exquisitely sharp edge to his knife, letting the lamp light run along the feathers of metal at its finest margin.

Sonja brought her knees together. "He is going to kill you."

Hoagg grinned at her over the edge of his knife, watching her squirm, recognizing her movements. Then he picked up his goblet and leisurely dribbled his wine onto the floor in front of her. He listened to it sprinkle, watched the woman across the cabin squirm and bite her own lip as a single tear traced its way down her smudged cheek. She closed her eyes as the warmth spread down her legs and droplets touched her ankles. His smile broadened as a yellow puddle formed between her bare feet, and he sucked another sliver of duck meat into his mouth.

13

At last, Ben and Simon trotted their horses over the swing bridge in front of the Canal Office at the northern end of Havre de Grace. Up Canal Street and onto Oyster, where waves of thinner mist were pushed through the fog by a faint breeze off the bay, showing store fronts and street lamps and then hiding them again. The clock in front of the Hardware chimed two melancholy sister notes as they passed the Tidewater Bank and Trust office, fully lit inside. Men's anxious voices spoke in the fog, roused out in the night and gathering just ahead.

Gathered within the yellow sphere under the street lamp in front of the Sheriff's Deputy Office, a dozen men pressed in toward Deputy Mattingly and Delbert Freidman.

Delbert raised his voice above the murmuring.

"They took Mrs. Pulaski, I said! And they nailed poor Isaac Pulaski's hands to the doorframe as a message to Ben. And they took his man, too."

Men's voices spoke over each other in anger.

"Who did this?"

"Took her where?"

"Why is this happening?"

"Where is Pulaski?"

"I am here," Ben spoke up. "Simon got away from them and is here with me."

The crowd surged around Ben's horse, firing more questions. Many ready to join the others in retrieving Sonja.

"No," Ben yelled. "Not yet! They have Sonja on board a ship in Spesutie Narrows."

"Who?"

"Why?"

"I need to go there. Alone," Ben yelled. "The man that has her is Randall Hoagg. He has a great hatred for me, and will kill her if I do not come."

"You can't go alone."

"We will come with you."

"Wait!!" The voice came out of the mist and then its owner stepped into the lamplight.

"Wait," Herbert Binterfield yelled again. "I will supply anything needed by any or all of you in order to rescue Mrs. Pulaski, but you must listen to Ben. I suspect he has a plan. Let's hear it!"

Ben and Simon traded wide-eyed glances. Simon shrugged his shoulders. Ben slid out of his saddle, then stepped into the middle of the group.

"Yes. Wait. Hoagg will hurt her if he thinks she might be taken from him. He wants me, but I do not believe that he will just let her go, once I am there."

Delbert grabbed the arms of men nearby.

"That man is a butcher, a devil! You should see the carnage he visited upon poor John Bartlett, and all the Pulaski livestock...everything was gutted. There is a sea of blood over the ground!"

Dan Bartlett grabbed Delbert's coat collar.

"What of John? John Bartlett? My Brother! What has been done to him?"

"He is dead, Dan. Cut open and left in the yard like an animal. I am so sorry to have to tell you."

"No! I was just there this afternoon. We're going oysterin this coming Saturday. You must be mistaken. Musta been someone else. Ya gotta be wrong, man..."

Ben placed his hand on Dan's shoulder.

"I'm sorry, Dan. I was just there. I wish Delbert was wrong about all this, but he is not."

Dan shook his head as he turned away, saying nothing else, and was consumed by the fog as he walked from them.

"Ben," Herbert said. "What do you need us to do."

"Binterfield, I don't need YOU to do anything."

Binterfield used his loud public voice. "This is not about you and me, Ben. This is about Sonja. All that I have is at your disposal."

Then he stepped close beside Ben, and whispered a question. "Does Sonja still have those two little moles on the underside of her left breast?"

Ben reached for his knife, but Deputy Mattingly heard the comment and grabbed Ben's arm.

"One day, Herbert," Ben whispered, "I will kill you."

Binterfield stepped back, holding his arm up in front of himself and speaking loudly, "Ben, I only wanted to help. Think of your wife!"

Mattingly stepped between them, still gripping Ben's arm. "Benjamin Pulaski, Delbert here says that maniac wants you to come alone to his ship, but this is a job for the Law. I will deputize some of these men and go get her off that ship as soon as this fog lifts."

"That will be too late."

Ben climbed back into his saddle and turned his horse onto Market Street. The voices in front of the Deputy's Office were muffled in the wool blanket of the fog and faded to mumbling, barely heard between the strikes of the iron horseshoes on cobblestone. The boardwalks on both sides of the street marked the edges of their sight, shown by the weak lamplight that bloomed in the mist around the tops of each pole like yellow dandelions in a world of swirling gray.

Simon brought his horse close beside Ben.

"Ben, Adam Tuttle can get us to Spesutie Island, fog or no fog."

"How do you know that?"

"He said never to tell this, but on Sundays he rows to that island looking for Lafayette's gold."

"That's just an old wives' tale, Simon."

"Does that matter, if he can get us there?"

"Not one damned bit."

"So how were you planning on getting out there?"

"Adam Tuttle. I just didn't know about his gold hunt."

Minutes later, Ben and Simon left their horses among the trees and made their way down the narrow pathway to Adam Tuttle's Boat Shop.

A dry, cracking voice echoed within gray rough-cut plank walls. "What the Hell do you want?"

"It's Ben Pulaski and Simon Bond, Adam. We need your help."

A meager candle flame sparked to life from inside and floated up to their faces as the door creaked open. "Yeah. It's you. So? What the Hell do you want in the middle of the goddamned night?"

"Some men took Sonja and I intend to get her back. She's on a sloop in Spesutie Narrows."

Adam left the door open as he withdrew back into his workshop that also served as his home. He pulled down a lantern and lit the wick from his candle. "You boys just tell me what I can do to help," he said, blowing out the candle.

"Fog's bad tonight. Can't see ten, twelve feet ahead. Figured you'd know how to get there through it."

"I've seen you do it," Simon whispered. "Looking for gold."

"You don't keep a secret for shit, Simon Bond. And after all that time I let you stay here..."

"And worked me like a dog."

"And I paid you same as my stupid nephew..."

"Simon, Adam, all this later. Adam, can you get us there in this fog or not?"

"Blackest night or fog filled day, don't make no difference, Benjamin. I was your daddy's best carpenter and second best navigator. I can get you over water just like following deer shit through the woods."

Within five minutes, Ben and Simon sat forward in Tuttle's newest rowboat, pulling oars in unison, pushing the boat across Concord Cove. Tuttle sat at the tiller, not even glancing forward of the boat, concentrating on the brass compass sitting next to the lantern on the seat board in front of him.

"Almost perfectly due South, with not quite two degrees easterly. That'll take us to the isthmus. Ya know, the Narrows ain't really a Narrows any more. North end is silted up. Got a little beach walkway from the mainland to the island."

Neither Ben nor Simon was listening to Tuttle. A soft southerly breeze gave slight assistance to their work. Backs leaned together, pushed hard by their legs braced against the boat ribs, biceps and shoulders pulling the oars hard against the thole pins. They dug the oar blades full into the water, pushing up a small white wake at the bow, shoving the boat as fast as it would ever go.

Tuttle spoke into the compass. "There was a servant that stole one of those little bags of gold from Lafayette during the Revolution. He headed south from Havre de Grace. Stole a dugout canoe down there where the shanties are now. I found it years ago in the upper end of the narrows, almost completely buried in the silt and mud. I found that canoe and I found this."

He pulled up a chain from around his neck and lifted up a gold coin, holding it next to his face. A hole was drilled near its upper edge to accept the neck chain. It gleamed in the lantern light. Words in another language were engraved near the upper and lower edges. In the center was a fleur-de-lis, the symbol of the French monarchy and benefactor of the Marquis de Lafayette.

Adam plopped the coin back inside his shirt and shook his head, his lips pressed together into a thin line, his revelation completely ignored by Ben and Simon.

"To Hell with'em," he muttered.

Adam checked the compass closely then listened intently to the sounds beyond the boat.

"Oars up," he whispered.

No sooner had the oar blades reached upward, than the keel of the rowboat hissed through the sand and came to a halt on a narrow sand beach. Adam looked at the spread of sand on either side.

"Just about dead center, gents. Just like I said."

Simon followed Ben out of the rowboat. Ben handed him one of the rifles.

"Adam," Ben whispered, "I need you to go back to town and bring the Deputy and as many man as you can, to this spot."

Ben and Simon pushed the bow of the rowboat back into the water, and Adam took the oars for the long row back, against the freshening wind.

Simon stepped toward the bushes that grew along the ridge of the little spit, but Ben grabbed his arm, pulling him back.

"I'm sorry, Simon, but I need you to stay here."

"No!"

"Yes, Simon. I need you here. Sonja and I will probably be chased, and a gunshot from the bushes could hold them back."

He handed his rifle to Simon.

"This won't be very useful to me. One bullet won't do much, and it would just draw them all to me. You keep this with you."

"Ben..."

"Please. Simon. I trust you with my life. With you here, I know we will have a safe way out..."

"No..."

"And you can guide the others in when they get here."

"Ben, I can help. You can't do it alone."

"Simon, I think it is the ONLY way to do it. Please. Protect my way back out."

Simon released a heavy sigh. He and offered his right hand to Ben. They shook hands in silence and Ben moved off through the bushes, resting his hand on the ivory handle of his knife.

---<>---

"Shut her up!"

Hoagg stood in the fog near the port wheel on

the Raven. He reached out and clutched the damp wool coat of his new first mate, pulling him near to his own face.

"I want this ship quiet, Johnson. What the hell is going on down there?" Hoagg noticed the clean rag tied around Johnson's usually bare forearm. "What happened to you?"

"That Bitch, Cap'n. We need ta cut her throat and be done with her. She's like a bobcat."

"No man touches her! I want her fresh and clean when Pulaski comes to watch. Then you can do what you want, but not a second before! Do ya hear me?!"

Before Johnson could do more than nod and swallow, Hoagg was near his face again.

"I'll gut the man touches her before I let him! And I'll gut you for letting him!"

"Ain't nothing gonna happen to her before you say, Cap'n. Don't you worry about that. But, God damn, that's one mean bitch. Thought she was half done for, all limp and hanging her arms when we carried her from your cabin. Before we knew it, she grabbed Jenkin's flayin' knife and cut a half-yard gash 'cross his back. Cut my arm open just getting the damned knife outta her hand."

"Why didn't you let Jenkins get his own damned knife?"

"He was tryin, but then she jumped in close and opened his lip almost to his eyeball. Jenkins keeps a real sharp knife, you know. Cook's trying to sew him up now, but he'll probably fester and die in a week or two. He's cut up pretty good. But we got that knife away from her and got her locked up below."

"Where?"

"We had ta put her back in your cabin."

"What? I will..."

The crashing and thumping from below deck rose to a pitch, sounds of wood on wood as Sonja beat against the door of the cabin. A moment of silence then the sound of shattering glass shot through the mist.

"God damn her, she's smashing my whiskey bottles, Johnson!" Didn't you tie her to something down there?"

"Well, not really, Cap'n. You told us we couldn't hurt her and she was kickin and scratchin' and bitin', and we just tossed her in there and locked her up."

Johnson took a half step back rubbing the ring of teeth marks in the tender area between his thumb and forefinger, hoping to avoid being sliced yet again. Hoagg reached down for the handle of his long knife as another crystal crash exploded into the air at the stern, followed by a splash of water. Hoagg could only wonder what possession of his she had just tossed through his cabin window, but stopped his own motion for his knife.

He grabbed Johnson's coat in both hands.

"Quick! Get down there! And take her far below decks! I'll..."

Johnson was already on the move toward the steps. He spoke over his shoulder as he grabbed nearby men and rushed down the companionway.

"I know, Cap'n, I know what you'll do."

"No, you don't',Johnson! You'll pray for death, if she gets away!"

Thumps and crashes continued for only seconds longer and then there was silence again in the fog. Hoagg twisted his head one way and another searching for the slightest sound. A single scream of pain pierced the air, ...a woman's scream. The scream reached the farthest edges of the cove.

---<>---

Ben heard her scream and fell to his knees in the muddy shallow water along the northwestern shore of the Narrows.

"God damn you, Randall Hoagg." A hoarse whisper rasped through clenched teeth. Anger and fear filled his eyes with tears. "Hold on, Sonja. Please hold on."

He rose and then stumbled again in the muddy water as slimy sediment sucked at his feet, the ooze of long trapped sand and dirt and decayed leaves letting his feet sink several inches into the muck with each step. Sediment and bird droppings covered the rocks along the bank, giving him no surface for a foothold. The painful knot on his left shin warned him to stay off the rocks. Even the footing in the muck was mixed with pumpkin sized rocks that twisted his ankles or jammed his toes as he tried to walk. Each fall took him back into the water up to his shoulders. Each recovery meant he stood back up into the chilling mist, and his body became cooler still.

Another rock ledge extended into the water in front of him. He reached out to it, to guide himself into deeper water and around this next point. The texture of the surface was irregular and not like smooth rock at all, and he leaned closer as his hand explored higher up and found a vertical edge to grip. A flat-bottomed boat stuck out into the water, its other end pulled up onto the unseen bank. Ben peered into the boat and could see only two or three inches of water. Stepping around the end of the boat he welcomed the firm sand his feet found. Around the other side, he followed the boat up onto a small sandy lip tucked under low hanging branches. Laying on the small beach, their ends touching the dead grass and weeds on either side of the sand, lay two oars that obviously belonged to the boat. Ben crouched under the tree limbs and listened closely for the owners of the boat.

I am coming, Sonja.

---<>---

Sonja rolled over in the darkness, retching onto the bare floorboards she could not see. Her wrists were tightly bound, the coarse strands of hemp scratching at her skin and her hands growing numb. Her feet felt swollen under the binding at her ankles. There was not enough circulation in her limbs. She was losing the sense of touch. A third rope was tied tightly to her wrist binding that kept her from rolling onto her other side. The pain in the pit of her stomach felt like a toothache, ready to engulf her entire body. She pulled against the rope at her wrists and felt the line tug at its limit. She was tied to something on the wall of this blackened room. No light, or even a hint of gray seeped into the room. She was in total blackness.

The space smelled of tar and mildew, rotting hemp and putrid bilge. Her shift and bloomers were soaked to her skin and she trembled with chill in the dank room. The mist had wet and frizzed her hair and now it had matted against her head. Something crawled over her leg, something with little feet and whiskers that touched and sniffed at her to identify its new roommate. She kicked her legs and jerked her entire body to scare it away, and hoped it was not hungry for bites of her. She sniffed the aroma of fresh urine, knowing it was hers. Depression and fear and melancholy approached the edges of her consciousness and she was again the little girl fallen into the narrow well of her uncle's farm in North Carolina. She would rather they had killed her than put her in this black hole to slip in the mold and retch and her own urine. She had been in a frenzy in the cabin above, fighting back at the men who had killed John and nailed the hands of her precious Isaac.

This is what God allows to happen to women who cannot keep their children.

The men had run into the cabin grabbing her and throwing her to the floor, holding and tying her feet, and bringing the dirty rag to gag her mouth. Her only remaining act of defiance was her raging scream at them and then the man had driven his fist into her belly. She spasmed without breath as they tied the rag over her mouth, the air completely vacant from her lungs from the blow and the rag suffocating her frantic gasps for air. There was no recollection of her coming to this place, only of awakening and being here. Maybe it was not even a place but a nightmare from which she was unable to wake. She rolled onto her back and prayed for God to finish his work; kill her and let her go to hell and be done with it.

---<>---

Ben waited several minutes beneath the

branches of a huge Cypress. It was the only large cypress on the island, had seen it before from the Bay side, even used it as a landmark to find the second channel when fishing. Knew exactly where he was. He kept his head down, intently listening for the sound of footsteps on the isthmus behind him or in the shallows before him. The boat was not a ships boat, but local, the wood old, slippery and heavily notched.

It is not from the Raven.

The fog opened for a brief moment, letting starlight illuminate his surroundings. He pushed one of the oars with his foot, rolling it over in the sand. The ground under the oar was a dry silhouette of the oar.

This oar has been lying here a while. Before the fog.

There were no foot prints near the boat except his.

This boat is abandoned. Been here since before the last rain.

In the center of the boat he discovered two tattered canvas coats. One was small, the size of a child, the other larger than Ben and damp, but welcomed cover from the seeping mist, and he quickly slipped into the coat. It had only one button that Ben matched to the open loop on the other side.

Pushing off while he stepped into the boat, he grabbed up one of the oars and used it as a rudder to steer. The cypress told him exactly where he was. The water was deeper near the western shore.

That's where Hoagg has to be.

The fog closed in again, blocking out the stars. A charcoal gray curtain hid everything around him. The little sandy beach and the huge cypress faded into the mist behind him and he floated into a rocking world where vision ended with the edges of the old wooden boat. He would not let his mind follow the question his brain had asked. Had the little boat been abandoned because it could no longer float?

The force of the push from land took the boat only a few yards into the mist. He slowly worked the oar grip back and forth, twisting the handle slightly in toward each stroke, causing the oar blade at the other end of the shaft to move through the water painting, spooning, just below the surface, pushing the boat forward. Within minutes he ghosted to another steeper bank emerging from the fog, but there were only trees on the nearby fog. The Narrows must be longer than he estimated, surely he could not have drifted passed the ship in the fog. The thought terrified him that he did not know which direction to go next.

Have I overshot my destination? Am I short of it? How much more time to save Sonja? How much of it will I throw away going in the wrong direction in the damnable fog?

He held his breath and forced his ears to find what his eyes could not. The sound of his own heartbeat and his own breathing faded from his mind as he concentrated, closing his eyes, reaching out into the mist with his hearing. He heard the sound of the drops falling from the trees before him, some hitting wet leaves and pine straw, other falling into the shallow water in front of the bank.

Clomp.

There! What was that? A footstep? Yes, wooded heel on ship deck, wood on wood.

He listened for more. A man coughed. He opened his eyes to see the man that must be right in front of him but only saw the light gray shroud that covered them all. The sound was slightly above him. A mumble. A piece of a voice, less than a word, keeping it low but having to speak to an officer or shipmate. It had come from his left, and it was close. He had crossed the cove just above the ship at anchor. Delicately he slipped the oar deeper into the water, easily, slowly poling himself slightly closer to the sound of the ship. The oar soon lost its touch on the bottom as it fell far below the surface of the water and dropped deep into the trench Hoagg had discovered for his ship. Another cough dipped into the fog as the boat drifted closer to its source.

"Shut th'Hell up," a voice grumbled."

"Ah cain't help it."

The fog ahead of him became slightly darker. The darkness extended high over his head. A yellow glow blossomed in the upper region of the darker fog. Ben stepped forward in the flat bottomed boat, reaching out just in time to catch the trailing edge of the ship's rudder. The stern windows of the Captain's cabin were a few feet above him. He could see the break in the light that was the window frame columns between the windows, but could not see through the mist to see any details of the cabin. Ben twisted at his grip on the rudder forcing the boat into a slow swing to bring it under the rake of the stern, to block it from possible view, using the angle of the ship's stern as an overhang above him. The bow of the boat finished its arc around Ben and gently nudged against the hull, causing a subtle but noticeable 'thunk'. Ben tried to freeze all motion of the boat, but his effort was countered by the boats buoyancy, causing it to 'thunk' a second time.

"Damn it to Hell," cursed a voice above. "Tell those bastards to keep it quiet out there!"

"Yes, Cap'n " another voice said. Boot steps on shattered glass was muffled in the fog above Ben.

Ben clenched his fist.

Hoagg!

"Clean this mess up!" the first voice ordered.

More boot heels across shattered glass and a door closed. Ben moved the boat back out, but heard the squeak of metal hinges above him and held his position. Loose glass shards still held within the window frame fell into the water near Ben. Someone gently tapped a wood handle or stick within the frame to loosen and dislodge the rest of the glass. Glass being swept, and another shower of glass sprinkled through the yellow lit fog above him and fell into the water, just missing his boat. The tiny splashes reverberating in the fog. Heavy boot heels and the cabin door was opened again.

"God damn you for a stupid son of a whore," Hoagg growled. "Don't throw it out of the damned window, you shit! We're trying to keep this goddamned ship quiet. Remember?"

The yellow light vanished and two sets of footfalls crossed the cabin floor. The door was pulled firmly shut.

Ben slipped the boat out from his hiding place and put one foot onto the steering chain that ran to each side of the rudder. Grabbing tightly onto the lower edge of the opened cabin window he pushed the boat away, sending it back into the fog, in the direction he had come. Pushing with both feet on the wet chain, he reached for the inside edge of the window to pull himself up. The sharp prick of glass slivers ran deep into his fingers of his left hand, but he kept his grip and joined it with his right forearm and wrist to make his way into the cabin. Light from the hall outside the cabin door came through the wood slats venting in the lower half. He had enough light to see the longer sliver stuck in the underside of his middle finger. He pulled it out with his teeth and spat it on the floor. The floor was damp, large swaths of splattered liquid stained the walls, and the room smelled of spilled whisky and rum. Shattered bottles, cups, and mirrors littered the cabin.

Good for you, Sonja.

An old Navy cutlass hung from its hooks on the cabin wall. He took it down, hefted its weight and looked closely at its blade. The meager light coming through the door slats danced along the razor edge of the blade. He turned and looked carefully at the spray of broken glass across the plank flooring seeking a pathway with the least noise and the least pain for his bare feet. Secured to another hook on the wall to his right hung Hoagg's great coat, and on the deck below it were his foul weather boots. Ben sidestepped to the coat, and stepped into the left boot. It was a good fit, and he welcomed having the leather sole between his battered feet and the glass. He twisted around to raise his right foot over the other boot when the sound of footsteps grew in the hallway outside and the door swung wide open.

Ben was spread eagle with his back to the door

looking over his shoulder as Johnson came through
the doorway with broom in one hand and bucket in
the other. His feet continued their progress as the
skin around his eyes grew in surprise, throwing his
eyebrows up while his jaws dropped to open his
mouth. The man spun on his heel dropping the
broom and bucket and grabbed for his knife, and
turned his head back to call for his mates. His
wooden heel rested on several layers of shattered
glass shards coated with spilled whisky. The pile
slipped apart, taking his footing away and sending
his leg flying into the room, his foot arching up into
the air.

Ben pulled his knife from its sheath, spun on
his booted foot and leapt across the glass ignoring
the slices to the bottom of his bare foot, pushing
away from the wall at the incoming man. The
cutlass tip barely cleared the cabin overhead in its
shining arch toward Johnson's face. Johnson
brought his knife blade up to fend off the flashing
blade as Ben fell into him, driving his own knife
deep into the man's throat, cutting his windpipe,
and slipping between neck bones in his spine. Both
bodies fell onto the glass covered floor. Ben was on
top, driving the blade deeper with the power of his
shoulder. Johnson's call for assistance died in his
throat below Ben's knife, the air hissing out of his
neck around the blade. His eyes looked frantically
into Ben's and then rolled up into the back of his
sockets, his mind freed to wander the remaining
seconds while his body finished dying. Ben rose and
had to place his knee against the dead man's chest
to pull his bloody knife out of his neck. He wiped
the blade and then his palm on the dry area of the
man's shirt, and limped over to the cabin door. No
one was in the lighted hall. Ben closed the door and

limped to the other boot. Holding his knife and cutlass in the same hand he pulled three slivers of glass from the bottom of his foot and slipped gratefully into Hoagg's other boot.

---<>---

In the darkness of the cable tier two decks below Ben and at the bow of the ship under the water line, Sonja rolled onto her side, using her resurging anger to drive away her despair. She reached out with her bound feet, twisting and turning them to fight their numbness and find the edges of this place, to find a door, anything she could use to free herself.

He was close. She could feel him near her.

Her feet touched something in the darkness. Something with a wooden handle rolled along the deck away from her feet. She slid as far as the rope would allow her and searched in the blackness for the thing she had touched. Arching her toes to hook the tool in the darkness, she herded it along the damp wood floor bringing it closer to her. The tilt of the deck in that space was only slight, but enough to release it to run away again twice before she could trap it with her toes. She brought it far enough for her bound hands to reach down and grab it. She ran her fingers over it trying to give her mind enough information to form a picture of what she had, and then grinned to herself in the blackness. Only twice before had she held one of these, but she remembered it. This must be where they store the heavy ropes for the ship's anchor and such, almost reciting one of Ben's many descriptions of his years at sea. The tool helps men weave splices and untie heavy knots in troublesome hemp ropes.

I know this! It is a spike, a Marlin Spike.

At last, she had something to help herself, something to use, to be ready.

14

Ben opened the cabin door into the brightly lit hallway. Steps led down deeper into the ship on either side of the landing, and led up to the main deck directly in front of the cabin door. He tilted back the lamp cover bracketed on the wall and blew out the flame. The darkness that he brought with him spread along the companion way, his face screwed up and unrecognizable to anyone who knew him. A wild animal with steel eyes, his breath short, his mouth tasted of brass. He had not felt these things since China. Swore he would never again. Horrible memories surged forward.

I will not come back from this. Not this time.

He let himself slip into it. His teeth clenched, his brow lowered, looking at the world from under them. Tension coiled every muscle in his body. His breath quickened. He slipped up to the lower steps of the companionway. His knuckles were white. His grip locked around both knife and cutlass. He took several more deep breaths, blowing them out slowly, feeding the furnace and driving away the reluctance. He felt the rough braid wrapping on the cutlass handle, and the smooth ivory handle of his knife. Three more deep breaths and then silently mounted the last steps to the main deck.

You will not come back from this.

Knowing what would come. Had let the monster out in China. Had sworn never to let it out again. A steam whistled erupted within his brain. Its shrill scream soared higher and higher, until it passed beyond hearing. His face stretched around a lunatic's grin and he flung himself into the madness.

---<>---

Sonja held the handle of the Marlin Spike within her fingertips, guiding the tapered steel tip along the surface of the hemp ropes tied around her wrists, searching for a knot to work loose. Twice she lost her tenuous fingertip hold on the spike and dropped in the darkness. She was unable to find the knot with just the Marlin tip. She needed to feel the surface of the rope; to find the knot; to know where the rope dove into the knot, where to push in the Marlin tip. Only then could she begin to work the spike between the coils, the first boundary between two layers of the same line forming the knot. Again, she dropped the spike. She was asking too much of her fingertips. The muscles in her hands and forearm were beginning to tremble and cramp. She brought her wrists up to her mouth. She kissed the coarse prickly fibers with her lips and probed the surface with her tongue to know the shape of the knot, to find the final twisted loop snapped together by the man they had called Johnson. The hemp was damp and mildewed. It had been used for foul work. The taste of it gagged her. She spit out in the darkness and rubbed her tongue along the fabric on her shoulder. She spit again and took in a deep breath, forcing herself to taste the rancid binding again.

There! What was that? Yes!

The loop end, the very end of the rope hanging loosely just beyond the last knot, the first to untie. She began to work the metal tip into the knot, using her lips to guide the work, reassured by the prickly hemp.

---<>---

Ben stepped into the mist, bathed in the cool moisture. No one cried alarm or was even close enough to notice him.

Hoagg. Kill him first. Stop all this. Kill Hoagg. Find Sonja.

Faint yellow spheres of light quivered in the mist around the ships lanterns. The coarse hemp lines running along the main sail boom directly overhead and the deck board seams at his feet were the only details to him. He was only one more dark form in the fog. Ben stepped on toes toward the wheel. Hoagg would not be far from there. A form neared him coming toward the stern. The face materialized out of the mist within three feet of Ben, the man's eyes widening in surprise then narrowing down as he recognized an intruder and reached for his knife. Ben slashed out with his own, opening the man's throat, a huge bright red mouth erupting below the man's chin. Even as blood spewed down his chest, the sweeping cutlass edge chopped deep into the man's skull just above his left ear, the cracking bone vibrating the cutlass handle. The man sank to his knees, dead on his way down. Ben stepped by him, prodding the fog with his knife tip for the next man to come, and prying the cutlass blade up and out of the dead man's head as he stepped forward. The man's face had just been sewed shut from another wound, but Ben discarded the observation for later thought, if he lived to rethink it.

Another man came out from the mist. Ben stepped into him, the cutlass tip shoved high into his abdomen and curving up into the heart. Ben's knife slashed out at his throat, creating another grotesque ruby orifice that would say no words. Ben pushed the man's chest back with a bloody fist holding his knife, sliding him backward off the steel blade, the wound sucking at the steel as it withdrew. Another form. Another face.

Where were the yells?

Two deaths in near silence and still he moved toward the wheel.

"Keep it quiet," a voice whispered. "Watch yer damned feet!"

The tip of the cutlass was still in the dying body slumped before him as Ben slashed his knife at the next man. The man saw the blade coming, dropped the loop of hemp rope he was carrying. He jerked his head around, moving his neck away from the arc of the blade, the knife edge only cutting fine hairs on his skin as it swept by. The man's chin went down as he reached for his knife. Ben jabbed his knife back at the man's face. The knife blade found flesh from ear to nose, opening the layer of blood and yellow tissue that had padded the cheek. The tip of the man's nose sailed into the air among a flock of bloody droplets chasing after it. Ben's blade continued its course even after furrowing the man's face.

Anger exploded within the seaman, allowing

him to ignore the wound and block the pain. He brought his own knife up at the throat of his attacker, missing the man but slamming forearm against forearm. The collision jolted Ben's knife from his bloody grip and it fell to the deck. The seamen grinned, his teeth showing through the hideous gash in his cheek. He stabbed forward to kill the unarmed man in front of him, but missed the flash of steel in the lamp light above him. He felt the shattering of his own skull before the pain exploded from the crown of his head, knowing his skull had been split and watching helplessly as the deck boards rushed up to his face.

Ben twisted the cutlass to free its blade, heard the bone cracking. He snatched up his knife and returned it to its scabbard, then continued his move toward the wheel, wiping blood from his hands and his face. Another form arose in the fog, motionless. Ahead of the form, the ship's wheel came into few.

Hoagg!

He gripped the heavy cutlass with both hands, holding the blade high overhead, closing the distance to the form. Shoulders, arms and back muscles contracted, with pushing legs he drove the blade down, wanting to slice the man all the way to the deck. Ben released a guttural snarl as he drove the blade down through the man, only skimming his head, taking scalp and ear. The blade snapped through collarbone and ribs, carving the arc of Ben's swing through the man's chest, down and to the side. Blood sprayed out, creating a crimson rainbow in the yellow light from the lantern above. The cutlass completely separated the shoulder and outer chest in an eruption of blood, cutting out at the wheelman's waist and dropping the body onto the deck in two parts. Blood drenched Ben's face, blurring his vision. In wide-eyed horror, the man opened his mouth to scream as the arc of the blade continued another quick loop, hacking his throat open and almost severing his head.

Ben wiped his eyes with his fingertips, could barely see. Looked down at the body.

Not Hoagg.

He twirled around. Saw nothing before him in the convoluted fog. He bent down, taking up the dead man's shirt sleeve, slicing a rag from it with the cutlass and wiping his face with it. He turned to face the bow.

Men yelled through the fog from outside the companion way entrance, one of the bodies had been found on deck. More men from below yelled into the mist. Another found dead in the Captain's Cabin.

"Shut up!! All of you! Pulaski's on board! Catch that sonofabich and bring him to me...NOW!"

Hoagg! He is up ahead. More men with him.

Ben ran back toward to the Captain's cabin, jumped over the companionway and stepped up onto the low cabin roof.

Cutlasses were yanked from a rack on deck. Men without a cutlass pulled their own razor sharp knives or found belaying pins to wield as bludgeons. Groups of twos and threes moved toward the stern of the ship, coming toward the wheel.

"I wanna cut him up some before we git him to the Cap'n," one of the men said.

Around the wheel, the mist momentarily feathered thin again, showing a vague outline of the wheel as a dark shadow. The closest man raised his cutlass and stepped toward the shadow but slid in the blood of the last man Ben killed and fell to the deck. The next man had his cutlass at the ready and stepped over his fallen shipmate to confront the shadow. Even as he moved beyond his cursing shipmate, he swung his heavy blade in a killing arc, bringing it down with both hands onto the form and feeling the bite of the blade go deep. The others surged around him with blades at the ready, an array of steel razors directed at the form in the mist. Another reached out to prod the form with the tip of his knife while the cutlass attacker fought to withdraw his own blade and absorb the pain of the impact within his wrists.

"Done killed the starboard wheel, Frenchie," said a voice as the men gathered around the ship's wheels. Frenchie rocked the cutlass blade back and forth out of a two-inch deep slice in the wooden wheel, where the blade had buried. The same voice spoke back from the stern, pushing his words toward Hoagg.

"He ain't back here, Cap'n."

"Find him, God damn it," Hoagg spat, no longer rasping, but in full command voice. "And bring that bitch up from below."

Four men moved back toward midships where Hoagg had planted himself on the cargo grating above the hold, leaving Frenchie to pull his blade from the wheel. His face stinging from humiliation and his chest filling with rage, he wanted to be the one who brought up the woman.

"I'll get her." He said into the fog.

Hoping she would give him a reason to give her pain, to slice her enough to terrorize her and vent his anger, but not so much the Captain would really care. He had helped carry her on board and down in to the cable tier, had felt her body under her thin clothes, firm in the secret spots. Maybe he would take a little time with her to...

But he never finished the thought. The man yanking on his own cutlass never saw Ben or Ben's blade. Stepping across the cabin roof and running toward the lone crewman on toes, Ben grunted as he swung the cutlass with both hands toward his head. The two bodies were almost passing each other. Frenchie looked up and back when he heard Ben. Ben was leaning beyond the man, adding final leverage to the cutlass, pushing hard with his legs, putting his full weight into the blade. The full force of Ben's shoulders and legs drove the cutlass blade completely through the man's neck. The head was propelled by the violence of the impact, and sent bouncing forward along the deck, onto the main cargo hold grating and tumbling into Hoagg's legs.

Hoagg shrieked at his men. "You just passed him! He's right there! Get him!!"

Hoagg pulled the pistols from his belt, cocked both and fired one back toward the stern.

"Get him! Get him!"

The ball buzzed through the mist near Ben's head. He dropped down onto the deck to get behind the wheel, slipping in fresher blood adding more to the pool already spreading there. He regained his feet and dashed back toward the companionway. Hoagg threw himself toward the companionway

249

with his remaining men following. Ben slipped again on the top step, losing his cutlass and trundling down the steps. Seeing the form moving below decks, Hoagg fired his other pistol, sending the other ball into the framework of his upper cabin. Ben ignored the firestorm in his side from the fall and recovered his sword. Hoagg heard the rasp of the cutlass blade dragged across the deck below. Pulling out his knife and followed by his men, Hoagg eased down the companionway steps to his cabin. The door was slightly open, bloody footsteps spotted the companionway landing, and there was a noise from inside. Hoagg threw himself against the cabin door slamming it against its frame, throwing the outer deadbolt closed and locking Ben below.

"I've got you, Pulaski! I've got you," he screeched.

---<>---

Adam Tuttle's compass rested unattended near the tiller of the large ships rowboat pulled up onto the northern shore of the island. Its pilot and its passengers had already gathered their weapons and followed Simon into the murky waters of Spesutie Narrows. Having the luxury of many eyes, a better pathway was discovered near the Narrows Quickly, the group pulled themselves out of the fetid water and made their way along the old path. Mattingly had deputized eight men, but they were accompanied by other angry men. Two men and two women came from the shanties at the edge of Concord Cove, carrying wood cudgels and iron knives. The women easily kept pace with the men, finely sharpened fish knives ready to bite deep into the people who stole family away from them in the night. Tuttle trotted at the far end, wheezing, stopping briefly to catch his breath, the ancient flintlock fired during the second war with Britain jostling in his grip as he ran. He could not let these people go without him, could not stay in bed when these people, these neighbors of his, went to fetch back family twice stole from their freedom. He felt the throbbing pain in his chest and along his neck, but would not stop. God would not let him come home with this undone, would not let him drop lifeless in the dirt path on this island. He clenched his teeth against the pain and sucked in the wet air between them and trotted after the others.

A gunshot echoed through the fog, and then another. Simon increased his pace and the group stretched apart along the length of the dirt path. Adam Tuttle clenched his tattered wool nightshirt into a ball against the base of his neck where the throbbing worsened after the sound of the gunshot. He glanced into the lighter grayness above him.

"Don't you let me fall, you hear? I ain't done yet!"

---<>---

After following Tuttle's group to the north end of the island, Aaron sailed the *Ugly Boat* along the eastern shoreline to the southern end of the Narrows. Without a keel, the *Ugly Boat* could manage water far shallower than any other boat in Havre de Grace. The large pile of coal tossed onto the Concord Cove mud near the shanties gave the boat all the buoyancy it required to get close enough to see the shore in the fog. A dozen more armed men from the canal basin and the shanties stood on the deck, peering into the fog. More eyes to keep the boat near the shore, but not too near.

The wind was faint, but blowing blessedly from the north and steadily filling the spread of canvas to capture it. A voice whispered from the bow, passed back to Aaron at the tiller.

"The Narrows are up ahead. Bear to the west."

No sooner had Aaron pulled the tiller back than the sloping square bow of the *Ugly Boat* hissed up onto the sand spit sticking out into the Bay like a tongue. Aaron ran forward to the bow to look down onto the shallow water and sand beach.

"She's hard aground. Might move her off at high tide, but that's still three or four hours away."

"Well, that's it then," said Nathan Brown. "We walk from here."

"It ain't far," said Carl Bowman. "I fish around here sometimes, and I spent a few years feeding sailors on a schooner before I opened the tavern. If there's a schooner backed into that narrows, she's not damned far. This is probably close enough."

A man dropped a plank off the bow and men started trailing each other down to the sand.

Forrest McMallery squatted down over a bulky bundle on the deck.

"We gonna take this thing?"

Aaron looked around the deck as he lowered the sails to flap loosely from the boom. McMallery followed his eyes and smiled.

"They took all the other stuff. Nathan swears he knows how to sight it. Fired it himself back in '15, before the Brits got too close."

Aaron gave the boat another quick glance, making sure the rowboat tied at the stern was still secure, then joined McMallery. The man and the boy lifted with a single grunt shared between them and shuffled down the plank with awkward half-steps. Nearly to the planned destination, they had carried the bundle as far as Aaron's trembling arms and legs would allow. At the sound of the gunshots Aaron dumped the heavy weight unceremoniously onto the swamp grass and mud at his feet. McMallery sensed it coming and stepped away from it as it fell, shaking his arms and rocking his neck after the release.

"Didn't mind the stop at all, young Mister Pulaski, but please do let me know if you decide to drop that again."

"Yes, sir. Sorry."

They both looked around. Breaks in the mist allowed him to see the bow of the slave ship anchored less than a hundred yards from their muddy path. Resting his shoulders and back, Aaron leaned forward and braced his hands on his legs just above the knees. He stayed there breathing deeply until some of the aches left his lower back. Mr. Brown dropped his heavy sack near the same spot, watching its content move about settling onto the soggy ground. Two other men brought the wooden wheels and another brought the keg of powder. Brown pointed the last man toward the tree line behind them, whispering to him.

"Best set that over there, Jim. You might start filling those little canvas bags with powder, if you would, please. Use the wooden spoon, though – no sparks."

The man nodded and stepped a few yards away.

Two men held the wheels up as Forrest and Aaron lifted the bundle one more time. The wheel hubs were slipped onto the cannon trunnions, the bulky pins sticking out on either side. Nathan tapped wooden pegs into the holes at the end of each trunnion to hold the wheels in place. When the men stepped back to look at the cannon, one of them spoke in a strained whisper.

"Little two-pounder might help some, but not much. I just got a glimpse of the schooner. She heavy armed. Got three cannon on each side, four or six-pounders, I think. We need to stay well away from the mouths of those things."

"Won't be trying to punch holes in the ship, just even the odds with their crew," Nathan answered. "We got a couple two-pound shot, but the rest we brought were grape shot. It'll be like getting shot at by fifteen large muskets, all at once."

Forrest shook his head. "Seen it in town before, where we got it, but never seen it fired. Nathan, you sure it will work?"

"I fire it every July 4th."

---<>---

Simon worked his way among the pine trees along the western edge of the island moving south on the old dirt path in a fast moving trot. Mattingly and the others were not far behind. Simon silently cursed himself.

Should have stayed with Sonja. Shouldn't have left her. Didn't think when I bit on Wilson.

He shook his head as he ran.

The ship could not be far.

His pistol was tucked into his belt and he carried a boat hook like a lance across in front of him, his hands gripping the oak shaft as he trotted through the mist. The fog was thinning more, raising its veil to show him the forest and the Narrows just yards away.

My fault. Should have gone in Isaac's window. Helped him then. It may be too late for Sonja. Damn! Damn! Damn!

The faint light above the mist grew again. Between the trees, he could see the hull of a ship further up the Narrows. He quickened his pace, his knees and his ankles aching from the run, his chest pounding, and colored sparks dancing at the edge of his vision. Even as the pain increased he ran harder still.

"Damn" he muttered through ragged breath.

---<>---

Sonja took in another deep breath.

Keep calm, woman.

Blind in the darkness. Each time she thought she was farther through the knot and quickened her pace, she found she had passed a loop and had to work back along the intricate sailor's knot to where she should be. The loops at her wrist kept her from actually feeling the knot with her fingertips in the lightless tier. She learned the knot through her lips and the sensitive skin at their edges, rubbing again and again over the prickly fibers. Pressing the steep tapered tip into the core of each loop, she used her tongue to set it into the valleys between the lines. The whiskered visitor in the dark crawled across her leg again, only to be ignored this time as the human concentrated on the rope knots. Finding no hint of a worthwhile morsel, the rat ambled among the stored anchor lines and out through one of the many holes connecting compartments for its routine forage.

Sonja jerked her back straight.

Yes! Yes, by God! Yes!

At last, the rope tying her to the bulkhead was undone and she could move farther about the darkened room, only to find she already had almost total access of her little space. She reset her shoulders and forced herself to concentrate again on the knot at her wrist. She forced herself to ignore thoughts about the gunshots that had reverberated through the hull. Light exploded through the cracks of the door directly in front of her, only inches away from her feet. She closed her eyes tightly against the pain of the blinding light splashed into the blackness by a single candle in the next compartment. Surely, he had come for her. The cabin door swung open with a crash, a form leaned through the doorway, hands yanked at her legs, sliding her out of her dungeon.

"C'mon, Bitch," a voice growled. "Cap'n wants ya."

A sack was thrown over her head and down to her waist while a second set of hands grabbed at her, yanked off her bloomers and helped drag her out into a companionway. She cried out in pain as a heavy fist slammed into her side.

"Be still, Bitch, or by God I'll cut ya."

She believed him and was still as he tossed her over his shoulder and carried her up the stairs to the forward hatchway. A calloused hand gripped hard at her inner thigh, holding her to his chest and shoulder as he walked, exploring her with his thumb. His other hand played freely with her exposed buttocks.

" Findley, I ain't gettin no fun," the other man complained. "I get to carry her back down."

---<>---

Ben worked his way along another deck, deeper in the ship, trying to find a way forward, but the forward most companion way was closed off and locked on each deck. No normal schooner would have such an impediment from the lower decks, it was paramount for seamen to get to the upper deck at either end, in case a ship foundered. Only a slaver would have such an obstacle. It was another barrier between the small white crew and the large number of African "cargo" of slaves. Ben was free to move about only the stern of the ship, but was otherwise trapped, held prisoner within its aft decks. A face arose in front of him, lit by the glimmer of a nearby candle lamp. Ben raised the cutlass and lunged at the face.

"No," it shrieked. "Don't hurt me! I am prisoner!"

Ben froze as he recognized the face. The cutlass tip only an inch in front of the trembling mouth. He tilted his head, looking at the face. Blinking away the blood still sliding down into his eyes from his soaked hair. He carefully brought up the rag and wiped his eyes and mouth, squeezing the saturated rag, dribbling blood onto the deck.

"Briscoe?"

Briscoe did not recognize the strained voice. Only saw the face and torso, tattered clothing drenched in blood, still dripping bloody droplets tapping on the deck in the moment of silence. The blade so close to his face

"No, don't kill me. Please, I won't tell anyone anything. Just let me go, please!"

"Briscoe? How are you here?"

Briscoe looked closer at the face.

"Pulaski? Oh God. Are we rescued?"

"What the hell are you doing here?"

"I was taken, Ben. I had to deliver papers to the ship's captain, and, and he had me locked away down here. He's a madman!"

Ben stared at him. The cutlass tip still hovering in front of the man's face. Ben's elbow up and cocked, his face canting to the other side, his frown deepening. "What papers? You deal in land. Why would you have business with a ship captain?"

"Yes. Land. That's right. He wants land. Wants land for investment. Yes."

"You are selling him land?"

"Land? Yes. Land. But, but not me, no, Binterfield. Binterfield is selling Hoagg land. Yes."

"Hoagg has you locked down here?"

"Yes. Yes. Yes. See?"

Briscoe held up his bound wrists, and pointed to the pallet on the floor where the rope from his wrists ended at a knot through an iron bolt in the ship framing. Ben looked around in the faint light, lowered the cutlass, and shook his head.

"I'll want to know more of this later."

Ben blinked, turned to walk away.

Briscoe reached out. "No! Don't leave me! They will kill me."

Ben shrugged his shoulders and stepped toward the companionway back up.

"For God's sake, Ben! Don't leave me down here. They will kill me for what I have seen. Let me loose and I will tell Mattingly what they have done. I will be a witness for you. And for Sonja..."

Ben stopped and turned back toward him, Briscoe bobbed his head.

"Yes! I can be her witness, too. Can tell the law what happened here."

"Do you know where she is? Where? What HAS happened here?"

"I heard them say she was in the cable tier at the bow."

"Can I get there from down here?"

"No. The cargo hold is for slaves. Only access is from the top. The bow compartments are forward of the cargo hold. No way through."

Ben turned back toward the steps.

Briscoe called after him. "Cut this rope, please! Or give me a knife."

Ben withdrew his knife and tossed it on the pallet, then crept back up the stairway. Even as he tried to think of what to do next, he heard his name called out from the upper deck. He could not understand the other words, for the muffle of the cramped interior of the ship and the fog outside.

Ben worked his way back to the base of the companionway past the captain's cabin.

"Pulaski!"

Hoagg yelled again, standing on the grating over the cargo hold.

"I have yer sweet Bitch, Pulaski!"

Hoagg had men with muskets and boarding pistols standing by the aft hatchway. Two others stood beside him holding Sonja between them.

"Findley, go unbolt the door down there, so he can come out," Hoagg ordered.

The man hesitated.

"Git," growled Hoagg, "And then bring your ass back here. No one's cuttin him but me."

Findley dropped Sonja to her knees, pulled out his knife and trotted toward the stern. Stopping at the edge of the companionway, he looked carefully down the stairway. He slipped down to the landing in front of the cabin door and quietly slid the bolt back. Then he dashed back up to the deck, checking behind himself as he came back to Hoagg.

Hoagg smiled. "Come out, Pulaski! I don't want yer woman, it's YOU I need ta settle with. Come on out and I'll let the bitch go!"

Ben remained silent. Nothing he could say would intimidate or satisfy Hoagg.

"You don't come out," Hoagg continued, "and your last memory of your woman will be the sound of her screaming and me guttin' her like a fish, while you stand down there pissin in yer pants!"

Ben kept his silence only a moment longer

before making his decision. He knew they were both dead. He had failed.

"All right," yelled Ben. "I'm coming up."

15

"Take the bag off her," Hoagg ordered. "I want her ta see all that's coming."

Findley removed the sack, Sonja's hands were still tied together, her dirty fingers still laced across each other. He yanked her off her knees by her hair. Sonja let out a muffled cry as small patches of hair were ripped from her scalp. He held her up on her toes.

"You and your bastard man kilt my mate Jenkins," he whispered into her ear. "You're both gonna die real slow."

He punched her in her side again, cracking the rib he had damaged in the cable tier. Sonja dropped to her knees, the air pushed from her lungs. There were no sounds of help outside the ship. He knew Hoagg would kill Sonja. Knew Hoagg had no intention of letting her go.

In front of me, and as painful as he can make it.

Ben fingered his cutlass. "I'm sorry, Sonja," he whispered into the gloom of the stairway. "But I will make it as quick as I can. Maybe I can get to him..."

Ben stepped up onto the landing in front of the captain's cabin, the door swinging free. Remembered the wall where he pulled down the cutlass. Crossed pistols above it. He stepped into the cabin. They were still there. He tossed the cutlass onto the desk and pulled down the pistols. They were cap and ball.

"Pulaski! Get up here!"

Hoagg craned his neck to see over the edge of the companionway opening. The crewmen around him tilting their heads listening, fingering their knives.

"He ain't comin out, Cap'n," one of the men said. He yanked on Sonja's hair again to make her cry out, but she gave up no sound, keeping her hands tight against her abdomen.

"Cut her a little, Findley," Hoagg ordered, "Not ta kill, just enough to let Pulaski know his time has run out."

"Hey, Pulaski," Findley yelled. "Here's a little something fer Jenkins!"

Pulling Sonja up by her hair, he pulled out his knife and stuck the tip against her outer thigh. He pressed with increasing firmness until the tip broke through her skin and penetrated into her muscle. Clenching her teeth Sonja emitted only the slightest whimper and would not scream out.

Stay down there, Ben. Stay down there. He will kill us both anyway. Stay alive, Ben. Stay alive!

Findley forced the steel tip deeper into her muscle, twisting it slightly, but still she would not scream. Tears ran down her cheeks. Blood flowed from the corners of her mouth as she bit her own lip to endure the pain. Ben finished loading the second pistol. Several lead balls rolled around in loose powder on top of Hoagg's desk, the ripped bag that held them discarded on the floor. He quickly stepped back out onto the landing. Took deep breaths, blew the air out slowly. The edges of his vision rippling in toward the center. The rush in his ears reaching a higher pitch until the sound was almost gone.

Move quick. Hoagg wants a show. Wants to make it happen slowly, so he can enjoy it. Let them hesitate for just an instance. That is all I will need.

The curved tip of the knife blade was buried under her skin and into her muscle, blood ran down her leg and began to patter onto the deck, ran from her mouth and dripped from her chin onto her filthy sodden shift. The knife tip found her bone. Findley felt it. Scraped the tip against it, knowing the pain that would generate. The cry rose up from her bowels, even fighting it as it erupted, hating that she could not endure more. It exploded through her throat into the mist and fog, piercing their ears and even the souls of those that had them,

"N-O-O-O-O-O-O-O-O-O-o-o-o-o-o-o-o-o-o!!!!!"

Findley smiled like a child, withdrawing the blade from her leg. He wiped it on her shift and returned it to its sheath with a flourish, relaxing his grip and allowing Sonja to settle down onto the grating. He looked to the others, wanting the admiration in their eyes. His snicker of self-satisfaction was audible and echoed by the others nearby. This would be over soon enough. One of the men near the grating even began to think how his share would increase with fewer shipmates asking for it. Sonja's scream continued, and she sank toward her knees, but not onto them.

As Findley pulled her back up by her hair, she sprang at him. The Marlin spike tucked between her wrists. Its handle was nested within her palms, rotated in her hands. Grasping the handle tightly, the spike extended in front of her fists. She drove up with her legs and pushed out with her arms. She found her target. She pushed with all her weight and strength and rage. Her palm jammed the spike deep. She drove the spike into his eye socket. It pierced the jelly of the eye. It crushed through the fragile bone behind it and deep into his head until only the tip of the handle showed. Findley screamed. He released his grip and brought his hands up to his face, groping at the spike jammed into his head.

Her hands still tied together, Sonja shoved her shoulder against Findley and jumped off the grating. Three steps. She passed the wheels. Four more steps. She was at the top of the companionway. Hoagg's face twisted into a snarl, opened his mouth to give an order. Findley twirled down onto the grating, both hands at his face, clawing at the spike handle. Blood gushed between his fingers. Sonja lunged up over the hatchway, leaving a bloody footprint on its rim and took the four final steps along the cabin roof. Without slowing, she flung herself off the ship into the water.

She yelled out as she plunged down toward the deep channel "Ben! I'm free! I'm Free!"

Ben was crouched on the landing, mounting the steps when she jumped. He turned toward the stern window at the sound of her calling out to him. Her voice pierced the roar in his ears. She flashed by the broken stern window. He dropped the pistols in the doorway, took four long strides to the window bench and launched himself out of the cabin into the water below. Hoagg's foul weather boots were yanked from his feet as he hit the water. He followed her bubbles down into the darkness. His shoulders ached as he pulled himself deeper and deeper in the water. Farther below, Sonja's jump had taken her all the way to the bottom. Her feet hit the mire at the floor of the channel and it trapped her there. Her scream for Ben had cost her dearly. She had not had time to take in a deep breath to serve her during such a dive.

Get away, Ben! I will look after Alisha until it's time for you to join us. But not today, Ben. Get away!

Farther down Ben pulled himself deeper against his own buoyancy. The air in his lungs kept him from going faster and farther. He pulled and pumped the water past him, shoving him farther down, the trail of bubbles thinning out and the meager light fading in the deeper cooler water. He was slowing, reaching the limit of his dive, the air in his lungs keeping him from getting to her.

NO! Not without you!

He exhaled all the air from his lungs, sending them back to the surface where they belonged, and still pulled himself deeper into the cold water. Pulled at the water finding nothing, feeling the coldness of the deeper water, and then a faint touch on his face, lighter than a downy feather.

There! A hand!

He grabbed at it, but it flew away from his grip. He grabbed again, caught her wrists, the ropes still there, pulled her up, her feet relaxing and loosening in the mire, and she came up to him.

Have her now. Pull her up!

Lazily his arms went out, groped through the dark water, fingers barely moving.

Wake, damn you! Pull us up! Pull her up!

Bright colored spots danced at the edge of his vision, moving toward the center, swirling toward a drain. Blackness chasing them inward.

Pull! Pull! Kick! Kick!

Sonja rose in the water, but wanted only to sleep. She wanted to release the burning explosion eager to be freed from her chest, release the ache in her chest that only inhaling would satisfy. Jerk. Jerk. Something was still kicking in the water. Something was jerking on her wrists. She could feel him there with her. He would not leave her. She had always known that. She pushed with her legs, slowly then faster. There was the gentle caress of lace drifting across her face, soothing her, calming her. She kicked with her feet. There was light in front of her face. Lighter water was up above. She could see him above her, pulling the water down with his one hand, holding on to her with his other.

He needs help.

She kicked and kicked again. The water grew lighter.

They exploded through the surface. Gasping, gulping hoarsely, sucking air into their lungs, putting out the fire, driving away the blackness and the lights and the pounding in their heads. Ben grabbed the tiller chain bolted into the rudder with one hand. His arm was stretched to its limit up and out of the water. His other arm was wrapped around Sonja. They gasped and coughed, looking into each other's eyes. Coughing, still hungry for air, holding on to each other.

Explosions from above joined hot splashes near them. Men shot down at them from the cabin window, but they were too far under the slope of the stern for a clear shot.

Yelling and cursing roared across the deck above them.

"Get them! Get them," Hoagg screeched into the thinning mist.

A large splash in the water behind them, but they could not turn quickly enough to see this new threat. A hand rose out of the water next to Sonja, grabbed weakly at Ben, then at her. The face of the owner came back to the surface. The marlin spike was still in his eye socket, ruby water swirling from his eye. His face was white, near death, but not yet dead. Hoagg had him cast into the water, so much trash to be gotten out of the way. Ben kicked out, connecting with Findley's torso and pushing him away from the rudder. Findley's hand slipped back into the water. His other eye held open and glaring at them. His lips twisted into a snarl and still moving in silent curses as his face sank deeper into the water until it was gone.

Ben began moving around the edge of the rudder, pulling Sonja with him. At last his lungs had regained enough air that he could trust himself to whisper without gasping or yelling.

"We need to make it to the shore, it's only a few

yards, then we can run into the woods."

Sonja gulped more air, still refilling her own lungs, but nodded yes to him. On the other side of the rudder, he moved as far forward as the available grip allowed him a hold and the rake of the stern gave him cover. They needed to move toward the thicker brush beyond the bow, but the ramp down to shore from the ship was near the bow. Men with rifles lined the railings of the ship looking for one or both of their captives to surface or climb on shore.

Heavy boots ran down the ramp, wooden heels knocking on oak planks.

They are coming for us!

A shot echoed off the woods toward the bow of the ship.

"Let the Bastard go!" It was Hoagg's voice. "Briscoe ain't worth killin. Let him go suck on Binterfield's tit. Don't need him anymore."

Hoagg knows Binterfield. Knows Briscoe works with him. Doesn't need him anymore? For what?

Ben pulled Sonja's arm. He kicked out from the rudder, pushing as hard as he dared without creating a splash in the water to draw attention. They moved quietly along the length of the ship. Sonja kicked with her remaining strength. They swam drunkenly, but silently, farther down the shore, farther down toward the bow. They found a large bush twenty feet beyond the bow, half in shallow water. Otter had long played among the bushes and the animal trail gave them a covered crawlway onto the bank. They crawled several feet into the bushes and found the ground firmer, but the bush thinner.

From the muddy point just south of the *Raven*, Aaron had heard his mother's scream. Guessed his father was near her, trying to help. He readied his tools as he watched the men on deck with rifles looking out at the water and then occasionally out over toward the bushes. He could barely see them between curtains of fog as the folds opened and closed, giving only glimpses between agonizing moments. It would flash open for only a split second, let him see the ship under its lanterns, then close again. The wind was rising slightly and the gray above had taken a slight blue. The overcast sky above the fog was breaking up.

Pray God we get sun to burn this fog away.

Ben and Sonja crawled deeper among the small trees and bushes, making progress away from the ship, but also heading out toward the last cover of the bushes. Aching joints, and burning muscles made progress slow and difficult. One of the crew spotted the pair and called the others. Cracks and pops erupted from the deck as small clouds of burned powder drifted in the air and musket balls peppered the ground near Ben and Sonja. Ben pulled Sonja's hand.

"We'll have to run, do you hear me?"

"I can't, Ben. There is no running left in me."

He knew she was exhausted, but feared a musket ball bursting into her body if they stayed where they were.

"There they are," Aaron yelled. "Pa! Pa! Stay down!"

But in the noise, Ben did not hear the words.

With Ben and Sonja safely out of the ship, Forrest and Carl managed to set themselves up in tree limbs to see across the ship's deck. When the fog parted, they fired at the men on deck. The sailors took cover behind the cabin walls.

Hoagg ducked down behind the ships wheels.

"Who the Hell is that? You men, go pull up the gangplank!"

Three men scurried forward to pull up the bow plank. He grabbed the remaining man near him.

"Are the deck guns loaded?"

"Yes, Cap'n. Mr. Findley had us load'em with grapeshot yesterday before ye came back."

Hoagg grinned. "Excellent. Come with me."

They sprinted to the forward most cannon, adding chocks under the rear of the barrel, forcing the muzzle down in front. Together they pulled the rear of the carriage toward the stern, sighting the cannon toward the grassy point beyond the bow.

"Go to the next one. Do the same thing there," Hoagg ordered.

As the other man moved to the midship gun, Hoagg pulled down a nearby lantern, opened its glass case and held the flame to the fuse on top of the cannon. He dashed by the wheels to get away from the cannon's kickback, but the fuse sputtered out.

"Damn it to Hell! Fog's made it damp."

Lead rifles balls furrowed into the deck near him, followed by the crack of firing.

"Shit! Who is that??"

Hoagg ran hunched-back along the deck to the aft companionway and tumbled down the steps to his cabin. He found the pistols in the doorway. Found they were loaded and cocked. Set them both to half cock, and slid them under his belt. He discovered the ripped bag of powder lying on the floor next to his desk.

"Shit! Shit! Shit!"

But the bag was still half full, so he scooped it up, holding it closed between his fingers and dashed back up the steps.

The fuse at the first cannon was still smoldering, so he pulled it off and set it on the deck. Then he grabbed a powder quill from its slot in the cannon carriage, and brushed off the firing hole on top of the cannon. He drove the bird's quill down into the hole, clearing it of damp powder, then filled the hole with fine grain powder from the ripped bag.

Again, musket balls smacked into the ship near him and he jerked away from their impact.

"God damn it!"

He scooted beside the cannon carriage, out of its kickback and grabbed the smoldering fuse. Bringing up his shoulders, covering his ears with them as best he could, he touched the fuse to the powder. The explosion was tremendous. Men were never to be this close to the muzzle when a cannon was fired. Hoagg's head ached from the thunder.

The dawning mist erupted in brilliant yellow light. Flame and smoke thundered out from the muzzle. Trees and bushes were swept away in the fury. Branches snapped off. The air near the ground was alive with the whining of grape-sized lead balls tearing through the woods. The young trees where Forrest and Carl sat evaporated under them, sending them crashing to the ground, trapped in the consuming silence that came behind a cannon blast. Beyond the nearby trees, unseen from the ship, Nathan spun in the mist like a toy top and fell to the ground.

The sailors crouching behind the cabin stood up to enjoy the destruction of the nearby trees and bushes. Cheering the scream coming back out of the fog, gleeful that someone had suffered.

Aaron stooped beside Nathan in the lingering silent stupor, saw much of his left upper arm gone, ripped away from the bone, blood cascading down within the gash. He reached for him, but Nathan pushed him back, his mouth wide open, screaming, pointing at the small cannon in front of them. Nathan screamed again. This time Aaron heard him.

"Fire it! It's sighted. Light the fuse!"

Aaron stood frozen. Nathan grabbed his bloody arm with his other hand. Kicked Aaron's leg.

"Light it, Aaron! Light the cannon fuse!"

Aaron reached down for the little tin candle lamp. Tiny holes in the metal where meager light escaped into fading darkness from the stubby candle inside. Nathan kicked him again, then laid back, squirming as the numbing shock to his body slipped away and the monstrous pain galloped to his brain.

Aaron opened the little lantern and took out the candle, cradled the flame within the cup of his fingers and touched the flame to the short fuse on top of the little cannon.

Once again thunder exploded in the grey light. The tongue of fire lanced out and smoke tumbled toward the Raven. A piece of the railing ripped away from the side and flung itself across the deck. Several thumps against the masts and spars, more pieces of splintered wood tapping down on the deck around the crewmen.

"God damn it to Hell," Hoagg screamed. "Who the God damned Hell *is* that?"

In the trees beyond the stern, Forrest and Carl helped each other off the ground and made their way back toward the point. Finding Aaron kneeling next to Nathan, Carl yanked his shirt off and began ripping it into bandages for Nathan. Forrest grabbed Aaron's shoulder.

"Let's reload this thing, young man."

Briscoe ran headlong into them. Forrest grabbed him around the throat.

"No! No," Briscoe rasped. "I'm not with them. See, Ben gave me his knife to get away!"

He showed them the knife.

"Good, you can help," but before Forrest could say any more, Briscoe was gone around the point. Running like a madman.

Aaron grabbed two small bags of grape shot and placed them next to the wheel. He stepped over to the little pile of small canvas bags a few yards away. He hefted one little bag then picked up a second. Forrest had already used a gaff handle with a wet rag tied around it to sponge out the barrel for the next load. As Aaron slipped the bags into the mouth of the cannon, Forrest used the other end of the stick to push the bags to the deepest end of the barrel.

"How many little bags of powder did you use last shot?"

"One."

Then Aaron pushed the two bags of shot into the barrel and Forrest rammed them all the way back against the bags of powder.

"Un-huh. How many bags of grape did you use before?"

"One."

The two rotated the wheel to aim the cannon back at the ship. Forrest used powder from his own powder horn to fill the fuse slot at the top of the barrel and then shoved another short fuse into the middle of the little pile of powder.

Forrest stepped slightly away from the cannon, thought a second, then stepped back two more.

Men on the ship with muskets had come back to the railing near the bow, Hoagg behind them pushing them and screaming.

There was no cover left for Ben or Sonja, he had to pull, drag, somehow get her behind cover. The grapeshot from the ship had whizzed only inches above their heads. His hearing was only now coming back. Sonja was willing, but her exhausted battered body no longer responded to her demands. They were trapped where she lay in the open.

"There they are!" Aaron cupped his hands around his mouth and yelled to his father. Ben raised his head to look around, to find the direction to move for cover, and was amazed to see Aaron standing fifty yards away waving to him.

"Pławić!" [Get Down!!] he yelled again, using the Polish that his father had always used to keep his son's head safe from the swinging boom. Ben still barely heard, but then saw the mouth of the iron cannon standing beside Aaron.

Aaron yelled again. "Pławić!"

Understanding this time, he threw himself on the ground over Sonja. The candle went down as soon as Aaron saw his father dive for the ground. The roar of the cannon was almost deafening compared to the pop and crack of the rifles and pistols. The double bag of grape shot sprayed almost everything on the bow of the ship, peppering the sides, penetrating where the wood was thinner, cutting sail lines and hitting two of the men standing at the rail. One fell to the deck writhing in pain holding the shattered remnant of the left knee, his foot dangling uselessly by tattered strips of skin.

Ben and Sonja rose again to stumble toward Aaron. Musket fire erupted from the wooded area beyond the stern of the ship. Mattingly had watched the firing on the ship and saw the impact of the old 'Potato Battery' relic pilfered by the canallers. He finally believed what was happening and had lined up the Havre de Grace men behind stout trees. Pop and crack, more muskets flung lead balls at the ship's crew. Another crewman slumped over the rail as the musket fire finally began to take its toll on the ship. Ben and Sonja managed to move a few feet closer, and Aaron prepared to run out to assist them, but Ben waved him back. "Stay there, we are coming to you!"

Briscoe saw the *Ugly Boat* wedged onto the sandy beach and ran toward it, bumping into Isaac. Before Isaac could speak, Briscoe had gone on. Isaac would not stay safely at the barge. His hands bleeding through the bandages, Isaac cradled more bags of black powder in his arms. Half stumbling, he ran on toward the gunfire.

Forrest slapped Isaac on his shoulder and bent to the task of reloading the cannon. "Not much too this, lad."

A figure stepped to the bow of the ship carrying two muskets. Hoagg himself came to kill Ben, but first would kill the bastard shooting the cannon at his ship. Forrest completed the reload and stood to look at the target.

"This time, let me see ya shoot, lad. May be the last time fer years I get ta see one of these little babies do their true duty."

Aaron pointed at the figure on the ship's bow and Forrest turned to look.

"There you are, you bastard," Hoagg said along the barrel of the musket. He loosed the lock and the air around him filled with the smoke as the musket fired, sending the ball almost a hundred yards to its target. The ball smashed into Forrest's chest, sending him onto his back in the soft grass. Aaron and Isaac stared at the fallen man lying on the ground, his eyes shut tight against the force of the impact. Isaac snatched up the smoking fuse that had dropped from Aaron's grip and slapped it against the touch hole of the cannon. Again the air erupted with the explosion of cannon fire, filled with dozens of lead balls ripping through the air to the bow of the ship, but Hoagg had already thrown himself to the deck and avoided the carnage meant for him.

Isaac and Aaron knelt beside the red bearded blacksmith. His eyes were shut tight and his arms thrown high above his head. His head lay there on the damp ground, much as Isaac had seen him only hours before as he had stepped up and removed the nail from his hands – and he had winked. Then his eyes opened, emeralds framed by the flaming red hair and beard, and he looked at the boys and winked. He brought his arms down and thumped his chest with the knuckles of one hand. The metallic sound was unmistakable. He sat up and pulled the curved iron plate from under his shirt, turning the front to see where the bullet had only dented the surface. The smashed ball was wedged into the crater created by its impact. He pried the ball from the plate with his fingernail and smiled at the boys.

"I'm a blacksmith," he said. "I know about such things."

They grinned as Aaron helped the man stand. "But, it still hurt like hell, I tell you," Forrest said.

Faces fell as they noticed the cannon had split several inches along the length of its barrel, near the mouth.

"No use left in that one," Forrest said. "Might as well drop it in the bay. Made for the Revolution, you know. Really too old ta be firing now."

Mattingly's group fired again from the tree line. Then, seeing the sailors scramble away from the railing, they rushed forward. Among the deputized men, Anthony Renowitz, looked for a sign of Ben. The last cannon fire had cleared the deck and he was sure any survivors ought to be ready to yield. He and others propped the discarded gangplank up against the midship opening. He was up the plank and the first onto the deck, seeing the backs of the few remaining men dashing down the hatchway. He ran into the opening and yelled for the men to surrender. Hoagg screamed from behind him, Anthony was too far ahead of his group to have their protection at his back.

"Renowitz! You sonofabitch! Does every bastard I hate live in this fuckin' town!"

Hoagg came from the far side of the bow driving the old boarding pike ahead of him, its long iron spear tip ran into Anthony before he could complete the turn to face him. The tip entered him just below his ribs and drove deep as Hoagg threw his weight behind it. The tip buried into a rib at his back and then snapped it in a sickening grinding crunch as Hoagg shoved the spear tip through the bone and deep into the wooden cabin wall in front of him, impaling Anthony where he stood. Anthony screamed out in pain. He tried to reach around with his hand to free himself from the spear.

Simon hopped onto the deck as Hoagg pinned Anthony to the cabin outer wall. He dropped his empty pistol and took up one of the cutlasses thrown down by the crew. Hoagg was still leaning into the shaft trying to drive the spear deeper when he heard Simon's footsteps, but too late to move. Simon brought the blade down, taking off the end of the shaft and Hoagg's right hand. Hoagg shrieked and rolled onto the deck, grabbing his empty wrist, fighting the pain and the blood loss and trying to move away from Simon's blade. Knowing Hoagg was finished, Simon threw down the cutlass and went to help Anthony.

"Take it out! Take it out," Anthony begged.

Simon grabbed the shaft and leaned back, pushing with his legs, wrenching it from the wall and pulling it from Anthony's side. Anthony fell to his knees as the tip was withdrawn. He leaned against the cabin wall, keeping to his knees, grunting in pain.

Simon knelt next to Anthony, his large hand gently holding Anthony's head next to his own. "Don't you worry none, Anthony. Don't be whinin over a little pinprick. You be out getting drunk with the boys in no time."

"Liar. Could always tell when you're lying," Anthony whispered.

A man cried out at the gang plank. Simon looked up to see one of the men from town , falling to his knees, grabbing at a gaping bloody line spreading across his belly. Hoagg lumbered down the plank with the cutlass dangling from his remaining hand, trying to squeeze the blood loss at his other wrist. Simon grabbed up the pike he had pulled from Anthony and ran to the rail, just as Hoagg touched onto the ground, heading for the northern tree line. Simon heaved the staff into the air with all the strength his body and his anger could give. It flew high the air, arching down, finding its target.

The spear punched through Hoagg's chest and buried its tip deep into the ground. The force knocked him to his knees and pinned him to the spot like a insect on display. Hoagg dropped the cutlass into the mud. He remained on his knees, examining the shaft that ran from his chest into the ground. Too much pain to fall forward, not enough remaining strength to pull himself off the pike. He grabbed desperately at the staff with his remaining hand. His shoulder blade was immobilized by the spear. Curses and spittle filled his mouth and the air in front of his face.

Simon walked down the plank and casually stepped in front of Hoagg, so the man could see him. He squatted down in front of Hoagg and looked close into his face. Hoagg grunted for each breath, sensed the presence of another person. He opened his eyes and stared at Simon's face. It took a moment before he could focus on the dark face in front of him. When he felt Hoagg recognized him, Simon smiled.

"Doesn't look like we're going to make it to Charleston after all, Hoagg."

Hoagg looked into Simon's face. Blood seeped from his mouth and dribbled down his chin. "I coulda got a thousand dollars for you, nigger."

Simon picked up the cutlass from the mud.

Mattingly yelled from the deck of the ship. "I am arresting him. He is my prisoner!"

Simon stood up, holding the cutlass with both hands, the blade arched over his shoulder.

"Not for sale, Hoagg.".

"Don't do it!" Mattingly yelled.

Simon raised his arms and shoulders.

"No! You can't kill a white man," yelled Mattingly.

Hoagg twisted his head to look up at Simon and spit.

Simon's arms made a wide sweeping arc. His muscles rippled as he drove the cutlass forward. The blade barely slowed as it sliced through neck muscle and bone. Hoagg's head dropped onto the ground next to him, where it bounced down the little slope into the water, and the waiting crabs.

"Simon! You are under arrest for murder!"

16

Aaron and Isaac dashed to their parents and helped bring them back to safety around the point. Ben and Sonja limped to the soft grass and dropped to their knees. The blood seeped out from Sonja's knife wound in her leg, red blossoming out in the wet fabric of her shift, a rivulet trailing along her calf and onto her ankle. She pressed her hand against it, pulling in a strained breath as she lay back onto the grass. Ben leaned over her, lifting the ragged edge of her shift and moved her hand just long enough to inspect the opening. Aaron and Forrest reloaded their muskets and stepped back toward the tree line to stand guard, watching for any movement from the ship or anyone coming around the point. Harper was bent over Nathan, wrapping the gaping wound in clean bandages and giving him a drink of laudanum from a small green bottle to help with the pain. Then he moved up to Sonja.

"Let's have a look there, Sonja."

"What happened to Mr. Brown, Wallace?"

Harper only shook his head as he examined Sonja's wound.

"Rather ragged edges there. Doesn't look like it was quick."

"No. The bastard enjoyed working it against my bone."

Harper squeezed the wound open to examine its interior. Sonja grimaced and jerked her hand up to his.

"Sorry, my dear, need to have a look in there."

He frowned and reached for his medical bag. He withdrew a pair of tweezers and brought them over the wound. He looked into her eyes.

"Brace yourself, Sonja. I need to pull something out of that wound."

Harper slipped the tweezers deep into the opening. Sonja whimpered and tears slipped down from the corners of her eyes as Harper worked. Ben grabbed her hand and held it tightly. Harper withdrew some debris from the wound, gave Sonja a quick glance and re-inserted the tweezers. He brought out more dark debris, and re-examined the opening.

"Not sure what all that is, Sonja, but we need that opening cleaner than it is."

He reached back into his bag and pulled out another small bottle. He uncapped it and held it over the wound, then looked into Sonja's eyes again.

"Brandy. This will sting quite a bit."

As he poured the alcohol into her wound, black debris floated to the surface and slid down the skin on her leg. Sonja gritted her teeth, but emitted no sound. Behind Harper, Nathan Brown moaned as he reached his other hand across his chest, holding his hand in the air just above his ruined arm, knowing he could not stand the pain if he touched it, making a fist. His wounded arm had gone numb below his elbow, but the banshees of hell still gnawed in his wound. Sonja leaned back against Ben's shoulder as Harper bandaged her leg.

"We need to get that wound flushed out again, as soon as we get back to Havre de Grace."

Nathan moaned louder as the pain increased. Harper patted Sonja's arm and moved back to Nathan. Ben let Sonja slip gently back down into the thick grass and stood over her. Above him, the fog was disappearing into the sunlight. He looked up to see the soft blue of an almost cloud-free spring sky. He turned his head toward Aaron and Mac.

"What's happening on the ship? Can either of you see?"

Forrest leaned forward, eyeing the activity on the deck. A couple deputized men were looking around the deck at the bow, looked out and saw Forrest, waved at him.

"Seems like the others from town have taken the deck. Can't see much more than the bow, but they seem to be walking around feeling safe. Mattingly is struttin around, acting pleased with himself."

"What?"

"Yep, Ben. Seems to be under control up there."

Ben looked down into Sonja's eyes, she was letting them close and breathing easily. He kneeled down and kissed her cheek then spoke softly into her ear. "Rest here. Catch your breath. I think it's over. I'm going back on the ship to speak with Mattingly."

She opened her eyes wide, started to rise, but Ben gently patted her shoulder and eased her down on the grass. "Just rest. We are all safe now."

Ben stood and glanced at Harper working over Nathan, shook his head and frowned, then turned his attention toward the tree line. He walked to where Forrest and Aaron stood. He slapped Forrest on his broad shoulder while he threw his other arm around his son.

"Well done, men."

Aaron smiled into his father's eyes, but retained a frown over his own.

"We are all right, son. Thanks to you and the others Tuttle brought back. Although I was really surprised to see you here. And Forrest. Who stayed with Isaac?"

Aaron shook his head. "No, Pa. Tuttle landed on the north end of the Island. I followed him in the *Ugly Boat*, and then steered east to bring her down to the point, well, almost to the point. And...uh...Isaac came with us."

"*YOU* sailed the *Ugly Boat*. *WITH* Isaac?"

"Yeah, and others. We came in two groups. Deputy Mattingly led one group, and...well...I led the other."

Ben's eyes flicked between the two. Forrest nodded in agreement and released a short belly grunt.

"He'd a swum otherwise. Surely knows how ta handle a sail boat. It was him said we had ta bring the little cannon from town. Nathan there knew where the powder and shot was kept."

Nathan released a terrible cry and Harper looked back over his shoulder. "Need some help over here! Think his artery has ruptured."

The three men dashed to Harper's side as Harper reached one handed into his bandage bag, muttering to himself, "Should have brought more of these damned things. Lift him up by his shoulder."

Hands from three men scooped up behind Nathan, raising him to a sitting position, while Harper frantically wrapped bundles of cloth around his bloody arm. Nathan screamed again. On the ground where he had laid, Aaron rested one knee in a deep pool of fresh blood. Harper flung a strip of bandage around his upper arm, tied it and yanked the knot tight. Nathan screamed. Blood spewed from under the bandages and rained down into the pool around Aaron's knee. Harper made another double loop around the upper arm and shoulder, flinging the already bloody strip through his armpit and over the shoulder again. He yanked another knot into place and tied it. Twisting his head around on both sides of him, he scanned the nearby ground.

"Hand me that thick stick!"

Forrest snatched it up and handed it to Harper who shoved it under the last two loops. "Need a tourniquet!"

Harper twisted the stick, binding the cloth strip, twisting it tighter and tighter around the armpit. Nathan's chin slumped forward onto his chest.

"No," Harper yelled, and he twisted the cloth strip tighter yet.

The dripping blood slowed. The knees of all three men holding him were soaked in his blood. A stain of blood seeped up the back of Nathan's pants. His palms lay flaccid on the blood soaked grass. Harper tilted Nathan's head back, pried open his eyes and examined the pupils, then held his ear to the man's mouth.

"Looks like the bleeding has stopped, Doctor Harper," Aaron said.

Harper looked at the ground then up into the sky.

"There is no more to come out, son. It's all there around your knees. Let's move him onto fresh grass."

They pulled him a few yards away and laid his limp body back onto unstained grass. Harper kneeled over him and gently closed Nathan's eyelids with his fingertips. He stood up, inhaling deeply and then exhaled a long ragged breath.

"God damn it," he muttered, then walked slowly to the nearby shoreline and kneeled in the shallow water. He rinsed his hands, letting the blood swirl away, blood on the Chesapeake, mixing with his own tears, drifting into the Bay.

Sonja crawled through the grass the few feet to get to Nathan. She sat by his side and held his hand. Tears ran down her cheeks, and she wept aloud. Aaron sat down next to his mother and put his arm around her shoulder. Isaac came back around the point and stood next to his father. The bandages around his hands frayed, loose and dirty, dried blood mixed with the dirt.

"Did Ma know him," he whispered.

"Yes, Son. He was a good friend to both her and me."

And he was Sonja's only witness to prove that she had not robbed the bank. Binterfield will come at us with a vengeance, now.

Simon Bond stepped up to Ben, speaking softly.

"Ben, I need to say goodbye."

"What?"

"The Deputy wanted to arrest Hoagg, but I killed him."

Ben turned to face him.

"You killed Hoagg?"

Simon nodded his head.

"Sorry I didn't get the chance to do that earlier, but the man needed to be killed, Simon."

Simon looked around the point and back toward the ship.

"Well, Mattingly wants to arrest me for killing a white man..."

"That's nonsense. Hoagg was a murderer and a lot of men came here from town to do just that."

"Yeah, but I was the one that did it, and the Deputy is coming after me."

"Let him come! You did us all a favor."

Simon's voice slipped into a hoarse whisper.

"Ben, you are as naive as ever. If they lock me up, I'll be hung. If they don't hang me for this one, they'll hang me for the one in St. Mary's County. Sooner or later the people here will know who I am, and then the ones from St. Mary's will come for me."

"I will do what I can, but we both know that is very little. I am sorry, my friend."

"Well, I have to go. I can't stay here. I need to take the row boat trailed behind the *Ugly Boat.*"

"Of course, take it, but what about Toby? What about him needing mahogany instead of oak?"

"I don't have that choice anymore, Ben. I have to run, and I can't take him now. Give him the best oak you can."

Ben offered his hand and Simon stepped in front of him to shield the view from others before taking it.

"Maybe we'll get together again someday, Ben."

Then Simon stepped back and crushed his hat in his hands, bobbing his head like a demoralized field hand, saying "Yassah, yassah." He looked up at Ben from under his eyebrows, winked, then turn and left.

"Go on, now," Ben yelled after him. "Do what I told you."

Ben put his hands gently on his sons' shoulders.

"You stay close to your Ma. Come get me if anything else happens." Then he walked around the point to the Ship. At the top of the gang plank he met Deputy Mattingly holding a clipboard and taking inventory of the people held captive in the hold.

"Where's your boy, Pulaski?"

"Which one?"

"Your boy, not one of your sons."

"Oh, I sent him trotting around to the barge to fetch blankets for my wife and the body of Nathan Brown."

"Brown? Man that clerked for Binterfield? He dead?"

"I am sorry to say it, but yes, he is. Grapeshot from the ship here tore off most of his left arm. He bled to death out there."

"Well, better than festering from rot and taking a week to die. Always better quick than slow. Who else came down on that barge of yours?"

"McMallery, Doc Harper,-"

"Doc Harper out there? Good! We need him up on the ship right away. Got two of my deputized men badly injured. One was belly cut by Hoagg before your boy cut his head off. The other was run through by the same spear that pinned Hoagg to the ground. They're both in bad shape, under shade over there on the other side of the cabin."

Mattingly stepped to the other rail.

"Stanley! You go around the point beyond the bow of this ship and holler for Doc Harper. He's over there with the other group. Get him up here quick as you can."

Ben moved beyond the cabin, where a piece of canvas was attached to the cabin roof near one of his own bloody footprints. A man bent under the canvas, which was tied to the rail at its other end. The feet of two other men spread out from under the shade where they had been pulled against the low cabin wall, propping them up. Ben moved around to the far side of the cabin to see the men's faces, looking to see if either face was familiar.

"Anthony!"

Ben flung himself onto his knees next to his friend. Anthony Renowitz was deathly pale with a bloody strip of canvas wrapped around his chest and his right arm. A bandana had been folded several times and wedged under the knot of the canvas bandage. A large teardrop blossom of blood stained the material. Anthony's expression was screwed tight in obvious pain. He tilted his head and forced open one eye to look at Ben.

"Hoagg get away?"

"Only down the gangplank. Apparently Simon used the same spear Hoagg used on you to impale Hoagg to the ground down there."

"He dead?"

Ben smiled. "Gotta be. Simon took off his head. Mattingly's angry about that."

"Good."

"What the hell was wrong with you? You shouldn't have come here with Mattingly's deputies."

"I *am* one of Mattingly's deputies. Couldn't miss a chance to rescue you and kill Hoagg."

"I appreciate you saving me, Anthony."

"Shut the Hell up. Give me some water."

Ben reached for the nearby water bucket and offered the ladle to Anthony. He snatched the handle with his left hand, holding it to his lips until the cup was empty. He gasped for air after swallowing the last mouthful, and coughed blood onto his lap. He glanced at the splatter on his lap and looked up at Ben.

"How's Sonja?"

"She's been stabbed in the leg. Lying in the grass around the point, but I think she will be all right. Harper already tended to her."

"Good thing you know a doctor, Benjamin. Your friends don't fare well."

"Especially the stupid ones..."

The man next to Ben leaned back and tossed a cloth over the face of the man sitting next to Anthony. His lower chest and abdomen and the folded cloth across his belly were all saturated with blood. A rivulet of thick blood spilled over from the puddle between his legs and following the slope of the deck, slowly wending its way to the edge of the ship like a night slug. The man tending him left his boot print in the rivulet as he stepped away and passed Doctor Harper hurrying toward him.

"No need for the first man. George is dead," the man said

Doctor Harper settled onto his knees next to Ben. "Let's lay you down, Anthony."

Anthony moaned as Ben and Harper pulled him away from the cabin wall and laid him on his back. Harper untied the bandage to examine the wound.

"Can't stitch you up yet, Anthony. I need to

cauterize that wound and it's unlikely I can do it here."

Ben glanced around the ship's deck.

"I'll bet she has a small smithie shop on board. Not enough to make manacles, but enough to fix pins and fashion spikes and such. I'll go see if I can start a fire in the coals."

Doc Harper nodded toward Ben and then turned his attention back to Anthony.

"It would be better to do it sooner than later."

"Aw, shit," Anthony muttered.

Harper pulled the cork from the brandy bottle, and squeezed the margins of Anthony's wound.

"This will hurt some."

As the pain shot through Anthony's upper chest like lightning strikes, he screwed his face in and grunted through clenched teeth.

"Save me a mouthful of that."

Down in the bow, just at the forward edge of the slave hold, Ben found the small bricked kiln with a miniature air bellows attached at the bottom. The bellows had a wooden handle that allowed the ship's blacksmith to force fresh air up into the coals to create the heat necessary to soften iron. He scooped a couple pounds of coal from the nearby bin and tossed them into the kiln from the top. Not knowing what the smith routinely used for starter, he snatched down the overhead lamp and poured half its contents onto the coals. Digging around the shelves on either side of the compact forge, he found a flint and striker, a length of unused iron bar, and next to that a pair of tongs. He struck the flint, starting the fire in the oil among the coals, then began pumping the bellows. As the fire shot up through the coals, he laid the end of the iron bar on the spot where they had already begun to glow white hot. The bar was round as a thumb and a foot long. He pumped the bellows again and again.

Moments later a hand pressed on his shoulder. Ben jerked around to find Isaac standing in the doorway of the cramped little shop. Ben's face was bright red and sweat dripped down his forehead and cheeks.

"Doctor Harper wants to know if you are going to be much longer."

Ben leaned aside, letting Isaac see over his shoulder. The air was folding and shimmering over the red hot end of the iron bar. The blasting heat of the little furnace lunged out at Isaac face and he stepped back into the narrow companionway.

"Tell Harper I'm almost ready to come back up. Tell him to get Anthony ready. Why are you on board?"

"Ma wanted me to come look for you."

Isaac disappeared from the doorway. Ben had thick leather mitts on both hands. He grasped the iron bar from its cooler end with the tongs and forced the handles together between his two-handed grip. The upper half of the iron bar was red hot and its tip had transcended into yellow-white. He left the inferno of the smithie shop and moved into the companionway and up the steps, holding the near molten iron ahead of him like a bowsprit.

The air on deck felt like a winter chill after the heat of the furnace, but the heat of the iron rod still baked his face. Watching his feet carefully, he stepped near the cabin area. Anthony was laid on the roof of the cabin. Hearing footsteps, Harper stepped back slightly to let Ben get closer.

Anthony tilted his head up and watched Ben approach. "Aw. Jesus Christ."

Harper came close to Ben. "Ben, I think the best way to do this is for me to guide your arms, so you maintain your grip on that rod. Yes?"

Ben took in a deep breath, then let it out. "Yes."

Harper turned to the men standing nearby. "Arms and legs, gentlemen. And stay out of Ben's way."

"Is this really necessary," Anthony asked, a tremor in his voice.

Harper stepped behind Ben, his huge frame almost engulfing Ben like a brown bear. He gripped Ben's forearms, rotating them until the rod was vertical and the red hot tip was pointing straight down. Harper spoke calmly and quietly into Ben's ear.

"Ben, we need to do this together. Slow, steady and straight. All the way down. All the way through to the cabin roof. Steady down and steady up, and not too fast. We must singe every blood vessel and purify every piece of tissue. But, we cannot linger or the tissue will stick to the rod. Do you understand?"

"Yes."

Harper lowered his voice to a whisper. "You cannot hear the screams, you must only hear my voice. You are my hands and we will save him. But, if we do not do it right, it will not work, and his pain will be for nothing."

"No. Wait. Let's talk about this some more," Anthony pleaded.

Harper looked at the men helping him. "Arms and legs, gentlemen. Arms and legs. He must be still, so we can save him."

The first hiss was like a water bubble dropped on the top of a fire-fed iron stove. Anthony whimpered, and bit on the leather strap placed between his teeth. Then the sound of fresh bacon laid in the bottom of a hot pan. Anthony surrendered a moan that scaled to higher notes as the bar slipped deeper. Then the popping sound searing fat meat and the bubbling of deep frying grease. Anthony screamed. The rod slipped deeper. Ben wanted to snatch it away from his friend; to yell how sorry he was, then the frying of more raw meat. The air became pungent with the smell of fried human flesh and vaporized blood. Anthony screamed, his voice reaching notes beyond human hearing, but his mouth wide open and air clawing out from his chest, his breath tainted with the scent of his own fried lung and blood. There was a gurgling in his voice and then nothing. His voice went silent. His body relaxed into unconsciousness.

Finally, with Ben in his own hell, he felt the rod tap against the roof of the cabin. A faint hint of molten tar, then the slow rise back up began. The hissing continued. The feel of the metal dragged over charred surfaces crawled up through the body of the rod and into Ben's hands. The pop and bubble of searing remaining vessels and blood drops slowed, and with a final faint hiss the bar came above the wound. Harper released his grip on Ben's forearms, and stepped around him to examine Anthony. Ben looked around, met Sonja's eyes, saw the tears on her cheeks, felt the wetness of his own, and walked slowly away from the cabin. He dropped the bar into a water bucket, heard its last angry hiss before the splash. Ben took in a deep breath and set the tongs and gloves on the deck, then slid down next to them and rested his forearms on his knees. Sonja sat next to him, with Isaac and Aaron joining them. Harper spoke over his shoulder.

"Excellent."

Mattingly stepped near the Pulaski's, looking directly at Ben.

"Need to talk, Ben."

Ben rose and slowly followed Mattingly.

"It was against my orders, Ben. Hoagg was under arrest. Your Simon will have to answer for killing him."

"We all came here to do that, Mattingly. Any one of us could have done it. Would've been glad to do it."

Mattingly nodded his head in agreement, looking around the deck, the several pools of blood drying in the morning sunshine. "You do most of this, Pulaski?"

Ben looked across the deck. Stared at places where he had murdered men during the night. Saw them fall again in his mind, blood gushing out like whale spew. Saw himself drenched in human blood. Stepped toward the pools of blood near the wheel.

The monster is out. Can I put it away again? Will it let me?

"Pulaski," Mattingly said.

Ben rubbed the palms of his hands, flicking away the blood that was not there. He squeezed the edges of his shirt, trying to wring out the blood. He stopped before the largest pool, but could not remember which man he hacked to death at that spot. The pool, thick as dried tar, smelled of rotten meat, rising in the heat of the sunlight. Ben leaned over the spot. Saw his reflection.

God cannot forgive this. I promised him I would never kill again, if I could just come home. I brought it here with me. It will never go away.

"Pulaski!"

Ben turned back toward Mattingly with a jerk. "Yes?"

Mattingly swept his clipboard in an arc over the bloody stern deck. "You do all this?"

He stared at the Deputy for a long moment. "Yeah, and one down in the cabin. No, no. I think one pool belongs to a man with a Marlin Spike in his eye socket. That would be Sonja's handiwork. I brought her to that."

Mattingly blinked, his eyelids fully open, his eyes meeting Ben's.

"Don't think I'd want to get on her wrong side."

"No. You do not, Deputy." Ben smiled, but the smile did not reach his eyes.

Mattingly spun around as the train of captives began coming across the deck. They had waited with manacles still locked to their wrists and ankles while a deputized man searched for the keys in the captain's cabin. Mattingly stopped the first man by pressing the blunt end of his pencil against his chest. The man had skin the color of onyx, sprinkles of grey hair just showing above his ears and furrowed rows across his forehead. His coarse shirt and pants were nearly shredded off.

"What's your name, boy. Who do you belong to, boy ?"

"Cephus, and I ain't belong to no one but mysef and God. Massah Smith hissef manumissed me in 18 and 18 on this here island. And these here men on this ship, these animals, they kilt my youngest son and stole my oldest! Said they cut his throat and throwd his body out yonder in the Narrows. Throwd him out like he was trash! Laughing cause they knowd the crabs eat him. What you gonna do about that? Huh? What you gonna do about that?"

"Don't you sass me, hear?"

Then Mattingly took in a deep breath and let it out slowly.

"I'm sorry about your son. But know this: Those men are going into the same manacles we just took off you. They're going to jail in Bel Air and probably hang."

"You gonna do that? You really gonna do that to white men cause they kilt my Timmy?"

Mattingly's shoulders sagged and he lowered his voice.

"No. Because they kidnapped a local white woman – and stole personal property. But, they'll still most likely hang. Be glad for that."

"I ain't propty. I a man," Cephus said.

"Maybe so, Cephus, but you can't charge a white man in court. Go along, now."

The man shuffled across the deck, still stiff

from weeks in shackles, limped down the gangplank followed by the others who had been set free. Mattingly walked to the stern of the ship and yelled down to one of his deputized men.

"Clifford! You round up Tuttle. Tell him we'll need him to ferry some folks back to town. Probably have to make two or three trips."

"Haven't seen him since dark, but I'll go find him. Town's gonna have to pay him for that," the man said.

"Damnation," Mattingly muttered under his breath. "Pulaski! How many men came up on your barge? Six? Seven?"

"About, I think."

"You haul tons of coal in that barge of yours, don't you? And you got to go back through the canal basin, right – just to get home?"

"Yes."

Mattingly smiled. "How about you take all these 'rescued victims' back to town?"

"Be glad to."

Mattingly sprinted back to the stern to recall Clifford, but the man was already gone back into the woods looking for Tuttle. Seeing another deputized man, he yelled at him.

"Stanley! Lead all these people coming down. Take'em around that point beyond the bow and put them on board Pulaski's barge."

Ben was still standing before the edge of the stairway down to the captain's cabin. Staring down at all the splashed blood, now dried brown and cracking in the sunlight. His actions in the dark racing through his mind over and over.

"What'd you use, Pulaski?"

Ben did not look away from the blood.

"A cutlass."

Mattingly looked around the deck, noting the places where full grown men had been hacked to pieces. Their bodies had already been pushed overboard into the water by his men and other volunteers from town, but the enormity of the blood-letting was painted in large splotches on the deck, the rails, the cabin walls and the steps. He shook his head.

"All this. One man. One Cutlass. And you not a scratch on you. Not a drop of blood on you."

"Cold water washes away the blood, but not the act."

"I would have liked to see that Captain Hoagg stand trial for all this. You know, he came into my office - Bond! Simon Bond! Is your boy named Simon Bond? I have a notice about a Simon Bond. Hoagg looked at it. What's your boy's full name? I stopped him last winter and he said it was something else, not Bond. Had papers, I think. He got a last name? Is his name Simon Bond?"

Ben looked out toward the bow of the ship.

"No. His real name is Silas. I forget his last."

"You got papers on him? Bill of Sale."

"No. He said he was freed. Showed up at my place a couple years ago. Him and an Irishman name Mickey showed up about the same time I started on the canal. Never saw either one before that. Hired them for barge work."

"Maybe the Irishman knows his last name?"

"Don't know. He left a while back. Went up into Pennsylvania. Haven't seen him since."

"Well, when Simon gets back with your blankets, you send him to me. Slave or free, he goes to jail for killing Captain Hoagg."

"Deputy! Deputy Mattingly." The voice came from the bushes beyond the stern.

Mattingly returned to the stern rail and saw Stanley Beecham waving his arms.

"Don't worry with Tuttle, I don't need –"

"Found him lying on the path, not far from the boat. He's about dead. I think he's dying."

Mattingly looked around the deck to continue his conversation with Pulaski, but Ben was gone.

17

Not far from the muddy bank where Ben had climbed out of the Narrows during the first hours of this day, he found Adam Tuttle. The trail, now a beaten path, held numerable footprints going in both directions. Adam Tuttle lay on his back with his head resting in the lap of a black woman known to Ben as Hattie. Ben acknowledged the woman and kneeled next to Adam, placing his hand on Adam's chest.

"What happened, Adam."

"Believe he had hissef a heart attack," Hattie said.

Adam opened his eyes and frowned up at the woman.

"Bull shit, old woman. Just a palpitation."

"Ain't the first time I had to come care for you, you grouchy old coot."

Ben smiled at the conversation.

"Sounds like you are in good hands, Adam. You need anything?"

Adam shook his head, then Ben looked the

question into Hattie's eyes.

"My man, Ulysses, done made it off that ship. He's gone to bring back a bag from Mr. Tuttle's boat. Told me Simon chopped that captain's head off. You see that?"

"No, but I heard."

"Told me the Sheriff gonna arrest Simon cause he killed a white man. That evil man stole my Ulysses. He needed killin, bastard of a man, but it's against the law for a black man to do it."

Adam attempted to sit up.

"Let me up, woman. I'm fine."

She placed the palm of her hand on Adam's forehead.

"You ain't got a temperature, and your heart ain't hard beating. You had pains in your chest and left arm. You had a heart attack, old man, now you rest a bit."

"I need to be out of this mud..."

"You need to lie still, or they gonna bury you in this mud."

She faced Ben.

"I got a leaf in my bag to go under his tongue, then he'll be ready to get up. What you gonna do?"

"Ma'am? What do you need me to do for Adam?"

"I'm doing for Mr. Tuttle here. What you gonna do for Simon? You gonna let them hang him? He told me you his friend."

"I am. He's already gone, Hattie. Mattingly

won't find him."

"He taking Toby with him?"

"You know about Toby?"

Hattie chuckled and shook her head. "Lord, but you folks still think we don't know nothing unless you tell us."

Ben smiled and looked down at Tuttle. "Toby will be looked after."

"You bring him to me. Hear?"

"Bring him to my place," Adam said.

Hattie nodded in agreement.

"Might as well do that, Mr. Pulaski. I'm gonna need to stay with this old fool for a couple days. Done it before. Need to make sure he don't kill himself."

Adam reached over and patted her hand.

"You're a good neighbor, Hattie."

"Just don't want you stinking up the cove if you die."

A large bull-shouldered black man stepped from the brush holding a small leather bag. He nodded to Ben, then kneeled down next to Hattie. After he handed her the bag, Adam reached up and gently grasped his wrist, guiding his hand toward Ben.

"This here is Ben Pulaski. Friend of mine. Knew his daddy. Also a friend of Simon's."

Ulysses took his hand and smiled at Ben. "Ulysses. Good to meet you."

Hattie withdrew a small bunch of sprigs tied

with a piece of string, snapped off a half dried leaf and brought it to Adam's mouth.

"You suck on this foxglove for a little bit, Mr. Tuttle."

He obediently opened his mouth and raised up his tongue so she could slip in the folded leaf, then laid his head back down. She patted Adam's head and then laid her hand on Ulysses' forearm. He covered her hand with his own. Hattie and Ulysses shared a brief silent moment simply looking into each other's eyes and smiling.

"Adam, Doc Harper is on the Raven. Why don't we take you there," Ben suggested. Then looking at Hattie, he added, "not that he'll do any better than Miss Hattie here."

She just chuckled. "You are so full of shit, Mr. Pulaski. But that's probably a good idea, since he's there."

Ulysses carefully lifted Adam to his feet, and with Ben on the other side, they began to walk him back toward the ship.

"Legs are still a little wobbly. I guess I can put up with you two walking with me," Adam said.

Fifteen minutes later, Tuttle was perched on the deck of the Raven sitting on a stool brought up from the captain's cabin. Hattie and Ulysses had hurried away to join the others moving onto the *Ugly Boat*.

Adam crinkled his nose. "This ship smells like the only outhouse in a town full of the runs."

"It's a slaver, Adam," Harper answered from Anthony's side. Anthony was awake, freshly bandaged, and most of his way through a bottle of whiskey snatched from the captain's cabin when the stool was brought up.

"Slaver," Anthony called out. "Yep. That's what the damned thing is!"

Harper relieved Anthony of the bottle. "That's enough, Anthony. Don't want you thinning out your blood just yet, and I think you've had more than enough."

Anthony showed a frown at Harper. "Let's discuss that again the next time somebody pushes a red hot railroad spike into *your* shoulder. Eh?"

McMallery and Aaron finished wrapping sailcloth between two poles and pinned it together as a stretcher for Anthony. Ben and Harper helped Anthony onto the stretcher, then Forrest and Aaron took him down the gangplank.

Mattingly watched the men carry Anthony toward the point. "They going to have any trouble getting him up on your barge, Pulaski?"

"No, we have gangplanks as well, and plenty of room on the deck to rest him."

"Well, I'm taking my other deputies and the prisoners back to town in the launch Tuttle steered here this morning. Just enough room for us. I'll leave it at Tuttle's place in the Cove."

He turned to face Tuttle. "You're going back with Pulaski, right."

Adam nodded his head and slipped the bottle of whiskey out of Doctor Harper's hand as he passed. Harper followed the stretcher down, and waved his hand over his shoulder. Mattingly followed the doctor with his gaze.

Coming up the gangplank, Stanley Beechum brought up the trailing end of the thick hemp rope that had been tied to a tree on the peninsula, and casually dropped it on the deck.

"Don't know what that was for," Stanley muttered.

Adam sat up straight and smiled at the men. Mattingly noticed Beechum and pointed him to a small wooden travel locker sitting in the middle of the deck. "Take that down with you, Stanley. It has the ship's log and any papers I could find." Mattingly smiled back at Tuttle, then turned to Ben. "You staying on board a while, yet?"

"Yeah, we'll just rest here a while. Aaron will get the *Ugly Boat* back to Havre de Grace safely, land all its passengers, and then come back for the four of us. We are in no hurry to go anywhere for now."

Mattingly nodded in agreement and moved toward the gangplank.

"Might be going pretty soon, though," Adam said.

"Believe he's drunk already, Ben. Don't let him fall overboard."

Ben smiled and waved as Mattingly stepped down the plank. Watched him take several steps northward, then the gangplank fell completely into the water with a tremendous splash.

"Anchor ain't down, Benjamin," Adam said.

Ben stood up and looked around. The larger tree on the peninsula side slowly edged toward the stern of the ship.

Ship's moving.

"Crew has abandoned her, Benjamin, and she's afloat on her own. No log book. No papers."

Ben looked at the sun, then at the water level at shore. "Slack water is leaving. Tide's going out!"

"She's a moving derelict, Benjamin. She slips out inta the current and she's a hazard to navigation..."

"But, no, she isn't..."

"Yes, she is. Ain't nobody on board but you, me, Sonja and Isaac..."

"But Adam, that can't possibly mean anything here. This is a cove..."

"No, it ain't. It's still a Narrows on all the maps..."

"That would be silly..."

"Silly, my ass! You want her or not?"

Ben looked around the deck. Dried blood pools showing where each man was murdered in his frenzy. "I don't know."

"What?" Sonja asked.

"What's happening? What's going on," yelled Isaac.

"She's afloat," said Ben

"What's yer orders Cap'n?" Tuttle asked with a laugh.

The Raven slipped slowly down toward the point. A fourth of the length drifting slowly beyond it.

Ben looked up at the sky.

God help me if I choose to stay within this nightmare.

Ben took in a deep breath, then blew it out. "Drop anchor," he yelled.

"You best do it on your own, Benjamin. On your own PERIL!"

Ben dashed to the bow of the ship, found the bolt holding the bow anchor to the side of the ship. Found the retaining pin holding the bolt in place. Found the heavy mallet used to knock the pin loose.

"Hey, Mattingly," Tuttle yelled. "you watching this?"

"What the hell is going on up there?" Mattingly yelled from the shore as many of his deputies and prisoners turned to watch the ship sliding toward the bay.

Ben raised the mallet high over his head.

Tuttle shook his head 'no'. "Not yet, Benjamin."

"What on earth is going on, Ben?" Sonja yelled.

"What, Pa? What is it?"

Tuttle held up his hand at Ben. "Wait, Benjamin. Not yet!"

"What is happening up there?" yelled Mattingly.

Tuttle stood near the railing at midships, looking out over the point with one eye open and one eye closed, gauging their position. "Almost. Almost."

Ben still held the mallet in mid air. All on the

ship was silence except for the faintest breeze drifting among the empty rigging. Overhead a seagull screeched. Isaac asked the unanswered question again, as the midship of the Raven drifted beyond the point at the mouth of the narrows. "What?"

"Now, Benjamin. Now," Tuttle yelled.

Ben grunted as he strained his chest and shoulder muscles, pulling down the mallet with all his strength, slamming it down on the chain catch and driving out the retaining pin. The four ton anchor dove down into the waters in front of the bow with a crash, burst through the shallow water and embedded itself into the thick muddy bottom. Ben slipped a holding peg into the winch, stopping the chain from running out any farther. The bow of the ship pulled slightly toward the east, as her forward movement was checked by the anchor. Ben ran to the stern of the ship, saw Mattingly, most of his deputized men, and the Raven's remaining crewmen standing in shackles, gawking at the little strip of open water between the shore and the ship.

"You are all witnesses! You are all witnesses!"

"To what," yelled Mattingly.

"This vessel was without sail and without her crew. There is no Captain's log aboard her and no papers of ownership. She was adrift, due to no effort on the part of her Salvors, and over half way out of the Narrows on her way into shipping lanes. We, the Pulaski family, and our ship's carpenter, Adam Tuttle, do hereby claim her as a derelict, under maritime salvage laws."

Mattingly stood on the shore with his mouth open.

Ben raised his hands. "We claim this vessel as our own!"

Sonja and Isaac stared in silence at each other with open mouths and wide-open eyes, then both looked toward Ben in confusion.

Adam Tuttle slapped his hands together and danced a sitting jig with his feet in front of his stool. "Honey-Fuggled them all! But she still smells like an overfull shithouse."

18

"Ben Pulaski, what the Hell are you babbling about?"

"No babbling, Deputy Mattingly. This ship was unattached to land and floating at the mercy of the current. She's a derelict and I claim her under the rights of salvage."

"You're just plain crazy, Pulaski, and I don't have time to fool with this nonsense now! I'm taking my prisoners and deputized men back to town. You can stay on board to guard this ship, if you want — Matter of fact, I'll be glad to deputize you for that!"

"Absolutely not, Mattingly! I'm on board by my own volition."

Mattingly threw his hand at Ben and turned toward the northern tree line, giving orders for the men to march back to the launch that brought him through the dense fog hours ago.

"Ben," Sonja called to him. "What are you doing? How can you claim this ship – why?"

"It's maritime salvage law, Sonja." Ben swept his arms over the deck. "When Beechum brought the mooring line on board, he set the ship free, and he was a deputy when he did it."

"Right as rain," added Tuttle. ."..and when the gangplank fell away there was no way for Mattingly to come back on board. Plus he took all ships papers that might say who the owner is."

"And with the crew already off because of Mattingly," Ben said. "– and no one ordered by him to assume command of the ship..."

."..and the current taking her out of the Narrows," Tuttle said.

."..she was abandoned to the peril of the sea." Ben finished the sentence.

Sonja shook her head.

"I still don't understand."

Ben walked over to her and held her shoulders.

"Sonja, even though we were spitting distance from the shore, in that instance this ship met the legal criteria for an abandoned ship. Same as if at sea. Anyone saving her can lay claim to rights of salvage ."

"You want a *slave* ship?"

"No. No. No. I would like to have her for cargo. Take shipments to Baltimore, Philadelphia, Norfolk. And bring goods back here from those ports. We would make a fortune. Our family would be set."

Sonja looked around the deck. Frowned up into Ben's face.

"How could you want to own such an evil thing as a slave ship?"

"We would clean her up. Open the companionways through the mid ships. Her slave hold would be converted for material cargo. Her design is perfect for that!"

"And you think they will just give her to you?"

"Sonja. There is no "they" for an abandoned ship."

"Well now, Benjamin," Tuttle added. "If they find an owner, he can lay claim to the ship, although..."

"Although," Ben continued, "he would be compelled to reward me greatly for saving the ship. Any sailor knows that."

"Reward you how, Ben?"

Tuttle put his finger in the air and cleared his throat dramatically.

"Been a part of something like this before. Back in '27. If the captain or the owner challenges the claim, there would need to be a split. But, seeing how the captain's head lies in the shallows beyond the stern, there'd only be the owner to claim. They would split the value of this ship between the owner and the Salvor – that'd be Ben. So half each."

Isaac stood between Tuttle and Ben. "Half of what, Pa?"

Tuttle answered the question. "Half the value of this ship..."

Tuttle looked around the deck, then up at the masts and rigging, along the sides where the cannon sat, then down at his feet. He scratched his head, then looked back at Isaac. "Figure it cost thirty, maybe thirty five thousand dollars to build this schooner. So, it's value is as it is, not to replace. So, let's say she'd sell for thirty thousand. Then that'd be fifteen thousand dollars for the owner, and fifteen for this here crew. Half for the captain, and half for the crew ta split..."

"No. Even split among us. Three thousand, seven hundred and fifty dollars for each of us," said Ben. "I've always been good at numbers. And yes, Adam, it would be equal all around. I wouldn't have thought of it without you."

Isaac squinted his eyes at his father.

"For each, including me?"

Ben smiled. Looked into Sonja's eyes, then nodded to his son.

"Isaac, you proved your manhood last night and again this morning. You have earned an equal share to any man alive."

"What about Aaron?"

"And you just proved yourself to be an honorable man as well, Isaac. You, me and your mother will share equally with him."

"as will I," said Tuttle.

While silence settled among the little group, as each began entertaining fantasies with more money than any of them had ever seen, Adam spoke again.

"'Course, now we need to occupy this ship until a court rules on our claim, or the law accepts her on our behalf awaiting a maritime court ruling."

Tuttle laughed a full belly laugh, then coughed several times, putting his hand to his chest as he coughed. Sonja went to Tuttle's side, laying her hand against his forehead and cheek. She turned her face toward Ben, a frown descending over her eyes.

"Ben, I saw blankets on the captain's bed. Could you please bring one up for Adam?

"Oh, I'll be alright, Mrs. Pulaski..."

"Hush, Adam. Let Ben get you a blanket. You men would walk around carrying your left hand in your right one, until a woman made you sit down."

Adam opened his mouth, but before he could speak Sonja tapped under his chin with her fingertip and had him close it again. Ben trotted back up the steps with the blanket and helped place it around Adam. Sonja used that same fingertip to direct Ben's attention to her face and gave him an almost imperceptible shake of her frowning face. Ben placed his hand on Adam's shoulder.

"You still need to get home, Adam, so Hattie can help you feel better."

Sonja's finger popped against Adam's chin even before he could speak. He just smiled in obedience, a clear indication of how poorly he felt. Ben slapped his hands together.

"Well, let's explore this awful smelling boat and see if we can find anything useful. I may have to stay on board a couple days."

Ben, Sonja and Isaac moved in different directions to explore the ship for supplies and items they may need. Down in the galley, Ben discovered several casks of salted meat and biscuits. After nearly thirty more minutes trying dozens of keys from the captain's cabin, Ben was finally able to enter the nearby storage areas, containing a treasure trove of supplies.

She must have been getting ready to go to sea.

Needing fresh air, Ben escaped from the cramped cubicles and putrid smell hanging in the air like rotten meat. Even as he made his way up, he knew the smell would never be gone. It would be like wearing the coat off a decomposing corpse. Even with it off the body, the stench would linger. He stepped onto the deck gulping the cool fresh air flowing through the rigging, bringing the scent of saltwater from the southern Bay. The sun was high overhead, bathing the world in golden light, the once omnipresent fog now only a memory in the minds of the people who endured it. Looking out beyond the bow, he noticed the stubby mast of the *Ugly Boat* drawing close. He twirled around, scanning the deck of the Raven, widening his eyes and growing a large smile.

"Aaron. *Captain* Aaron, that is. Ahoy, sailor!"

They came over the railing like happy pirates. Aaron broke away from the group hug between Sonja and Isaac to meet his father. Ben took him in a bear hug that lifted him off his feet.

"I am so proud of you, Son. You and Isaac, both. Did you get everyone to their destination? Who came back with you?"

"Forrest and Jeremy McMallery, and uh, well, and Maggie Freidman..."

Ben gave the barest smile at the last name, and traded quick glances with Sonja, who had her own smile poorly contained. Relieved to have other information for his father, Aaron continued.

"As for destinations, we laid poor Mr. Brown at the Undertaker's – Doc Harper told them he would settle with them later. And of course, all the people who had been kidnapped were quick to go home once their feet touched the dock. Oh, and Pa, I think someone took our rowboat. The line to it was cut and the boat gone when we sailed back to town..."

"Not to worry, son. I told Simon he could take it..."

"No, but he didn't take it, Pa. He waved to me from the woods here when we sailed north. No, we found it floating on the Susquehanna flats, with nothing in it."

Simon did not take it. He is still on the island? Who took the boat? Briscoe!

"Did you bring it back here with you?"

"Sure, Pa."

"Good boy, er, good man, Aaron. Please leave it pulled up on the shore when you go back."

"Aren't you going back with us?"

Ben explained the need to stay on board the Raven because of his claim on the ship. He would stay on the ship alone, and send everyone else back to help Adam home.

"The Hell I will," Sonja said and crossed her arms in front of her. "This ship stinks like an outhouse, but I'm not leaving you to yourself tonight."

Ben smiled.

"Yes. I would like that."

He turned toward Aaron.

"Isaac needs to be seen by Doc Harper, and it

wouldn't hurt for him to have a look at Mr. Tuttle, if the old man will allow it."

"Well, it won't take long to get back to town. The wind has gotten fresh out of the south. We'll be there in just a few minutes."

Ben looked up at the few clouds in the afternoon sky. The clouds were gliding north, the canvas of the furled sails shifted in the wind, and he called over to Tuttle.

"Adam, isn't there a requirement for salvors to take derelict ships back to port?"

"Yep. At least to make the attempt, barring foul weather."

Ben called Forrest and Jeremy up on the Raven to assist loosing the main sail.

"I want to show just enough canvas to catch the wind and push us back into the narrows," he explained.

Together, they pulled down on the line running up the mast to the main sail pulley. Slowly, the wooden spar attached to the top of the sail rose until a fourth of the sail was exposed to the wind. Almost immediately, the ship began to drift backward into the narrows, until its movement was checked by the bow anchor.

"Pay out the anchor chain, Mac. That'll give us enough play to back up."

The Raven edged back silently, until she was sitting almost exactly where she was before her shore line was brought on board.

"Lower the main sail," Ben yelled as he ran to the stern to release the stern anchor.

Adam had stood at the rail while the others worked sails and anchors.

"Nicely done," he said to all.

"Should we go get that gang plank up from the shore?" Forrest asked.

"Nope. Need to keep her untied from land, and manned only by her salvors. That's the law."

Sonja placed her hand on Ben's arm.

"Are you sure you want to do this?"

"Sonja, if you found a gold coin lying in the road, what would you do?"

"I would buy a thousand yards of blue silk," she said with a broad smile. The wind tussled her hair, drawing it across her lower face like a veil and her eyes sparkled.

"No. You would not do that, Sonja. You would want to find its rightful owner."

"And how would I do that? Give it to the first person I came upon?"

"No. You would let it be known that a coin had been found. The true owner would be sincere and most likely desperate to have such a thing back."

"And if no one came to claim it, it would be ours, Ben. Is that what you mean for the ship?"

"That, or more likely, a substantial reward. More than enough to pay for a seat at a university," he whispered to her.

Mac, Jeremy and Aaron pulled the bow line on the *Ugly Boat* to bring it along side of the Raven.

"Aaron," Ben said, "Do you think you are ready

to take the *Ugly Boat* to Annapolis with that load of coal?"

"Sure, I can do that, Pa, but there isn't as much coal as we took on. I'm sorry but I had to throw out-"

"I know that, son, and I understand. Maybe you and Jeremy can reclaim at least some of it? And, you know who to take it to in Annapolis. You've gone there dozens of times. Are you up to doing all that tomorrow?"

The excitement practically glowed off his young face.

"I can do all that and then some."

Ben placed his hand on Aaron's shoulder.

"All right, CAPTAIN Pulaski, you take these other folks home this afternoon, and then take our coal to Annapolis tomorrow morning-"

"And Isaac can help with-"

"No. I want him to stay home with Toby."

"Isn't Simon going to do that?"

"No. He can't go back now. Maybe not for a long time. Maybe not ever. Mattingly means to arrest him for killing Hoagg. That's why you are leaving the rowboat. Now say nothing more about Simon or the boat. Do you understand?"

"Yes, Pa. Do you need me to bring anything more for you or Ma?"

Ben noticed the satchel of fresh clothes and other things Aaron had brought aboard for their return home.

"There are provisions for a dozen sailors and a

hundred slaves on board this ship. Your mother and I will want for nothing. Still there might be something of a womanly nature she would like you to bring, so do ask her."

He glanced back at Maggie Freidman, standing patiently by the wheel and frequently flipping her eyes in Aaron's direction.

Ben added, "And you might as well develop skills in fetching things for the ladies."

Sonja met Ben's gaze, her eyes sweeping between Ben, Aaron and Maggie, suppressing a small smile, as Aaron walked across the deck to her side. Moments later, Ben and Sonja stood at the bow of the Raven, with their arms around each other's waist, watching the *Ugly Boat* tack out of the Narrows. Then her sails caught the wind solidly, swinging her blunt bow around and taking her north toward to Havre de Grace. Aaron and Isaac waved from the stern. Sonja slipped away and made her way down to the captain's cabin.

When Ben entered the cabin, Sonja was on her hands and knees scrubbing the deck near the post where she had been tied.

"You don't have to do that, Sonja."

She spoke without looking up.

"Yes, I do."

Ben kneeled down beside her.

"Then, I'll help you..."

"No," she said through gritted teeth. "I will not come back in here until this spot is cleaned. And I must do it."

Ben rose and went to the broken windows and

pulled in the frames. Reaching out, he pulled closed the outer shutters, leaving only the single lamp at the desk giving light. He found a broom in a small closet and began sweeping broken glass toward the rear of the room. Sonja stood up and dropped the cleaning rag into the bucket, then carried it to the rear, opened the shutter and threw the entire bucket out the window.

"It smells like blood and piss in here."

Ben looked around the cabin and slipped his hands into his pockets.

"Do you want to find another room to stay in tonight? There are other smaller cabins, and they are all ours for the choosing."

She folded her arms as she walked toward him, shaking her head wearily. "No."

She leaned her body against him, resting her head against his chest and wrapping her arms around his waist.

"I want to stay in here to prove to myself that he is dead. Besides, the bed looks inviting."

They both looked in the corner of the cabin where the large bed hung from stout chains attached above corner. Sonja stepped away from him and began searching through cabinets built onto the walls. Within the fourth cabinet she found clean folded linen, which she pulled out and held to her nose. Turning back to Ben, she pointed at the bed.

"Let's take those dirty things off the bed and throw them out."

Ben shook his head as he yanked material off the bed.

"Let's put them in a pile somewhere to burn tomorrow. I don't want to fill the Narrows with debris that someone will have to pull out."

She nodded and brought clean sheets and blankets from the cabinet. He stood there momentarily patting his shirt and pants, ones brought to him by Aaron. He found the little parcel, withdrew his pipe and pouch and stood there fingering them. Sonja looked back over her shoulder as she flattened out the fabric, and smiled. He showed her what he had in his hands.

"Maybe I should take this up on deck," he said and turned toward the door.

"Please don't, Ben. I don't want to be alone in here." Then she laughed. "Just sit down and light the damned thing."

"But...I know you don't like the smell..."

"It will be better than the other smells in this cabin, and in this ship. And besides, it will be far closer to normal than we have had in days."

He took her in his arms and drew her to him. They stood in silence, drawing in the scent of each other, the fresh clothes and the smell of soap; luxuries enjoyed individually in the cramped black smith compartment, bathed in the warmth of the little furnace. Tears flowed down her cheeks and onto his shirt, and she sobbed, but only the once. Then she pushed him gently away.

"Go sit. Let me finish making the bed. And let's open the shutters."

Night came quickly and the long undulating waves from the bay slipped into the Narrows, gently rocking the Raven with lazy swells. They lay together with the lamp put out, watching the low-lying stars through the broken windows drift back and forth in slowly repeating arcs. Sonja drifted off to fitful sleep, as moonlight laid soft shadows across the upper deck, that moved slowly.

Ben sat up in the darkness, then went up onto the deck. He found another bucket and scrub brush, tied a line to the bucket handle and threw it overboard for more water. For each bloody pool he dashed a bucket of water, then went down on his knees to scrub the deck. With each brush stroke he pleaded, "No more."

Three hours later, Sonja stepped up onto the deck as Ben scrubbed the last pool. His chant had become a childlike plea, drifting over the deck, amidst uncontrollable sobs.

"No more. No more, God. Not again. No more."

Sonja slipped beside him and put her hands on his shoulder, urging him up off his knees.

Holding each other tightly, they both released their suffering. Standing alone on the deck of the Raven, they shared their anguish and merged their tears until they could cry no more, then found their way back to bed and sleep at last.

Near dawn, footsteps pattered on the deck.

"Someone has come aboard," Ben whispered, rolling out of bed and grabbing a cutlass.

19

The half moon was still well above the horizon when Ben stepped barefoot onto the deck, crouching low, the blade of the cutlass floating in front of him. He halted, staying within the shadow of the cabin, panning across the deck, looking for anything that should not be there. Most of the lower rigging and the deck to his right was absorbed into the silhouette of the eastern tree line beyond the ship. Anyone could be there. To his left, across the Narrows and away from the nearby land, the deck was bathed in starlight and moonshine. A shadow slipped away from the outermost wheel. Ben kept to his spot, the blade drifting up over his right shoulder, his forearm and shoulder muscles tensing to strike if necessary.

"Who are you?" Ben demanded.

The shadow froze in position.

"Benjamin?"

Ben knew the voice. Had known it for almost thirty years. He stood into the night light, lowering the cutlass and shifting it to his left hand as he stepped to greet his friend.

"Simon. Did you not find the boat down there."

"Of course. And the oars, and the provisions, and the blanket, and the knife. Aaron is very generous."

"You heard us? You were watching?"

They shook hands.

"I decided it was just you and Sonja up here. I wasn't sure at first, but after Aaron left, it seemed so to me. Still, I wanted to be careful that one of Mattingly's deputies had not stayed on board."

"I wish you had left Hoagg for me, or for Mattingly..."

"Not after what he did to Anthony. Not after all he did in China, and even before that..."

"But, now what, Simon?"

"Well, I sure as hell can't drag a little boy around with me trying to hide from the law..."

"No. I understand that. What will you do? Maybe it's time for you to make your way into Pennsylvania?"

"No. I'm going south, not north. St. Mary's County..."

"That's almost like going into Alabama or Mississippi..."

"It's where Lettie is. I get her, then I go north."

Sonja stepped up onto the deck wrapped in a blanket and moved almost silently to Ben and Simon. The men turned toward her as she placed her hands on their arms.

"There are pistols and rifles on this ship, Simon. Take what you need. Go get your woman."

Without another word, Simon made his way down below.

Ben put his arm around Sonja, and stood there waiting.

When Simon returned to the deck, he held a stuffed leather bag and had a rifle slung over one shoulder. He shook hands with them.

"When you head back north, Simon, if you come by here, we will help you."

Without another word, Simon turned away and slipped into the darkness. They could hear him climbing down the side of the ship and step into the rowboat already waiting along side. Heard the gentle slapping of the oars in the water as he rowed away. They walked to the rail at the bow, looking out at the bay, black water undulating in reflected moonlight, outlining a man in a rowboat pulling the oars rhythmically, pulling himself south. They stood there, felt obligated to do that, to give vigil until the small image crawled around the next point of land and was gone from their sight.

"Damn it to hell," Ben whispered.

"Poor Toby," Sonja added.

After heavy sighs shared by both of them, they made their way down the steps to the landing in front of the captain's cabin. Sonja entered and lit a lamp, then joined Ben in the ships galley where he made them coffee. Walking around the well-lit galley area, she was amazed to find a horde of supplies to sample. For months-long voyages with dozens of crew and hundreds of slaves, the food would only be just sufficient, but within Sonja's experience of barely feeding herself and her sons before Ben came back, this was a treasure trove. She found a sharp knife, slid it into her waist band and patted it gently. Hanging from an iron hook in the overhead beam of the smallest storage room was a generous side of smoke cured pork. Sonja hefted the meat off its hook and almost stumbled out to the cook stove and carving table. Letting the meat fall from her shoulder and slam onto the wood surface with a resounding 'thud', she faced Ben and slapped the meat.

"I want Bacon!"

Making use of the large iron cook stove, bolted to the deck and surrounded by bricks, Ben found a large frying pan, while Sonja discovered the locations of baking pans and flour. An hour later, they sat on the upper deck near the bow at a table and chairs brought up from the cabin. The sun peeked among the trees of the peninsula and seagulls dived at the waters beyond the point. They sipped coffee, still nibbling at the remaining bacon and biscuits.

"I ate far too much," said Ben.

"Yes. Me, too. A luxury we have seldom experienced, Husband. One that was once only a dream, unlikely to come true. And tomorrow morning, if we are still here, I want to repeat the sin of gluttony. At least, one more time!"

Leaning across the table, he smiled at her and laid his hand on hers, squeezing it gently. He looked directly into her eyes, lingering in his view, then opened his mouth to speak. Her eyebrows rose ever so slightly, a hint of smile peeked out at the corners of her mouth.

"Ahoy, Raven!"

The shout boomed up from the land near the stern.

Ben closed his mouth and walked toward the stern rail. Sonja exhaled, closed her eyes and pulled her hand from the table.

"Ahoy Raven!"

"I'm coming," Ben shouted back.

Resting his hands on the rail, Ben looked down at Deputy Sheriff Mattingly, but said nothing, waiting for the deputy.

"Can you lower a gangplank for me, Pulaski?"

"Nope."

"We need to talk."

"I hear you perfectly well from here."

"George Milton was waiting at my office door when I got to it this morning. Adam Tuttle sic'd him on me, but he said he represented you."

Ben scratched his head. "Really? What did he have to say?"

"A hell of a lot..."

Mattingly rested his hands on his hips, stamped his foot and looked around where he stood, then back up at Ben.

"Sure would be easier to talk with you if we could get face to face."

Ben hesitated a moment, looking back up the narrows where he crossed from the isthmus two nights ago.

"Tell you what, Lyle, there's a rowboat back toward the isthmus. Not far I don't think. You probably passed it coming down. It leaks a little, but will suffice within the Narrows here. You go get that, or go back to whatever you used to get to the isthmus and come around the southern point of the peninsula. I'll let you on board either way, but I'm not connecting this ship to any shore."

"Why the hell not? Why the hell do I have to go to all that trouble just to get ten feet from where I'm standing right now."

"You know damned well why, Lyle. Especially if you talked to a lawyer this morning. This ship is in salvage!"

"Sounds like maybe Milton has already been out here, as well."

"No. I just know what a seaman knows."

Mattingly turned around and spat behind himself, then stamped his foot again. "Hell and Damnation, Pulaski!"

Then he marched up the pathway north, and followed it around the curve into the tree line. Forty-five minutes later, he rowed around the low lying point where Ben and Sonja had sought cover in the fog. Ben saw him from the bow and motioned him to come around to the water side of the ship, where he had lowered a boarding ladder. Soon Mattingly came over the bow railing, his face beet red from exertion and anger.

"You're still mad at me for taking your knife from you that day, aren't you? I had to do that, Benjamin. You would have killed Binterfield! You and I know that for sure."

He turned his face to Sonja, noticing she carried a large knife in her belt.

"And this lady would be a widow all over again."

Sonja reached out her hand and touched his shoulder with her fingertips. "And I thank you for doing that, Mr. Mattingly."

Mattingly's lips moved silently, he blinked and looked down at his boots. "Well, er, I appreciate you saying that Mrs. Pulaski. I, er..."

Ben glanced at Sonja, nodded his agreement. "I no longer begrudge that, Lyle. It was your duty, and you were right to do it. So what do you need to discuss with me this morning."

"Well, um, before I came here, I stopped in to see old Judge Jessup up on Adams Street. He no longer sits as Circuit Court Judge in Bel Air, but he is kind enough to provide advice to the Sheriff's Department."

Sonja placed her arm around Ben's waist and leaned against him. Ben folded his arms in front of his chest.

Mattingly cleared his throat. "Judge Jessup says that since Hoagg's death occurred as the result of a legal arrest, and since your actions appear to be within maritime law, I am to collect..."

"Legal arrest," Ben repeated. "Does that mean there is no charge on Simon?"

"No, it does not, Ben. The Judge said just that, since the captain won't be available to contest your claim. Now, I am to make an official list of your crew for submission to the Maryland State Maritime Court. Those are the names that will have a legal share of any award.

"Happy to do that. We can list them right now."

Ben invited Mattingly to sit at the table near the bow, while he dictated the names to the deputy. Mattingly slowly wrote the names, his stomach growling loudly as he sat so close to the remaining biscuits and bacon.

"Mr. Mattingly," Sonja said. "Please do help yourself to our bounty."

Mattingly snatched a biscuit with two fingers like a snake strike and used his other fingers to hook three slices of bacon.

"I've not yet broken my night's fast, due to this legal business, Ma'am. Thank you so much."

She patted him on his back and went below to fetch him a cup of coffee.

Mattingly pointed a half eaten biscuit at Ben.

"This is wonderful, but your Simon will still likely hang in Bel Air, when we catch him. And don't tell me he may not be Simon Bond, like you don't really know if he's got a last name. I've already had a couple citizens confirm that he is. I am going to believe that you just didn't want to lose your boy from your barge work, so don't do anything to make me think you somehow wanted to hide him from the law. Understand?"

Ben gritted his teeth and nodded in silence. Sonja returned with coffee and set it next to Mattingly, sensing the coolness between him and Ben and showing her question in silence to Ben. Mattingly nodded thank you to Sonja and sipped the coffee. When he finished his list, he turned it around toward Ben, tapping the paper with his finger.

"Need you to sign right there."

Ben scrutinized the list, his lips moving slightly as he struggled through the names, then he turned the paper back around, tapping one of the names.

He had his chest out and his back straight.

"You misspelled that one."

Mattingly leaned over the paper.

"Damned if I didn't."

As he lined through the name and re-wrote it at the bottom of his list, Sonja beamed a smile and wide-eyes up at her husband, while Ben looked seriously out at the bay with his chin up, pretending he did not notice her expression.

Can't read everything, but by God I can spell my son's last name – It's mine!

Sonja peeked over his shoulder at the list as Ben signed it. Mattingly slipped it into his pocket, thanked Sonja for the breakfast and crabbed down the rope ladder back to his rowboat. Ben and Sonja stood at the rail as he rowed away. She looped her arm around his.

"You listed me as a crew member."

"Of course."

"I would get a share of yours, like a wife is supposed to."

As Mattingly rowed farther away he yelled back to the ship. "Oh! Mr. Milton informed me that he would be out here this afternoon."

Ben waved his acknowledgement to Mattingly, then turned to face Sonja. "If we get possession of the Raven, that list will make you one of its owners. How many women do you think own ships?"

She looked up at him through tearful eyes, and he pulled her close to him.

"Maybe a queen somewhere," he said, then noticed the knife she now carried. "or a damned buccaneer woman."

"A buccaneer woman? Well, you just remember you said that the next time you make me angry."

He held up a hand in mock surrender.

"Woman, I tracked your trail of bodies and blood from Lapidum to the deck of this ship. I will never make you angry again."

He put his arms around her and they both laughed, both knowing his pledge was a lie and both walking together in rhythm down into the cabin.

-- <> --

The afternoon was still young when Mr. George Milton, Esquire, came on board with several documents for review and signatures.

"I'm lucky the winds are light, Ben. Otherwise, that would have been a far more challenging row than I could handle. Too much time in offices and court these days. It has been too long since I had oars in my hands."

George was very positive about the likelihood of Ben obtaining a significant portion of the ship's value, but had insufficient information to venture a guess about ownership. As they talked, Aaron made his return trip from Annapolis and came on board. The steamship Pocahontas was again anchored in Whitehall Bay, near the mouth of the Severn River, paying far more for coal than the Annapolis colliers. Even with only a partial load of coal in the holds of the *Ugly Boat*, Aaron still received more payment than Ben had received with a full load before the price war.

Ben signed the papers formally proclaiming himself and his crew as salvors of the Raven, 'a derelict ship found unmanned by the captain or crew and adrift in Spesutie Narrows'.

"Ben, bear in mind this will take time, probably months. And, you must stay in possession until you are granted legal recognition of your claim. This ship is not known here, nor are any owners. At this point, we don't even know the home state of her registration. "

"We will stay as long as it takes, but hopefully it will not be for months. And George, please consider tying on to the *Ugly Boat* and riding back with Captain Aaron and his curious crew."

"Happily, Ben. I suspect that if I try to row all the way back to Havre de Grace, I will never make it."

Within the chortles floating around the deck, Ben pulled gently on his son's arm and added, "Your Mother will need to stop by Doc. Harper's on her way home. I fear her wound may cause her trouble if it is not doctored further."

Against her protests of abandoning her husband, and the promise she elicited from Aaron that he would bring her back the following day, Sonja allowed herself to be taken on board the *Ugly Boat*. She waved from the stern as the pudgy boat caught the wind in its mainsail and slipped around the point out of view, trailing George's rowboat behind it like a lone duckling.

At nightfall, the wind settled into stillness, and the smoke from the cook fire in the galley drifted straight up from the terra cotta chimney at mid ship. Ben helped himself to more bacon and ugly flour misfits that might have matured into biscuits under Sonja's gentle skill. Still they tasted like bread – of sorts, and he enjoyed them with the bacon, sitting by the table at the bow, watching the stars turn themselves on in random patterns in the darkened sky. After eating his fill and starting his pipe, and alternating it with sips of the rum he had discovered in a cabinet below, he began to doze in his chair. Unable to fight off the sleep any longer, he stepped down the companionway and into the cabin. He fell asleep even as he sank into bed, sliding down into deep sleep through brief jumbled dreams like slipping under cake icing. There, he fell into that warm cocoon where slumbering children frequently visit and adults rarely find.

Early the next morning, as Ben stood on deck, Aaron scampered up the side of the ship to swing out one of the cargo booms over the *Ugly Boat*.

"What all do you need that for, Aaron?" Ben asked.

"Ma brought all of Lapidum with us this morning!"

"Just what we need, Ben," she said. "Mr. Milton told you this might take months."

"Did you stop by Doc Harper's, Sonja?"

"Yes. He gave me a salve to rub on the wound, and told you not to worry too much about it."

Aaron and Ben pulled on the line to bring up a cargo net full of boxes, and bundles. The cargo was set on the deck and Aaron pulled away the netting. Ben stood there with his hands on his hips slipping glances between it and Sonja, with his eyebrows arched in unspoken question.

"You'll be glad I thought to bring all this. Just you wait and see," she said.

And he did. And he was. Spring slipped toward summer, while Ben paced the deck of the ship waiting on the decision. After a few days with Adam and Hattie, Toby was taken in by Cephus, the man who lost his son to the pirates. Ben rotated with Aaron keeping a Pulaski on board the Raven. Adam had recovered enough to escape the iron love of Hattie and managed to row out to the Raven and visit Ben a few days, until she found him. Anthony's wife, Camilla, came down from Philadelphia to watch over his recovery. When he recovered enough to travel, he sent a document to Ben, deeding him ownership of the Wilhelmina and asking him to continue in its philosophy.

Isaac's wounds had healed well under the close scrutiny of Wallace Harper. Wallace had commented how lucky Isaac had actually been, since no bone or tendon had been destroyed. The hard scars on his hands were simply souvenirs of a horrifying time, he had said. It was near the time for Isaac to begin his journey to West Point and he had agreed to accompany the Renowitz's on the train trip to Philadelphia .

In late May, Aaron stayed onboard the Raven, while Ben, Sonja and Isaac rowed across the Susquehanna Flats to Perryville. Isaac turned his head in every direction, trying to see as much as he could. The train cars rolled off the top of the SS Maryland where its track extension merged aligned with the Cecil county tracks. Moving train cars across the Susquehanna River was the only task the steamship ever performed. She was specially designed for that one purpose. The railroad men pushed the cars up to the back of the northbound steam engine and were locked in place by an engineer. The engine was far too heavy to ride atop the steamship, so the same engine that brought the cars from Philadelphia for the southbound train earlier, would now take the cars of the northbound train back to Philadelphia.

Ben and Isaac assisted the attendants placing Anthony's stretcher in the second car. Isaac was eager that he find the seat planned for him, but it was already reserved for him by name. The Renowitz family had secured the entire car for the trip to Philadelphia.

Sonja could only occasionally gain Isaac's attention. "He is far too young to be doing this, Ben," she said. There was slight tremble to her voice.

"Sonja, he is the same age I was when we married."

"You were much older then. Sterner. Older not in years, but – something..."

"I had been in war, fought other men; been bloodied and took blood."

"Oh Ben, I can't bear to think of him in a war!"

"We are at peace, Sonja. The closest thing he will ever see to war is already behind us, on Spesutie Island. In New York, he will learn to build bridges and stout walls; march men in parades to drums and trumpets. He will never see a real war."

"Promise?" she asked.

Ben's mind flashed with images of dead men, clawing up from the swamps of Georgia, the gutters of China, and slipping out between the deck beams where he could not scrub their blood away.

"Of course," he lied. They both knew he could not keep such a promise, but the pretense eased the parting.

The railroad conductor yelled, "All Aboard!", and the milling crowd began to split awkwardly into groups, those with bags and those who could only wave goodbye. Isaac dashed back to his mother for a quick tearful good-bye, while she let hers flow openly and he quickly wiped his out of sight. Ben almost had to tackle his son as he started to charge away, but he was able to grab him in a bear hug and whisper in his ear, "I am so proud of you, son."

"More!" he mumbled into Ben's shoulder

"Proud," he said into his son's ear, then pulled him down so he could kiss him on the top of his head, and then he was gone.

Isaac mounted the steps as the car began to move. The engine shrieked its whistle and blew out a steam cloud that almost engulfed the entire train. As the car moved through the cloud, Isaac leaned out from the top step, found his mother's eyes with his own and waved goodbye.

Ben and Sonja returned to the Raven, to maintain their vigil of claim. Spring fell into a hot humid Maryland summer, full of mosquitoes and fireflies, Honeysuckle scent and marsh fumes, rain and swelter. In July, a letter came from Annapolis, informing Ben his case was scheduled to be heard by the court. And still they were there.

---<>---

Into August, Herbert Binterfield sent one of his clerks for Briscoe, but the clerk returned alone after being unable to find him. It was later in the evening, long after closing time when Briscoe knocked on the back door near Binterfield's desk.

"Where the hell have you been," Binterfield snapped as he opened the door and allowed Briscoe in.

"I had some problems with one of my properties that I had to settle."

"YOUR Properties! Briscoe, you forget. YOU have no properties. This bank owns it all, and your company is only an onion skin I wrap around my properties to keep noses out of my affairs."

"Yes, sir."

"Now when I call for you, you drop everything and get your worthless ass over here. Do you understand me?"

"Yes, sir."

"Good. I want you to double the rent again on the Pulaski farm. Start the new rate the first of September."

Briscoe sighed, "Certainly, sir."

"Very well. It's time we discussed what happened out on Spesutie Island..."

"Yes sir, I was in fear for my life with that maniac..."

"I don't give a God damned about all that. I want to know if you gave him anything in writing."

343

"No, sir, but he did have that list you wrote out."

"You should have got that! Don't think for one second that I don't know how you ran like a woman and rowed back here while the real men in the town were out there on Spesutie Island."

"But not you, Sir."

"What do you mean by that, Briscoe. Don't you dare think you can..."

"There is something from the ship you need to see, sir – something I've been hiding."

Binterfield began to sit down, ignoring Briscoe and focusing his attention back to the ledger spread open on the top of his desk, extending his hand blindly toward Briscoe. Briscoe stepped around the desk, reaching into his pocket.

"This is something I should have given you a while back, Herbert."

Binterfield's head snapped up, a frown crossing his brow and a snarl curling his lip as Briscoe's face came within inches of his.

Binterfield stood up straight. "How dare you..."

Briscoe shoved the shiny blade into him with all his strength, reaching his left arm around Binterfield, pressing his body into the blade. Binterfield's eyes widened as their chests pressed against one another. The knife blade, sharpened for hours on the smooth stone in Briscoe's apartment, slid easily through the fabric of the coat, vest, and cotton shirt. The blade tip ran through the skin and fat. It dove through and beyond the stomach, slicing open the aorta and then sinking its tip into Binterfield's spine. Binterfield tried to scream.

Briscoe leaned him over like a ballet dancer laying out his partner, and placed him gently on top of his desk. Briscoe cupped his left hand around Binterfield's throat, squeezing it shut. Not enough to kill, just enough to stop the scream.

Binterfield tried to speak, his eyes were frantically looking around, one hand grabbing at the center desk drawer. He had been here before, under that Pulaski woman. It would never happen again. He grabbed at the drawer handle, fingers flying angrily at the handle. Got it open. The reworked corner of the drawer was empty, the derringer out of place.

Briscoe laughed and drove the blade higher up within Binterfield's abdomen, slicing in and out, cutting his way toward his chest. "It's in my pocket," he said.

Binterfield lay back on the desk, paralyzed by the damage, but still alive. Briscoe straightened and took in a deep breath. He yanked open the vest and shirt, loosened and pulled down the trousers and finished his work. The lightning bolt design was the best he had done. He had much better light to work under this time.

"Practice makes perfect," he whispered to himself. When he was satisfied with his design, he smiled and patted Binterfield's cheek, then drove Ben Pulaski's knife into Binterfield's heart. Outside, he washed his hands in the horse trough behind the bank. He casually walked home, humming to himself.

---<>---

Deputy Lyle Mattingly stood beside the big mahogany desk examining Binterfield's body.

Morning sunshine streamed in from the front window. The distraught clerk had moved back to his stall at the front of the bank. He looked over ledgers that no one would ask for today, doing whatever he could to remain away from the back office. Dark blood pooled on the plank floor around the desk, crusting over in some places, but still dripped lethargically in elongated tears from the edges of the desk. Mattingly took keen interest in the knife handle standing up from the blade impaled into the dead man's chest.

"I know that knife," he said to himself.

Later that day, he rowed out to Spesutie Island, and retraced the pathway to the stern of the Raven. He stood in his usual spot and called out for Ben Pulaski, then told him of the murder of Herbert Binterfield.

"Can't say I'm either surprised or disappointed, Lyle," Ben said.

"Didn't expect it to be otherwise. Ben, you got proof you were on board all last night?"

Sonja and Adam leaned out so Mattingly could see them up on deck.

"We were here together all night," Ben said.

"Can you tell me where your ivory handled knife is?"

"I lost it during the fight with Hoagg's people. I think Sam Briscoe took it."

Mattingly exhaled, pulled out a small notebook and pencil. He made a brief entry, then turned to walk away, waving over his shoulder with one finger as he left.

"Good riddance to Binterfield and Hoagg," Sonja said at Mattingly's back, watching him go. "Both were pirates, just Binterfield plied his thievery from his Bank."

---<>---

The rest of summer was peaceful, without the worry of new schemes from the Tidewater Bank and Trust. Aaron tied canvas covers over the stern and bow areas of the Raven, so they could sit in the shade and enjoy the soft breezes off the bay. Ben's screaming nightmares were fewer and Sonja no longer wore a knife in her waistband. September was blessed with an extension of summer.

Ben sent monthly rental payments to the bank, he wanted the bank completely out of their lives. Business was slow for McMallery's blacksmith shop, so he agreed to let Jeremy work on the *Ugly Boat*. Ben offered full wages, Forrest thought he should have none as an apprentice, but the two finally agreed to half wages. Coal prices had steadied at levels before the collier's price gouging. With the Wilhelmina in tow behind *The Turtle*, the Pulaski's were still achieving healthy profits. Aaron convinced his father to hire another deck hand. George Milton assisted them in listing the barges and employees under the name of the 'Pulaski Shipping Company'.

Aaron bartered well with the merchants of Havre de Grace and Wrightsville for the goods he purchased in Annapolis. Aaron and Ben traded between the barges and the Raven, and with each trip up to Wrightsville, Anthony's secret space in the Wilhelmina took a few more escaped slaves across the line to Pennsylvania. The slave catchers remained at the Line, but grew accustomed to the

Pulaski barges and rarely gave them other than cursory inspections.

Margaret Bartlett was welcomed into her sister's home when the new lock tender arrived. He was a widower with seven children, who filled the lanes and alleyways of Lapidum with laughter and skinned knees.

Ben installed smudge pots in the slave holds of the Raven, encased in brick walls and bases, and burned juniper and pine needles for weeks to mollify the stench of slavery. When the wind blew south, smoke would billow from the gratings and sweep over the bow, kissing the rigging with the scent of pine rosin. They left August, then September behind, welcoming a gentle autumn and keeping their vigilance on board the Raven through October and into November of 1843. And still they waited.

By November 8th, still no ice settled on the bay. Sunrise painted the yellow and red trees lining the Narrows in golden light under a perfectly blue cloudless sky filled with seagulls diving for fish. Autumn had finally yielded to her obligation and settled herself fully in residence with crisp cool air, resurrecting fond memories of old wool shirts and sweaters. Sonja came aboard wearing her favorite wool shawl, retrieved from its warm weather exile in the cedar chest at home.

The *Ugly Boat* sailed into the Narrows with all sails filled by a brisk northerly wind. Yelling and screaming and the sound of banging pots bolted across the narrowing distance to the Raven. Sonja and Ben dashed to the bow. The *Ugly Boat* was travelling far faster than she should be.

"Good god," Ben shouted. Then louder at the oncoming boat. "Veer away, God damn it! You're going to ram us!"

Red faces yelled in chorus at them from the deck of the *Ugly Boat*. Adam Tuttle held up a rum bottle and shrilled like a savage. Aaron waved wildly from the stern. He was standing barefoot on the storage box, one foot was resting on the tiller and steering with his toes. He too, had a bottle in his hand.

Ben shook his fist at the oncoming boat.

"What the – Veer off, I tell you!" He turned toward Sonja. "They are going to ram us!" Then he pushed Sonja back from the bow, knocking her off her feet and down in a painful thump onto the deck.

"Damn it, Ben!"

At the last possible moment, Aaron shouted "Jeremy!", and pushed the tiller hard to the right. The boat slid across in front of the Raven and over the shallows. Jeremy immediately released the bow anchor and dropped the sails, snugging the bow of the *Ugly Boat* downward almost to a perfect stop. The stern of the *Ugly Boat* swung against the Raven with a gentle thump near the side ladder. Aaron launched himself from the boat onto the ladder and popped over the railing like a chattering red-faced frog, trading calls with Ben.

"They approved it, Pa!"

"The Court?"

"Yes!"

Mac, Jeremy, Adam and Maggie danced around Ben.

"They approved our claim, Aaron?" asked Ben.

"Yes!" he screamed

"How much? What percent are we allowed?"

"All of it, Pa!"

"What?"

Sonja shoved into Ben, slapping his shoulder with both hands.

"You almost broke my tail bone, Benjamin!"

She continued to slap at Ben. He pushed her hands down as they came, ducking her swings, struggling to look back at Aaron.

"All of what, Aaron?"

"All of the ship, Pa. No one else claimed it! It's ours!"

Sonja screamed the question. "It's ours?"

Ben pulled her close to him as the crowd from the *Ugly Boat* surged around them singing a jumble of different songs all at the same time.

"It's ours, Sonja," Ben said to her.

She slapped him softly on his shoulder, and hugged him tightly. "It still stinks."

"The cargo won't mind," he said. "Not the cargo we will carry within her."

They hugged each other in the center of the jumping crowd. Sonja spoke into his chest

"Can we go home now, Ben?"

"Yes."

Bibliography

Blood On The Chesapeake is a work of fiction. Although no academic work is directly cited, I would be neglecting due homage to interesting sources of historical information that I read while developing this book, without sharing a bibliography with the reader.

Anbinder, Tyler , *Nativism & Slavery, The Northern Know Nothings & Politics of the 1850s,* New York, Oxford University Press, 1992.

Bates, Bill, *Images of America, Havre de Grace,* Charleston: Arcadia Publishing, 2006.

Brewington, M.V. , *Chesapeake Bay Sailing Craft,* The Calvert Marine Museum *and* The Chesapeake Bay Maritime Museum, Printed by the Anthoensen Press, Portland, 1986.

Carey, George G., *Maryland Folklore,* Centerville, Tidewater Publishers, 1989.

Cumbo-Floyd, Andrea, *The Slaves Have Names,* Amazon Digital Services LLC, 2013

Dwyer, Eddie, *A Trip Into Yesteryear and a Tale of Granpa's Life Aboard a Canal Boat,* The Havre De Grace Record.

Glatfelter, Heidi L., *Havre de Grace in the War of 1812 'Fire on the Chesapeake'*, History Press, Charleston, 2013.

Harford Historical Bulletin, Number 58, *The Tidewater Canal: Harford County's Contribution to 'The Canal Era'*, The Historical Society of Harford County, Inc., Fall 1993.

Jay, Peter A., Editor, *Havre De Grace - An Informal History*, Havre De Grace, Sparrowhawk Press, 1994.

Kopczewski, Jan Stanislaw, *Kosciuszko and Pulaski*, Warsaw, Interpress Publishers, 1976.

Levine, Bruce , *Half Slave and Half Free - The Roots of the Civil War*, New York, Hill and Wang, Noonday Press, 1992.

Phillips, Christopher, *Freedom's Port - The African American Community of Baltimore, 1790-1860*, Chicago, University of Illinois Press, 1997.

Shaw, Ronald E., *Canals for a Nation - The Canal Era in the United States 1790-1860*, Lexington, The University Press of Kentucky, 1990.

Stranahan, Susan Q., *Susquehanna – River of Dreams*, Baltimore, Johns Hopkins University Press, 1993.

Sydnor, Charles S., *The Development of Southern Sectionalism 1819-1848,* Louisiana State University Press, 1948.

The Susquehanna Museum at the Lockhouse, Havre de Grace, Maryland.

ROBERT F. LACKEY lived in Havre de Grace, Maryland, for 23 years, spending many afternoons exploring the remnants of the Susquehanna and Tidewater Canal. He was a member of the Susquehanna Museum at the Lock House, and served a period as publisher for its newsletter. After moving to Havre de Grace from North Carolina in 1993, he fell in love with the little town sitting at the mouth of the Susquehanna River and head of the Chesapeake Bay. The area is rich in history and watershed culture reaching back to the beginning of the country. Among the many historic themes coexisting within the nearby sites and lanes, the Canal Era drew the author's attention first. Stepping outside technical writing to complete his first novel, *Pulaski's Canal,* Robert began a family story that has blossomed into a family saga. **Blood on the Chesapeake** is the first of several sequels to follow *Pulaski's Canal.*

"I wandered the trails and historic marker sites along the old Susquehanna and Tidewater Canal route, and it was easy for me to picture families centering their lives around the canal, the way community centers spring up along the interstates today. Of course I was drawn to the simpler times, barges only moved at three miles an hour, but my research identified not only the hard demands and historical challenges of that simpler life, but the richness of the world the people lived in then. Having access to the original gateway Lockhouse, still maintained by the local historical society, was an absolute thrill and it gave me my first backdrop.

Once the core characters of the story tumbled out of my imagination and onto the computer screen in front of me, they almost took on their own life. They frequently went in directions I had not planned in the earlier part of the day, but evolved as the story evolved. Ben and Sonja, and their sons Isaac and Aaron, ARE the 19th century. Ben was born on the first second of January 1, 1800. The Pulaski experience encompasses the national experiences of that century, but from the eyes of a Maryland family on the canals. Much as today's national news is perceived from the living rooms and household budgets of American families.

Now they are dear friends, and I look forward to keeping their story going through the years after 1843. We will experience the changes that occurred in our country over the next two or three decades through them."

Robert is a member of the Historical Novel Society, the Surf Side Writer's group, and the South Carolina Writer's Workshop. He is currently conducting research for the third Pulaski book, tentatively titled **Raven's Risk**. He is planning additional sequels to follow the Pulaski family through the coming trials they will face in the 1800's. He has written other books under his pen name, Pug Greenwood: **Tooey's Crossroads** (Humorous short stories with a country flair, 2009), **Bim and Them** (Children's adventure, 2011). He now lives with his wife Sandi in Murrells Inlet, South Carolina, and divides his time between their beach house and the secluded writer's cabin he built in Southern Virginia.

Please follow Robert's Facebook^(TM) page:

https://www.facebook.com/RFLackey.author

Other books by Robert F. Lackey and Pug Greenwood are available through Amazon.com, BarnesandNoble.com, Booksamillion.com, and other internet book sellers. Kindle versions are available through Amazon.com.

Share your thoughts about this novel. You can email Robert at

Rflackey.author@gmail.com

Made in the USA
Charleston, SC
24 April 2016